"Oh, so you think
why you're laugh

Micah wasn't intereste~~d in Susannah, and she~~
certainly wasn't interested in him—not that way.
They were just hanging out together, helping him
through a tough time until he was able to return
home.

She'd do well to keep that thought front and center.

When he returned and presented her with the shoe,
she grabbed it from him with a curt "I'm going to get
even for this."

But his response was a mere whisper that sent
goose bumps down her arms. "You look awfully
pretty in the moonlight, Susannah Beiler."

Which set off every emotional alarm she possessed.

Was he flirting with her?

What was she doing standing in the moonlight with
Micah Fisher? She was supposed to be keeping an
eye on him—keeping him out of trouble.

Micah said, "Let me gather up our stuff. Then we can
walk back by the road. It'll give our clothes time to
dry off a bit."

But a small part of her wished the night could go on
and on…

Vannetta Chapman has published over one hundred articles in Christian family magazines and received over two dozen awards from Romance Writers of America chapter groups. She discovered her love for the Amish while researching her grandfather's birthplace of Albion, Pennsylvania. Her first novel, *A Simple Amish Christmas*, quickly became a bestseller. Chapman lives in Texas Hill Country with her husband.

Jo Ann Brown has always loved stories with happily-ever-after endings. A former military officer, she is thrilled to have the chance to write stories about people falling in love. She is also a photographer and travels with her husband of more than thirty years to places where she can snap pictures. They have three children and live in Florida. Drop her a note at joannbrownbooks.com.

VANNETTA CHAPMAN

An Unlikely Amish Match

&

JO ANN BROWN

An Amish Arrangement

LOVE INSPIRED
INSPIRATIONAL ROMANCE

LOVE INSPIRED®

INSPIRATIONAL ROMANCE

Recycling programs
for this product may
not exist in your area.

ISBN-13: 978-1-335-40247-9

An Unlikely Amish Match and An Amish Arrangement

Copyright © 2021 by Harlequin Books S.A.

An Unlikely Amish Match
First published in 2020. This edition published in 2021.
Copyright © 2020 by Vannetta Chapman

An Amish Arrangement
First published in 2017. This edition published in 2021.
Copyright © 2017 by Jo Ann Ferguson

This edition published by arrangement with Harlequin Books S.A.

For questions and comments about the quality of this book,
please contact us at CustomerService@Harlequin.com.

Harlequin Enterprises ULC
22 Adelaide St. West, 40th Floor
Toronto, Ontario M5H 4E3, Canada
www.Harlequin.com

Printed in U.S.A.

CONTENTS

AN UNLIKELY AMISH MATCH

Vannetta Chapman

This book is dedicated to Ms. Peggy Looper, who inspired in me a real love for the art of storytelling.

Being confident of this very thing,
that he which hath begun a good work in you
will perform it until the day of Jesus Christ.
—*Philippians* 1:6

But when he was yet a great way off,
his father saw him, and had compassion,
and ran, and fell on his neck, and kissed him.
—*Luke* 15:20

Chapter One

Susannah Beiler was carrying a to-go bag holding half of a cinnamon roll in one hand and her coffee in the other when she stepped out of Cabin Coffee and started across the street. At that exact moment, a large Ford pickup truck careened to the curb. Her friend Deborah pulled her back with a laugh and a smile. "Wouldn't do to have you flattened on the streets of Goshen on this beautiful spring day."

After all she'd been through the last two years, it would be ironic. Susannah shook off that thought and would have walked across the street that was now clear, but Deborah stepped back under the canopy of the coffee shop and nodded toward the truck. "Do you ever wonder why people act like that?"

The music was blaring at such a high level that the vehicle was practically rocking. The truck sported a bright blue paint job with streaks of lightning painted down the side, a large chrome bumper and spinning tire rims.

"Why would you jack it up so high?" Susannah

crossed her arms, tapping her right index finger against her left arm. Sometimes she felt like she didn't understand other people at all.

"And who would want to purchase such big tires? They look as if they'd fit a tractor."

"*Ya*, I'm not sure what the point is."

They glanced at one another when a young man jumped out of the truck, empty fast-food bags and soda cans trailing after him. He noticed the girls, smiled in a cocky *Englisch* way and then realized they were staring at the litter that had escaped from the truck.

"Oops." He snatched up the trash and tossed it into an adjacent trash can before once again flashing them both a smile.

He was a bit taller than Susannah, but then, most men were. He was also built like the mule her *dat* kept to watch over the goats—stocky and muscular. Blue jeans, a T-shirt that sported the logo of some rock and roll band, and sandy-colored hair flopping into his eyes and curling at his neck completed the picture.

Deborah laughed, but Susannah shook her head.

She couldn't abide rude people, and this guy seemed oblivious that the truck was obnoxious and the music was too loud.

The driver of the truck had put the vehicle into Park and jumped out. He had bright red hair sticking out from his ball cap, but other than that he could have been a twin to the first guy. As Susannah and Deborah watched, he walked up to his buddy, and they performed some complicated handshake.

"Take care, man."

"You know it." The first guy reached into the truck and snatched out a ball cap and a faded backpack.

"Later."

"Much."

The driver hopped back into the truck and sped away. The sandy-haired guy winked at Susannah and Deborah, pulled a cell phone out of his pocket and proceeded to stare at it as he walked in the opposite direction.

"Clueless," Susannah said, rubbing at the brow over her right eye. "He'll be lucky if he doesn't fall off the sidewalk the way he's staring down at that phone."

"Maybe."

"Are you kidding me?"

"I'm only saying that just because he's different doesn't mean that he's bad."

"I didn't say he was bad."

"Uh-huh, but the look you gave the both of them would have frightened a small child."

"Really?"

"Definitely. You've always been able to do that—stop someone in their tracks." Deborah linked their arms together and turned them toward her buggy. "Are you sure you don't want to be a teacher?"

"I'm not sure of much, but I am sure of that."

"Which is just as well, because you're a fabulous quilter."

"Danki."

"Off we go to the fabric store, then."

Which cheered up Susannah immensely. Even if she didn't purchase anything, being around bolts of fabric had a way of encouraging her on the darkest of days.

During the worst of her chemotherapy treatments, she'd often stopped into the local fabric store simply to enjoy the smell and touch of new fabric. When she was too sick to piece or quilt, she'd sometimes sit with a basketful of different-colored cotton swatches, dreaming of what she would sew as soon as she was better.

There was something about brushing her fingertips over the cotton, envisioning the pattern she would use and the quilts she would make and picturing the smiles on tourists who purchased them. Quilting was her way of spreading joy, and wasn't that what a person of faith was supposed to do?

Deborah was describing her *dat* having to battle his way through a thicket of thorny brush to free a goat that had managed to become ensnared. The goat had taken one look at Deborah's *dat* and scampered off in the opposite direction, leaving him wondering why he'd thought he needed to save the animal in the first place. "'Goats are resourceful animals, Deborah. Never forget it,'" Deborah finished with a spot-on imitation of her *dat*. She always could tell a good story, and they were both laughing by the time they reached the fabric store.

Susannah enjoyed the rest of the afternoon.

She forgot all about the *Englischer*.

And she arrived home humming a tune and feeling immeasurably better than she had when she had awakened that morning. Some days she still woke terrified that the cancer had returned, certain that she was about to be plunged back into the cycle of doctor's visits and tests and treatments. Some days were still harder than others.

But her day had improved, and her mood had lightened with it.

"Mind fetching the mail for me?" Her *mamm* had been up since before sunrise—they both had. While Susannah did her best to help with household chores, her *mamm* often shooed her away, telling her to go rest or step outside for a while or spend an hour in her quilting room. At the moment, her *mamm*'s apron was a mess, her hair was escaping from her *kapp* and her hands were covered in bread dough. Two loaves were already baking in the oven and two she'd finished kneading sat on the counter.

Sometimes Susannah wondered why they still made the bread from scratch, since loaves were certainly cheaper to purchase at the grocery store. She did love the smell of fresh-baked bread, though.

"And please take your *schweschdern*. They're full of energy today."

Sharon and Shiloh dropped the dolls they were playing with and ran toward the front door.

"Sweaters first," Susannah said. Though it was the last week of April, the afternoons cooled quickly. The twins reversed directions and ran for their cubbies. When the girls were born, her *dat* had placed cubbies in the mudroom with their names marked at a level they could now easily read.

"They sound more like puppies on the loose than children," Susannah said.

She adored her little *schweschdern*. Her *mamm* had been twenty when Susannah was born and forty when the twins came along. They were the siblings she never thought she'd have, and she prayed every day that they

hadn't inherited the gene that had caused her ovarian cancer. She didn't want anyone else to have to endure such a thing, especially not her *schweschdern*.

"Like I said—full of energy. I wouldn't mind if you stayed out with them a half hour or so, give them time to run some of it off."

Susannah thought her mother was one of the most hardworking women she knew, but twin five-year-olds could wear anyone down.

"Finish that bread and then sit down with a cup of tea. I have a feeling you've earned it today."

The twins catapulted back into the kitchen.

"I'm ready." Shiloh reached for her hand.

"Me, too. I wonder if we have a letter from *Mammi*." Sharon dashed to the front door.

"Don't run too far ahead," Susannah called out.

The girls looked identical—white-blond hair, blue eyes and a thin build. The only physical difference that was easy to spot was that Sharon had freckles and Shiloh didn't. Their personalities were quite opposite. Sharon was always running ahead—energetic, enthusiastic and fearless. Shiloh preferred to hang back and carefully watch. She also liked holding hands, while Sharon proclaimed that was for babies.

By the time Susannah and Shiloh descended the front porch steps, Sharon was already waiting at the lane—hands on her hips, a scowl on her face and a whine in her voice. "Why are you so slow? Come on already."

The day was one of those glorious spring days that Susannah often daydreamed about in the winter. The leaves were a green so bright they caused you to blink,

and the flowers planted earlier that month had burst into a rainbow of color. The sky was blue, the sun shone brightly and the weather was cool enough to require a sweater but without a cold north breeze.

Perfect.

They picked wildflowers as they rambled down the lane.

Both girls stooped to watch ants carrying tiny pieces of grass.

And they fed carrots to Percy, their buggy horse, who was grazing in the field that ran alongside the lane.

Susannah's mind called up all the things she had to be thankful for—her family, her health, a community that had supported her through a difficult time and now a perfect spring afternoon.

Ten minutes later, they reached the mailbox. Susannah had her hand inside, trying to reach to the back, where it seemed at least one piece of mail always managed to land, when Shiloh stepped closer and Sharon began to bounce from foot to foot.

"Someone's coming," Sharon said.

Susannah shielded her eyes against the afternoon sun, at first curious and then disbelieving and finally completely confused. What was *he* doing here?

Micah Fisher had taken his time finding his way out to the farm. He'd figured that as long as he was in town, he might as well check things out. Then he'd realized he was hungry again, so he'd stopped by the coffee shop where the two Amish ladies had been standing. He ate a leisurely lunch and used the time to charge his

phone since he wouldn't be able to do so at his grand-parents' farm.

The sun was low in the western sky by the time he hitched a ride to the edge of town. The driver let him out at a dirt road that led to several Amish farms. He'd never been to visit his grandparents before. They always came to Maine. But he had no trouble finding their place. His *mamm*'s instructions had been very clear.

As he drew close to the lane that led to the farmhouse, he noticed a young woman standing by the mailbox. A little girl was holding her hand and another was hopping from foot to foot. They were all three staring at him.

"Howdy," he said.

The woman only nodded, but the two girls responded with "Hello"—one whispered and the other shouted.

"Can we help you?" the woman asked. "Are you... lost?"

"*Nein.* At least I don't think I am."

"You must be if you're here. This is the end of the road."

Micah pointed to the farm next door. "Abigail and John Fisher live there?"

"They do."

"Then I'm not lost." He snatched off his baseball cap, rubbed his hand over the top of his head and then yanked the cap back on and down to shield his eyes. "Say, don't I know you?"

"Absolutely not."

"But I've seen you before...in town, when I first arrived. You were standing outside the bakery with a plain-looking girl."

"If you mean Amish, we all are."

"No, I meant plain." He smiled to suggest he was teasing, though honestly the other girl had been so pale as to be translucent and had worn the traditional white *kapp* and a gray dress. She could have been a cloud or a puff of fog or a figment of his imagination.

But the girl in front of him?

She wasn't someone you'd quickly forget—daring brown eyes, a *kapp* pulled so tightly that not a hair escaped, which only served to accentuate the exquisite shape of her eyes, bright color in her cheeks and a sweet curve to her lips. Her dress was a pretty dark green with a matching apron.

And she was his neighbor?

Perhaps *Gotte* had provided him an ally through this trying time of his life.

Micah stepped forward and held out his hand. "I'm Micah—Micah Fisher. Pleased to meet you."

"You're not *Englisch*?" Instead of shaking his hand, she reached for her other sister. They had to be siblings from the way they looked up at her and waited to see what she'd do next.

"Of course I'm not."

"So you're Amish?" She stared pointedly at his clothing—tennis shoes, blue jeans, T-shirt and ball cap. Pretty much what he wore every day.

"I'm as Plain and simple as they come."

"I somehow doubt that."

"Since we're going to be neighbors, I suppose I should know your name."

"Neighbors?"

"*Ya.* I've come to live with my *daddi* and *mammi*—at

least for a few months. My parents think it will straighten me out." He tugged his ball cap lower and peered down the lane. "I thought the bishop lived next door."

"He does."

"Oh. You're the bishop's *dochder*?"

"We all are," the little girl with freckles cried. "I'm Sharon and that's Shiloh and that is Susannah."

"Nice to meet you, Sharon and Shiloh and Susannah."

Sharon lost interest and squatted to pick up some of the rocks lining the caliche lane. Shiloh hid behind her *schweschder*'s skirt, and Susannah scowled at him.

So, not an ally.

"I knew the bishop lived next door, but no one told me he had such pretty *doschdern*."

Susannah's eyes widened even more, but it was Shiloh who peeked out from behind her skirt and said, "He just called you pretty."

"Actually, I called you all pretty."

Shiloh ducked back behind Susannah.

Susannah narrowed her eyes as if she was squinting into the sun, only she wasn't. "Do you talk to every girl you meet that way?"

"Not all of them—no."

"And do you always dress like that?"

"What's wrong with how I'm dressed?"

"And why did you arrive in a pickup truck?"

"Because a friend offered to bring me."

"An *Englisch* friend?"

"Say, what is this—the third degree? It feels like it,

and as far as I know, I've done nothing to land me in trouble."

"Yet." Susannah snatched up Sharon's hand and turned back toward the bishop's house.

"It was *gut* to meet you," he called out, knowing it would fluster her. Just his luck that the girl next door would be a killjoy. He'd met enough Amish girls like her to fill the back of a pickup truck twice over.

They were so disapproving.

It rankled him.

It also made him want to do something reckless, like throw a party or take off for points unknown or walk back to town and see a movie. But he didn't do any of those things. He didn't know anyone to invite to a party—yet. All of Goshen was unknown, and he wasn't even sure they had a movie house. Plus, he had no money to pay for a movie.

He sighed heavily, considering what lay before him. He'd promised his parents that he would come to Goshen and stay for at least six months. He realized he might as well walk up to the farmhouse. There was no point in avoiding it, but first he pulled out his phone, tapped the Snapchat button and held the phone up in front of him.

"I've arrived at the far reaches of northern Indiana. Let's hope I can survive life on the farm." He made what he hoped was a hilarious face, added a filter and frame, and then clicked the post button. Sticking the phone into his back pocket, he trudged down the lane toward his grandparents' house and what was probably going to be the longest six months of his life.

* * *

Susannah wasn't going to bring up the subject of their new neighbor to her parents. She actually was trying to forget him. She liked her life exactly as it was. The last thing she needed was trouble living next door, and Micah Fisher definitely looked like trouble.

They'd paused to bless the food and had just begun passing around the dishes of ham casserole, fresh bread, carrots and salad when Sharon starting chatting away about their encounter with Micah.

"He's tall and he talks funny."

"He wears a crazy hat," Shiloh added.

"And he wanted to shake Susannah's hand, but she didn't want to."

"And he said we were pretty—he said we were *all* pretty." Shiloh pulled in her bottom lip as she concentrated on cutting up her ham into small bites.

Her *dat* helped Sharon to scoop a spoonful of carrots onto her plate. "John mentioned to me that the boy was coming to stay with them for a while."

"He hardly seems like a boy." Susannah felt a slow blush creep up her neck when both her parents turned to stare at her. "What I mean is that he seemed to act like a *youngie*, though plainly he was older—I'd guess around twenty."

She could tell that her explanation hadn't cleared up anything, so she backed up and told them of seeing him in town, of the truck and the trash and the *Englisch* clothes. She didn't bring up the cell phone. That felt like tattling. No doubt his grandparents, and her *dat*, would know about it soon enough.

"Not everyone is as settled as you are, dear. I believe

Gotte used your illness to mature you." Her *mamm* buttered a piece of bread—hot, fresh and savory. Perhaps homemade was better.

"And hopefully to make you even more compassionate toward others." Her *dat*'s smile softened his words. "No doubt Micah is trying to find his way as many of our youth are—though, as you say, he's hardly a *youngie* anymore. Just turned twenty-five, if I remember correctly from what John said."

"The same as you." Her mother looked pleased, as if sharing the same age would make them best pals.

Susannah didn't think that was likely.

Her life had finally settled down. She had no desire to complicate it with the likes of Micah.

The rest of the meal passed in a flurry of conversation. Sharon chattered on about the kittens in the barn and how she was planning to name each one. Shiloh had read another of the picture books from the library, and she insisted on describing it in great detail. Her *mamm* reminded Susannah that church would be at the Kings' on Sunday, and that they had agreed to go over and help Mose prepare on Saturday. And her *dat* described a young mare that had been brought in for shoeing. "Four white socks and a patch on her forehead—pretty thing."

Susannah heard the conversations going on around her, but her mind kept volleying between the log-cabin quilt she'd started the day before and the new neighbor next door.

She didn't want a new neighbor.

Why couldn't things stay as they were?

She couldn't have explained what made her think

so, but somehow she was certain that the comfortable rhythm of their days was about to change.

And then, as if to confirm her thoughts, her *dat* said, "Oh, I forgot to mention that Micah is going to be working in my shop a couple hours each afternoon. Perhaps we can have him over for dinner sometime."

The smile on her *mamm*'s face told Susannah there was no use arguing with that.

Well, she'd just have to endure Micah's presence though she did not and would not approve of his *Englisch* ways.

Her *dat* had said he was staying awhile.

Micah had mentioned a few months.

Surely it couldn't be for a terribly long time. He wasn't moving in, and he hadn't been carrying any luggage, just the denim backpack. With any luck, he'd be gone by the first day of summer.

As was his habit, her *dat* took the twins out with him to do a final check of the animals. Susannah and her mother were cleaning the dishes when the conversation returned to Micah.

"Do you think you might like him?"

"Oh, I'm pretty sure we're polar opposites."

"Not always a bad thing."

"It's not going to happen, *Mamm*." The words came out more harshly than she'd intended. "We've spoken of this. I don't believe... That is, I'm sure what you're thinking of isn't *Gotte*'s plan for me."

"You mean marrying."

"*Ya*. I mean marrying."

"Because of your cancer—which is gone."

"Gone, yes, but it could come back, and more than that, the whole experience has left me changed."

"In more ways than one." Her *mamm* turned to study her though her hands remained in the sudsy water. "You've turned into a fine young woman, Susannah—a godly woman."

"You're changing the subject. Any man—any Amish man—would want a houseful of children." Susannah refused to meet her mother's gaze. Instead, she focused on the plate she was drying.

"Just because Samuel felt that way doesn't mean every man feels the same."

"We both know that Samuel and I were…mismatched. His breaking up with me, it was hard, but I felt immediately better once it was done."

"But…"

"But I learned, *Mamm*. I learned that men have certain expectations from marriage."

Why was it that speaking of this always brought tears to her eyes? She'd grown accustomed to the facts—to the limitations—of her life, but it seemed as if a certain part of her heart remained bruised. "How does the proverb go? 'No woman can be happy with less than seven to cook for'? I suspect no Amish man can be happy with less than seven to provide for."

"Children come to us in different ways."

"You're speaking of adoption—which is rare in an Amish community."

"Rare but not unheard-of." Her *mamm* wiped her hands on a dish towel, reached out and put a hand on each of Susannah's shoulders, turning her toward her.

Susannah couldn't resist the need to look up, to look into her *mamm*'s eyes and face her dreams and fears head-on.

"I'm only saying that you shouldn't assume you know *Gotte*'s plan for your life. Our ways are not *Gotte*'s ways, and that's something to be grateful for."

Once Susannah nodded that she understood, her *mamm* picked up another dish and slipped it into the dishwater. Susannah swiped at the tears that had slipped down her cheeks, feeling foolish and wishing she could keep a better rein on her emotions.

Her melancholy wasn't about Micah. It was about her parents' expectations for her life. Micah, she felt nothing except pity for—and perhaps a tad of irritation.

"Just wait until you meet Micah, then you'll understand."

"Will I, now?"

"I'm more likely to marry Widower King."

"Who is a fine man and a *gut* addition to our community."

"And he's thirty-five years old."

"Is he, now?"

They shared a smile. Her *mamm* knew very well how old Mose King was and that Susannah didn't have an ounce of romantic feelings for the man.

"You wouldn't have to worry about not being able to have children," her *mamm* joked.

"Indeed—six would be plenty, especially when those six are three pairs of twins."

"And all boys."

"All of them *full of energy*." Susannah purposely used her mother's words from earlier that afternoon.

They finished cleaning up the kitchen and walked onto the front porch to watch for her *dat* and the twins.

"I understand your not being interested in Micah, though you'd do well to remember that our first impression of someone isn't always the best."

"Fair enough."

"There's something else you should know, though."

Susannah sank into the rocker beside her *mamm*. She thought that twilight might be her favorite time of day. Something in her soul felt soothed by watching the sun set across their fields and her *dat* walking hand in hand with the twins toward the house.

"Micah's parents have been corresponding with Abigail and John. When it was decided he would move here, they shared the letter with both me and your *dat*. He's had a bit of a hard time, which is why he's here."

"Okay." She said the word slowly, tempted to add an *I thought so*.

"What I'm saying is that Micah will be here for at least six months—"

"Six months?" Susannah realized her mouth was hanging open and snapped it shut.

"And he'll be here helping your *dat* every day, so it could be that *Gotte* has put him in our path for a special reason."

Susannah stifled a groan.

"There's a real possibility that what Micah needs most is not a girlfriend but simply a friend, and that's something that we can each be."

Chapter Two

~⌒∂~

Micah's first night with his grandparents went fairly well. It was the next morning that things took an unpleasant turn, when they laid down the law, so to speak.

His *dat*'s parents were in their midsixties—not too old to farm, but old enough that they should be slowing down. That wasn't happening. His *daddi*, John Fisher, was built like an ox. Micah's mother had always said that Micah inherited his size from the man, but Micah didn't see it. He was as muscular as the next guy, but his grandfather's forearm look like corded rope. *Forearm*—singular. He'd lost his right arm in a harvesting accident when he was just twenty years old. It had made him tough and intolerant of weakness of any type.

He was also a very serious man. Micah couldn't imagine that they'd come from the same gene pool.

Abigail Fisher was stern as well, but with a soft spot for her grandchildren. Growing up in Maine, Micah had seen his *mammi*'s letters arrive weekly. They always contained a paragraph addressed to each of the eight

children. Her Christmas presents were always mailed well before Christmas Day—practical items, lovingly made. And his *mammi* and *daddi* visited occasionally, though certainly not every year.

In truth, Micah felt as if he hardly knew his grandparents, and though he loved them as he thought grandchildren should, he didn't think they had much in common. In fact, from the expression on his *daddi*'s face he wasn't sure the man really wanted him there. So why had he agreed to this ridiculous plan? How was Micah supposed to become a different person—*a more mature person* in the words of his *dat*—by living in a different state for six months?

Daddi didn't look up until they'd finished eating. Then he cradled his coffee mug in his left hand and waited until he was sure he had Micah's attention. "We expect you to work every day."

"Okay. That's fair." Micah brushed his hair away from his eyes and sat up straighter. "I can start looking for something today."

"No need to do that. I have it all arranged."

"All arranged?"

"To begin with, you'll be expected to carry your share of the work around here—the same as any grown man. I realize that will be different from what you're used to back home. I'm aware that your parents have coddled you."

Micah frowned at the last biscuit on his plate and focused on not saying the response that immediately came to mind. His thoughts scrambled in a dozen different directions, trying to think of a way to forgo the lecture that was surely headed his way.

"It's true, Micah." His *mammi* peered over her reading glasses at him. "There's no need to look hurt when your *daddi* is only stating the obvious. I spoke to your *dat* and *mamm* about this on several occasions."

"This?"

"She's referring to the way your *schweschdern* spoiled you—all of them did, really. It's not a surprise, you being the last child and only son."

Micah had seven older *schweschdern*, and it was true that they doted on him. He'd never washed a dish or helped prepare a meal. If he suddenly had to cook for himself, he'd probably perish from starvation. When he was young, he'd thought that was the life of every Amish boy, but as he grew older he'd learned his situation was a bit unique. The entire family had treated him as if he was a special gift left on the doorstep on Christmas morning.

Spoiled? *Ya.* He had been, but who in their right mind would turn that down? What was he supposed to do? Ask his siblings to be mean to him?

"You'll work with me in the fields every morning," his *daddi* continued. "There will be no more sleeping in."

Micah nearly choked on the sip of coffee he'd been in the process of swallowing. His *mammi* had called up the stairs at 5 a.m. sharp to wake him. That was sleeping in?

"After lunch you'll go to the bishop's and help in his farrier shop."

"The Beilers are *wunderbaar* people." His *mammi* might have winked at him, or she might have a twitch in her right eye. Micah couldn't tell. "This way you'll be learning two trades. Your *daddi* can teach you everything about farming—"

"Something your *dat* should have done already."

"And the bishop can teach you about horses."

As if he didn't know about horses. He was Amish, in spite of the way they were speaking to him. Micah felt the hairs on his neck stand on end, like a cat that had been brushed the wrong way. Why had he ever agreed to come to Indiana? What they were describing sounded worse than boot camp, which he only knew about from his friend Jackson, who had given him a ride from Maine.

Up before the birds.

Early-morning drills.

Work all day.

Collapse into bed at night.

Rinse and repeat.

His *daddi* gulped down the rest of his coffee, pushed his chair back and stood. The sleeve of his right arm had been sewn into a pocket, so that his stump rested inside it. He held his left hand in front of him—palm down—and made an invisible circle that included the three of them as well as the empty chairs, which he supposed his cousins had occupied before moving to Maine. In fact, it seemed the entire family was there, so what were his grandparents still doing in Goshen?

"We are your family—your *mammi* and me and all of your kinfolk here in Goshen. Your family in Maine loves you, as do we, but it's time for you to grow up, Micah. It's time to become a man."

And with that pronouncement, he turned and strode from the room.

Micah pulled in a deep breath, pushed himself away from the table and started across the room after him, but *Mammi* called him back.

"Best go upstairs and change first. I put proper clothing in your dresser and on the hooks. Your *daddi*—well, he won't abide the blue jeans and T-shirts."

The day seemed intent on continuing its slide from bad to worse.

"Anything else I should know? Any other changes I need to make?" He tried to sound lighthearted, but the words came out sarcastic and gruff. Too late to bite them back, and his *mammi* didn't seem to even notice.

"When you're done with the day's work, I'll cut your hair."

"What's wrong with my hair?"

"And he knows about the phone. As long as it isn't in the house—as long as he doesn't see it—he'll tolerate it. Just don't push him."

"I shouldn't push him?"

"He's old-fashioned, I know."

"You think?"

"But he's also a fair man." She stood and walked over to where he waited. His *mammi* barely reached his shoulders, but she was a formidable woman, and for some reason he couldn't identify, Micah wanted to make her proud. Reaching out, *Mammi* put a hand on his shoulder and waited until he met her gaze. "He's a *gut* man, and he cares about you. I suspect the changes will be difficult at first, but in the end, you'll thank him."

Micah seriously doubted that.

A quick glance at the clock told him it wasn't 6:30 a.m. yet.

The day was shaping up to be a long one.

He cheered himself with the thought that he only had 179 to go.

* * *

By the time they stopped for lunch, Micah was yawning and eyeing the hammock strung up in the backyard.

"Thomas expects you at one o'clock sharp, so you best hurry." His *daddi* nodded toward the sandwich on Micah's plate. "You can eat that on your walk over."

Micah started to protest but then realized he'd probably prefer eating alone. At least he wouldn't have to listen to his *daddi*'s plans for their work the next day. He was too tired to even consider more fieldwork, and the day wasn't half-over.

Why had he never listened to the stories of how severe his *daddi* was?

If he had, he wouldn't have agreed to this exile.

He tried to hold on to his bad mood, but the weather was fabulous, and he had over a dozen comments on his social media pages. He'd fetched the phone from the barn as soon as he'd left the kitchen. He paused at the fence line long enough to answer the comments and snap another picture to post.

It would probably be a bad idea to take the phone over to the bishop's. Thomas Beiler was no doubt even more strict than Micah's *daddi*.

He glanced around for a place to hide it, but all he could see was fence line and fields, so he shoved it into his back pocket. Fortunately, on his way to the bishop's shop, he spied Susannah coming out of a small building set next to the house.

He called out to her and then jogged to where she was waiting.

"Do me a favor?"

"Like what?"

She was holding a basketful of fabric scraps. He pulled the phone from his pocket, picked up the stack of fabric and dropped the phone, then covered it back up. "Keep that for me until I'm done working."

"Why would I do that?"

"So I won't get in trouble on my first day in your *dat*'s shop."

"If you knew you would get in trouble, why did you—"

"Thanks, Susannah. You're a peach."

Instead of smiling, she glared at him, which caused him to laugh.

"I don't see what's so funny."

"You are. You just don't know it." He turned and walked backward so that he could point at her. "You're going to be my new best friend."

"Oh, I doubt that."

"You'll see."

"Uh-huh."

"Just don't use up all my battery playing *Candy Crush*."

"What is…"

But he never heard the rest because he realized it was five minutes past one and he was late. No doubt the bishop would relay that to his *daddi* and he'd be given extra chores, or perhaps they'd deliver yet another lecture. He absolutely hated lectures. It was difficult to sit there and act respectful and pretend to listen. He just did not understand old people. Best to avoid such a confrontation, so he broke into a run.

He was surprised when Thomas greeted him with a smile and no rebuke. "I was happy to hear you'd be here for a few months. I can use the help."

"Don't know as I'll be that much help."

"Does your mind work?"

"Excuse me?"

Thomas tapped the side of his head. He was tall for an Amish man, probably close to six feet. His beard was peppered with gray, and crow's-feet stretched out from his eyes. He struck Micah as a man who smiled easily.

"Does your mind work? How did you do in school?"

"Oh, I did fine."

"Then the work won't be too hard for you to learn. It's difficult physically... I'll give you that. But anyone who is willing to learn the trade will always have a job."

"*Ya*, always plenty of horses when Amish are around," Micah joked.

"Exactly. Now, let's get to work on Widower King's buggy horse."

Micah had never considered that he'd be straddling the leg of a thousand-pound beast. He'd lived around horses all of his life, but feeding a horse or harnessing it to a buggy was one thing. Getting that horse to raise its foot so you could trim away its hoof was another.

"A horse's hooves are like our fingernails. They must be trimmed and exfoliated." Thomas proceeded to show him how to cut off the excess growth, then clean and check the hoof for overall health. "It's important that the horse trusts you. If you appear confident and act like you know what you're doing, the horse will relax."

"But I don't know what I'm doing."

"You will. Soon enough you will. See this triangle-shaped thing at the bottom of the hoof?"

"Sure."

"That's the frog. It acts as a shock absorber of sorts. We need to clean it up. Don't want any ragged ends."

"Why?"

"*Gut* question. We clean it so the dirt and muck is able to get out of the foot easier. Next we trim the hoof wall. Hand me the curved blade there on the shelf."

Micah quickly did as asked. When Thomas was finished, he used a hoof nipper to trim the outside of the hoof wall, and then a rasp to even out everything.

"I never realized there was so much detail to shoeing a horse."

"Few people do—they count on their farrier. Think of it as job security." Thomas looked up and smiled. "Now let's see what sized shoes we need."

Susannah was tempted to find an excuse to visit her *dat*'s shop. How was Micah doing? And did he know anything about trimming hooves or shoeing horses? She knew firsthand that what her *dat* did was hard work. She'd sat in his workshop often enough and even helped him occasionally. She loved being around the animals whether they were buggy horses or workhorses.

It took her an hour to separate her fabric scraps by size and color. It was amazing what could be salvaged from one project to use in another. The process soothed her until she picked up the last piece of fabric and spied Micah's phone in the basket. Why did he have such a

thing? How much did he pay for it? And who did he stay in touch with?

Other Amish rebels?

Someone in his family who had left the faith?

Or maybe an *Englisch* girlfriend?

She dropped the phone into her apron pocket. It didn't matter to her what Micah did with his phone, and she would set him straight that it wasn't her place to keep him out of trouble. She didn't think he was going to fit into their community very well. She didn't think he even wanted to.

There's a real possibility that what Micah needs most is not a girlfriend but simply a friend...

Remembering her *mamm*'s words caused her to feel a twinge of guilt. Perhaps he had a good reason for having the phone, though she couldn't imagine what that might be.

She didn't have to wait long to find out.

She was pulling laundry off the line while Shiloh and Sharon played on the trampoline when Micah came walking around the corner of the house.

He headed straight to the water hose and preceded to roll up his sleeves and wash his hands and arms. He even swiped some of the water on his neck, wetting the hair that curled there, and then he doused his face.

"We have indoor bathrooms."

"I like washing up with a water hose."

Susannah handed him a clean hand towel.

"Danki."

"Gem gschehne."

He rubbed his face dry, then his arms, and finally

remembered that water was dripping down his neck. When he was finished, he held up the towel and asked, "Where should I—"

"I'll take it."

"Do you need help with the laundry?"

She inclined her head toward the empty clothesline.

"I could help fold."

"Do you know how to fold clothes?"

"How hard can it be?" He peeked into her basket. "Oh. Looks like you've already folded everything."

"It's easier to do while you pull the items off the line."

"I knew that."

"Sure you did." She moved closer to the trampoline so she could keep an eye on the girls.

Micah followed and plopped down on the grass. For reasons she couldn't quite fathom, she did the same. It wasn't that she was interested in Micah, but she was curious as to what made him tick. How did he become so unorthodox? And why? What was the point of rebelling against their conventions?

"Actually, I know nothing about housework." He picked up their conversation as if there hadn't been a long, awkward silence. "I'm the baby of the family."

"Is that so?"

"Seven older *schweschdern*."

"What was that like?"

"I loved it, but apparently…according to my *daddi*, I was spoiled and it's time for me to grow up and become a man."

"Ouch."

"Yeah. Hence my exile here in Goshen for six months."

"When you say it that way, it sounds like a long time."

"It is a long time—a lifetime practically." Micah leaned forward and lowered his voice. "Not sure I'm going to make it if every day is like today."

"Why's that?"

"It's all so...grim."

The sun was setting in a beautiful splash of color, the horses were pastured in the field, Sharon and Shiloh played happily a few feet from her, and dinner was nearly done. "I don't understand."

"What?"

"Grim. How can you call this..." She took an exaggerated gaze around them. "How can you call it grim?"

"The work is endless."

"You didn't enjoy helping *Dat*?"

"Actually, that part was rather interesting."

"But..."

"But I'd already spent five hours in the field. I've done nothing but work all day. And tomorrow will be the same. It's just so...boring."

She fought the urge to defend their lifestyle, even their farm. So what if he didn't like it? Why should she care what Micah Fisher did and didn't like?

"If excitement is what you want, then *ya*, I agree that Goshen isn't the place for you."

"I knew you'd understand."

"And the work is endless because it's a farm. That's pretty much the definition of farmwork."

"I do not see the point."

Susannah didn't know what to say to that, so she asked, "How did it go working with *the horses*?"

"Better than I thought it would be. I only got kicked once."

"Once usually does the trick."

"You've helped your *dat* shoe horses?"

"Of course."

"Not exactly girl's work."

"So now you're a traditionalist?" She reached into her apron pocket, retrieved his phone and dropped it into his hand. "Except for that…"

"Have you ever owned a phone?"

"Nein."

"Did you play around on mine?"

"Of course not."

"It's not going to burn your fingers, you know."

"And yet it's forbidden."

"It's discouraged. There's a difference." He winked at her.

She refused to let his charm muddle her thoughts. "Does that usually work?"

"What?"

"Winking at girls."

"Not sure I wanted it to work. I was just being… friendly."

"Ah."

He stuffed the phone in his pocket and said, *"Ah,* what?"

"That's what people who flirt say…that they were just being friendly."

"So you think I was flirting with you?"

Susannah almost laughed, but she didn't want to en-

courage his silliness. The twins continued to jump on the trampoline, giggling and calling out to one another.

"Watch me, Susannah. I can flip." Sharon jumped and then fell onto her back. "Did I do it?"

"You didn't do it," Shiloh said.

"I did, too. Tell her, Susannah. Tell her I did."

"Almost. Keep practicing."

Micah flopped onto his back, staring up at the sky. "Your *dat* isn't what I expected."

"How so?"

"Well, he's a bishop."

"Ya."

"I thought he'd be more conservative."

"Don't tell me he was watching TV again while shoeing the horses."

Micah propped himself up on his elbows, then smiled at the twins, who were trying to get his attention. "I mean he seems rather open-minded. He asked all about our community in Maine, which many of the old folks don't even want to know about. They think it's much too progressive."

"Is it?"

"I don't think so. Plus, look at this place." He waved at the backyard. "Trampoline for the kids."

"They need somewhere to play."

"A new little modular house."

"That's my sewing shop, where I quilt."

"I wondered what all those pieces of material were for."

"They're scraps and they're for sewing."

"Do you have an electric sewing machine in there?"

"I do not." Her cheeks warmed, not because he was teasing her but because of the way he was looking at her. She stood and picked up her laundry basket. "Dinner will be ready in a few minutes. I assume you're staying."

"I wouldn't miss it."

Sharon jumped closer to the edge of the trampoline and held onto the netting, which prevented her from falling out. "Come and jump with us, Susannah."

"Yeah, come and jump." Shiloh was actually sitting on the trampoline, not jumping. She was careful even there, as if the thing might throw her onto the ground.

"It's time to help with dinner. Come on inside."

"Just five more minutes…please."

It always made her smile how their voices could become one when they wanted something. Usually Sharon and Shiloh seemed like complete opposites, but when they joined together, they reminded her of two halves of the same whole.

"I have to go in, and you know *Mamm* doesn't like you out here alone."

"I'll stay with them," Micah said. "Unless you need me to help cook."

"Have you ever cooked before?"

"Nein."

"Then no—we don't need your help."

"I'll just stay here, then. I promise to keep an eye on them."

Actually, he did better than that. By the time she'd climbed the porch steps and looked back, Micah had removed his shoes and was pulling himself up onto the trampoline.

Not that he could ingratiate himself to her by playing with the girls. His comments had bordered on rude—first calling them progressive and then boring. Or, had it been the other way around? Regardless, he obviously didn't like it here and she didn't think he'd last even a week.

Which was absolutely fine with her.

The longer he stayed, the higher the risk he would be a bad influence on someone in their community. The last thing her friends needed was an Amish bad boy complete with long hair, *Englisch* phone, ball cap and blue jeans. Though he had been wearing more traditional clothes today. Where had those come from? Were they stuffed in his backpack?

Not her business.

She guessed he'd probably grow up eventually, but she didn't think it would be today or tomorrow or anytime in the near future.

That boy was trouble with a crooked smile.

The sooner Micah Fisher was out of their lives, the better. If he needed a friend, he could find one back home in Maine.

Chapter Three

By the time Sunday rolled around, Susannah's feelings regarding Micah had grown even more complicated. He'd shown up the second day with a fresh haircut but the same born-to-be-wild attitude. Her *dat* was happy with his work, but Susannah was growing increasingly uneasy around him. Micah reminded her of a wild horse temporarily corralled. It was only a matter of time before he broke out and then his grandparents would be heartbroken and her *dat* would be in need of another helper.

She spent much of the service praying that God would forgive her uncharitable feelings and clear the confusion in her mind. Since her *dat* was the bishop, she was aware that she was scrutinized more closely than others.

So even as her mind wandered toward Micah, she kept her attention on the person preaching.

When it was time to pray, she closed her eyes and petitioned her heavenly Father for clarity.

When it was time to sing, she stood and raised her voice with the others around her.

And as soon as the service ended, she hurried toward the serving area, not pausing to give their new neighbor a second glance. She worked at filling cups with water and lemonade. When she saw Micah walking toward her, she quickly changed tables to help with salads. It wasn't that she was avoiding him, but he would simply want to tell her more about Maine, a subject she'd heard quite enough about. When she finally had a few free moments, she snagged Deborah.

"Care to walk out into the pasture?"

"I can think of nothing I'd rather do." Deborah jumped up from her seat and grabbed her sweater from the big bag she carried around. Deborah was the only Amish person Susannah knew who carried what amounted to a baby bag though she had no baby. It was sometimes quite amazing what Deborah could pull out of that bag.

"Tell me about Micah," Deborah said as soon as they were out of earshot of the others.

"What's to tell?"

"Does he seem to be behaving himself?"

"*Dat* hasn't complained."

"I'm not surprised. Your father is the bishop. Of course Micah would be on his best behavior around him."

"*Ya*, I suppose."

"Betty heard that Micah had an alcohol problem when he was living in Maine. That's why his parents sent him here."

"Alcohol?"

"Or maybe it was drugs… She wasn't really sure." Susannah sighed and pressed her lips together.

"You might as well say it," Deborah teased.

"Then I would be as bad as Betty."

"Oh. So you don't want to be a gossip, which you would be if you pointed out that Betty is a gossip."

That was such a convoluted statement that it made Susannah laugh, which helped her relax a little. "I guess I was thinking that Betty has been somewhat bitter since Joshua left the faith."

"And left her for an *Englisch* girl. I saw them in South Bend the other day."

"At the college?"

"*Ya.* They looked…um…close. Arms wrapped around each other. Kissing in public." Deborah made a wide-eyed, somewhat disgusted expression.

"Your *dat* is still consulting at the college?"

"He is. Their agriculture students want to know all about our Plain and simple ways."

Which caused them both to laugh.

"Perhaps they should come help in the fields—then they'd really understand."

"They're actually going to do that sometime in the next few weeks."

"Seriously?"

"Uh-huh."

"You're going to have *Englischers* traipsing around in your fields?"

"We are."

"Maybe we should send Micah over. He seems to speak their language."

They'd made it to the corner of the property where Mose King had made a bench out of a felled tree. After

checking that there were no critters hiding beneath it, they both sat down and studied the scene in front of them.

Most of the women and a good number of the men were spread out in chairs under the trees.

Boys of all ages were playing baseball, with a few of the men standing on the edge of the ball field, providing sideline advice.

The younger children were in a play area that Mose had made for his own children. It looked like a school playground. There was a seesaw, a swing set and even a sandbox that he kept covered with a tarp when it wasn't being used.

Susannah thought that playground was a sign of something—thoughtfulness, adoration, maybe devotion. "*Mamm* thinks Mose would make a *gut* husband."

"I'm sure he would...for someone his own age."

"*Ya*, my sentiments exactly."

"That's another thing I heard about Micah. He was apparently dating an older woman—who he dumped, and according to the grapevine, that wasn't the first relationship that he broke off for no reason."

"There's always a reason."

"I suppose."

"It's kind of sad that we're so interested in everything he did wrong there."

"Are you defending him?"

"Not at all. It's only that... Well, *Mamm* reminded me that everyone deserves a fresh start. Don't they?"

Deborah pulled her skirt up an inch or so and proceeded to pull stickers from her socks. "I guess. The

only thing is that I'd rather these people who need a fresh start get it somewhere else."

Which pretty accurately mirrored Susannah's thoughts, though somehow, spoken out loud, they sounded rather judgmental and unfair.

"What do you mean?"

"I guess I was thinking that what Micah Fisher does in Maine is his own business, but what he does here… Well, here he stands to hurt other people with his actions."

"Meaning what?"

Deborah shrugged and pretended to look for something in her purse. Susannah put her hand on top of the bag and left it there until her friend looked up.

"What aren't you telling me?"

"Apparently Micah sneaked out of his house on Friday night and met up with Caroline Byers."

"I have trouble believing that's true. He's been here less than a week. How could he—"

"I heard it from Caroline herself. She said it was harmless. Said they just happened to be downtown at the same time to hear a local band, but Betty heard them talk about meeting up again on Thursday."

Susannah had at least a dozen questions, but none of them really mattered. Most of them were none of her business. She settled for asking, "Her parents let her do that?"

"*Nein.* She sneaked out. Are you even paying attention?"

"I am now." Susannah jumped up, crossed her arms and paced back and forth in front of Deborah. "Caro-

line is young and impressionable. I can see how she'd fall for someone like Micah in a second, but I'm not sure that's a *gut* idea."

"Finally."

"Finally what?"

"Finally you're paying attention and concerned. I mean, the guy practically lives at your house. Maybe you could say something to him."

"I'm not sure that I could, or even that I *should*."

Deborah began to fiddle with her *kapp* strings, something she only did when she was holding back.

"What else?"

"Well…one of the boys claimed they saw him smoking."

"He doesn't smell like smoke, and I should know… He's eaten with us three times now."

"There was also talk of his carrying a flask in the back pocket of those blue jeans and…you know…taking a sip now and again."

Susannah flopped back down beside Deborah. "I don't know if I'm more aggravated about the gossip—"

"Unless it's true."

"—or Micah's behavior."

That sat between them a few minutes until Susannah realized they needed to start back to help put out a snack for the children. It was nearly three in the afternoon and some of them would be going down for a nap soon.

They were halfway toward the main group when Deborah asked, "Are you going to talk to your *dat*?"

"*Nein*. He wouldn't want to hear about it unless it was something I saw myself. He has no patience for

gossip." She turned abruptly so that Deborah nearly bumped into her. "If anyone else talks to you about Micah, about his behavior, you tell them to come to my *dat* directly. *Dat* will speak to him, but only if the report is a firsthand account."

"Okay. I should have done that to begin with. I guess I was a bit stunned by it all."

"Understandable, but now that we know about his reputation we need to take steps to protect our *freinden*."

"What kind of steps?"

"Well, I can keep a closer eye on him when he's at our farm. I can certainly watch for the smoking and drinking."

"I doubt that he's likely to do either of those things around your *dat*."

"But there would be signs, and I just don't..." She looked toward the picnic tables, where she should be helping. Instead, she tugged on Deborah's arm and pulled her in the opposite direction. "It's just that I don't want him to be unfairly judged. He seems like a *gut* guy, just a bit lost."

"Reminds me of my *bruder* when he was on his *rumspringa*."

"Exactly."

"Only Elias was seventeen at the time."

"And Micah is twenty-five."

A shout rose up from the baseball field, where none other than Micah had apparently hit a home run and was jogging around the bases to the cheers of all watching.

Susannah pinched the bridge of her nose and

squeezed her eyes shut. After taking a deep breath and letting it slowly out, she tried to shake off the feeling of trepidation. It was a beautiful Sunday afternoon, and so far at least, Micah had done nothing against their *Ordnung*—at least nothing she'd witnessed.

"We'll give him a fair chance but keep our eyes on him."

"Sounds reasonable." Deborah nodded so hard that her *kapp* strings bounced.

"And above all else, we'll make sure that he doesn't set his ball cap at any of the girls in our group."

"Like Betty."

"Or Caroline or any of the other girls we've grown up with. The ones who aren't married... Well, some of them are too quick to fall in with a guy."

"Their biological clocks are going ticktock."

"Exactly."

Deborah tucked her arm through Susannah's. "The good part is that he's not planning on staying, from what I've heard."

"He said as much to me, as well. Hopefully he can serve his time at his *daddi*'s and then go home to break hearts."

"*Gut* idea. We don't need any of that sort of drama around here."

Which echoed what Susannah had been thinking. Personally, she'd experienced enough tragedy in the last few years with her cancer diagnosis, treatment and the breakup with Samuel. She knew firsthand what it was like to have your dreams ripped away, to have your heart shredded to the point that it felt raw. If she had

anything to do with it, that would not be happening to her friends. Even if it meant she had to take matters into her own hands.

The following Thursday, Micah had finished shoeing a dappled gray mare under the watchful gaze of Thomas. Then the bishop had been called off to visit with one of the old-timers who had taken a turn for the worse, and before Micah knew it, he was being babysat by Susannah.

"I can take the man's money and put it in the box."

"What man?"

"The man who owns the mare."

"Yes, but you don't even know the man's name. Mr. Hochstettler has been bringing his horses here since I was a *kind*. *Dat* likes for our customers to have personal service."

"They're Amish. Where else are they going to go to have their horses cared for?"

"Not the point, according to *Dat*. The point is that we treat every customer as if we value their business— which we do."

"Fine. I didn't remember the man's name, but you could tell me that and leave."

"Do you know the mare's name?"

"*Nein* and what difference does that make? Are you going to tell me that the mare needs to feel valued, too?"

"Of course she needs to be valued. Have you ever owned a mare?"

"Never needed to. I had my parents' buggy horses to use in Maine, and I have my grandparents' here."

"But one day you'll be a man with your own family and your own horses." Susannah had been grooming the mare, which definitely did not fall under the services of shoeing a horse in Micah's opinion. She stopped what she was doing and pointed the brush at him. "When you have your own horses, you'll understand why it's important to appreciate them and treat them with respect."

Micah rolled his eyes and then started laughing. He couldn't help it.

"What?"

"Nothing."

"Just say it."

"You couldn't even see over that horse if you weren't standing on a crate, and yet you're lecturing me."

"What does being short have to do with anything?"

Micah raised his hands in surrender, but he continued to laugh. Most days Susannah aggravated him, especially when she reminded him of his nagging sisters. But then, other times, he caught a glint of mischievousness in her eyes, and he wondered what else was going on underneath her perfectly starched *kapp*.

"Say, I'm thinking about asking Caroline Byers to this weekend's spring festival in town. What do you think?"

"Terrible idea." Susannah resumed brushing the mare, but much more vigorously.

"Why's it terrible?"

Now her lips were forming a tight, straight line, as if they'd been glued together. He knew that expression well enough.

"Just say it. What's the problem?"

"She's too young for you, that's what!" Susannah

brushed the mare so vigorously that it turned its large muzzle toward her. "Sorry, Smokey."

"Smokey?"

"That's her name. If you'd bothered to find out, you would know that."

"You seem awfully cranky all of a sudden."

"I'm not cranky!" She jumped off the crate, cleaned the horse brush with a metal tool and slammed it onto the tool shelf. Next she picked up the currying comb, which looked somewhat dangerous the way she was brandishing it in his direction. "Pick a girl your age, Micah."

"Wow. Okay. Well, I hadn't thought of it that way, but I guess I see your point. How about Betty Gleich?"

Susannah closed her eyes as if praying for patience and shook her head so hard he feared her *kapp* would pop off.

"What's wrong with Betty? I know for a fact she's over twenty-one."

"She's twenty-two, and she just went through a rather rough breakup."

"What does that have to do with me?"

"Did you not say only twenty minutes ago that you only had—and I quote—one hundred and seventy days left in this awful place?"

"Sounds like something I might have said."

"Obviously you hate it here."

"You don't understand. If you'd been to Maine, then you'd appreciate how much more beautiful it is than your much-loved Indiana. If you could experience the hunting, the fishing, the wildness of the place. It's just—"

"You'd be in your precious Maine right this minute if you hadn't been banished."

"Ouch."

"Again—your word, not mine."

"Fine." He named off four other perfectly eligible girls, all of whom Susannah disapproved of him dating for the most ridiculous reasons and sometimes for no reason she'd share at all.

His mounting frustration was threatening to get the better of him. He tried to mentally order himself to calm down, but the way Susannah was frowning at him was not helping matters. "What is your problem?"

"My problem?"

"You know, I don't need your permission to date someone, but now I'm curious. What's your beef?"

"Beef?"

"Apparently I'm not *gut* enough for any of the gals in your district."

"It's not a question of whether you're *gut* enough for them."

"Then what?"

"You're leaving, that's what. You're leaving, and they'll get attached to you, and then it will hurt them when you go."

"I'm not proposing to them, Susannah. I'm asking them out on a buggy ride."

"One thing leads to the other."

Micah threw up his hands and walked out of the farrier shop. The sky was dark and brooding, a perfect reflection of his mood. Well, Susannah Beiler was not the boss of him. He could ask out whomever he liked.

He stomped back in to tell her that and caught her with her cheek pressed against the mare, a look of utter desolation in her eyes. Now he felt like a heel, and he didn't even know what he'd done.

"Hey…it's not that bad."

She stood up straighter, gave the mare one last pat and returned the crate to its place along the wall.

"You can't expect a guy to hang around for six months and not go on a single date. Surely you can see that."

"Why?"

"Why? Because it's not natural."

"There's nothing wrong with being alone, Micah."

"Maybe not for you, but I haven't decided I want to be single the rest of my life—apparently you have."

"This discussion isn't about me."

Now her chin rose as if she needed to defend herself—oh, the many faces of Susannah Beiler. If she ever came down from her high horse, she might be an interesting person to get to know.

"Look, I'm sorry." He yanked off his hat and stared at it—a straw Amish hat. Why couldn't he wear his ball cap? Glancing up, he realized Susannah was waiting. He forced himself to refocus on the problem at hand. "I didn't mean to offend you, but you're so…"

"What?"

"Serious. You're so serious, and life is just waiting for us to enjoy it." In three long strides, he was at her side. Grasping her by the shoulders, he marched her toward the open barn door. "See that? The clouds and the rain and the turbulence?"

"I see it."

"But behind all of that are more things that we can't begin to imagine—sunshine and new experiences and memories waiting to be made. Life is out there, Susannah. We're supposed to be living it."

"And you can't do that without dragging some poor girl along with you?"

"Why should I?"

Susannah rubbed at her forehead as if she'd quite suddenly been slapped with the worst headache imaginable. Finally, she pulled in a deep breath and turned to stare up into his face.

"Then take me."

"Huh?"

"If you must take someone on these jaunts around our little town, take me."

"But…you don't even like me."

"That's beside the point."

"No, I think that is the point."

"You're not looking for love, Micah. We both know that. You're looking for a buddy to pal around with, and there are plenty of men your age in our district."

"All paired up. I've already tried that route."

"Then take me, like I said."

"You're going to pal around with me? Miss Susannah Beiler, who does everything by the book? That should be a load of fun."

"I do not do everything by the book."

"You cleaned the horse brush before putting it on the shelf. Who does that?"

"You're changing the subject. Is it a deal or not?"

"A deal?"

"I go with you to enjoy life, and you leave the girls in my district alone."

"Wow. There's a proposal that is hard to turn down."

"So it's a deal."

She held out her hand, which reminded him of meeting her out on the lane, offering his hand and her refusing it. He couldn't help laughing as he clasped her small hand in his large one.

"Fine. It's a deal, but you're going to regret it."

"I have no doubt that is true." And then she turned and strode toward the house.

"I thought you needed to be here when Mr. Hochstettler came by," he called out to her.

Rather than bothering to answer, she simply gave him a backward wave.

So, he was going to date the bishop's daughter.

Or rather, *not* date her.

It would be like having a chaperone along every time he went to town. He kicked the door of the barn, startling the mare.

"Easy, Smokey. It's just me, doing a stupid thing to top off another stupid thing."

One hundred and seventy days.

Somehow, that seemed like an even longer stretch of time than it had an hour ago.

Chapter Four

Susannah went with Micah to hear a music duo on Friday. She had to resist the urge to remind him that they were Amish and their *Ordnung* strongly discouraged listening to worldly music. But she didn't have to point that out. Micah taunted her with it as soon as they were in the buggy and driving away from her parents' farm.

"Guess your *mamm* and *dat* didn't want you to go tonight."

"Why would you say that?"

"First of all, because it's with me."

"For reasons I can't fathom, my parents have taken a real liking to you."

"Huh." He looked pleased for a brief moment, but then he slouched his shoulders and rammed his hat down on his head. "Wish I could say the same for my *daddi*."

"I'm sure your *daddi* likes you."

"*Nein*. He might love me. He's supposed to love me, but like me? I'm pretty sure that isn't the case."

"Why would you say that?"

"A guy can tell."

"Give me an example."

"Okay." He pulled the buggy out onto the main road, then glanced at her and smiled, as if he was sure he could prove his point—even though his point was that his own *daddi* didn't like him. "I asked him to go fishing, and he said no."

"Maybe he was tired."

"I asked him to play checkers, and he said no."

"Maybe he's not good at checkers and hates losing."

"I even asked him if he'd like to walk outside with me and see an owl's nest that I found."

"Maybe he doesn't like owls."

Micah laughed, stretched like a cat and looked immensely proud of himself. "Enough about my problems, but admit that your parents did not like the idea of your going to an *Englisch* concert."

Susannah shrugged and refused to make eye contact.

"Oh, my gosh. You never had a *rumspringa*!"

She shook her head and closed her eyes. He really was incorrigible. She wasn't about to explain that she'd been going through her cancer diagnosis and treatment when her friends were enjoying their running-around time.

"I hit the nail on the head. I knew they didn't approve of your going to hear Jason Wright and the Red River Posse band."

"What does that even mean? Red River Posse?"

"Well, a posse is a group of individuals who are sort of deputized. You know, they help out the sheriff."

"And Red River?"

"In Texas."

"And Jason Wright?"

"I think it's a play on the word *right*, like being right, not wrong."

"Ridiculous."

"Uh-huh." Now he did looked pleased. "Just as I thought. You're going to hate it."

"I might not hate it. I happen to like music."

"You do?"

"Sure. I've been known to hum a melody as I sew."

"What kind of melody?"

"Uh…the only kind I know. Songs from church." She rushed on when he gave her an I-told-you-so look. "That's not the point. Did you specifically pick this to do tonight because you thought I'd hate it? Are you trying to—" she waved a hand at the passing roadside "—ditch me?"

"Oh, no. You're not getting out of this that easily by saying that I'm trying to ditch you. Uh-uh. I'm not ditching anyone. I'm glad that the bishop's daughter is having a night out on the town. Besides, you're my only option if I'm not allowed to date anyone else."

"I'm not the boss of you, Micah."

"Exactly. But you know how to put the pressure on, just like a woman."

"Oh, good grief."

"So if I'm being pressured not to date other girls in your community, then you have to stick to our deal."

"Fine by me."

They rode in silence for a minute, but then Micah

returned to his original question. "So, were your parents upset…about where we were going?"

"*Nein.* I'm a grown woman. I can go wherever I want."

"But you've already joined the church."

"Which doesn't mean I can't enjoy an evening in the park."

"Uh-huh."

"If a band happens to be playing, there's no rule that says I have to cover my ears."

"I see."

"It's not like I have a radio hidden away in my sewing room."

"Already I'm corrupting you."

She slapped his arm, but in truth it was a relief to get away from the farm for an evening. It had been a long time since she'd done something that didn't involve her family or her girlfriends or her sewing. She loved all those things, but it felt good to do something different. Maybe Micah was a bad influence or maybe he could be for some people, but she would be more careful than that. She had decided not to worry about anything this evening.

She actually had fun at the park. There were booths set up where people were selling homemade items like jewelry and T-shirts and even ball caps. Micah put one over her *kapp* that was pink and had the word *Princess* spelled out in glitter. Susannah told the woman it was beautiful and carefully placed it back on the table.

The local pizzeria had a booth where they were selling giant slices, but Micah insisted on buying a large

pizza. Susannah couldn't remember the last time she'd eaten two slices of pizza, but when Micah dared her to eat another piece she actually found she was still hungry. Maybe it was from all the walking around they'd done.

And the music wasn't so bad. They saw a few other Amish families enjoying the fine May evening, though none were actually sitting up front listening to the band like they were. She waved each time she saw someone from their district.

"What's wrong?" Micah nudged his shoulder against hers. "I rather liked that song. It was all about bull riding, which I saw once in Maine. Maybe you'd prefer love songs."

"Oh, it's not that. I waved at the Kings."

"Mose King? Isn't he the one you told me was a widower? The guy your *mamm* wants you to marry? Point him out to me. I want to see if he has hair sprouting out of his ears and uses a cane."

She slapped his arm. "Not Mose, his brother and sister-in-law—Frank and Ida. I waved when they looked toward us, but they turned away as if they didn't see me."

"They probably didn't see you." Micah nodded his head to the left and right. "Lots of people here."

"I guess you're right."

He pulled back and widened his eyes in mock surprise. "Excuse me? Could you say that again?"

Which made her laugh, and then she stopped worrying about the Kings.

Susannah helped her mother clean their house the next day. Since it wasn't a church weekend, they were

having dinner for their closest neighbors—which would include Micah and his grandparents.

"I'm interested to see how they react around him," she confessed to her mother as she dumped the pail of dirty water on the flower beds.

"What do you mean?"

"Well, according to Micah, his *mammi* is strict but kind."

"Abigail is a *gut* woman."

"But his *daddi* is beyond strict. Micah says he doesn't think his *daddi* cares for him very much."

"Why would he say such a thing?"

Susannah shrugged, then plopped down beside her mother in the porch swing. The twins were playing with a set of jacks on the far side of the porch. The sight of their heads nearly touching as they leaned over the jacks and ball made Susannah extremely happy. Was it just two years ago that she was worried she wouldn't see them grow up to be young girls? Yet, here they were. She was thankful for that, for every day she had with her family.

"Where'd you go?" her *mamm* asked softly.

"Just thinking about how grateful I am to still be alive."

"I thank the Lord for that very thing every day when I rise and every evening when I go to sleep. It's a frightening experience to almost lose a child."

Susannah cornered herself in the swing so she could study her mother. "I guess it's easy for me to forget how hard that time was on you."

"That's the thing… When tragedy is in our past we

do forget about it, but it changes us, Susannah. Just like you are a more serious young woman—a more grateful and mature one—because of your illness. I'm changed, too, as is your *dat*. We realize more than we ever did before how precious each day is."

They pushed the swing for a while as the girls' laughter spilled toward them. Susannah's mind drifted back toward Micah and his grandfather. As if sensing the turn in her thoughts, her *mamm* stood up and brushed dirt off her apron. "John Fisher loves Micah. I have no doubt about that. I didn't know him before the accident…"

"The one where he lost his arm?"

"*Ya.* I didn't know him then, but I imagine it changed him just as your experience with cancer changed you. We can never know how a person's path through this life twists and turns. We only know where they are right now. But John? Well, it's been hard for him."

"Because of his disability."

"That and probably how strangers look at him—no one wants to be pitied."

"I hated when people looked at me that way—when I was going through the worst of the chemo."

"John has endured those looks all of his life. People mean well, but sometimes they allow your disability to define you, and none of us want that." She reached for Susannah's hand and pulled her off the swing. As they walked inside to prepare lunch, she added a final comment on the subject. "John does love Micah. Abigail has shared with me that they are both worried about

the boy, and John intends to do his best by him. Sometimes that's not an easy thing."

That evening Micah took her moonlight fishing. As they walked across the back fields to the pond, Susannah felt as light as one of the swallows darting through the last of the sunset. She realized in that moment that she felt happy, really happy for the first time in a long time. Glancing at Micah, she wondered if that had anything to do with him.

But that thought was ridiculous.

It wasn't Micah that was changing the way she looked at things.

But it could be that doing things she wasn't used to—going to the park and listening to bands and fishing in the moonlight—was pulling her out of a lingering depression that had started when she'd first been diagnosed.

"Tell me you're not thinking of changing your mind." Micah shifted the backpack across his shoulders. "I even brought *Mammi*'s cookies and coffee."

"I'm not going to change my mind, but I don't believe we'll catch anything. You can't fish by moonlight."

"Can, too."

"How do you know if you've caught anything?"

Micah reached into his pocket and pulled something out. As he shook his closed fist, she heard a jingle sound.

"Bells?"

"Yup. Small ones." He was carrying two fishing poles, and he waved them in front of him. "Plus, I rigged these up with fluorescent line."

"Now, that was a waste of money."

"You won't think so when we catch a lot of fish."

They didn't catch a lot of fish, but somehow that didn't matter too much to Susannah. Sitting on the dock in the moonlight, she thought that she hadn't ever seen a more beautiful evening. The moonlight resembled the soft glow from a lantern. If she focused, she could just make out the fishing line stretched out from Micah's poles. He'd attached the bells on the end, and each time they rang she laughed.

"You're scaring off the fish."

"I'm sorry, but I've never fished with a bell before."

"Have you ever fished before?"

"Some." She almost said "before my cancer," but then she realized she hadn't told him about that part of her life. Did he know? Had someone else told him? Maybe not. Maybe that was why she liked being around him. Micah didn't treat her as if she might break.

A few minutes earlier she'd thought he was going to make good on his threat to push her into the water. He'd only stopped when she'd grabbed one of the poles and said she'd take it with her. She enjoyed people treating her like a normal person. Maybe that was what she'd been missing.

"Oatmeal cookie for your thoughts?" He held up a cookie, and when she reached for it, he moved it out of her reach. "Uh-uh, you have to tell me what you were thinking about first."

"Right. Okay. Well, I was thinking about something my *mamm* said, that hard times change a person."

"Ya?" He handed her the cookie and then scooted

the thermos of decaf coffee closer to her. "What kind of hard times?"

"I guess it could be anything, but the point is that you're not the same afterward. Maybe you start out carefree and end up serious. Or maybe you start out sure of everything, every turn your life is going to take. Like you have it all planned out. You know?"

"I've never planned much," Micah admitted.

"Say you did, and then something happened to change everything."

"Everything?"

"Ya."

"Huh. I guess that would make me more cautious." He reeled in a little of the fishing line, then asked, "Is that what happened to you? Is that why you're such a rule follower?"

"I'm not a very good rule follower. I went to a concert with you last night."

"And it didn't corrupt you a bit."

"True, but I need to be careful, or I might start singing about pickup trucks and mud on my boots."

She picked up one of her flip-flop sandals, waved it at him and then sat it back down. "Imagine that—an Amish woman in cowgirl boots."

Micah picked up the other shoe and studied it. "This looks nothing like a boot. Maybe if I threw it into the water, it would change and become a boot."

"Give me that shoe back."

But Micah had already jumped up and was holding the flip-flop over his head. "This? You want this?"

"Micah, don't you dare…"

"Sounds like you're issuing an ultimatum."

"I need that shoe to walk back to the house. You don't want me walking barefoot through the fields."

"It's good for a person to walk barefoot. Helps you to feel connected to *Gotte*'s green earth."

Susannah was standing on her tiptoes, trying to wrestle the shoe from his hands, and Micah was moving backward to avoid her, a big dopey grin on his face. Then he took one too many steps backward at the exact moment that she rested a hand on his chest so she could keep her balance and reach up higher with the other hand. His eyes found hers just before they splashed into the water.

She came up sputtering, shocked that she was now thoroughly wet. Then she heard something that was becoming quite familiar to her—Micah's laughter.

He pointed at her head. "You have moss on top of your *kapp*."

"Oh, so you think that's funny. Is that why you're laughing?" She reached down into the water, grabbed a fistful of the slimy green stuff, then lurched toward him and tossed it on top of his head. After that, it was rather a free-for-all of water splashing and moss throwing.

Micah was the one who noticed that her flip-flop had drifted toward the middle of the pond. He swam out to it with sure, easy strokes. She waited near the dock in the moonlight, standing in water up to her waist and wondered where he'd learned to swim like that. His shadow in the moonlight reminded her of a large fish cutting through the water.

It occurred to her that Micah was a nice guy and a good-hearted man. He was certainly not difficult to look at. That

thought caused her cheeks to burn with embarrassment, and she was grateful for the darkness. He wasn't interested in her, and she certainly wasn't interested in him—not that way. They were just hanging out together, helping him through a tough time until he was able to return home. She'd do well to keep that thought front and center.

When he returned and presented her with the shoe, she grabbed it from him with what she hoped was a curt "I'm going to get even for this."

Walking out of the water, she paused at the edge to put her shoes on her feet and squeeze water from her dress. She didn't realize he was behind her until he spoke—his mouth close to her ear and his words a mere whisper that sent goose bumps down her arms. "You look awfully pretty in the moonlight, Susannah Beiler."

Which set off every emotional alarm she possessed.

Was he flirting with her?

Did he think she had been flirting with him?

What was she doing standing in the moonlight with Micah Fisher? She was supposed to be keeping an eye on him—keeping him out of trouble.

Before she could work any of that out, Micah said, "Let me gather up our stuff. Then we can walk back by the road. It'll give our clothes time to dry off a bit."

The route would be longer, but Susannah found she didn't mind.

A small part of her wished the night could go on and on.

Micah whistled through his Sunday morning chores, maybe because he knew they were going over to the

Beilers for lunch. There was something about Susannah that intrigued him. It wasn't that he was falling for her—she was much too serious to be his type—but she was easy to be around.

And she was a challenge.

He was honest enough to admit that he loved a good challenge.

The morning devotion time with his grandparents was a bit trying. His *daddi* had an obvious focus in mind. They began in the book of Psalms, reading how *Gotte* would establish the work of their hands—whatever that meant. Then moved to Proverbs, where they spent a good twenty minutes on a verse about sluggards and how such persons were doomed to an unsuccessful life. Finally, they ended up in Colossians, where Paul wrote that whatever they did they should do with all their heart.

Micah tried to stay focused.

He didn't fidget or peek at the clock in the kitchen even once.

But he did feel resentment building in his soul. Did he not work hard every single day? What did his grandfather want from him? And why had his parents banished him to Indiana when it was obvious that he belonged in Maine?

By the time they'd finished the final prayer, Micah was feeling agitated and needing to burn off some steam. He felt like he could hit a baseball a hundred times and still have energy to spare.

"We'll be driving the buggy over to the Beilers'

place." His *mammi* had followed him into the mudroom, where he'd grabbed his hat and jammed it on his head.

"*Danki, Mammi,* but I'll walk."

He didn't wait for an answer.

He didn't bother to explain.

He needed out of there and away from their disapproving stares.

Being outside in the sunshine helped. He wasn't normally a morose person. Sometimes, though, he felt backed into a corner. For the life of him, he could not understand what people wanted from him, what they expected. He chewed on those thoughts for the first half of his walk, but as soon as Susannah's little sewing shop came into view, his mood improved.

Last night had been fun.

He'd almost kissed her just to see what it would be like.

But the way her eyes had widened… Well, it had caused him to pat her awkwardly on the arm and walk away.

Had Susannah never been kissed?

Why wasn't she dating?

She was a smart girl with a pleasant personality. She apparently was a very good quilter, as there were often people stopping at her little shop to purchase quilts. She was patient with her sisters, and she was pretty to boot.

Why wasn't she married?

He forgot that question and his aggravation with his grandparents as soon as he started helping Susannah carry out food to the picnic tables. Her little sisters— Sharon and Shiloh, who looked so much alike that he

still couldn't tell them apart—had taken a liking to him. They followed him like baby ducks waddling after their mama.

In truth, they reminded him of his own *schweschdern* back in Maine—they were older, but he rather missed having them around. He could always make them laugh, and they thought he was ever so clever.

Shiloh and Sharon helped him and Susannah set up a volleyball net.

They insisted on showing him the new kittens in the barn and the baby goats in the pasture.

They sat beside him as everyone ate lunch.

"You need to finish eating, Sharon." Susannah nodded toward her sister's plate with a stern look.

Which, of course, made Micah laugh because Susannah looked so serious and Sharon looked so frustrated. And then he remembered that Sharon was the one always running ahead. She also had freckles sprinkled across her cheeks and the bridge of her nose.

"Why are you laughing at me, Micah? I don't want to eat. I want to play."

"*Ya*, but the playing is not going anywhere, and you need to eat to have lots of energy."

"*Mamm* always says I have plenty of energy."

"That's because you knock things over a lot," Shiloh commented as she was carefully attempting to cut a piece of ham with a knife and fork.

"Want some help with that?" he asked.

She nodded enthusiastically, but Susannah shook her head in disapproval. "How will she ever learn?"

"How will she learn what?"

"*If* you do it for her, how will she learn?"

"I'm watching him do it, Susannah."

"*Ya*, you're watching, but your hands are smaller. When your hands are bigger you'll be able to do it yourself."

Shiloh studied her palms, then held them up for all to see. "Still small."

He couldn't have said why he felt so comfortable around Susannah and her sisters, but the afternoon flew by. Micah's grandparents left early, *Mammi* claiming she had a terrible headache.

"Is she okay?" Susannah asked.

"She gets migraines sometimes. Says the only thing to do for them is lie down in a dark room."

"Should you have gone home with them?"

"They'd probably rather I didn't." He laughed at the look of dismay on Susannah's face. "What I mean is that it's quieter when I'm not there."

"How much noise do you make?"

"Not that much, but they're used to living alone."

"How did they end up here without any family?"

"Their oldest daughter—my *aenti* Grace—married and moved to Maine when the Unity community was first established in 2008."

"How did she happen to meet a fellow from Maine?"

"Her husband, Otis, had been looking for cheaper land, moving every few years, trying to find a less crowded area. Lots of eligible men in Maine and not a lot of women, since the communities are smaller. My other *aentis* had soon married and moved there, as well. Then my *dat* would visit, and the way he tells it, he loved

being out in the wild. In fact, that's our family motto. It's sort of a joke. *Less people and more wild animals.*"

Susannah rolled her eyes and shook her head at the same time. Ha! He was getting to her.

"My *dat* says he wouldn't want to live anywhere else, that he's glad I grew up there."

"But you weren't born there?"

"*Nein*. I was actually born in Wisconsin."

"Wisconsin?"

"Before he settled on Maine, my parents moved every few years. According to my *mamm*, they'd move to a place, get settled and then the community would double in size and my *dat* would start looking in the *Budget* for another place to move."

"So why haven't your *daddi* and *mammi* moved to be with the rest of the family?"

"That's a really good question, one that I've been asking myself, but I haven't figured out the answer. Maybe they were waiting to see if we'd all actually stay there."

"Sounds like your *dat* plans on staying."

"*Ya*, he does. The problem is that the other communities in Maine are quite strict. Fort Fairfield, which is the northernmost district, was originally a Swartzentruber district."

"I've heard of them. More conservative?"

"Much. They're not allowed to hire drivers unless it's for an emergency, no close relationships with non-Amish people and their clothes are even more Plain." He bumped his shoulder against hers as they walked to-

ward the adjacent field. "That pretty peach color you're wearing wouldn't be allowed."

"I can't imagine you living in a community that strict."

"Well, where we live in Unity isn't that strict, but there's still the influence of the other groups."

"Maybe that's why you're such a renegade."

"I'm a renegade?" He stopped in his tracks, hands on his hips. "You have offended me deeply, Susannah Beiler."

"Sure I did."

They walked to an old swing suspended from a tall maple tree. "Have a seat."

"What?"

"Sit down. I'll push you."

"You want me to get in the swing?"

"Sure and certain. It'll make you feel free. Make you feel as if you could touch the sky." He stepped closer. Already he was learning that she spooked easily. Susannah was accustomed to her personal space. Anytime he stepped within that space, she looked like a colt about to bolt. Rather than let him in her space, she plopped down into the swing and raised her feet.

"So push me already."

Soon they were both laughing, and Micah was wondering if he could talk her into fishing again. But they were interrupted by Sharon, who ran up and said, "*Dat* wants to see you both. In the house."

"Are we in trouble?" He was kidding, but the look on Sharon's face said that he might have nailed it with his question.

"Both of us?" Susannah asked.

"*Ya*, that's what he said. I have to go. We found a bird nest over by the barn, and I'm watching the babies try to fly." She fairly screamed the last part as she ran in the opposite direction.

"Does she ever slow down?"

"Only when she's sleeping."

Apparently their afternoon free time was over. Micah pulled Susannah to her feet, and they trudged toward the house, in step with one another.

"Any idea what this is about?" He tried not to sound worried. Why should he be worried? It wasn't as if he'd never been called in to see the bishop before. He should have expected this, though somehow he'd begun to hope that things could be different in Goshen.

"*Nein.*"

"Your *dat* didn't say anything at breakfast?"

She shook her head, glancing at the adults gathered around the picnic table.

When they walked into the house and saw that Thomas was there with one of the other preachers— some guy by the name of Atlee—Micah sensed they were in trouble. He could understand why he might be. Not that he could think of anything in particular, but there was always something. It was actually rather a surprise that he'd made it nearly two weeks without being reprimanded by someone.

But Susannah? He couldn't imagine why she'd been called in.

"Have a seat." Thomas indicated the couch, so they sat side by side. Thomas sat in a rocker, and Atlee was

in a rather large upholstered chair. He was a small older man, and the chair pretty much dwarfed him.

"I'll get right to the point," Thomas said. "I've had two different families come to me this morning with concerns about your behavior."

"Mine?" Susannah's voice screeched like a hoot owl.

It made Micah smile, which caused Atlee to frown.

Micah quickly schooled his expression in an attempt to appear more serious.

"Can't think of any reason there would have been concerns," Micah said. "I pretty much just worked all week."

"And I was working on that new quilt order I had."

"I'm sure you both did work very hard." Thomas's expression softened. "This was about the weekend, beginning with Friday night at the park."

Susannah crossed her arms and frowned. "I can't think of anything we did wrong at the park."

"Perhaps we shouldn't think of this as right or wrong, but rather something that someone saw and was concerned about. You two are old enough to realize that it matters how we're perceived by the community at large. We're to be examples of Christ, and we're to set ourselves apart from the world."

"Of course." Micah stared at the floor, because if he looked up, Thomas would see that he was about to lose his temper. He just had no patience for this sort of thing.

"You went to the park in town?" Thomas asked.

"*Ya*. I told you that, *Dat*. You said it would be fine."

"And you stayed to hear the concert?"

"In fact you moved and sat up front, if accounts

are correct." Atlee studied them through large round glasses.

Micah blew out a noisy breath, then he sat up straighter. "We did, and I asked Susannah if it was all right before we did so."

"And I told him it was. *Dat*, there's nothing wrong with listening to music. We didn't get up and dance. We didn't waste money on a CD that we could bring home and play on a hidden music player we keep in the barn."

Thomas sighed heavily, then scooted to the edge of the rocker, his elbows braced on his knees.

"Why do we sing?"

Micah glanced up, wondering if this was a trick question. He was surprised to see a twinkle in Thomas's eyes when he'd expected to see condemnation.

"To express our moods," Micah said.

"Because it lifts our spirits," Susannah added.

"All right. Those are both *gut* reasons. But you've forgotten the Biblical reason—to give glory to *Gotte*. Singing, it's an act of worship, just like when we pray or observe communion or when we wash one another's feet."

Micah shifted uncomfortably in his seat. He wasn't sure where Thomas was going with this. This wasn't the standard lecture he'd received back home from his bishop or his *dat* or even from his *daddi*.

"We're even admonished to keep singing in the Bible. Paul told us to encourage one another with psalms and hymns and spiritual songs." Thomas paused, then added, "I suspect that isn't what you were listening to at the park."

"Nein," Susannah said softly.

"More like songs about pickup trucks and mud and boots."

"Ah." Thomas slapped his leg, as if they were finally getting to the crux of the matter. "We could relate to that if it was a buggy instead of a pickup truck."

When Micah dared to look at him again, he was grinning. "We want to be separate from the world, though I've been known to listen to a country tune myself once in a while. You both know Jethro. He gives rides to Amish folk, always has his radio turned to country music. I heard a lady named Alison Krauss sing 'Amazing Grace' once. It was beautiful indeed."

"So why are we in trouble?" Micah asked.

"I didn't say you were. I only said people were concerned."

"Then there's the matter of last night." Atlee cleared his throat and pushed up his glasses. "Perhaps we should move on to that."

"All we did last night was fish, *Dat.* You knew we were going to do that. You even reminded me not to get my line caught up in the brush."

"This has more to do with you coming home in the dark at a very late hour, apparently in clothes that were soaking wet."

And there it was. The line they had crossed. Micah knew that he always managed to find it, but this time he'd dragged Susannah with him.

Thomas spent the next twenty minutes leading them through scripture that directed them to be separate, to be set apart, to be holy. By the time he finished, Micah

was feeling appropriately chastised. He thought it might end there, but then Thomas stood and delivered his final decree. "Perhaps we should continue this conversation after you've had some time to think on it. I believe a weekly meeting might be appropriate—between the three of us. Do you agree, Susannah?"

"Sure."

"Micah?"

What could he do? Micah agreed. He couldn't leave Susannah to endure the punishment alone, though spending an hour each week being lectured didn't sound like his idea of fun. At least it would be with Thomas and not Atlee. If he'd been told he had to spend an hour with the frowning old guy, he might have been tempted to throw in the towel and walk back to Maine.

Chapter Five

The Goshen Amish community held a barn raising on Friday and Saturday of the following week. Of course, Micah had been to plenty of barn raisings and home raisings, too, for that matter. In Maine, their community was small, which meant that everyone pitched in when there was a need. But the fact that they were small also meant that raisings took a week to complete. Everyone showed up on the first day and then people worked on it as they were able throughout the week until it was completed. Apparently in Goshen they did things differently.

He dropped his grandparents off near the main house, then parked the buggy.

"Where did all these people come from?" he asked Elias Yoder, who was directing buggies.

"There are twenty thousand Amish in Elkhart and Lagrange counties."

"And they're all here today?"

Elias laughed as he chalked a number on Micah's grandfather's buggy—#321. *Wow*. There were 321 fami-

lies here? He'd actually thought he'd get to spend some time with Susannah today. He'd be lucky if he even saw her.

That thought fell away as he fastened his work belt around his waist and hurried toward the construction area. Though the sun had barely peeked over the horizon, the sound of hammers striking nails rang out and the south wall of the structure was already taking shape. He glanced over to the long string of picnic tables near the house.

The women made quite an image, reminding him of worker bees. They were wearing gray, blue, pink, peach, even green frocks—though everyone's head was covered with the same white *kapp*. There looked to be a hundred or more of them there, many holding babies on their hips and ranging in age from the infants to an old woman he passed, who had to be a hundred if she was a day.

The concerns of the previous week fell away.

He forgot about the meetings he was required to attend with Susannah's father.

He stopped worrying about the many ways that he managed to disappoint his *daddi*.

And maybe for the first time, he let go of his wish to be in Maine.

Micah checked in with the master engineer, who assigned him to the west wall that was just being laid out. The foundation had been poured two weeks earlier. Lumber and hardware had been delivered beforehand as well, and sat waiting to be used in large organized stacks. He passed a group of men sawing floor joists

to length. A group of *youngies* would carry the measured and cut boards to men standing on the foundation. Micah suspected that given the amount of workers they had, the frame, including the roof beams, would be in place well before lunch.

Soon he was intent on his section—finishing out the frame and finding a rhythm with the large group of men in his section. Someone started singing, and soon his voice was joined by another and another. Micah became totally focused on the hammer, the nail, the song and the rising sun warming his back. He didn't realize that sweat had drenched his shirt until one of the young boys walked up with a tray of cups and water. He took two, pouring one over his neck and downing the other.

Then the second master engineer was calling out that it was time to begin the actual construction of the wall. The boards were measured and cut. Micah scrambled to the top with a dozen other men as others from the ground lifted the boards into place. The planks were positioned vertically—Micah hammered from the top as a younger guy he didn't know hammered from the bottom.

An hour later, he was once again being offered water. As he gulped it down, he looked around the roof area where he was working. An old man with white hair stood on his left and a young teen on his right. Both reflected the same grin that he felt on his own face.

And then they were working again. Micah straddled a beam so that he could nail from the outside. He looked down and counted four others doing the same. They must look like a ladder of Amish men.

He had no idea how much time had passed when he

climbed down and stepped back, trying to take in the whole of what they'd done. "It's like building a house of cards," he murmured.

"Pretty much," the old guy to his right agreed, grinning and straightening his suspenders. "Much sturdier, though."

Soon they were both back on the roof again. The morning passed without Micah even being aware of it. When he heard the lunch bell ring, he scrambled down to the ground, but then he stood there as the tide of workers swept past him. He stared up at the frame of the barn, which was now completely intact.

It really was amazing what could be done when people worked together.

Almost without realizing what he was doing, he slipped his cell phone from his back pocket and took a selfie with the barn rising behind him. Only when he touched the photo button and heard the click did he realize that what he was doing was generally frowned upon. So he stuck his phone back in his pocket and strode off toward lunch.

He'd put it on Snapchat later that evening.

One picture wouldn't hurt anything.

And it wasn't like anyone else in the group had a phone or a Snapchat account. What they didn't know wouldn't hurt them, and it wouldn't land him in trouble, either.

Or, at least, that was his thinking at the moment.

He spied Susannah twice during lunch. Both times he tried to catch her attention, but she didn't see him. Or at least she pretended not to see him.

Was she upset about the meetings they had to attend with her *dat*? He tried to remember if they'd talked about it, but she had been curiously absent when he'd worked in her *dat*'s farrier shop. He'd thought she was simply busy, but maybe she was avoiding him.

He didn't have much time to dwell on it. Before he'd even cleaned his plate, men were returning to work. The afternoon passed as quickly as the morning had. By the time he climbed down from the roof, he was sore in a way that he hadn't been in a very long time. He supposed that farming and shoeing horses didn't use the same muscles as construction. It wasn't that he was getting older. His age had nothing to do with it.

He looked for Susannah as he made his way to fetch the buggy for his grandparents. When he asked Elias, who was once again helping folks with their buggies, he learned that the Beiler family had already left.

Possibly she was avoiding him. So what? Maybe she'd decided that being his sidekick was too risky. The thought depressed him terribly. Hadn't they had fun? Hadn't she enjoyed the evening in the park and the time they'd gone fishing?

He knew she had. She'd laughed and smiled and the serious Susannah had slipped away.

But he didn't doubt that she was making an effort not to spend time with him, which was fine. He'd see her on Sunday. They had the church meeting, and there was no way she could avoid him there.

Fortunately for Susannah, Sunday morning dawned dark and rainy. She could volunteer to stay inside with

the babies after service. Then she wouldn't have to deal with Micah.

So she was pretty surprised when she was sitting with Deborah, rocking babies in the Gleichs' front living room, and Micah stepped inside.

"Uh-oh. Looks like someone found you," Deborah said under her breath.

If he felt uncomfortable in a room full of babies, Micah didn't show it. But then was he ever uncomfortable? That was part of his problem—even places where he didn't belong, he still seemed to enjoy. No, that wasn't quite right. Micah Fisher was a man intent on savoring every single moment of a day, and she couldn't really blame him for that. She admired it in one way, but then there was her *dat* to think about...

"Deborah, Susannah. *Gut* to see you both."

"Is there something we can help you with, Micah?" Deborah smiled sweetly and nodded to the fussy baby in her lap. "Or maybe you had an urge to rock a *boppli.*"

"I could if you need me to, not that I have any experience. I somehow managed to avoid babysitting my nieces and nephews when they were still infants. Come to think of it, I don't think I've ever—"

Deborah stood and held the crying infant out to him. "Jeremiah is teething and none too happy about it. Maybe he'll respond better to a man. And here's his Binky, which he won't take from me, and also his blanket."

And with an obvious wink at Susannah, Deborah picked up her giant purse and fled the room.

"That was embarrassing," Susannah muttered.

"What was embarrassing, and how do I get this kid to stop crying?"

"First of all, stop holding him at arm's length as if he's a fish you just caught."

"Oh."

"Closer. Snuggle him like you would a newborn."

"I don't know how to snuggle a newborn."

"Okay. First, sit down." She'd been rocking Mary Lynn, a sweet six-week-old whose *mamm* looked as if she was going to fall asleep on her feet. Susannah laid the child in a playpen that had been set up in the corner of the room, covered her with a blanket and then returned to Micah's side.

He was staring at Jeremiah as if he'd never seen a crying baby before. As for Jeremiah, his cries had reached a fever pitch.

"Sit."

"Here?"

"Sit and rock. I'll fetch a bottle."

When she returned to the room, it was quiet. Micah had the baby lying on his belly across his knees and was rubbing his back.

"Huh."

"*Huh*, what? Did you think I didn't know how to quiet a baby?"

"Quite obviously, you didn't. You said as much when you walked in."

"True, but I tried this once with a puppy I found that seemed miserable. I think he'd eaten some hamburger that had gone rancid…"

"Please don't tell me any more."

"The thing had vomited once, and he started howling. Mutt looked so pitiful that I finally went to the front porch and put him across my knees, just like this. And it worked, just like with…" He stared quizzically down at the child.

"Jeremiah."

"*Ya.* Anyway, I've been looking for you."

"Have you, now?" Baby Hannah was happily lying on her back on an old quilt and trying to catch her toes, but Susannah picked her up anyway. She suddenly needed something to do with her hands.

"Come on. Out with it. You're avoiding me."

"Why would you say that?"

"Because it's obvious you are. What gives?"

Susannah sighed. There was simply no avoiding difficult conversations with Micah. He was too direct.

"I've never been called in by my *dat* before."

"I figured as much."

"And I didn't like it one bit. Plus, I'm ashamed that I embarrassed him."

"You didn't embarrass him. I don't think he even really cared. It was that old guy, Atlee, who was stirring up trouble."

"I'm the bishop's *doschder*, Micah."

"And that means you can't have any fun?"

"That means I'm held to a higher standard."

"Sounds like pride to me. Didn't we learn at our meeting on Monday that pride is a sin?"

"Now you're mocking me."

"*Nein*, I'm not."

Baby Jeremiah had fallen asleep, and apparently Mi-

cah's knees had, too. He raised the baby to his shoulder, trying to mirror the way that Susannah was holding Hannah. It was such a funny sight, Micah juggling a baby and a blanket and a pacifier, that Susannah had trouble hanging on to her anger.

Anger.

The sermon that morning had been on anger. *The wrath of man does not work the righteousness of God.*

Susannah sighed. It seemed that in matters of Micah, whether she turned left or right, she was facing some sort of dilemma.

"I'm sorry we got in trouble about the picnic and the fishing, but as your *dat* said, it wasn't that we did anything wrong, only that we weren't thinking of how it might be viewed by others."

"So you were listening."

"Of course I was listening. I like your *dat*."

Which made her smile. He said it so simply, as if it were an obvious fact. "I like him, too."

"So would you like to go a movie next week?"

"Uh-uh. No way."

"It's a cartoon. Nothing at all racy about it."

"I'm not going to the movies."

"So you're setting me free to ask someone else? Our deal… It's over?" He smiled slyly at her. "Because I think your friend Deborah might have a thing for me."

"That is ridiculous."

"Is not."

"She left the room as soon as you walked in."

"So she's a little shy."

He was incorrigible. But then again, she had agreed to

be his sidekick for as long as he was here. Come to think of it, how much longer was he going to be in Goshen?

"Any news on your moving back to Maine?"

"Now you're trying to get rid of me?"

"I did not say that."

Micah's laugh was sincere and hearty. It came from somewhere deep down in his belly. She'd never met anyone as good-natured as he was. In fact, if she were honest, Micah Fisher was a complete mystery to her.

Tuesday morning Micah still felt like he was in something of a funk. He hadn't been too surprised when Susannah turned him down for going to the movies. It wasn't forbidden, as long as they attended something G-rated or possibly PG, depending on the story. While it was true that most Amish folk didn't waste money on things like movies, it was understood that *youngies* needed to be away from the farm occasionally.

But he'd known before he asked that Susannah wouldn't go. He'd paid attention to her reaction when her *dat* and Atlee had first called them in for The Lecture. That was how he thought about it—with capital letters. It wasn't his first reprimand and probably wouldn't be his last, but it was Susannah's first. There was no doubt about that.

She'd gone instantly rigid.

Sure, she had supported him, but as the meeting had worn on, her shoulders had tensed and she'd clasped her hands so hard that he was afraid she was going to cut off the circulation.

And then in the days immediately following, she'd started avoiding him.

The plan was for them to meet with Thomas every Monday, which they had done twice now. It hadn't been as terrible as Micah had feared. They'd discussed the *Ordnung* in general, events they were looking forward to and how they were feeling about their circumstances. Micah wasn't big on talking about feelings—he had them, same as everyone else. But what was the point in dwelling on them?

Did he feel like he'd been cast out from his home? Yes.

Did he struggle against the restrictions of the *Ordnung*? Yes!

Did he wish to remain Amish? Well, yes, of course he did. He simply didn't understand why it had to be so difficult and confining.

And so, he dithered. That was the only word for it and one his grandmother used—in fact, she'd accused him of that very thing just the day before. *Micah, I love you more than the breath in my lungs, but you can dither more than any man or child I've ever met.* He'd waited until he was in the barn brushing down the buggy horse to look up the meaning on his phone.

Webster's online claimed it meant to be indecisive.

Well, the fact that he was standing in a horse stall using his cell phone pretty much confirmed that he was indecisive—at least about whether to join the church and commit to following the rules of the *Ordnung* for the rest of his life. Moreover, he didn't see why he had to make a decision now. What was the rush? He prob-

ably had sixty years stretching in front of him. There was plenty of time to settle down and be a good Amish person.

In the days immediately following The Lecture, he'd told himself none of this mattered.

He often found himself once again calculating the date until his six months was up, but just looking at the days on the calendar filled him with dread. The immense amount of time that was left before he could even think about returning home, the idea of working every morning in the field and every afternoon in the farrier shop, the fact that he and Susannah hadn't done anything fun in nearly ten days…it all depressed him.

On the Tuesday after he'd talked to her in the nursery, he decided he might go crazy if he didn't take a few hours off from the farm. Fortunately, he'd finished up in the farrier shop early. Thomas was having a business meeting with the other members of church leadership—something about the benevolence fund. Micah had the afternoon free, and he'd seen on his phone that the sports store in town was having a clearance sale.

Few things cheered him up like a new hunting rifle or crossbow or fishing gear. His home town of Smyrna was located in the northeastern part of Maine, and was well-known for its fishing opportunities—whitefish, three kinds of trout and two kinds of bass. Just thinking about the fall fishing cheered him up, and he did have a little extra money in his pocket from working for Thomas. Certainly it wouldn't hurt to spend part of it, and he could stop by Jo Jo's Pretzels for a snack afterward.

The thought of a few hours in town had him humming to himself. As he cleaned up and shelved the tools in Thomas's shop, it occurred to him that the only thing that would make his plan better would be if Susannah went along with him. Not that he thought of her in any romantic way—she'd made it quite clear that she wasn't interested in dating—but the girl needed some relaxation time.

Whistling as he walked across the yard, he stuck his head into Susannah's sewing shop, but the place was empty. In fact, it was terribly neat, as if she hadn't been there all day. He started to climb the steps to knock on the front door, but he didn't want to wake the twins if they were napping. They probably weren't, but since it was so quiet, they might be.

Then again, maybe Susannah was around back, working in the garden. He walked down the steps of the porch, around the house, and stopped short when he saw her sitting on the bench next to the garden.

She was sitting in the sun, her head back and her eyes closed. Something caught in Micah's throat. Susannah was a beautiful woman, and she didn't seem to be aware of that fact at all. But it wasn't that awareness that caused him to stand perfectly still staring at her.

She must have washed her hair and was drying it in the sun. Her *kapp* lay on the bench beside her, and as he watched, she reached up a hand to run it through her hair—her beautiful, short brown hair. Then, as if she sensed him there, she turned to look at him. Her eyes widened, and Micah knew that there was no backing

out of the situation. So instead he did what he always did: he plunged forward.

It would seem that Susannah had secrets of her own, and he was about to find out exactly what and why she'd been keeping them from him.

He strode over to where she was sitting and straddled the bench. He didn't say anything, deciding to let her lead the conversation, but it was hard to just sit there and wait. He had an overwhelming urge to reach out and run his fingers through her hair. He could see now that it only fell an inch past her ears. The look was so incongruous—an Amish woman with bobbed hair—that he honestly didn't know what to say.

When he'd waited as long as he could, he finally stated the obvious, "Must be hair-washing day."

"*Ya.*"

Maybe it was the way she looked up shyly at him, but Micah could no longer resist. He reached out and ran his hand over the top of her head, trailing the golden brown strands to her neck. Her hair felt like silk in his fingers. He wanted to run his fingers through it, but he knew that would be inappropriate, so instead he crossed his arms and said, "Short hair looks *gut* on you."

"That's it?"

"What?"

"That's all you're going to say?"

Micah shrugged, doing his best to look nonchalant. "I suppose there's a story there, but if you wanted to tell me, you would."

"Astute."

"I am all ears, if you have an urge to share. Finished

my work in the shop, cleaned up everything and was just…you know…hanging out."

"You want to go somewhere."

"Maybe."

"And you don't want to go alone."

"I go places alone."

Susannah's grin spread, but then she spied her *kapp* sitting between them and snatched it off the bench.

"Your hair's almost dry."

"Doesn't take very long, not like when I was younger."

And then, he did what he'd told himself he wasn't going to do—he asked.

"Why's your hair short, Susannah? I'm the renegade here, so I know you didn't cut it because of a dare or a wild urge."

"*Nein*. Nothing like that."

"You don't have to explain if you don't want to."

A look of vulnerability crossed her features. Her customary mask—the one that said she knew what the answers were and had no doubt how things would turn out—slipped. Then a bird called out from a neighboring bush, broke the spell and the proper Susannah was back.

"It's not such a mystery, and honestly I didn't know that you didn't know. Maybe I did realize you didn't know, but then it seemed awkward to bring it up."

"What don't I know?"

She looked left, then right, then out across the garden. When he didn't rescue her from the discomfort of the moment, she met his gaze and said simply, "I had cancer."

It was the very last words he would have expected to come out of her mouth.

"What? When?"

"Diagnosed two years ago, just before my twenty-third birthday. We didn't catch it early enough, so I had chemo before and after the surgery."

"Chemo?"

"*Ya.* It caused my hair to fall out." She ran a hand over the top of her head, as if she needed to assure herself it was no longer bald. "It's growing back quicker than I thought."

Her voice had dropped to a whisper. "Soon no one will be able to tell."

"Who cares about your hair?" The words came out more abruptly than he'd intended. "What I mean is, your hair looks *gut* that way, but more important, how are you? Are you still sick? And why did you never tell me this?"

"Why would I tell you?"

"Because we're friends!" Micah wanted to jump up and pace back and forth, but he forced himself to remain seated. When Susannah still didn't look at him, he put a hand on each of her shoulders and waited until she finally raised her gaze to his. "We're friends. Right?"

"*Ya.* Of course."

"So tell me about this. How do you feel? Will you need more surgery or more chemo? And what is your prognosis?"

"Fine, probably not and *gut.*"

Micah let his hands fall to his side. There was something about the way that Susannah was looking at him

that made him squirm. As if she were waiting for him to figure it out. But figure what out?

Then it occurred to him. Like a bolt of lightning illuminating a dark night, his mind put the pieces of Susannah's puzzle together.

"This is why you don't date?"

Susannah became suddenly interested in the dirt under her thumbnail. "Maybe. I guess."

"That's ridiculous."

"How would you know?"

"Because it doesn't matter."

"It does matter."

"No, what matters is what type of person you are and whether you have feelings for someone—not that you had cancer and are now in recovery."

Susannah tapped a finger against her lips. Her eyebrows were pulled down into a V, and her eyes seemed to be glistening. Was she going to cry?

"I can't have children, Micah."

"What?"

"Because of the type of cancer I had, I can't have children."

"What does that have to do with anything? Why would that make you decide to stop dating?"

"Because there's no point."

"No point?"

She looked at him directly now, her chin up and her eyes daring him to argue with her. "We both know what that means to an Amish family, to an Amish man. Sure, I dated before my diagnosis, but now I understand—"

He cut her off, his impatience suddenly overpowering his vow to let her tell the story in her own way.

"You understand what exactly? That no one would want you? Because that's foolish and… Well, it's wrong."

"Is it?"

"Yes!"

"I don't exactly have men lining up at the door."

"Maybe because you keep everyone at arm's length."

"Or maybe because they would want children." Her anger was winning out over her embarrassment.

Micah was almost relieved to see the return of the Susannah he'd come to know—obstinate and strong-willed, sure, but not heartbroken. One more minute of the heartbroken Susannah, and he would have pulled her into his arms and embarrassed them both.

"Not all men want *kinner*."

"All Amish men do. Trust me, I know."

She leaned her neck forward, twisted her hair into some sort of knot and then secured it with bobby pins that were lying on the bench. How did women do that? He couldn't brush his own teeth without looking in a mirror.

She adjusted the *kapp* on her head, then turned and stared at him, as if she was daring him to push further.

Fine.

He'd push.

Because Susannah needed to realize that any man would be lucky to have her as a *fraa*, children or no children.

"Not everyone wants children, Susannah. You can't not date because of that."

"Of course I can, and that's a personal decision, thank you very much."

"So what do you see as your future? Living with your parents the rest of your life? Hiding in your sewing room and making quilts for other families because you don't deserve to have one?"

He knew he'd hit a nerve by the way she catapulted off the bench.

"I'll thank you to keep your nose out of my future."

"Oh, really? Because you're pretty intent on sticking your nose in mine."

"I have been trying to be your friend."

"You've been trying to corral me, to keep me away from anyone in this stupid town, to keep your girlfriends safe from me as if I'm some kind of ogre that might corrupt them."

But Susannah wasn't listening to him anymore. She was storming away as if they were an old married couple having a fight. He didn't know if he should follow her or not, but by the time he made up his mind that he should, she'd gone into the house and slammed the door quite forcefully behind her.

Which pretty much ended any conversation they were having.

Chapter Six

"You haven't talked to him in two days?" Deborah yanked on the yarn she was knitting with. It was a pastel color and self-striping. She was making a baby blanket for her *schweschder*. Someone in Deborah's family was always about to have a baby. It was a good thing that she was a fast knitter.

Susannah had stopped by to drop off some hot pads and aprons she'd made from fabric scraps. Deborah's family had a good-sized produce shed where they sold everything from fresh vegetables to eggs to knitted items. Susannah kept a corner table filled with quilts, pot holders, aprons, even table runners. Though she offered to work one day a week at the shed, Deborah's parents insisted there was no need. They had twelve children, so there was always someone willing and able to work a few hours.

She'd brought along an infant quilt that she was hand sewing the binding to. As she knotted her thread and pulled it through the back of the quilt, she tried to think how best to answer Deborah's question.

"It's a simple yes or no."

"Yes. We haven't spoken since Tuesday."

"Because you're embarrassed?"

"I don't know. Maybe?"

"Why would you be embarrassed, Susannah? It's not like you dyed your hair pink."

"Indeed."

"Anyway, I think I know what's really going on here."

"Oh, you do, do you?"

"It's so obvious." Deborah waved a knitting needle at her and then stuck it back into her next stitch and tugged again on the ball of yarn. "You have a crush on Micah Fisher."

"I do not!"

"I think you do."

"And I think you've been staring at that ball of yarn too long, because you're sounding a little crazy."

"You don't want him dating anyone else."

"Of course I don't. He's trouble wrapped up in suspenders."

"Okay. That sounded plausible when you first told me of your plan to tag along with him. I even admired you for sacrificing your free time to keep him in check."

"I do not keep him in check. Trust me on that."

"Many in our community were perhaps too quick to believe the rumors about Micah, and I'm embarrassed to admit that I might have been one of them. You have to admit that he is…different."

"Oh, I'm aware of that."

"Does he still have the phone?"

"Of course."

"Still wearing *Englisch* clothes?"

"He occasionally swaps out his straw hat for his base-ball cap."

"But none of those are actual crimes." Deborah finished the row she was knitting and turned the blanket to purl in the opposite direction. "After he first arrived, when he was sneaking out of his own house, I thought he wouldn't last more than a week."

"The trouble he does manage to get into is so..." Susannah stared down at the needle and thread in her hand, trying to remember what she was doing with it. "Trivial. That's what it is—trivial. Silly stuff."

Deborah stopped knitting and waited for Susannah to look up at her. Lowering her voice, as if she could cushion the blow, she asked, "Did you hear about his picture in the paper?"

"What?"

Deborah reached down into her large purse. She pulled out a paperback book, what looked like a sand-wich wrapped in wax paper, a bottle of water and a tube of hand lotion.

"Doesn't that bag hurt your shoulder?"

"Mostly it sits on the ground."

"I still don't understand why you carry so much around."

"If you had eleven siblings, you'd understand."

"I suppose."

"Here it is." Instead of looking pleased with herself, Deborah's expression said that she wanted to apologize.

She didn't, though. Without saying another word, she handed a copy of the local newspaper to Susannah.

"Why would I want to read about the city's contract for a new water tower?"

"Not there." Deborah reached over and flipped the paper so that Susannah could read below the fold. "There."

Susannah actually felt light-headed as she stared down at the photo of Micah standing in front of the barn that was only partially completed. He was wearing his usual cocky smile. In the background it was plain to see several other Amish workers picking up tools or climbing down from the roof. If she guessed, Susannah would say he'd taken it as they were breaking for lunch.

"I can't… I can't believe he'd do this."

"Trivial, as you say, and yet plenty of folks in our community are upset about it."

"Why did you wait so long to show it to me?"

"You've only been here a half hour."

"Still, I would think you'd have pulled it out as soon as I climbed down from my buggy."

"I'm not any happier about this than you are." Deborah resumed knitting. "I don't like being the bearer of bad news."

"I just… I can't believe Micah would do this. He submitted it for photo of the week?" As she continued reading, her mouth dropped open in disbelief. "He won fifty dollars?"

"So it says."

"He doesn't even need the money. I know he's making plenty from my *dat*, and besides, he rarely has time

to spend it, since he's working for his *daddi* in the mornings and with the horses in the afternoon."

"It wonders me."

Susannah refolded the paper and held it out to Deborah.

"I'm sorry," Deborah said.

"For what?"

"Ruining your day."

"I'm glad you showed me." Susannah stared down at the paper that they were now both holding, then she jerked it back. "Maybe I should keep it, if that's all right with you."

"Sure. Of course."

Susannah set the offending newsprint down next to her purse. She tried to focus on the quilt in her hands. Sewing always relaxed her. It was immensely satisfying to see random pieces of fabric become something that would warm or comfort another person—often a person she didn't even know. She slipped her needle into the binding of the quilt, pulled it through, then slipped it into the quilt itself. The ladder stitch was one of her favorites, invisibly closing the two seams together. If only life were so easily patched.

Deborah cleared her throat. "So, about your crush…"

"I do not have a crush on Micah."

"Then why did you wait so long to tell him about your cancer? Why did you wait until he stumbled over the fact?"

"I don't know, honestly. I thought about telling him—a few times. But always it seemed like such a downer, or like I would be asking for sympathy."

Instead of answering, Deborah raised an eyebrow and motioned for her to continue.

"And I didn't want his sympathy. You have no idea how tiresome it is to have people pat you on the hand and ask 'how are you getting along, dear?' in that syrupy-sweet voice."

"They mean well, I'm sure."

"Of course they do, but I'm not fragile. I'm not going to break in two simply because I had cancer. In fact, you know what?" She tugged three more stitches through the binding, tacked down the corner and then stowed her needle by rocking it through both layers of fabric. "I do like being around Micah, or I did, because he didn't know about my cancer. He treated me like he would any other woman."

"Ah."

"Ah? That's your response? Ah?" Susannah realized in that moment that she'd been avoiding examining her feelings toward Micah. Was she afraid that she was falling for him? That was ridiculous. Micah Fisher was not her type, and even if he was, he wasn't staying in Goshen. Still, there was something about him that she'd never encountered before in the few men she'd dated.

"What response did you expect?"

"I don't know. I thought you might understand. You know how it was when I first found out."

"I'm the first person you told."

"And then when Samuel broke up with me."

"He didn't deserve you. By the way, I heard that girl from Shipshe he was dating dumped him."

There was a time when news of Samuel caused her

heart to twist, but Susannah realized she wasn't really interested in his dating life. Sometime between their breakup and now, she had moved on.

"I never felt around Samuel like I do around Micah."

"Oh, my. That sounds serious."

"*Nein*. It's not like that. I keep telling you. It's less like when you have a crush on someone and more like I can be myself. Not Cancer Survivor Susannah but... just Susannah."

"I suppose it makes sense."

"What does?"

"This strange attraction you two have, and don't deny that he likes being around you, too. It's plain as day to anyone with eyes and a brain."

Susannah folded her quilt, stuffed it into her sewing bag and sat back in the lawn chair. "Please explain."

"Micah is attracted to you—"

"He is not."

"He touched your hair."

"Whatever. Probably he was in shock. Go on."

"Micah is attracted to you because you're not a risk taker. You're a rule follower. You're the ultimate challenge to a guy like him."

Susannah felt an irrational urge to cover her ears, and yet, didn't she want to hear her friend's opinion? Deborah had always been the one person who would be completely honest with her. Even during her illness, when she was bald and exhausted and looked terrible, Deborah had been refreshingly candid. Instead of claiming she looked fine, Deborah had suggested they add color to her wardrobe. Then she'd proceeded to knit

incredibly soft hats and scarfs in blues and greens and lavender, claiming the color gave her a healthier glow.

Susannah didn't know if it had helped her glow. She'd never really thought of herself as a glowing type of person. But the small gifts definitely lifted her spirits, that and the fact that her friend had been honest with her.

"You're an attractive woman, Susannah. And it's not prideful for me to say that about you. It's only prideful for you to think it of yourself." Deborah paused, stared out at the tables laden with goods to sell and then glanced back at Susannah, a smile tugging at the corners of her mouth. "Or maybe pride isn't involved at all. Maybe it's just an observation."

"Danki."

"Where was I?"

"You were explaining why Micah is attracted to me, something that I have to tell you I don't see at all."

"What about the night you were fishing, when you thought he was going to kiss you?"

"I should never have told you that."

Deborah frowned down at her knitting, paused to count her stitches, placed a marker and resumed working on the row. "We've been telling each other about first kisses since we were fourteen."

"You and Josiah behind the schoolhouse."

"Uh-huh." Deborah grinned at the memory. "As I said earlier, I think maybe you and Micah started out as enemies…"

"Scripture reminds us to have an attitude of kindness to all."

"Then whatever you felt for one another moved to friendship when you began to understand each other."

"We're also called to be friends to one another—love your neighbor as yourself."

"And now it's blossoming into something more than mere friendship." Deborah focused on the row she was knitting with a flourish of needles and waited.

Susannah had no idea what to say. Was it possible that Deborah was right?

"Comments? Insights? Objections?"

Susannah felt an unexpected release of the tension she'd been carrying around for some time. Her shoulders relaxed and the headache that had been teasing her all morning dissipated. She had the sense that she was letting go of something that she'd been holding on to for a long while, perhaps since she'd first talked to Micah standing in the road leading to their respective houses.

"It could be you're right. I'm not saying you are, but I will say that I feel...confused. Some days I do find myself thinking that Micah would make a fine husband, and yes, occasionally I drift off into daydreams about that."

Deborah smiled, but she didn't interrupt, and she certainly didn't say the four dreaded words: *I told you so.*

"I realize how silly that is. He's not even staying here in Indiana. If you could hear him go on and on about Maine."

"I have. We all have." Deborah set aside her knitting, walked over in front of Susannah's chair and squatted in front of her. "It's okay to enjoy this time with Micah."

"It is? But—"

Deborah put her hands over Susannah's. "Maybe it will lead to something else and maybe it won't. All we know for certain is that *Gotte* brought you two together during this time in your lives for a reason."

"But I have no idea what that reason is."

"That's okay."

"Then what am I supposed to do?"

"How about you do the simplest of things? Just savor it and stop worrying about where it might or might not lead."

Micah nearly swallowed his gum when Susannah walked into his *daddi*'s barn early that evening.

"I thought you weren't talking to me."

"Why would you think that?"

"Because you walked away."

"Oh, yeah. I did."

"Not that I blame you. I overstepped. I tried to lecture you on your life when my own life is a mess."

Instead of denying that, she simply said, "I might have overreacted."

Which was all the apology he was going to get. But then, maybe she didn't owe him an apology. Maybe he owed her one. Regardless, Susannah seemed to have moved on.

Micah had been oiling and mending one of the harnesses. He set it aside and studied her as she stood there in the doorway to the barn, the last of the day's light splashing over her. She was a sight for sore eyes, that was for certain. He'd tossed and turned until midnight the previous evening, wondering how he was going to

survive the remainder of his Indiana exile without Susannah by his side.

"My parents used to have tiffs," he admitted.

"Did they, now?"

"Couple of times a year. Nothing terrible, just a bit of a row and then an awkward silence for the remainder of the day."

Susannah looked intrigued. "My parents never fight, not that I'm aware of."

"Could be because my *mamm* has a temper, or because my *dat* is more stubborn than any mule you will ever encounter." He walked past her, out into the fading sunshine. Watching the sun set in the west, looking out over the fields, he realized that Indiana had a certain unique beauty. Not that it could compare with Maine, and not that he'd ever want to live here, but he could understand why people did. "It used to upset me when I was a *youngie*."

"What did you do?"

"What most Amish *kinner* do. I ran to my grandparents. This would be my *mamm*'s parents. They moved up to join us in Maine after the first year. You'd think that they would be on her side."

"They weren't?"

Micah shrugged. "Couldn't ever tell, but I do remember what my *daddi* said to me after one particularly loud argument my parents had. I was sitting out near the pond, but not fishing. He came over and told me not to worry. He said if my parents were perfect, they wouldn't have married each other. But since neither

one was perfect, I could rest assured that they would forgive each other."

Susannah started laughing, and then Micah started laughing, and then he knew that everything was okay between them. They both sat on the bench under the barn's overhang.

Susannah bumped her shoulder against his. "No perfect people in your family, huh?"

"Not a single one."

"Mine, either."

"Which, I suppose, means we're not perfect."

"Not even close." Susannah pulled a folded sheet of newspaper from her pocket. "And now that we've established that neither of us is perfect, we should probably talk about this."

Micah stared at it, dumbfounded for the space of a few seconds. Then he hopped up, walked across the barn and retrieved his phone from the shelf where he usually stored it. He returned to where Susannah was and attempted to turn it on, but nothing happened.

"Problem?"

"It's dead."

"Ah."

"I don't think I've even used it since the workday at the barn." He waited, expecting her to begin scolding him for using it at all. When she didn't, he sat back down beside her. "There was a time when I checked it every day. Who am I fooling? I checked it every hour. I thought… Well, I guess I thought I was going to miss out on something."

"How so?"

"Well, I have *freinden* on different chat apps."

"Real friends?"

Micah shrugged his shoulder. "They seemed to be at the time, and maybe they were. Or they could have been, if our lives had connected in a more tangible way. I don't know. At the time that I bought this phone, I was feeling like no one understood me. And suddenly there was this virtual community where people did understand. It was nice."

"And now?"

"Now I don't know if any of what goes on through this device is real."

He scrubbed a hand over his face. "If I were to be honest? Now I would rather spend time with you and Deborah and even her *bruder* Elias."

"I didn't know you'd spent any time with Elias."

Micah didn't try to explain that Elias was okay but he enjoyed his time with Susannah more. He didn't know how to say that without making a fool of himself. As he mulled over that fact, Susannah studied him, and he almost fell over when she started laughing.

"Are you sure you're feeling all right?" he asked. "You're acting a little odd."

"It just occurred to me that your chat apps aren't so very different from the *Englisch* pen pal that I have."

"Now you're just tugging on my suspenders."

"*Nein.* It's true."

"How did Susannah Beiler, bishop's *doschder*, end up with an *Englisch* pen pal?"

"Jayla was in the hospital when I was… We shared a room for a while."

"Did she have cancer, too?"

"*She did.* She's older than me by a few years, African American and already had one *boppli*. We're as different as two people can be."

"Like me and my *freinden* on Snapchat."

"Maybe, which I guess is part of what I like about writing to her. She helps me to see my life from a different perspective."

"And you still exchange letters?"

"We do. We've even met up for coffee a couple of times, when she was back in town for treatment. She lives over by Millersburg, so it doesn't happen as often as I'd like, but I always look forward to seeing her. And her letters—it cheers me up just to see her return address on an envelope." Susannah reached out and poked his phone with a finger. "So, how were you going to learn more about the picture you took from the phone?"

"I was just going to check and see if I could figure out how this happened." He picked up the paper again and stared at it, as if doing so would make the puzzle pieces fall together.

Finally, he handed it back to her. "I don't know how that photo ended up in the paper."

"But you took it?"

"*Ya.* Plainly it's a selfie that I snapped. I even remember taking it. I was thinking I'd like to show it to my family when I get back to Maine."

"Why?" There was no condemnation in her voice, only curiosity. "Surely you have barn raisings in Maine."

Micah was shaking his head before she even finished. "Not like here. That..." He nodded toward the

paper she was now holding. "That was a completely different experience for me. In Maine, our communities are much smaller."

"You still help one another."

"Of course, but a barn isn't raised in a day. We might have one big workday at the beginning, but the majority of the work is done as people are able over the period of a week or two." He stood, paced back and forth in front of her for a minute and finally leaned against the barn post, crossing his arms. "I don't know how that picture ended up in the paper, and I know nothing about winning fifty dollars."

"But you think you can figure that out through your phone?"

"Maybe."

Susannah stood and straightened her apron, then stepped closer and smiled up at him. "Perhaps we should go to town tomorrow."

"Town?"

"I heard Dairy Queen has a special on their ice cream."

"Do they, now?"

"Personally, I could go for something cold and chocolate."

"I could probably charge my phone while we're there."

"Exactly."

"What time should I pick you up?"

"We can go whenever you finish your work with my *dat*."

Micah couldn't believe how much his mood had

lifted since she'd stepped into the barn. Did Susannah's opinion of him matter so much? And why wasn't she more angry about the picture? She was always lecturing him about staying within the guidelines of the *Ordnung*, but she hadn't said a word about it since arriving. He knew that asking her wouldn't yield answers, and maybe the *why* didn't matter so much after all.

When she'd arrived, the sun was just beginning to set, but while they'd talked, twilight had crept over the fields.

"Let me hop inside and tell my grandparents that I'm going to walk you home."

"I'm pretty sure I can find my way."

"Still…" And rather than explain, he jogged toward the house, returning in a few minutes with a flashlight, a napkin filled with a few of his *mammi*'s brownies and a quart jar full of milk.

"Didn't expect you to bring a picnic."

"Just thought you might like something sweet."

They stopped at the top of the small hill that sat just inside the boundary line on her parents' property. Susannah was wearing a sweater, and Micah had on a jacket. He slipped it off and put it on the ground for her to sit on.

"Seriously?"

"Wouldn't want you to get your dress…" And then words seemed to fail him as he looked at her in the soft light of the moon. The stars shone as if they'd been flung there particularly for the two of them. He thought of kissing her, then wondered why he'd even have such a

thought and then wondered if she'd want him to. Finally, he thrust the brownies at her. "Hope you like walnuts."

"I love walnuts."

They didn't speak again until they'd finished the snack. Passing the quart jar back and forth felt curiously intimate. The brownies were still warm, the milk cold and the sky above them offered a spectacular canopy of the heavens.

He didn't want to push, didn't want to spook her away again, but he wanted to know. For some reason he couldn't put his finger on, he needed to know. And since she didn't seem in a rush to get home, now was as good a time as any. Now might be the best chance he'd get. So he crossed his legs at the ankle, leaned back on his hands and asked what he'd wanted to ask since the day he'd walked up on her drying her short hair in the sun.

"What was it like?"

"Cancer?"

"Being afraid that you might die. How did you get past that every day?"

"I guess during those first few weeks, I was just in shock."

"You didn't realize something was wrong before your diagnosis?"

"Not initially. I became worried when I started losing weight, had trouble eating and then there was the pain." She placed a hand on her stomach.

When she didn't continue, Micah reached for her hand and entwined their fingers together.

"And you had surgery?"

"Ya." Her voice was a whisper, practically a caress.

"That must have been frightening."

"The diagnosis was probably the worst part. After that, it was simply a matter of weighing my options. And my parents were very supportive for whatever I wanted to do."

"Did you have options? Other than the surgery?"

"Not really. But if I'd said I needed time, if I'd wanted to wait, my parents would have understood."

Micah stared down at their hands, which he could just barely make out in the darkness. He rubbed his thumb over hers. "I would never have guessed that you'd been sick."

"Is that so?"

"You're so spunky."

"Spunky?"

"I guess I was a little afraid of you when I first met you."

Susannah began giggling. Snatching her hand from his, she covered her mouth…until she'd worked herself up to a full belly laugh.

"Not that funny."

"It…it sort of is."

Which was followed by more laughter, and Susannah gulping for air, which started Micah to laughing, though he couldn't have said what he was laughing about.

But suddenly it didn't matter why they were laughing, sitting on top of the hill, the stars spread out before them like grains of sand on a beach.

It occurred to Micah then that he should step back. The be-careful voice in his head asked what he thought he was doing.

She's not your type, buddy.

She's out of your league.

She's the bishop's daughter, and don't forget you're heading back to Maine as soon as possible.

As they walked toward her parents' home, he realized that most people he knew would agree with that voice of reason. But when had he ever listened to reason or cared what other people thought?

Never.

And he didn't plan on starting now. He might be in trouble with her *dat* for the picture, but he suspected things would be even worse with his *daddi*. In fact, the picture on the front page of the *Goshen News* might be the final straw. Micah understood he should be worried about that, but at the moment he would rather keep his attention on the beautiful woman walking at his side.

Chapter Seven

When Susannah suggested going to town to charge Micah's phone, she had thought she could sneak away from the farm for a few hours. Normally that wouldn't have been a problem. Unfortunately, the next day her *mamm* was called to a neighbor's to help with a sick *aenti* and her *dat* was attending a monthly meeting of area bishops.

"I'm stuck with these two," she explained to Micah.

"Hey! You're not stuck with us. You love us." Sharon was sticking flower seeds into pots, though in the process, more dirt ended up on her than around the seeds.

Shiloh was sitting on the back porch step, writing her letters on a tablet. "Does this look right, Susannah?"

"Sure it does."

"I think the tail of my *g* needs to hang down more." She flipped the pencil around and began vigorously erasing.

"Those two are yin and yang." Micah sat in the rocking chair beside Susannah. He kept watching her, like he wanted to say something, but then he would look away.

Perhaps he didn't want to talk in front of Sharon and Shiloh—little pitchers having big ears and all of that.

"Yin and what?"

"They're like flip sides of the same coin."

"Oh, *ya*. They look alike but often act very different."

"Which one is more like you?"

"I don't have freckles like Sharon."

"You called them stardust." Sharon put her dirty hands on her nonexistent hips and cocked her head. "Remember?"

"She has *gut* hearing."

"Yes, they both do."

Shiloh remained focused over her tablet. "I don't have freckles, either, but you said I had the stars in my eyes."

"Yes, you do, Shiloh."

"You told them that?"

Susannah's mind was spinning, trying to keep up with three conversations at once. She finally gave up and focused on Micah. "The point is that we can't go to town for ice cream."

She knew she'd made a mistake the second the words slipped out of her mouth. Her *schweschdern* might be complete opposites on some things, but at other times they merged together into one entity. This was one of those times.

"We want to go for ice cream."

"We did all our chores."

"And you promised we'd do something fun."

"And planting flowers isn't that much fun."

"And I love ice cream."

Micah looked as if he were going to burst out laughing.

Fortunately, he held it in or Susannah would have been tempted to dump one of Sharon's pots of dirt over his head. Laughing at the girls convinced them they were entertaining, and from that point there was no turning back.

"We could take them with us," Micah suggested, which pretty much sealed her fate for the day. There was no stopping her twin sisters when they had another adult on their side.

Susannah insisted they walk next door with Micah while he fetched his *daddi*'s horse and buggy. "It'll wear these two out, and as you've noticed they have a lot of energy."

Sharon had repeatedly dodged ahead of them and circled back. As usual, Shiloh stuck close to Susannah's side, though at the moment she was hopping from foot to foot.

Micah's *mammi* actually clapped her hands when they walked up to the front door. "It seems I haven't seen you girls in ages."

"We're going for ice cream."

"Micah's going to take us."

"If he can borrow the buggy."

"Well, of course he can." She reached out and put a hand on both girls, ushering them into the house. "Come in. Come in. Susannah, it's been too long since you stopped by."

Soon they were settled around the kitchen table, and Micah had explained why he wanted to use the buggy. "But only if you don't need it."

Mammi smiled at the girls, then turned her attention to Micah. "I had planned to go and visit Miriam

Hochstettler, who's had a flare-up of her rheumatoid arthritis."

"We can go another day."

"Nonsense. You go on out and tell your *daddi* that you need the buggy. I can visit Miriam tomorrow."

"But—"

"*Nein.* I insist. These two girls look like they've been working hard all day. They've earned a treat."

Susannah couldn't help laughing. "Sharon certainly does look as if she's been working hard. There's more dirt on her apron than in the pots of flowers she was planting."

"Nothing that won't wash out," Abigail assured her.

"And I've been writing my letters," Shiloh chimed in.

"Aren't you a smart girl."

"We have to go to school next year." Sharon's voice dropped an octave and she ducked her head. "Whether we want to or not."

Which earned a laugh all around.

Micah moved to the back door to go and bring the buggy around. As an afterthought, he turned back to Sharon and Shiloh. "Do you girls want to help me?"

He started laughing as they dashed out the back door ahead of him. "I'll take that as a *yes.*"

Susannah and Abigail caught up on what was happening on both farms—which wasn't much.

Glancing at the kitchen clock, Susannah said, "I suppose I should go on out. I don't want to keep Micah waiting."

"Or the girls. They seemed quite excited."

Susannah walked with Abigail out to the front porch, where they sat and waited for Micah to bring the buggy around.

"I've been meaning to speak to you regarding Micah. We appreciate your befriending him."

"Micah's an easy person to like."

"That's what we're a little worried about."

"What I mean is that he's a hard worker and he has a *gut* attitude. Even my *dat* says so."

"I agree with both of those points, but you and I both know that Micah hasn't made up his mind on some very important life choices."

"I'm not sure what you mean."

Abigail set her rocker in motion. "Oh, I pray every day that all of my *family* will stay in the faith, but not all do. That's a truth to be reckoned with."

Susannah started to protest, but Abigail raised a hand to stop anything she might have said. "You're young yet, so it's hard for you to imagine."

"I do have *freinden* who have joined the Mennonite church."

"And it's not my place to say whether that is right or wrong. *Gotte* directs each path. However, if what I know about you and your family is correct—and we've lived next door to each other all of your life—then you have no plans to leave our church or our community."

"*Nein.* Of course not. Well, I've always thought of myself as Plain, and I suppose I will stay in Goshen. Where else would I go?"

"My point is Micah may not stay in our faith."

"He told you that?"

"His actions told me that, and you would arrive at the same conclusion if you'd get the stars out of your eyes."

Susannah sifted through her memories of time spent

with Micah, searching for a way to defend herself. She finally settled for "I do not have stars in my eyes."

"Looks that way from here, and normally I would be thrilled at the thought of having you as a part of the family."

Susannah jumped to her feet at the word *family*. Fortunately, Micah pulled the buggy up in front of the porch at that moment.

"I have to go."

"Just remember what I said, Susannah, and guard your heart."

Those words bounced round and round her mind as she climbed into the buggy, made sure the girls were sitting back properly, and listened to Micah discuss a horse he had shoed that morning. Only she wasn't really hearing him.

She was thinking about Abigail Fisher warning her to guard her heart.

The day was warm, and Micah needed to charge his phone, so they ate their treats inside. Susannah and Micah sat on one side of the booth, Sharon and Shiloh sat on the other.

It took a few minutes for his cell phone to come to life. When it did, Micah started punching buttons. Sharon and Shiloh seemed not to notice. They were busy licking at the ice cream cones while at the same time coloring the place mats that the girl working the front counter had given them. Susannah glanced around the restaurant. It was plenty full for three in the afternoon.

One couple sat in a booth across from them. Their

young child in a highchair was leaning forward to touch the screen of some small tablet. Across the restaurant another toddler, surely not yet walking, was crying and reaching for his *mamm*'s phone. Even the employee who was supposed to be bussing tables had pulled out his phone and was staring at it, the cluttered table in front of him temporarily forgotten.

She hadn't really paid attention to how much *Englischers* used their electronic devices. What were they looking at? What could be so fascinating? She glanced again at her *schweschdern*. They were adorable, their heads practically touching as they worked on a puzzle on the color sheet. Both were wearing white *kapps* and blue dresses with blue aprons, and for a moment Susannah realized how different they must look to *Englischers*.

She knew it wasn't her place to say who was right or wrong. Her *dat* had often reminded her *not to judge lest ye be judged*. She thought she knew what was right for her, but did that mean that other ways were wrong?

Why did there have to be a right or wrong anyway?

Some people chose to be farmers, some woodworkers. Some people were *Englisch* and others were Amish. What mattered was how they treated one another and how they lived their lives. She glanced at Micah and once again heard Abigail's words. *Guard your heart.* Was she falling in love with Micah Fisher? And even if she was, who was to say that it would end badly?

It probably would end badly.

He was definitely moving back to Maine as soon as possible.

She couldn't imagine living so far from her family,

even if he did care about her in that way, which was by no means certain.

Micah turned off his phone and focused on his sundae.

"Well?"

"Well, what?"

"Did you figure it out?"

"Oh, *ya*. I figured it out."

"And?"

He looked at her and smiled as he shoveled in another rather large spoonful of ice cream. "I'm suddenly starved. I could eat two of these."

"You're suddenly avoiding the subject. Out with it."

Micah wiped his mouth with a napkin and cornered himself in the booth so that he could look directly at her. "I took the selfie and posted it to Snapchat the day of the barn raising. As I told you, I haven't even used the phone since."

"So how did it get to the paper?"

"A friend of mine—an *Englischer*—managed to capture the photograph and then he sent it into the paper, pretending to be me."

"Why would he do that?"

"I might have mentioned that I'm running a little low on money."

"My *dat* is paying you."

"*Ya*, and I give all of that money to my *daddi* as I should, since he's feeding me and providing me a place to stay. But that doesn't leave anything for…" He glanced at the girls and cleared his throat, then leaned

closer and lowered his voice. "Doesn't leave anything for dating."

Susannah felt her cheeks flame red. She would have stopped it if she could, but she'd always blushed when she was embarrassed. Micah was looking at her as if she was the most important thing in the world, and he definitely noticed her sudden fascination with her ice cream. Instead of saying anything, he squeezed her hand and went back to eating.

He didn't ask her out.

And he certainly didn't clarify what he'd meant.

She had no idea if she was relieved or disappointed.

As they were loading the girls back into his buggy, Micah noticed a car pull up in front of the Dairy Queen and drop off an older woman who toddled toward the door. Micah hustled over to the door, opened it wide for her and spoke to the woman.

When he jogged back to the buggy and climbed in, Susannah said, "What was that about?"

"An idea."

"What kind of idea?"

"The *gut* kind, of course."

"We want to play I Spy," Sharon said, leaning forward over the seat.

"Best sit back," Susannah said.

"Can we play?"

"I spy with my little eye…" Shiloh was practically bouncing on the seat.

The sugary treat must have given both girls an added burst of energy.

Sharon's voice went up an octave. "I wanna go first."

"But I already spied."

"Did not."

"Did, too. I spied that cat over there." She pointed with her finger to a ginger cat sitting on a picnic table.

"Okay, I know what you spied—a cat. Now it's my turn. I spy…"

Micah figured it was best to play along, so they spent the ride home spying another horse and buggy, a red car, two boys riding bikes and even a woman pushing a child on a swing. It wasn't an easy game to play in the buggy, as the thing the person spied was often left behind. When the girls became frustrated, he changed the game to fifty questions, which went much more smoothly.

By the time they reached Susannah's place, he understood how the girls managed to wear her out. He'd barely pulled the buggy to a stop when both Sharon and Shiloh tumbled out. They clamored up the porch steps, rushing to show their *mamm* the paper place mats they had colored.

"Those two are a handful."

"I told you so."

"They're cute, though."

"You don't mind that I had to bring them along?"

"Why would I mind?"

Susannah shrugged, and he wondered if she was thinking what he was thinking. But if he asked, she'd probably just deny it. Susannah was traditional, and she wouldn't admit to wanting to kiss him or even wanting to be alone with him—not that she'd ever lie, but she wouldn't want to be forward.

As if to confirm his thoughts, she blushed prettily and then glanced away. "I should go fetch the clothes off the line."

"I'll help."

Micah set the brake on the buggy and tethered the horse to the hitching post Thomas has fashioned in front of the house. Then he followed Susannah to the backyard, thinking about the girls he had dated before, the girls back home. They had been quite different from Susannah. They'd been flirty and immature. He could see that now. They'd covered their insecurities up with bold words and *Englisch* clothes, but they hadn't shared their dreams or fears or hopes for the future.

They'd tried to prove to him they were different, that they were *the one*. The pressure to choose and settle down with one girl had begun when he'd turned twenty-one. His parents didn't understand what he was waiting for. Honestly, he didn't know, either. He'd always felt different from everyone else.

Now he wasn't so sure about that.

Underneath, wasn't everyone the same? Everyone wanted to be liked, to be respected and to have their opinions count.

But it was more than that.

Everyone wanted to connect in some authentic way. Maybe that was what he'd been looking for on social media. He wasn't certain. He only knew that he wasn't finding satisfaction there, but when he was with Susannah, that itch felt as if it was being satisfied. Just watching her fold clothes brought a goofy smile to his face, and he was powerless to stop it. He was confused

about his feelings when he was around her, but he was also content for the first time in his life.

How could he feel both things at the same time?

Susannah laughed when she saw the way he was folding the towels.

"Do not tell me I'm doing this wrong."

"Okay."

He looked at the neat stack she'd placed in her basket, then at the towel he'd folded into a football shape. "I'm doing this wrong. Show me."

Instead of pointing out he most certainly did not know the proper way to fold clothes, she walked over to where he was standing.

"Hold the towel up like this."

He picked up a towel and mirrored what she was doing.

"Now fold it like this."

He thought he did what she did, but looking down, he must have twisted it somehow.

Susannah started laughing—a sound he dearly loved to hear. "This is impossible," he growled.

"Of course it's not. All you need is practice."

"Uh-huh."

She quickly folded the last of the towels, and they carried the two baskets of fresh laundry to the back porch.

"Are you going to tell me what your *gut* idea was? The one you had when you held the door open for the *Englisch* woman?"

"Hmm... I'd rather wait and see if it pans out."

"So, you're not going to tell me."

"I will say this..." He stepped closer, glanced at the

windows to be sure no one was watching and then dipped his head and kissed her softly on the lips. Why did she taste like strawberries? He didn't ask about that. Instead he said, "If it works out, I'll have the money to take you to dinner."

"Will you, now?"

He wanted to kiss her again, but Sharon and Shiloh sprinted out the back door, squealing and running to the swings that had been set up under the branches of a large maple tree.

Susannah stepped toward the porch. "I should probably help with dinner."

"And I need to go and talk to my grandparents about that newspaper thing."

"I suppose it would be best if they hear about it from you before a neighbor takes them a copy."

"And I'll talk to your *dat* tomorrow when I come over."

Which he realized was a change in how he did things. Usually he avoided such conversations. But what was the point in that? Best to stay ahead of trouble if that was even possible, though in this case it might already be too late for that.

Micah knew the minute he stepped into the house that he was indeed too late in beating the bad news home. A copy of the *Goshen News* sat on the kitchen table, where supper should have been. His *daddi* and *mammi* were sitting at the table, obviously waiting for him.

"I was coming home to talk to you about that." He slid into a seat at the table.

When his *daddi* finally looked up, Micah's heart sank. He saw an entire world of emotions in the set of his mouth, the weariness of his eyes and the frown lines that seemed permanently etched on his forehead.

Mammi sat with her hands cradling a cup of coffee. Supper was on the stove, but apparently no one was expecting to eat anytime soon.

His *daddi* sighed heavily, as if he were carrying the weight of the world and needed to set it down. "We're disappointed, Micah."

"But I can explain."

"How can you explain that?" His voice remained a low growl.

Micah could have handled a raised voice. Hadn't he just told Susannah about how his parents would holler at each other? But always, always they would make up before darkness fell on the day. No, what his *daddi*'s voice told him was that he'd already made up his mind, already decided on his judgment and there would be no arguing.

Still, he had to try.

"I did take the picture."

"With the *Englisch* phone."

"I had never been to a barn raising with so many people, and I wanted to show my *schweschdern*."

"We make quite an effort to keep the *Englisch* photographers at bay, only to have you splash our doings on the front page of the local paper." *Daddi* grabbed the paper from the table and shook it at Micah. "I don't know what you were thinking, but I do know that I warned you."

"But I didn't—"

"We are to remain separate, Micah. Do you not understand what that means?"

"I did *not* send that picture in to the paper."

"Now you're denying taking it?"

"*Nein.* I took it, but someone else sent it in."

"That makes no sense."

"It was a friend of mine."

"An *Englisch* friend, no doubt."

"He thought he was helping me. He thought I could use the money, but he didn't ask me first. I had no idea he would do such a thing."

"You should have considered that possibility before you took the photograph." *Daddi* dropped the paper and slapped the flat of his palm against the table. "If you hadn't taken it to begin with, we wouldn't be having this discussion."

"What is so wrong with people seeing that we help one another?" Micah knew his temper was winning out over his common sense, but he couldn't help it. He couldn't sit there and not defend himself.

"Go and get the phone."

"What?"

"You heard me. Go and get the phone."

Micah didn't have to go and get the phone, since it was still in his pocket from having gone to town. He handed it to his *daddi*, thinking that perhaps he was going to keep it awhile or hand it over to the bishop or mail it back home to his parents. He never once thought that the man would drop it on the floor, stand and crush it beneath his foot.

"Are you crazy? Do you know how much that cost?"

"Perhaps you should learn to use your money more wisely, then." He didn't bother to pick up the pieces. Instead he snatched his hat off the hook on the wall. "I'm warning you again, Micah. You step outside the lines one more time—"

"And are those lines that you've drawn? Or the bishop? Because last time I spoke with Thomas, he was quite happy with my work."

"Your work—yes. But your actions outside work? You should stop and consider the repercussions of those, Micah. As far as I'm concerned, you're on your last chance." *Daddi* didn't even turn to look at him. Something about the stoop of the man's shoulders pulled guilt strings in Micah's heart, and if he'd even turned and given him a hint of compassion he might have let his sympathy for his grandfather win over his anger.

But he didn't turn.

He didn't look at him.

And Micah quickly brushed away any such thoughts of sympathy. His *daddi* was obstinate and unfair. He did not deserve anyone's sympathy.

"Go against our *Ordnung* one more time, and you'll have to find another place to live."

"You're kicking me out?"

Now *Daddi* did turn. The stump of his right arm rested in the pocket that *Mammi* had sewn from the sleeve. His left hand was tanned and strong. At the moment he was using it to rub a circle on his chest.

"Maybe you should calm down, John." It was the first words his *mammi* had spoken.

"I'm fine." He never took his eyes off Micah. "The crops are in. I won't need your help around here except for feeding the horses and cleaning out the stalls."

"Meaning what?"

"Meaning I want you to find another job." And with that final jab, he turned and left the house.

Micah sat staring at the door his *daddi* had walked through.

Why did life have to be like this?

Why did his grandfather make a problem where there was none?

Mammi stood, fetched the broom and dustpan and swept up the pieces of phone. She held the dustpan out to him. "Want what's left of it?"

He waved her away.

"Your *daddi*…"

"I know. He wants what's best for me."

"It's true, Micah. Whether you can see it or not, it's true."

"Is it also true that he doesn't need me around here to help him? Or does he just not *want* me around to help him? Because it's pretty plain to me that he can't stand the sight of me."

"You're being unfair."

"*He*'s being unfair."

His *mammi* had never been particularly demonstrative with her emotions, but now she sat down beside him and pulled his hands into her lap. "He's a *gut* man, your *daddi*, and I won't have you disrespecting him."

Her words were softened by her touch as she reached out and untwisted one of his suspenders. "John's not a

proud man, but he sees things as black-and-white. He wants you to put away your childhood things…"

"By stomping on them?"

"Become a man and put away childish things."

"And get another job."

"Only for the mornings. You'll continue to help Thomas in the afternoons." She patted him on the shoulder, stood and walked to the stove. "Dinner will be ready in thirty minutes."

Micah wanted to say he wasn't hungry, but in truth his stomach was gurgling. Refusing to eat would be childish, plus he would go to bed hungry. There was no use trying to avoid his *daddi*, and he wasn't ready to move out. The thought hadn't really ever occurred to him.

He'd thought of moving home, but not of moving out.

Where would he go?

And how would he afford it?

Nein. He needed to find a way to make this work until he could return to Maine, which meant he needed a job. He remembered the older *Englisch* woman, the car that had dropped her off, the sign in the window of the car.

The idea he'd had would put extra money in his pocket and satisfy his *daddi*'s demands. As to whether they would approve of what he hoped to do, time would tell.

Chapter Eight

Susannah did not plan on telling her *mamm* about the kiss.

But as they were sitting at the kitchen table later that evening—her *mamm* knitting and Susannah stitching together the top of a nine-patch quilt—the details of the day came tumbling out of her mouth.

If her *mamm* was surprised, she hid it well.

"You've been kissed before."

"*Ya*, but it's been a while."

"Since before your cancer."

"Just about two years ago, which doesn't say much for my dating life."

"You know, Susannah, you're not damaged goods."

"Why would you say that?" Susannah pricked her finger with the needle, jerked her hand away and inspected it to make sure she wouldn't bleed on the fabric.

"I sometimes think that you have the opinion that no one would want you, that you're not whole."

"I'm not whole. The doctors removed part of me, leaving me not whole."

"Not true." Her *mamm* shook her head so vigorously that her *kapp* strings bounced. It reminded Susannah so much of Sharon that she couldn't help smiling. "You are fearfully and wonderfully made."

"Is now really the time to quote Scripture?"

"If it fits, then yes, it is."

Susannah ducked her head to better see the seam she was attempting to stitch. In truth, her mother's words brought tears to her eyes. Some days she hated that she cried so easily, that she was so emotional. Other days it seemed as if she was viewing life from a distance and couldn't feel a thing. She wasn't sure which was worse.

"After my diagnosis, Samuel treated me differently, almost as if I was contagious."

"It's obvious now to both of us that you and Samuel were not meant to be anything more than *freinden*."

"I wish it had been obvious then. At the time, the way he treated me and then our breakup… It just—well it hurt."

"And if I could have spared you that hurt I would have."

"It doesn't bother me much anymore, not really. I've moved on." As she uttered those words, words she'd probably said before, Susannah was surprised to find that they were true in a new way. Thinking of Samuel didn't bring the old ache that it had at one time.

"My point is that your cancer wasn't something that *Gotte* didn't see coming. It wasn't a mistake on His part."

"How could it have been intentional?"

"I don't know. Most of the whys in life I don't understand."

"What you're saying doesn't make any sense."

"Do you think that Caroline Byers's *bruder* is a mistake?"

"Because he has Down syndrome? Of course not."

"He's not damaged goods?"

"You know that no one thinks that." She glanced up to see her *mamm* studying her very closely. "A person who is born different isn't damaged in the way that a buggy might be after a wreck."

"I'm glad you feel that way."

"We all do. We all love Stephen. Have you seen how he is with their sheep? He's named every one, and they come to him when he calls them. Stephen isn't damaged. He's special."

"So *Gotte* didn't make a mistake with him?"

"I don't know why he's different, but the fact that he is doesn't cause anyone to love him any less. So no, I don't think *Gotte* made a mistake."

"You'd never throw him away."

Now her *mamm* was teasing her. Sure enough, when Susannah glanced up, she noticed a smile tugging at her *mamm*'s lips.

"I would not, and no one who knows him would."

"Then how are you any different?"

"I don't follow."

"Only because you're being stubborn."

Instead of asking her *mamm* to explain, Susannah allowed a silence to permeate the room. She became aware of the sound of her mother's knitting needles, the

crickets outside, the creak of her father's rocking chair from where he sat on the porch.

Finally, Susannah gave up on the seam that was growing increasingly crooked. She stood, heated water on the stove and brought two cups of tea and a plate of oatmeal bars to the table.

"*Danki.*"

"*Gem gschehne.*"

And those words, that tradition of gratefulness and kindness, seemed to loosen the cat's grip on Susannah's tongue.

"I don't think I'm damaged, but I do think I'm different."

"Every one of *Gotte*'s creatures is unique."

"And maybe it wasn't a mistake that I had cancer. Maybe *Gotte* has some grand plan, some greater good that will come from it."

"He used Balaam's donkey. I'm sure He can use your cancer."

"But I am different, *Mamm*. There's no more use in denying that than there would be in denying that Stephen is different."

Her *mamm* nodded and reached for an oatmeal bar.

"So what are you really worried about?"

Susannah sipped her tea, then sighed and closed her eyes for a moment. When she opened them, her *mamm* was studying her.

"That the kiss meant nothing to Micah and everything to me. That the kiss meant everything to both of us. That he doesn't understand the baggage that I

carry around with me—that there is a chance the cancer will return."

"And there's an even better chance that it won't."

"Regardless, I will not be able to have children."

Her *mamm* didn't answer right away. In fact, Susannah thought she wouldn't. They finished their snack, her *mamm* stood, rinsed their cups, covered the oatmeal bars with a dish towel and finally sat down across from her again.

"If Micah loves you—and I'm not suggesting that's true or that enduring love always follows one kiss—but if he does, then it won't matter to him whether or not you can have children."

"How can it *not* matter to him?" As hard as she tried to blink away the tears, they insisted on coursing down her cheeks. Her *mamm* reached forward and thumbed them away, then kissed her on the forehead.

"Because love doesn't work that way."

Micah spoke with Thomas early the next morning. As he laid out the details of his plan, he noticed Thomas's hesitancy and expression of skepticism.

"I'd like your approval to just try this—give it a few weeks, a month at the most. If it doesn't work, then I'll try to find employment at one of the businesses in town."

"And you've spoken to your *daddi* about this?"

"*Nein.* I wanted your approval first, and I also still need to speak with Widow Miller and finalize the details. Once everything is in place, I'll go to *Daddi* and explain the entire thing. You have my word on that."

Thomas clasped him on the back. "And you've prayed about this?"

"I have, and I feel that *Gotte* put this idea in my mind. I certainly would have never thought of it on my own."

"All from seeing a driver drop a woman off at the Dairy Queen." They were sitting in the farrier shop. Thomas had been working on his accounting books. He picked up a pen, clicked it twice and sat it back down. "Coincidence or possibly *Gotte*'s guiding hand."

"I honestly think it's something I'd be *gut* at. I have a lot of energy, it drives me crazy to sit still and I have an outgoing personality."

"That you do." Thomas glanced around his farrier shop. "I can take care of today's work. See if you can get the details of your plan worked out."

"Danki."

Micah was almost to the door when Thomas called him back. "Perhaps it would help if we switched your hours with me to the morning. That way you could work on your new business into the early evening when necessary."

"You'd be willing to do that?"

"Sure. Seems to me you'd have a more flexible schedule then, to accommodate your customers."

"What about our meetings, you know, where I'm learning to be properly Amish?"

"I suppose we can talk while we're working, like we are now."

Micah wanted to jump and shout at the same time. Instead, he smiled his thanks and headed down the lane.

Widow Miller lived two miles away. He'd be walking that distance twice a day, but Micah didn't mind. He could cover a mile in twenty minutes, and the exercise would do him good.

He'd met the older woman when he and Thomas had gone to her house to shoe her buggy horse. The gelding was not getting enough exercise and generally wasn't being looked after as well as he should have been. Nothing neglectful, really, but the horse could use a good brushing and the buggy definitely needed to be cleaned.

It took him ten minutes to explain his plan and another twenty to work out the details. Thirty minutes later, he was ready to go to the Goshen Library to make some flyers and copy them, but first he needed his *daddi*'s approval.

"Just once, why can't you do something normal?"

Micah had dared to hope that his *daddi* would be as open-minded as Thomas. Apparently that was hoping for too much. He tried to tap down his anger—count to five, take deep breaths, be patient. It wasn't working. He could feel his pulse accelerating and sweat running down his back.

How he would love to storm out of the barn, but that was what a child would do. He was a man now, and he was ready to act like one. He was ready to stand and fight for what he wanted to do.

"You want me to go and work at the RV factory? Or maybe you see me riding over to Amish Acres every day, showing *Englischers* what it's like to live simply."

"There's nothing wrong with either one of those jobs."

Micah took a deep breath. "I didn't say there was, but I think my idea is something I could be successful at."

"And Thomas approved of it?"

"He did. He even offered to shift my hours to mornings."

His *daddi* turned back to the plow blade that he was sharpening. He'd positioned the blade in a bench vise to hold it steady. It was amazing what the man had learned to do with one arm.

"And you'll be splitting what you earn with Widow Miller?"

"Fifty-fifty. Seems only fair since I'll be using her buggy and horse. Plus, it'll be better for the horse."

"So you explained."

Micah waited, and it seemed that his *daddi* had forgotten he was there. Finally, he raised his good arm and made a motion as if he was shooing away a fly. "I expect you to make good on what you told Thomas. If you're not seeing enough business in two weeks…"

"We agreed to a month."

"And if the widow is unhappy with the deal for any reason, then you abandon this plan and get a real job."

"Done."

If he'd been expecting his *daddi*'s blessing, he might have stood there a long time. Instead, he took his grandfather's grunt as permission, hitched their mare to the buggy and headed to town to make it to the library before it closed.

Susannah and her *mamm* had planned to go to a sew-in the following Monday. She hadn't seen Micah on

Sunday, but then perhaps his grandparents had lunch with someone else. It was their off Sunday. She was a little surprised that he hadn't stopped by, but then it wasn't like he'd promised he would.

The sew-in would be a nice distraction. Sharon and Shiloh were excited to see their friends, but if Susannah was honest with herself, she was rather dreading the entire thing. There was no doubt that she'd be grilled about Micah's comings and goings. He seemed to be the talk of the town these days, which just proved that very little was happening in May in Goshen, Indiana.

But her mother was looking forward to her day off the farm, and Susannah knew that begging off would make things harder since she wouldn't be there to help keep an eye on the twins. It would actually be selfish for her to do so when there was no good reason not to go, and besides she'd just have to face everyone at the next Sunday meeting. Might as well get it over with on a beautiful summer day.

The sew-in had been scheduled so they could complete half a dozen quilts that they planned to donate to the school auction held every summer. That event attracted *Englischers* with money to spend on authentic Amish items. The funds raised helped to pay for school supplies as well as any needed repairs to the building.

She found herself growing more excited as her *mamm* drove the buggy toward Widow Miller's, where the sew-in was to take place.

After they'd parked the buggy, Susannah asked Sharon and Shiloh to help her. "Can each of you carry in one of our lunch dishes?"

"I can carry the big one." Shiloh stood up straight and tall as if to prove her strength.

"Better give me the little one," Sharon said. "I drop sometimes."

"Both of you hold the dish with both hands and walk—don't run."

Taking their task very seriously, they walked toward Widow Miller's front porch and up the steps.

"They're *gut* girls." Her *mamm* hooked her arm through Susannah's. "You've been rather quiet today."

"Have I?"

"Anything you want to talk about?"

"I'm dreading everyone asking me questions about Micah."

"And why would you dread that?"

"First of all, because I'm not his keeper."

"But you are his friend, and it's normal for people to be curious."

"I suppose. And second, folks seem to assume the worst where Micah is concerned. I guess his first impression wasn't a particularly *gut* one."

"You can set the record straight."

And then they were in the widow's house, and the large group of women assembled there naturally separated into smaller groups by generational lines. Susannah supposed that was because friendships had formed many years ago, and there weren't that many chances to all get together and catch up. Sometimes it seemed to Susannah that she knew more about her cousins in Ohio than she did about someone living down the street.

She went out the back door. Two quilts had been

set up on standing looms. Around one was most of the sixteen-to-eighteen-year-old group. She remembered how she'd looked forward to these days when she was first out of school. She hadn't missed sitting in a school desk for the majority of the day, but she'd certainly missed seeing her friends. Watching that younger group brought a sharp pain of nostalgia that she hadn't expected.

Did she miss being so young?

It wasn't as if she was an old maid now.

But then she turned toward her group, which was gathered around a double-wedding-ring quilt that had also been placed on a quilt stand. They were situated more toward the side yard, with a view of both the back and the front of the house. It seemed to her that over half the group was pregnant. Many of the others had babies in carriers on the ground beside them. Only Susannah, Deborah and three other girls remained unmarried.

Perhaps she didn't really fit in with either group, which was a rather depressing thought. Regardless, there was quilting to be done.

She clenched her teeth and prayed for patience.

Strangely, no one asked her a thing about Micah.

There was plenty of "How are you today, Susannah?" and "What a pretty apron. Is that new?" and "I saw your *schweschdern* flitting around here. They certainly are growing."

She felt herself relax, so much so that when she saw looks passing between others—knowing looks—she convinced herself that it had nothing to do with her or Micah.

They'd sewn for most of the morning when she heard the clatter of buggy wheels.

Again the knowing looks, and then as one, they stopped sewing and turned their attention toward the front of the house.

And that was when she saw him. Micah was driving Widow Miller's buggy. When he pulled to a stop, he jumped out, walked around the buggy and helped out Old Sally. It was when he closed the buggy door after her that Susannah saw the sign.

It read Amish Taxi, followed by a phone number.

Micah had helped Old Sally up the porch steps. As he returned to his buggy, he stopped and waved—whether at Susannah or the group in general, she wasn't sure.

He looked inordinately pleased with himself.

And Susannah suddenly wished she could melt into the ground because conversations had erupted to her right and her left, and they were all about Micah and his new business.

She didn't have a moment alone with Deborah until they were eating lunch.

As usual, Sharon and Shiloh had finished in record time, so Susannah took her plate of food out to the picnic table that was situated next to the swings and see-saw, long ago remnants of a time when Naomi Miller had *kinner* and *grandkinner* around. Now all of her family lived in Shipshewana—close enough to visit, but not as often as she'd like. Susannah wondered why she hadn't moved with her family. Before she could think that through, they were surrounded by loud, en-

ergetic children. The afternoon was filled with a dozen girls and boys running and shouting and using up their abundance of energy.

Deborah nudged her with her shoulder. "You really didn't know?"

"I really didn't."

"It was the only topic of conversation before you got here, and then I tried to get your attention."

"You did?"

"*Ya.* I was…" Deborah pantomimed raising her hand above her head and bringing it back down over her *kapp*.

"Thought you were swatting at a bee."

"Word is he started this morning, but he put out flyers all over the community on Saturday."

"Good grief, word travels fast."

"You know the Amish grapevine."

Susannah momentarily covered her face with her hands.

"It's not so bad."

"Not so bad? Amish Taxi? It sounds like a bad joke."

"But it is honest labor, and to hear the girls talk, he had your father's approval."

"What?" Susannah's voice rose so high that both Sharon and Shiloh turned to look at her. She waved at them to go back to playing. "My *dat* knew and didn't tell me?"

"You've told me before that he's very private about things that he discusses with others."

"That's true."

"Seems to me it's honest work, and what else is he to do? The crops are in and…"

"And there are at least a dozen people hiring in Goshen to help with summer tourists."

"I suspect he'll have a line of folks waiting to ride in an Amish Taxi. He'll be helping with tourists plenty." Deborah started laughing and then, against her better instincts, Susannah joined her. It was rather funny if you thought about it.

It wasn't until they were all back home and had finished eating dinner that she had a chance to talk to her *dat* about it. Sharon and Shiloh were upstairs preparing for bed. Playing with the other children all day had certainly worn them out. They'd practically fallen asleep with their *kapp* strings in their soup.

"Seemed like a rather *gut* idea to me," Thomas said. "He's splitting what he earns with the widow, since he's using her buggy and horse."

"He is?"

"The horse needs more exercise, and Widow Miller can certainly use the money."

"She needs money?"

"It's not easy for the older ones." Her *mamm* filled their mugs with decaffeinated coffee.

"What do you mean?" Susannah asked.

"About what?"

"About it not being easy on the older folks. I thought we… Well, I thought that we provided for those in our community who had less."

"We do, as is right and proper." Her *dat* pointed an unlit pipe at her. He'd had it for as long as she could remember. She'd asked her *mamm* about it once. The pipe had been his father's. He only actually smoked it

once a day, only after the evening meal, and only out on the porch. "The Scripture tells us as much—to care for the orphans and the widows."

"Many of our elders have family close by, but for those who don't, finances can be tight. They'll never want for house repairs or groceries, but even Widow Miller likes to have a little extra change in her pocketbook."

"She has family in Shipshe."

"That she does, but there's some difficulty there. She doesn't ask them for extra because she doesn't think they have it."

Susannah shook her head. "We're getting off topic here. How is Micah's business even supposed to work?"

"Maybe you should ask him yourself." Her *dat* pointed the pipe toward the window, where she could just make out Micah crossing the field that separated her parents' home from his grandparents.

Susannah ignored the smile that passed between her parents, excused herself and met Micah before he'd made it to the porch.

"Amish Taxi? Really?"

"I'm sorry I didn't get a chance to tell you myself."

"You certainly don't owe me an explanation." The words came out snippier than she intended, so she looked up, down and around, and then asked, "Wanna look at Shiloh's kittens?"

Instead of answering, he entwined his fingers with hers, and that seemed so right, felt so natural, that she couldn't possibly hold on to her frustration. Fifteen min-

utes later they'd examined each kitten. There were five in all—four striped and one white.

"We never had any cats growing up." Micah ran his finger from the top of the white kitten's head, along its spine, to the tail. He was rewarded with a purr that resembled a small power motor. He glanced up at her and smiled. "This one likes me."

"You never had barn cats?"

"*Nein*. My *mamm* was allergic. If we had church in a member's barn and they had cats, she'd start sneezing and her eyes would water, and she'd have to excuse herself and go outside."

"You don't seem allergic."

"Guess not." He placed the kitten down next to the mama cat. They walked outside and stood looking at the near-dark sky.

Susannah could make out the first star, but there was still enough light for her to turn and study Micah. "Tell me how this new business of yours is supposed to work."

"Pretty simple, really. Widow Miller lets me know ahead of time if she will need the horse and buggy. Mostly she only drives to church or the grocery store or sometimes a doctor's appointment. It was one of the things that made me think of it. Her horse—Sunny Boy—needs more exercise. He almost seemed depressed when your *dat* and I went over to shoe him last time."

"Okay. So you walk to her house, harness Sunny Boy to the buggy and then…"

"I bought another phone, but not like the last one.

This one doesn't even have the internet. It's only for making and receiving calls." He had to explain to her about his *daddi* crushing his cell phone and insisting he get a job.

"I'm sorry, Micah. I had no idea he was so strict."

Micah shrugged. "I don't think it's about me as much as it is about him coming to terms with the changes around him."

"That's awfully mature of you to say."

"I've never been accused of being mature before." He stepped out from under the overhang of the barn. "Want to walk a little? For some reason, I'm feeling restless."

So they walked, and they talked some more as the moon rose and darkness fell properly over the fields.

He'd had a dozen rides his first day of business.

He'd made two hundred dollars.

Half of that he gave to the widow when he returned the horse and buggy.

Susannah thought of what her *dat* had said about helping the elderly. Micah was certainly doing that.

"This morning I worked a couple of hours for your *dat*, and when things slowed down, he told me to go on to town and get started on my new venture."

"I can see why my *dat* gave you his approval, but I'm a little surprised your *daddi* went along with it."

"Guess he felt like he didn't have a choice, since the bishop had approved."

"But he wasn't happy."

"Nein."

"Maybe he will be, when he sees how you're helping folks."

"Half of my customers were *Englisch*, just wanting to ride in an authentic buggy."

"That's pretty common around here."

"Not so much in Maine." Micah's voice turned somber. "*Daddi* thinks we should be separate. I'm sure that's the part of my plan that he doesn't approve of…as if being around *Englischers* will rub off on me. Next thing you know, I'll be wearing blue jeans and carrying a cell phone."

"You were wearing blue jeans the first day I saw you."

"True."

"And you had a phone in your back pocket."

"See? I'm already corrupted, so what harm can come?"

What harm indeed. Susannah had heard every possible scenario as she'd sat in the sewing circle. Everything from he shouldn't be alone with *Englisch* girls to he might put Timothy Zook out of business. Timothy ran a buggy ride for *Englischers* during the summer, and Susannah knew for a fact that he had more business than he cared to have. He had refused to extend his hours and had even cut his days back to three a week. Micah would actually be filling a gap that needed to be filled, and he'd be helping Amish folks at the same time.

She understood in that moment that Micah was a good person. It was only that he considered things from a different perspective than most. Who else would have thought of being an Amish taxi driver?

She walked over to an old tree that held a tire swing.

"Get in," he said.

"What is it with you and swings?"

"Just get in already. I'll push."

"I'm not even sure it will hold me."

Micah tugged on the rope, looked up at the limb and declared it sound.

He turned the tire upside down and ran his hand inside to make sure there was no water or critters, then he held it high as she wiggled her shoulders through. And the next thing Susannah knew, the tire swing was going up, then down and twirling and then back up again, and all of the responsibilities that she carried on her shoulders—or thought she did—fell away. Suddenly she was simply a young woman in a swing being pushed by a handsome young man. And above her the stars seemed to wink their approval.

Chapter Nine

What Micah didn't share with Susannah was that he was giving his grandparents half of his portion of the day's earnings. Out of two hundred dollars, the widow received one hundred, his grandparents fifty, and he kept fifty. It seemed like a fair enough arrangement to him. His grandparents were providing him a place to stay and feeding him. He also received a small amount each week for working with Thomas Beiler in the farrier shop. Between the two jobs, he felt like he was pulling his weight.

He would be lying to himself if he didn't admit that he thought his grandfather would thank him, or at least acknowledge in some way that he'd done well.

Instead, the next morning his grandfather had ignored the money sitting on the middle of the table. When his *mammi* brought it up, he'd simply grunted and told her to put it in the mason jar she kept in the pantry. "Something's bound to break soon, and we'll need it."

The meal passed in silence, the way most of their

meals did, and then without another word, his *daddi* stood, pushed in his chair and walked out toward the barn.

"Has he always been like this?" Micah asked.

"Like what?" His *mammi* stood and began clearing away the breakfast dishes.

"Solemn, taciturn, grumpy."

Mammi had her back to him as she filled the kitchen sink with warm water and then a splash of dish-washing detergent, but he could still make out the heavy sigh.

He carried the rest of the dishes to her and picked up a dish towel. "I'll dry if you wash."

Which seemed to ease her burden a bit.

Was it that easy?

Did helping with dishes make that big a difference?

Or was it more that his grandmother wanted to be seen, that she wanted to be thanked for her labors the same way that Micah wanted to be thanked for the fifty dollars sitting on the table? When was the last time someone had thanked her for making a meal or putting clean sheets on the bed or sweeping the floors?

"Breakfast was *gut*."

"*Ya?*"

"*Mamm* never did learn how to make biscuits from scratch."

Mammi started laughing. "I tried teaching her, and I know her mother tried, as well. She always seemed to forget at least one ingredient, and there aren't that many ingredients in biscuits."

"I might have starved if Becky hadn't taken over the cooking."

"Your *schweschdern* are all *gut* girls. It's funny when you think about it. I suppose we all have things that we're good at and other things that we never can quite get the hang of."

They continued washing and drying, and Micah was surprised to find that the silence between them felt comfortable. He realized he'd miss this when he went home—this time with grandparents that he barely knew.

"I wish I could figure out how to talk to him. Everything I say seems to irritate him one way or another."

"Your *daddi* never was much of a conversationalist."

"So it's not just me?"

"*Nein*, though…" She shook her head, as if she wished she hadn't started the sentence that she couldn't bring herself to finish.

"Might as well say it."

"It's only that he worries about you. Your *dat* was our only son, and now you're his only son."

"I'm supposed to carry on the family name."

"I don't know about that. If the Lord wills it…"

"But…"

"But you do have a responsibility to your family, even to your *schweschdern*."

Micah was shaking his head before she'd even finished. "They're all older than me. Trust me—they're not depending on me for anything."

"That's not true." *Mammi* pulled the plug on the sink water and watched it swirl down the drain. "It might seem that way now, because of your age. And you'll always hold a special place in their hearts because you're the baby *bruder* they hoped and prayed for. But when

you're older—when you're forty or fifty or sixty—it won't matter that you're the youngest. They'll look to you for advice. It's just the way Amish families are."

"Hard to imagine."

"I know it is."

The sun was peeking over the horizon, and he had chores to do before heading over to work at the bishop's. Hopefully, his afternoon would once again be full of taxi customers. He was looking forward to the day, and he felt some better about his grandfather. He might never understand him, but at least he could sympathize a little with what the old guy was going through.

He'd given his grandmother a quick hug, fetched his hat and was headed out the back door when his *mammi* called him back. "Keep an eye on him for me."

"Daddi?"

"Ya, just…let me know if you notice he's not feeling well."

"Is he not feeling well?"

"Nothing that he would admit to." She walked over to him, straightened his hat and stood on tiptoes to kiss his cheek. "But as you so clearly pointed out, he's grumpier than ever. It could be that he's feeling worse than he's letting on."

As he walked to the barn, Micah realized that it wasn't *Daddi's* amputated arm that *Mammi* was talking about. *Daddi* had been dealing with that longer than Micah had been alive. No, if he wasn't feeling well, it was something else, and it was something that he wasn't even talking to *Mammi* about. The question

was whether it was anything serious, and if it was, how they'd convince him to see a doctor about it.

The next day, Susannah stood and stared at the calendar on the wall. She'd had the day circled since her last visit, six months before.

"Are you sure you don't want me to go with you?" Her *mamm* was sewing new dresses for Shiloh and Sharon on the old treadle machine they kept in Susannah's shop. Susannah had offered to do it, but in truth, she was better with quilts than she was with garments.

"*Nein.* I can go by myself."

"We'll go with you, Susannah." Sharon was sitting on the floor playing with a ball and jacks.

"We can hold your hand," Shiloh said from her chair beside the sewing machine, where she was watching her mother sew each stitch.

"By the time you get home, these two girls will have nice new frocks."

"Because we're growing," Shiloh said.

"Like weeds. That's what *Dat* said. 'You girls are growing like weeds.'" Sharon's imitation of their *dat* caused everyone to laugh and eased the worry that Susannah was feeling.

As she directed their buggy horse, Percy, toward town, she realized she wasn't terribly worried about what the doctor would say. There was always a chance that her cancer would return, but wouldn't she know it? Wouldn't she feel different?

The fear of what might happen was something she'd learned to live with—at least some days. Other days

were a bit harder. All she knew for certain was that she felt better, healthier than she had in a very long time. Her cancer no longer was something that she thought about constantly. It no longer defined her, or at least she didn't think it did. She was enjoying being a normal young woman, and she wasn't ready for that to change. Not yet. Maybe not ever.

She'd stopped by for blood work the week before.

Today she would have an examination and then meet with the doctor to discuss her test results.

Dr. Kelly's office always made Susannah smile—it was decorated with pictures from her patients, some who were obviously quite young. The drawings sported stick figures holding a stethoscope, large hearts decorating each person and flowers taller than the people.

As the doctor walked in and picked up a folder, Susannah was overwhelmed by a fluttery feeling in her stomach—it wasn't fear exactly, but some emotion just as powerful.

"Your test results look good."

"They do?" The butterflies in her stomach scattered, replaced by sudden and total euphoria.

"Were you expecting something else?" Dr. Kelly had black skin, shoulder-length hair and kind eyes. She seemed ageless, but the picture of two teenage boys on her desk—boys Susannah could tell by one glance were her sons—indicated she had to be close to forty. "Talk to me, Susannah. Having you been feeling poorly?"

"*Nein.* I feel fine, and I wasn't expecting anything else. I always hope and pray the tests will come back fine, but I also try to prepare myself. You know…"

"Go on."

"Well, I try to weigh myself a couple of times a week to make sure I'm not losing weight, because last time…"

"I remember how thin you'd become when you first came to me."

"And I keep the journal you had me start…saying how I feel each day."

"That's good, Susannah. It's good that you're being vigilant about your health and keeping your appointments. Everything here looks fine. In fact, you seem healthier—and happier—than I've seen you in a long time."

Dr. Kelly waited. She didn't check her watch or tap her fingers against the desktop. If anything, she relaxed into her chair, indicating Susannah could take her time sorting through her emotions.

"Can I ask you a question?"

"Of course."

"How many of your patients, patients my age, go on to live happy lives—happily married lives?"

"That's an interesting question. I'd say roughly about the same percentage as those without cancer."

"Oh."

"I just read a study that Americans are waiting longer to marry, and more people than ever before are choosing not to marry at all. But that's probably not true among the Amish."

"It's not true among the Amish I know. Most Amish pair up by the time they're twenty, and they stay married for life."

Dr. Kelly sat there, her fingertips steepled together,

for another moment. Then she crossed her arms on the desk and leaned forward. "I can tell you my opinion, but it's based on purely anecdotal evidence."

Susannah nodded, though she wasn't completely sure what anecdotal evidence was.

"It seems that my patients put their lives on hold when they first receive their cancer diagnoses. If they're young and just beginning to consider marrying, they put that out of their mind for a while. If they're older and were thinking of retiring and traveling the US, they put that on hold. They press the pause button on their lives and deal with their cancer."

"And then?"

"And then the vast majority of them move on. They press the go button. They take up where they left off. Not all of them, of course. For some people, a cancer diagnosis becomes a new identity and changes the way they view every facet of their lives. They don't know how to move past it." She stood, smiled and walked around the desk, before sitting in a chair across from Susannah.

"I have a feeling that what you're experiencing, the thing that's worrying you, is that you are ready to press that go button. And if you're looking for my permission or approval to do so, then you have it. You've always had it. Now all you need is to find the courage to do so."

Susannah didn't remember driving home.

Once there, Shiloh and Shannon pounced on her, insisting she sit in the living room until they ran upstairs and tried on their new dresses. Her *mamm* knew she had good news before she said a word, and when

her *dat* came in for dinner, he immediately enfolded her in a hug.

"*Gotte* is *gut*," he murmured, and Susannah nodded her head in agreement.

The rest of the evening passed in a blur. It was when she was kneeling by her bed to say her prayers, which sometimes felt childish but mostly felt necessary, that she realized she was ready to push that go button Dr. Kelly had talked about. She understood in that moment that she was tired of worrying about what might or might not happen.

Would her feelings for Micah grow even stronger?

Did he feel the same?

What would they do when he moved back to Maine?

What if her cancer returned?

And beyond all those questions, there were several that had been in her mind since she'd first learned she had cancer. Would someone really want to marry her knowing that she couldn't have children? Would it be selfish of her to do such a thing? How would she know if any marriage proposal was motivated by true love or something done out of pity?

As she knelt there on the hardwood floor, she didn't receive any answers straight from heaven, but she did resolve to stop worrying and trust that God had a plan.

Micah's afternoons driving Amish and *Englischers* grew even busier than that first day. The following week, Old Eli actually flagged him down from the side of the road. "Heard you're giving rides, and my wife says I can't drive anymore on account of my cataracts."

"I'm headed back to town now. Want a lift?"

"That's why I'm standing out here flagging you down."

Micah generally didn't quote a price for his rides. People paid what they could—most offered something between five and ten dollars. It added up quickly. When he didn't have any Amish folks who needed a lift, he drove to downtown Goshen, parked near the Old Bag Factory and put his cardboard sign out.

Amish Taxi.

$10/person for twenty minutes.

Inevitably, there was a queue of people by the time he returned with the first passenger.

The day flew by. He lost track of how much he'd made, but he thought he'd exceeded the previous day's total. It seemed word was spreading quickly, and he already had rides lined up for each day the next week. After he'd dropped off the last *Englischer* for the day—a lady who simply wanted to drive through the countryside and look at the farms—he stopped by the general store.

"Can I help you?" One of the Amish girls from their church district was working the register. She looked to be about sixteen years old and had freckles across her cheeks and nose. Micah might have been introduced to her at church, but he couldn't remember her name.

"I guess I need a calendar."

"Like a wall calendar?"

"*Nein.* Something I can put in my pocket."

"I know just what you're talking about."

Unfortunately, they all looked pretty girlie to him—

the outsides decorated with flowers and hearts and motivational slogans. He settled for the one with kittens, since it reminded him of the white cat he'd held at Susannah's. He bought a pen as well, and at the last minute he spied a display of rose-scented goat lotion. "This stuff work?"

"I guess. My *mammi* uses it."

So he added a tube to his purchases. When was the last time someone had bought his *mammi* a gift? Probably not in the last ten years, since it seemed his *daddi* had been in a bad mood at least that long. He carried his purchases to the register.

"The calendar must be for your Amish taxi business."

"It is."

"I think what you're doing is so smart. Some people say it's a travesty—that's the word Ruth Lapp used when she was in here earlier—but I'm not sure what that means."

"It's bad."

"I gathered as much. Still and all, if you're going to be Amish in this day and age, you have to learn to adapt."

"Not something we're well-known for."

"I'm aware."

"I'm Micah, by the way."

"I'm Lydia." She smiled at him, her cheeks a rosy red.

Did she think he was flirting with her? The old Micah would have been. Maybe out of habit he'd done or said something that she'd taken the wrong way.

"Can you ring me up one more of those tubes of lotion?"

"Sure."

"It's for my girlfriend, Susannah Beiler. Maybe you know her?"

"*Ya*, I know Susannah. I didn't know you two were stepping out." She fetched another tube of the lotion, and then placed all of his items in a bag and counted out his change. "If it doesn't work out with Susannah, you know where to find me."

It was a rather bold statement coming from an Amish girl, but somehow the way she said it, the words seemed more friendly than flirty.

Instead of responding, he waved goodbye and moseyed out to the buggy. The week had turned into a fine one even if it had suffered a rocky start. Maybe by the time he got home, his *daddi* would have found something to smile about, or maybe he needed to stop worrying about whether that would happen. He hadn't caused the old guy's unhappiness; at least he hadn't caused all of it, so there was little chance he could help him get over it.

He returned the buggy and horse to Widow Miller, counted out her portion of the money and turned down oatmeal cookies and milk.

"*Mammi* serves dinner pretty early. Wouldn't want to ruin my appetite."

But as he drew close to his grandfather's place, he saw a van parked in the lane, and he knew that he wouldn't be eating anytime soon.

He rushed up the front porch steps, where his *mammi*

stood on one side of the screen door and a reporter for the *Goshen News* stood on the other.

"Micah, I've told this woman that we're not interested in being interviewed. Now, please see her off our property."

"Micah, I'm so glad to meet you. I'm Phoebe Jackson with the *Goshen News*."

The *Englisch* woman turned her attention toward him, and he tried not to squirm under her gaze. Her eyes were heavily made-up, and she had several earrings running up one ear. Her hair was cut in a short spiky style. Her lipstick reminded him of the pink taffy candy he'd loved as a child. She didn't look that much older than him.

"My editor sent me out here to ask a few questions about your Amish taxi business. Can you tell us how you got started?" She pushed the microphone in his direction and then glanced at a skinny guy, who looked to be about twenty and had terrible acne. "Charlie, you're rolling, right?"

"Uh-huh."

"So, Micah…"

Micah put out a hand and gently pushed her microphone down. Then he turned to the cameraman. "Charlie, stop rolling."

"But…"

"Stop, please."

Charlie looked at Phoebe, who nodded once—curtly.

"*Danki.* Now, if you'd be so kind as to leave my grandparents' property." He stepped off the porch to-

ward their van, and Phoebe followed as if they were tied together by some invisible string.

"But this is a big story, a human interest story. People want to know how you got started."

"They can take a ride in my buggy and ask me then."

"You're from Maine, right?"

"How did you know—"

"Do they have Amish taxi drivers there?" Phoebe had once again pushed the microphone in his direction. "I couldn't find anything on the internet."

Micah stared pointedly at the microphone until she took the hint and dropped it. "In general it's difficult to find Amish businesses online since we don't own computers."

"But…"

"Look, Phoebe, I appreciate that you need stories to fill your paper."

"It's called the news for a reason." She trudged back toward her van as she stuffed her microphone, notepad and pen into a large shoulder bag—eyebrows drawn together, pink lips in a pouty frown.

Micah sighed and followed her. "I know that you're only doing your job, but my grandparents are very private and very old-fashioned."

"And what about you?"

"What about me?"

"Are you private and old-fashioned, too?"

Micah shrugged. "A little of both, I suppose."

Charlie had loaded his camera in the van. Phoebe opened the door, tossed her shoulder bag inside and

then turned to give Micah a once-over. "Not too private to submit a selfie to our paper and win fifty dollars."

Micah shook his head. "I can explain that."

"What's to explain?" She hopped in the van and slammed the door shut, then rolled down the window. "Seems to me that if you're being paid for it, then you have no trouble being in the paper."

"I didn't submit that photo, and I'm sorry if I've offended you in some way."

"Oh, I'm not offended." She checked her lipstick in the mirror, dabbed at the corner of her mouth and looked again at Micah as she slipped dark sunglasses on. "I'm a reporter, Micah. I will get my story. In this instance, I'll just have to interview your customers since you're not willing to go on the record."

"On the record? What do you think this is…a television show?"

"So you know about those, too." She tapped a finger adorned with bright pink polish against her lips. "Are you sure that you're really Amish?"

Micah felt his temper spike, but for perhaps the first time in his life, he brought it under control.

Phoebe reached into her bag, pulled out a business card and held it out the window until he took it from her hand.

"If you change your mind, give me a call."

And then they were gone.

Micah stood there, watching the red taillights disappear down the lane and trying to figure out how he was going to explain this to his *daddi*.

Chapter Ten

As May gave way to June, Susannah and Micah settled into a pattern of sorts. He would come in the morning to help her *dat* with the horses. Before he left, he'd stop by her quilting room, and they would make plans for the evening or the weekend or whenever they could find time to be together. It was becoming increasingly more difficult because his taxi business was doing so well, or at least that was the only reason she could think of that would cause him to be out every evening. He was no doubt running *Englischers* around until sundown.

He didn't share the particulars of his business with her, but she could well imagine that by the time he returned the buggy, walked home and ate the cold dinner waiting on the stove, it was too late for them to see each other.

Susannah assured him that she understood, though he was looking increasingly exhausted. Dark circles had formed under his eyes, and it looked to her like he'd lost weight. When she asked him about it, he only said, "I have a plan, Susannah."

"Care to share it with me?"

"I do." He glanced at the watch he'd begun wearing. "But not yet. Not now, when I'm rushed. We need to talk soon, but when we're not in a hurry or distracted."

He was certainly both of those things. She shrugged as if *soon* was fine with her. "But how do your grandparents feel about your long hours?"

"I don't know. *Daddi* barely speaks to me. He probably hasn't said a dozen words since he smashed my phone with his work boot."

"And your *mammi*?"

"She seems preoccupied. He doesn't seem well, and I think she's worried about him. For reasons I can't fathom, he refuses to talk about it."

"Should he go to a doctor?"

"Maybe. She's suggested it, but he won't even consider seeing a doctor. The last time she suggested it, he glowered at her and said, 'Does it look like I'm bleeding, Abigail?'"

"I could ask my *dat* to go over and—"

"I don't think that's a *gut* idea. At least not yet. But *danki*." He pulled her to her feet and into his arms, lowered his head to hers and inhaled deeply. "I sure am glad you offered to be my buddy when I came to town."

"Is that what I am to you?" Her voice was teasing, but Susannah knew that he heard the seriousness behind her question. They had kissed on several occasions since her visit with Dr. Kelly, and she was trying to let things unfold naturally and at their own pace. Some days that was easier than others.

"Yes…" His lips found hers, and for a moment, she forgot what she'd asked.

Then she pulled away. "I'm not sure it's appropriate for buddies to be kissing."

"Is that so?"

"Maybe."

"I guess we need to change your title, then."

"And what would we change it to?"

Micah rubbed at his chin as if he couldn't think of the word. Then he snapped his fingers. "I've got it. Girlfriend. You'll be the girlfriend, and I'll be the boyfriend."

Susannah rolled her eyes and turned back to her cutting table.

"My boyfriend should get going then, or you're going to be late for your first taxi client."

He walked up behind her, slipped his hands around her waist and lowered his voice. "I have a plan."

"You do?"

"Yup. And if it works, and I think it will, then I will have plenty of financial resources. I won't be at the mercy of my parents or my grandparents. And then you and I will sit down and decide what happens next."

She pivoted in his arms, looked in his eyes and marveled that she'd managed to fall in love with someone she was hoping wouldn't stay in Goshen more than a few weeks.

For the next three hours she focused on the quilt on her design table. She was working on a patchwork-star quilt the librarian had hired her to make for her soon-to-arrive grandbaby. Unfortunately she was having trou-

ble focusing. Her thoughts insisted on wandering back over Micah's words.

What plan? What did he mean when he said *if it works*? And what was he thinking when he said they'd have to decide what happens next?

Was he hinting about marriage?

Was she foolish to jump to that conclusion?

And why hadn't she just asked him?

The questions tumbled through her head, but she soon pushed them away and immersed herself in the process of choosing fabrics, cutting squares and meticulously sewing them together. As for Micah, whatever his plan was, time would tell. He'd share the details with her when he was ready to. Until then she'd pray for patience, and that whatever he was cooking up was firmly in line with their *Ordnung*. The last thing they needed was another run-in with his grandfather.

Susannah woke to pounding on the front door and then the murmur of voices downstairs. She grabbed her robe and hurried to the living room, arriving in time to see Micah's grandmother leaving. "What is it? What's wrong?"

Her father had already returned to his bedroom, presumably to dress, since all of the lanterns seemed to be on.

"*Mamm*, what's wrong?"

"It's Micah." Her mother pulled her over to the couch. "He's been arrested."

"Arrested?"

"He's at the Goshen Police Department now. Abigail

came and asked your *dat* to go down to the police station and see if he could work out the misunderstanding."

"What misunderstanding? Why did they arrest him?"

"It seems there's been a robbery."

"What?"

"And Micah was in the vicinity. The police pulled him in for questioning and decided to book him."

"Can they do that?"

"Apparently."

Her *dat* walked into the room, kissed her *mamm* on the head, then did the same to Susannah. "Try to sleep, and if you can't sleep, then pray."

And then he was gone, leaving Susannah wondering what had happened and what, if anything, she could do about it.

Micah looked up when he heard Thomas's voice. He couldn't hear what was being said. When no one appeared in the hall that led to the cells, he finally moved back over to his cot and sat down.

He stared down at his ink-stained fingertips. The photographing and fingerprinting seemed to have happened days ago. He became convinced this nightmare of an evening would never end. Once his initial fear had subsided, a sort of numbness had settled over him. It was almost as if he was standing a few feet apart from himself—watching the arrest, booking and jailing happen to someone else.

He'd never been in an *Englisch* jail. It was both better and worse than he'd imagined.

Better because he wasn't forced to share it with any

petty criminals—the Goshen municipal jail allowed each person their own four-by-six concrete space. The stories of motorcycle gangs and hardened criminals roughing up the innocent Amish boy melted away into the night. No doubt, these stories were told to *youngies* to keep them on the straight and narrow.

And that was the worst of it. He'd finally committed his life to the straight and narrow, and look where it had landed him.

He heard footsteps and glanced up to see Susannah's *dat*.

"How are you, son?"

"I've been better. Did you come to get me out?"

"I came to try, but the officers are claiming they have video evidence."

"That I robbed the general store? That's not possible, because I didn't do it."

"Gut. Gut." Thomas reached into his pocket, pulled out an old pipe and stared at it a moment. Stuffing it back into his pocket, he glanced up at Micah and smiled. "My *dat* used to say the truth will out."

"The truth will out?"

"Ya."

"What does that even mean?"

"That given enough time, the truth will work its way out. If you didn't do this thing—"

"I didn't."

"Then you have nothing to worry about."

Micah looked around his cell—the small bed, the toilet and sink. It was all so humiliating. He turned his attention back to Thomas.

"*Ya*, I know. Just think, though. You're in good Biblical company."

"I am?"

"Paul and Silas spent time in jail."

"Oh, I suppose I remember that now that you mention it."

"Joseph, Samson, Jeremiah, Daniel, John the Baptist…"

"I didn't remember those, though I doubt they were in jail because someone thought they'd knocked over a general store."

"I would like to pray with you. Would that be all right?"

"*Ya*." Micah sighed and walked toward the bars separating them. "I could use some prayers right now."

He never expected to fall asleep, but he woke to someone in an adjacent cell complaining about instant eggs, and the guard telling him that this wasn't the Ritz. Whatever that was. He washed up at the sink, pulled the single cover up on his thin mattress and sat on the bed. Within a few minutes, a tray of runny eggs, cold toast and what had to be imitation bacon was delivered to his cell.

"Probably not what you're used to at home," the officer said. He almost sounded like he cared. The tag on his uniform said Officer Wright. The expression on his face said that he'd seen it all, and he probably had.

"*Nein*. It's not."

"Hopefully you won't be here long enough to get used to the food."

Micah cleaned his plate because he was starving.
His restlessness grew as he realized that he was miss-
ing his taxi appointments. No doubt everyone had heard
by now, though. He'd be lucky if anyone trusted him
enough to ride in his buggy.

His heart felt as if it dropped somewhere close to
the floor when he realized Susannah would have heard,
as well. He wished he could get a message to her. She
wouldn't believe him capable of doing such a thing. Su-
sannah was a fair person. She wouldn't turn her back on
him. Thinking of her made him feel better, and know-
ing he would see her again helped him to resist falling
into a state of despair.

An hour later he was sitting in an interview room,
Thomas next to him on one side of the table and two
officers sitting across from them. One was in uniform
and the other was in regular *Englisch* clothes.

"For the record, this interview is being recorded."
The man in *Englisch* clothes straightened the sheets of
paper in his folder. "Please state your name."

"Micah Fisher."

The man nodded toward Thomas, who tapped a fin-
ger against the table, smiled and said, "Thomas Beiler."

"And are you related to Mr. Fisher?"

"*Nein*, I'm his bishop."

"I'm Detective Cummings and this is Officer Decker.
This interview is occurring at 9:35 on the morning of
June 10." Cummings was tall and thin with red hair
that had been recently buzzed. Decker was a woman
in her forties and had yet to smile. "Mr. Fisher, please
confirm that you've been read your rights."

"As officers were slapping the handcuffs on my wrists."

"A simple yes or no will do."

"Yes, I have."

"You are being held on suspicion of breaking and entering of the general store."

"Which I didn't do."

"We'd like to go over your statement, and then we'll talk about what happens next."

"What happens next is you let me go. I did not rob the general store."

Thomas's hand on his shoulder caused Micah to shut his mouth, which he supposed was the good bishop's purpose for being there. He took a deep breath and scrubbed his hand over his face. If ever there was a time he needed patience, it was now. And he needed it fast!

"Understandably Micah is upset." Thomas's voice was quiet and his tone neutral. It worked to calm Micah down. "I'm happy to vouch for him. He's a *gut* worker, and he has never been in trouble before."

"We'll get to that. Again, just to confirm, Mr. Fisher, you waive your right to an attorney?"

"Yes."

Thomas nodded in agreement. "As I'm sure you know, we prefer not to become entangled in legal matters. Our goal is to remain separate and yet be *gut* members of the community."

"Yet you are entangled." Decker sat back, crossed her arms and waited until she was sure she had everyone's attention. "I've been on this police force for twenty-two years, and I appreciate and respect your culture. But you

know as well as I do, Bishop, that we've had our share of Amish teenagers step over the line."

"And we've always cooperated and done everything in our power to compensate anyone for damages and see that the youth received counseling as needed."

"We're not talking about underage kids drinking beer behind the Dairy Queen. We have video evidence of this young man robbing the general store last night."

"That's not possible, because I wasn't at the general store."

"All right." Cummings tapped a pen against his pad of paper. "Give us your alibi, then. We'll verify it and we can have you out of here in time for lunch."

"My alibi?"

"Tell us where you were and who you were with."

Micah opened his mouth and then shut it. "I can't do that."

"Why?"

"Because I can't."

Susannah's father tilted his head toward Micah and lowered his voice, though, of course, the detective and office could still hear what he said. "It would be in your best interest if you would—"

"I can't, Thomas. I just…can't."

"All right. We seem to be at an impasse here. Micah, for whatever reason, can't tell us where he was, but if I understand *Englisch* law correctly, he doesn't have to prove his innocence. You have to prove his guilt."

Detective Cummings nodded at Decker, who pointed to a television on the wall and then hit some buttons on

her cell phone. At first, the video was dark, showing little except for the front of the general store.

"This was taken from the store across the street twelve minutes before the alarm went off in the general store."

As they watched, a horse pulling an Amish buggy stopped in front of the general store. A young man stepped out, though the camera was too far away and the scene was too dark to tell who it was. The man was approximately Micah's height and build.

Decker paused the video. "Now, is there something you want to tell us?"

"*Nein*, because that's not me."

As they watched, the young man pulled out a crowbar, busted the lock on the front door and hurried inside. They couldn't see in the store or what was happening, but suddenly the wail of a siren could be heard on the video.

"That was activated by the alarm attached to the cash register," Cummings explained. "The owner disabled the security alarm to the front door because it kept going off at random moments, but he left the one on the cash register drawer."

The time meter at the bottom of the video continued to roll forward. Not long after the alarm went off, the Amish person ran out of the store, jumped into the buggy and drove off. Decker stopped the video and looked at Cummings, who focused on Micah.

"Son, it goes better for everyone if you just confess to what you did. Plead guilty, and I will personally speak with the judge and request the minimum sentence."

"I am not your son, and I wasn't the person in the video."

Cummings sat back with a sigh, as if it pained him greatly to hear Micah's words. Not even looking at Decker, he motioned for her to keep going. She pushed more buttons on her phone and another video came up, this time showing the opposite side of the buggy. The buggy had paused at a road crossing, directly underneath a streetlamp.

"A business on the next block has CCTV."

"What is that?"

"Closed-circuit television—it's a security measure so they can record any activity in or around the store when it's closed. We were able to pull this video and establish that it occurred in the same time frame as the first video, but it gives us a different point of view."

"So?"

Officer Decker looked at him for just a moment, as if he might be the dumbest person she'd ever encountered. Thomas had gone completely still, his eyes focused on the video. With a sinking feeling in his stomach, Micah turned his attention to it. He watched as the buggy came into view and then proceeded past the camera's field. Decker pushed more buttons on the phone; the horse and buggy moved backward. She then paused the video and zoomed in.

The first thing Micah saw was the scraped paint on the front fender. He'd asked Widow Miller about fixing it when he'd first started using her buggy. Her answer had been "Why? It travels the same whether the paint is perfect or scraped."

The second thing he saw was the passenger-side window, and taped to it was the sign that he had placed there, which read Amish Taxi.

He didn't know what Thomas said to the detective or what the detective said to him after that. His mind was spinning, and it was as if he couldn't process anything else.

It wasn't until he was back in his cell, until he heard the bars clank shut and the lock turn, that he managed to bring his attention back to the present.

Officer Wright had apparently escorted him back. Now Wright was studying him with a resigned look. "Guess you'll have time to get used to the food after all."

"What do you mean?"

"Do you have the money to post bail?"

"Nein."

"Neither does your bishop, apparently."

"So?"

"So that means you're staying until the judge is in court again, which will be two more days. Might as well make yourself comfortable." Officer Wright stepped closer to the bars, and something about his demeanor or the look in his eyes reminded Micah of the old men in Maine who sat around and told stories of the early days there. Something in his eyes spoke of experience and wisdom. Whatever it was, it caused Micah to listen—to really listen.

"I don't know what you did or why you did it. The why doesn't matter so much at this point, and I can guarantee you that Judge Johnson isn't interested in whether you were mistreated as a child or are suffering

depression. Johnson's an old-fashioned kind of judge. You do the deed, you pay for it."

"And what if I didn't do it?"

"Then you need an alibi, because from what I heard, they've got you on this one from three different directions."

Micah didn't answer. He was thinking about the buggy and the Amish man and the sign on the window.

"All I'm saying is that this place is not so bad. Food's terrible and you don't have TV or a library, but it's not that bad. But where you're going? It's not where a young man like you should spend a year or two. Do yourself a favor and wise up before the judge gets here."

And with those words of comfort, Micah found himself once again alone.

Susannah couldn't believe it. She tried to process what her *dat* told her. She could tell he wasn't holding anything back, but she couldn't believe what he was saying. There was no way that Micah was guilty of breaking into the general store.

She tried to speak to his grandparents. John Fisher took one look at her and headed to the barn. Abigail stepped out on the porch, but the conversation went nowhere.

"I know you love your grandson."

"Of course I do, but Micah has never seen the world as the rest of us see it."

"You're saying you believe he did this?"

"I'm saying he might have convinced himself it was

okay. I don't know. Sometimes what a person is capable of will surprise you."

"Have you been to see him?"

His *mammi* shook her head once, and that was the end of the conversation. She turned and walked back into the house, leaving Susannah standing there and wondering what to do next.

Visiting Deborah didn't go much better.

"He didn't do this, Deborah. I know he didn't."

Deborah held up her hands in surrender. "I don't want to believe it, either."

"He didn't do it."

"You said he's been out late a lot."

"So what?"

"So four other stores have been robbed in the last two weeks."

"What? And you think he did that? You think Micah was traveling up and down Goshen knocking over stores? Why would he even do such a thing?"

"You're the one who said that he has a plan. Didn't he say if it worked, he would have financial resources?"

"Which could mean a lot of other things besides robbery."

Deborah stopped separating dollar bills in the cash drawer of her family's vegetable stand. She walked around the table and put her arms around Susannah, who had determined she would not cry. She was not going to cry about Micah, because he did not do this.

"Have you tried to see him?"

"I have." She brushed her sleeves across her eyes.

"And?"

"He saw me the first time—that was yesterday. Told me that he didn't do this, and that he would be out by the weekend, so I should have the fishing poles ready."

"Maybe he will. Maybe he is innocent. I'm just so sorry you're going through this."

"Then he asked me not to come back."

Deborah stepped back, hands still on Susannah's shoulders, as if she needed to get a better look at her best friend's face. "Why would he say that?"

"Because he said that without an alibi…" The tears resumed streaming down her face. "Without an alibi, they just might pin this on him, and there wasn't anything he could, or would, do about it."

"All right. So we know where to start."

"What do you mean?"

"I mean, you're going to see him again this afternoon. Didn't you say the judge is in court tomorrow?"

"Yes."

"So go to him today. Go now. It's important that you see him before he appears before the judge."

"What am I supposed to do? What am I supposed to say?"

"You're going to convince him to explain where he was and who he was with."

Chapter Eleven

Micah didn't look up when he heard the guard open the outer door. Whoever was in the cell at the end of the hall had a large family. They'd all come to see him. He couldn't hear much of what they said, but what he did hear was like a knife in his gut.

"We know you didn't do this."

"We're going to get you out."

"Dad's working on the bail money."

"Mom knows a guy who knows a guy who's a lawyer."

Whoever that person was had a very engaged family—a family who believed in his innocence. Micah didn't know if the person was guilty or innocent, but he did know that he was a lucky man to have so many people on his side.

Only two people had come to visit Micah.

His bishop.

And his girlfriend.

He hadn't seen or heard from his grandparents.

He'd used his one phone call for the bishop, so he

hadn't spoken to his parents, and he wasn't sure he wanted to. What could he tell them? How could he explain this situation that threatened to change the course of the rest of his life?

And then the scent of rose lotion pulled him away from his dark thoughts.

If anything, Susannah looked prettier than the day he'd seen her standing by the mailbox with Sharon and Shiloh. She wore a light blue frock and a white apron and, of course, the ever-present white *kapp*.

"Why are you smiling?"

"Just remembering the first time I saw you without that *kapp* on."

"Five minutes," Officer Wright said. He offered to bring Susannah a chair, but she shook her head no and thanked him.

"Why did you come back?"

"Because I needed to see you." She pulled in her bottom lip, and he knew that she was fighting back tears, which caused his defenses to crumble.

He stared at the ceiling, and when he looked at her again, he'd regained control of his emotions. It wasn't that he was afraid of crying in front of her. He wasn't one of those guys who believed that men shouldn't ever show their emotions. It was more that he felt if he let go of the reins that were holding them in, he might never regain control again.

"Things were going too well," he whispered.

"What things?"

He only shook his head.

"Come over here."

Micah could hear the trembling in her voice, and it nearly undid him. He closed his eyes for a moment, but when he opened them she was still there.

"If you are going to do this to yourself, to us, then you owe me this much. Come over here and look me in the eye."

"I can't tell you where I was. I—"

"You can't tell the judge. I know. You said that before. But if you can't tell me the when or where, then you can at least tell me the why."

So he stood and walked to where she was waiting. They weren't supposed to touch. The poster on the wall proclaimed that rule loud and clear. But then Micah had never been good at following the rules. Susannah's hands were wrapped around the cell's bars. He ever so gently wrapped his hands around hers, figuring they had one minute, maybe two, before one of the officers came busting through reminding them to stand three feet apart.

"Tell me why." Her voice was soft, and when he looked in her eyes he saw a whole world of hurt.

But he also saw something else… He knew that she trusted him or at least she wanted to.

"I can't tell you where I was…"

The rattle of keys at the end of the hall told him the officer was coming through.

"I can't tell because I promised I wouldn't. I gave my word, Susannah. And what kind of man would I be if I couldn't keep my word? You deserve better than that."

She swiped at her eyes. "Okay."

"Okay?"

"*Ya*. Okay."

The officer separated them before either could say anything more, but what Micah saw before she walked away almost sent him to his knees because it wasn't judgment or disappointment or anger—it was love.

Micah stood in a type of waiting room next to his court-appointed lawyer. The man was definitely under thirty years old, and he looked as if he'd slept as little as Micah had. When Micah had refused to give an alibi, he'd only asked, "You're sure?" When Micah confirmed that he was very sure, the man—Rafael Rodriguez—had grinned and said, "Chances are you're going away to prison, but we're going to make them earn it."

He opened the door, and they walked into the main courtroom.

The judge had apparently been working for several hours already. He glanced at the clock, as if he was wondering whether he could take a lunch break. The man was in charge, wasn't he? Couldn't he just order the court adjourned? Or perhaps Micah was remembering the single court scene he'd watched on television wrong.

Judge Johnson was older, white haired, and Micah could tell in a second that he did not suffer fools.

The bailiff called Micah's case, and he and Rafael walked forward to stand before the judge.

It was a moment that Micah understood he wouldn't forget if he lived to be a hundred. It was surreal, standing there before a man who had the power to free or imprison him. There was a spiritual lesson here that wasn't lost on him—the power of forgiveness and the sacrifice of Christ standing before the one and true

God. He'd heard it preached often, but at that moment, he felt it clean through to his soul.

"Mr. Rodriguez, does your client still refuse to provide an alibi?"

"He does."

"Mr. Fisher, you are charged with aggravated burglary." Rafael had explained that *aggravated* meant he had a weapon—in this case, a crowbar that could be seen in the video and was used to break the lock on the front door. "How do you plead?"

"I plead not guilty, Your Honor."

Rafael had told him what to say word for word. They'd even practiced.

"I assume you still have no means to post bail."

"That's correct, Your Honor."

"Then I have no choice but to remand you to the Elkhart County Jail until..." He must have consulted a calendar, because he picked up some half-glasses, perched them on his nose and stared down at something. "Looks like it'll be July 18 before you can have a jury of your peers."

He took the glasses off and looked at Micah—really looked at him—for the first time.

"Mr. Fisher, you're certain that you want to remain behind bars until that time?"

"I don't see as I have a choice, Your Honor."

"You most certainly do. If you can prove that you weren't the person in the video..."

"Objection, Your Honor. The accused is not required to prove his innocence, but rather—"

"I know the law, Mr. Rodriguez." Johnson shook his

head as if he needed to rid himself of a pesky fly. "I've seen the video, and I have to say that the evidence here is strong. Strong enough to hold Mr. Fisher over for a trial."

"You can't know that's him."

"That will have to be proved at the trial. Until then…" He raised his gavel to strike it against the desk when someone spoke up from the back of the room.

"I can provide Micah with an alibi."

Relief washed over Micah in that moment because he knew that voice. His legs felt suddenly wobbly and his hands shook so that he had to clasp them together.

Rodriguez stepped closer and said, "Steady there. Don't faint on me, Fisher."

But Micah understood what Rafael Rodriguez and Judge Johnson couldn't—what they would very soon know. Micah understood that this nightmare was over, and that he'd be able to go home.

Thomas walked on one side of him, Susannah on the other, as Micah left the Goshen Municipal Jail.

"How about we have some lunch before we go home?" Thomas nodded at a coffee shop across the street.

Susannah squeezed his hand. "We heard the food wasn't so good in there."

"You heard right. I'm starved."

They ordered hamburgers, fries and shakes before they got down to business.

"Levi Hochstettler?" Susannah was sitting across from him. No doubt she wanted to be able to look into his eyes while he explained the last few weeks. "You were with Levi? I wasn't aware you even knew him."

After thanking the waitress for the shakes she left on their table, Thomas asked, "And why was that so hard to admit?"

"The first time I picked up Levi for a ride, he had me drop him at this old barn over on the east side of town. It was an *Englischer*'s place, from the look of it."

"What was he doing there?"

"Rebuilding the engine on a 1956 Mercedes."

"Levi always was *gut* with small engines," Thomas said.

Susannah leaned forward. "And you helped him?"

"Not at first, but after the third ride, he figured he could trust me." Micah had already consumed half of his shake. He didn't realize how bad jail food was until he was a free man and eating good food again. "I did some engine repair up in Maine, so I offered to lend a hand. This was last week, the same week that my business first got off the ground."

"This is why you've been so tired."

"I knew I was stretching it—burning the candle at both ends as the old folks say—but it seemed like too good an opportunity to pass up."

Thomas grunted, but he didn't interrupt.

"So I was helping Thomas in the morning, running my buggy service in the afternoon and helping Levi at night. We were about halfway through with the rebuild…"

"And then?" Susannah was twirling her *kapp* string, completely engrossed in his story.

"Then Levi found a buyer. An *Englisch* guy who was willing to pay top dollar."

"Which was, no doubt, a lot of money."

"It was, and the *Englischer* put down a deposit, so we knew he was good for it. But the problem was that he needed it for some race this weekend."

"A race?"

"Some race with old cars. They give you a map at the last minute. I didn't really understand that part."

"The Great American Race." Thomas smiled when they both turned to stare at him. "I'm a bishop, but I'm still a man. This race has been around since the eighties."

The waitress brought their food, and for the next few minutes, no one spoke as Micah made up for lost calories. When he finally pushed back his plate, Susannah and her father shared a smile.

"Don't say it, *Dat*."

"Growing boy needs his food."

They all laughed, and it felt good. Micah wanted to pull Susannah into his arms. He wanted to thank her for standing by him, but he understood that doing so in the middle of a burger joint in front of her father probably wasn't a great idea.

"So the *Englischer* needed the car fast. He was willing to pay good money and Levi was willing to share what he made." Susannah shook her head. "What are you not saying?"

"Levi's parents." The bishop ran his fingers through his beard.

"Exactly." Micah took up the story. "Levi's parents are quite strict. They were already unhappy that he was working on car engines."

"I've talked to them about that," Thomas said. "Levi

is good with his hands, good at fixing things. If he'd been born *Englisch*, there's no doubt he would have been an engineer of some sort. It seemed to me that allowing him to use those talents in a way that was acceptable would solve the problem."

"But it didn't?" Susannah had pushed her plate away and was again leaning forward, no doubt ready to pull the rest of the story out of him.

"I'm only sharing this because Levi told me as we left the courtroom that I should tell you everything." He glanced at Susannah but directed the next part to the bishop. "He's thinking of leaving the faith. Well, not leaving exactly. He has an *onkel* who is Mennonite and has a shop in Ohio. Says he can give Levi all the work he needs. But he insisted that if Levi really wanted to do it, then he would have to save the money for the bus fare as well as a deposit on a place to live. They have eight young ones, so there's no room at their house."

"But if he could sell the Mercedes…"

"Then he'd have enough money to go." Micah finally pushed away his plate. "He's going to come and talk to you tomorrow."

Thomas nodded as if that settled things.

"Okay." Susannah held up her left hand and began counting off points. "You were helping Levi. He was sharing the profits with you. You were definitely not in Widow Miller's buggy, and you did not rob the store…"

"I never doubted that," Thomas said.

"Why couldn't you just explain that to the judge?"

"Because I promised Levi I wouldn't tell. I gave him

my word that I would not be the one to tell his parents. He wanted to do it, in his own way, in his own time."

"You didn't want him to get in trouble? You were willing to go to jail for that?"

Micah didn't answer right away. When he looked at Susannah and Thomas, at these two people who had come to mean so much to him, he knew that he could be completely honest.

"I've been on the outside most of my life. I'm not really sure why. Rebellious nature that needs taming, or maybe…maybe I hadn't met the right person who could settle me down." He paused and looked directly at Susannah—smiled and resumed his story. "I know what it's like to walk a tightrope at home, and how important it is to have one person who you can trust with your real self, with who you really are. You two have been that for me, and I have been that for Levi. It was important for me to honor that commitment."

"When Levi stood up for you in court, when he provided your alibi, he also put himself on the line with his parents."

"Exactly."

"You know, Micah. The one thing that you can give and still keep is your word. It seems to me that you showed maturity and wisdom today."

Which seemed to settle the matter as far as Susannah and Thomas were concerned. Micah didn't know what would happen when he went home to his grandparents.

And he certainly didn't know who had stolen Widow Miller's buggy and broken into the general store, but he did know that it wasn't him, and that it was time to

do what Levi was doing. It was time to stand up and be true to who he was. He would probably never be a traditional Amish person, but he loved his faith and he had the support of the bishop for his Amish buggy service. If that wasn't good enough for his grandparents, then perhaps it was time he accepted he was bound to disappoint some of the people who meant the most to him.

Their disappointment might hurt, but it wouldn't change who he was.

Micah stared at his *daddi* in disbelief. "You can't make me do that."

"You're right. I can't. However, I can issue an ultimatum."

"An ultimatum?"

"*Ya*, for sure and certain."

"That's not… It's not how we do things."

"How would *you* know?" His *daddi*'s voice rose like a wave crashing over them. "How would *you* know how we do things? You've spent the last three days in an *Englisch* jail."

"For something that I didn't do."

"You have only one foot in our world. The other is firmly planted in the *Englisch*."

"That's your opinion."

"*Nein*, son. It's a fact, and I will not stand for it any longer."

Micah glanced at his *mammi*. Was that sympathy he saw in her eyes? Perhaps, and yet she didn't jump to his defense.

"You will inform Thomas of your decision to join the church on Sunday morning."

"I haven't made that decision yet."

"You will inform him on Sunday or before Sunday, or you will find another place to live—perhaps one of your *Englisch* friends will take you in."

His *daddi* pushed himself up from the table with his one good arm, and that was when Micah noticed that his hand was shaking. He shifted his left shoulder, as if it pained him. Micah had the sudden realization that his *daddi* was not a young man, that he was aging. He felt a stirring of sympathy for him, which was immediately wiped away by the man's next words.

"I've given you time, Micah. We all have."

"And I have done what you asked."

"You think this life is a game of some sort—a long procession of parties and reckless decisions and stepping back and forth across the line that our community has plainly drawn to keep us separate." He reached for his hat and crammed it on his head. "That is your choice, but I won't abide it a moment longer. We've all coddled you much too long. It's time for you to make a decision. Choose the life you wish to live."

And with that final declaration he stormed out the back door.

Neither Micah nor his *mammi* moved. Finally, she sighed and stood, beginning to clear away the dishes.

"Tell me you don't agree with him."

"Doesn't matter if I do or not."

"It matters to me."

Mammi placed the dishes into the sink and stood

there for a moment, staring out the window. When she turned back toward Micah, he saw such conflicting emotions in her eyes that it tore at his heart.

Was this really all his fault?

Was he tearing his family apart? The memory of his last week at home in Maine threatened to rise, but he quickly pushed it down. They'd understood him little more than his grandparents.

Instead of lecturing, *Mammi* walked over to where he sat, pulled a chair up close and sat so that their knees were touching. She reached for his hand and stared down at it a moment. When she finally raised her eyes to his, Micah's heart sank.

She was on his *daddi*'s side.

He knew what was coming.

"Your *daddi* isn't wrong, not in his intent. Perhaps his presentation could use a little work." She attempted to smile, but it slid away. "He loves you, Micah. We all do. However, you are twenty-five years old. You're a man, not a *youngie*."

"I know that." His throat was suddenly tight. He had to push the words out. "I know I'm not a child."

"And yet you so often act like one."

Coming from his *daddi*, the words would have stung. But the words were whispered by his *mammi*, and the look she gave him? It held only compassion.

"He's feeling older these days. The mornings are hard because he wakes so stiff, and then some mornings, like today, the indigestion bothers him."

"I'm sorry he isn't feeling well, but it gives him no right…"

"It gives him every right. He doesn't complain, and I'm not telling you this so you'll feel sorry for him. Though, of course, you should have sympathy for others, especially your family. I'm telling you this so you'll understand."

She ran a wrinkled finger under his suspender, straightening it, and patted his shoulder lightly. "What your *daddi* understands, which you don't, is that this life is but a fleeting matter, like a passing mist. You think that you have all the time in the world to decide the course of your life, but none of us has an unlimited amount of time to make our choices. Today is the day for you to make your decision."

She patted his shoulder again, then pushed herself into a standing position. That was when Micah knew that all was lost. She would not intervene on his behalf.

He felt numb all over.

Why did it seem that everyone was against him?

First that foolishness about the break-ins, as if he would do such a thing. And now this.

His *daddi* was actually going to force him to join the church. He'd actually been considering doing so, but now... To have it dictated to him put a sour taste in his mouth. He couldn't make a decision like that because someone said he must. It would be a lie.

The one thing you can give and still keep is your word.

Thomas's words came back to him like an arrow to the heart. When he made a decision to join the church, he was giving his word, so he needed to be certain. Didn't he?

And what was the alternative?

Or did he even have one?

Chapter Twelve

He spent that afternoon and the next morning in a bit of a fog. He saw Susannah when he stopped by her *dat*'s farrier shop, but he didn't speak to her of what was happening with his grandparents. He wasn't ready. What if she agreed with them?

There was little work for him in the shop, so he took off early and headed to town to hopefully pick up some Saturday passengers in his buggy service. He lasted less than an hour. After he took one Amish girl to the wrong store, and an *Englisch* woman asked why they were traveling in a circle around the same block, he knew his mind wasn't on his work. Apologizing, he dropped her off where they'd started—free of charge.

He simply couldn't focus.

The anger and sense of unfairness grew until he thought that he might explode. He picked up his Amish-taxi sign and made his way back across town, returning the horse and buggy to Widow Miller's and making his way to his grandparents' house. There he paced back and forth in the barn for the better part of a half hour.

Only ten thirty in the morning, and yet it felt like the day had lasted forever. He walked inside, looked around and headed back out. He was barely aware that he'd grabbed his hat from the mudroom, and he didn't realize he was walking toward Susannah's until he caught sight of her playing outside with her little *schweschdern*. Sharon and Shiloh spied him at the same moment and dashed toward him.

"We found a grass snake in the garden." Sharon grabbed one of his hands. "We placed rocks around him so that we can watch what he does."

"He can't get away," Shiloh added, standing close and worrying one hand inside the other. "I was scared at first, but Susannah says it won't hurt us."

He followed them to the edge of the garden. The grass snake was only a few inches long and bright green. He'd probably been sunning himself when the girls had noticed him and quickly built a perimeter— one that the snake would have no trouble sliding over or through, but Micah didn't bother telling them that.

"I'm going to get him some grass." Sharon bounded off toward the edge of the garden.

"Susannah said he eats frogs. I'm going to see if I can find one." Shiloh dashed toward the water trough they used to irrigate the garden.

"Watch out for snakes," Susannah called from her place at the north end of the garden.

"Too late for that advice." Micah plopped down on the ground beside her.

She rolled her eyes. When he didn't say anything else and only sat there brooding—that was the only word for it—she bumped her shoulder against his.

"What's wrong? Did your favorite baseball team lose last night?"

"Nein."

"I thought you'd be in a fine mood today, since you're no longer considered the bandit of Goshen."

"And yet I'm still the black sheep." The unfairness of it seemed to press down on him. Why couldn't people simply accept him like he was? Why couldn't he be Amish without following every one of their silly rules? Why were rules even necessary?

"Something has happened." Instead of pushing him, Susannah waited, which was something she was very good at.

It was one of the things he appreciated about her. While his mind dashed back and forth, her steady presence helped to calm him down. He stared at the garden for several minutes—a part of his mind hearing the girls giggling over the snake, a part of his mind still back in his grandparents' kitchen.

Finally, he blew out a noisy breath and told her everything.

Susannah wasn't exactly shocked at what Micah told her. She'd suspected such a thing might happen sooner rather than later, but she was disappointed that it had happened the morning after he'd been proved innocent of the break-ins.

"I'm a little surprised you're taking it so hard."

Micah jumped to his feet and began to pace back and forth. "Taking it hard? I'm about to be thrown out on my own."

"Just last week you were talking about having a plan and not being dependent on your grandparents anymore."

"But I need more time. I'm not… I'm not ready yet."

When she smiled at him, he collapsed on the ground beside her. "Maybe I should have seen this coming. I'm not sure, to tell you the truth."

"It seems to me that your grandparents are simply forcing the issue—an issue that you were already thinking about."

"They're saying I have to decide between being Amish or *Englisch*. That I have to decide now."

"They're saying if you're going to stay in their home, you have to decide now. No one can force you to make the decision to join the church, Micah. You can take as long as you need, but the process of deciding… Well, it must be hard on them."

He flopped onto his back and shielded his eyes against the sun. "I know you're not on their side. You've stood by me through all the ups and downs since I've been here. You even visited me at the jail."

"Twice."

He stole a peek at her and made a valiant effort to keep the perturbed expression on his face. "Twice," he conceded.

"You've had a difficult week. I definitely think you deserve a break."

He pulled up a handful of grass and tossed it at her, and Susannah couldn't help smiling. He had changed so much from the young man she'd seen step out of an *Englischer*'s truck in downtown Goshen. He had stepped into adulthood when he'd begun his own business, when he'd begun planning for the future, and certainly when he'd put his integrity over his freedom.

But the playful Micah lurked underneath, and maybe that was okay, too. Many adults were too serious. She loved that he was able to lighten her mood with a touch or a smile or a silly suggestion. Amish Taxi? She couldn't believe he'd come up with that. She was beginning to think of him as her Amish rebel. And rebels weren't such bad things—they kept everyone on their toes, weighing their decisions rather than following blindly along.

Still, she understood that it was hard to leave the carefree years of *rumspringa* behind, to embrace being an adult and accept responsibility for all of one's actions. Her cancer had forced that role upon her earlier than most, and something in Micah's upbringing had allowed him to put off any such change again and again. Perhaps it was because he was the only son in a family full of daughters. Perhaps it was simply his personality.

Regardless, she rather agreed with his grandparents that it was time for him to decide. They could have suggested such a thing a bit more tactfully, but John Fisher had never been known for his tact.

"You refuse to cut me any slack," Micah muttered. "Is that what you want?"

"*Nein.* I like that you're honest with me."

She shrugged and the look he shot her caused the heat to rise in her cheeks. Just like that, the subject of remaining Amish was behind them, and the playful Micah was back.

"You worry me when you get that look in your eyes."

Sharon picked that moment to dump two handfuls of grass onto Micah's stomach. He launched himself off the ground, chasing her around the garden until she fell

into Susannah's lap squealing and laughing. Shiloh had plopped down cross-legged beside them and rested her head in the palm of her hand.

"I think we should take our snake to the pond."

"Do you, now?" Susannah reached out to tug on her *kapp* strings.

"Actually, that's not a bad idea." Micah sat up straighter. "But I've heard that what snakes really like is rivers—especially grass snakes, because…you know, there's lots of grass growing on the banks of the river."

Susannah tried to catch his eye, but he was avoiding looking directly at her. "I don't like where you're going with this."

"It's Saturday. What else do you have to do?"

"I'm supposed to be minding Sharon and Shiloh while our parents are visiting church members."

"And you will mind them at the river."

Which, of course, started a chorus of "Please" and "Can we?" and "We promise to be good."

"No fair," she laughed. "It's three against one."

"I'll even help you pack a lunch." Micah pulled her to her feet, stepped close enough to scoot her *kapp* strings back over her shoulder. "Maybe we can wear these two out, and they'll take a nap."

"I hate naps," Shiloh murmured.

"We're too old for naps!" Sharon jumped from one foot to another. "Oh, I know. I'm going to get a box to put Simon the Slippery Snake in."

She dashed off toward the house in search of a box. Shiloh stood clasping her hands and watching Susannah. "Are we going? I think Simon would like the river better than our garden. If you think it's okay."

It was probably the look on Shiloh's face that made up Susannah's mind. She was such a sweet, serious girl—maybe too serious. A few hours at the river would do them all good.

"All right, but we need to be back well before dinner. I promised *Mamm* I would have food on the table by five. Besides, it's supposed to rain."

Micah waved away any concern. "A summer shower can't stop us from having fun."

Twenty minutes later, Susannah had changed the girls into older dresses, Micah had helped to pack the makings for a picnic lunch and they were traipsing across the field to the back of her parents' property. She'd left a note telling her *mamm* where they were going.

The clouds had begun building toward the west.

"Weather's changing." Susannah pointed the fishing rods she was carrying toward the darkening sky. Shiloh and Sharon were walking in front of them—Sharon carrying the box with the snake, Shiloh carrying an old quilt they would use to spread across the ground.

"Still a long ways off. We'll be fine, Susannah." Micah shifted the picnic basket to his right hand and slipped his left arm around her shoulder. His fingers trailing her neck caused goose bumps to cascade down her arm. She deftly stepped to the left, out of his embrace.

Micah laughed. His melancholy mood over the argument with his *daddi* seemed to have passed. She'd learned that was both a strength and a weakness of Micah's. He had the ability to move past things in a way that she envied. She tended to dwell on things too long.

But he also moved on without ever attempting to re-

solve the problem. She knew from experience that such a course was akin to kicking the can down the road. It only postponed what needed to be done, and many times that indecision had a ripple effect, causing even worse problems and more difficult decisions.

But now wasn't the time to tell Micah that, if it was even her place to do so.

He was laughing, assuring her that a little rain wouldn't hurt them and predicting they would catch enough fish to feed her entire family.

They crossed one field, then another. The path to the river that they used skirted around and then behind an abandoned barn. She hadn't been in that thing in years. Her *dat* kept saying he was going to tear it down, but looking at it now, she felt a rush of affection for the thing. It seemed to be leaning gently—its boards weathered to a soft gray, and she realized she enjoyed seeing it there. The old barn was a symbol of permanency, a fond memory from her childhood. She'd played in it many a summer as a young girl.

She led her way around it, then down the path that led to a lower pasture and the river. Perhaps Micah was right. Maybe it was the perfect day for a picnic.

Micah felt in his element walking toward the river at the back of the Beiler property. Perhaps the argument with his *daddi* wasn't as bad as he'd feared. Oh, he understood his *daddi* was serious, but as Susannah had pointed out…he'd been thinking of moving into town anyway. That had been part of his big plan—independence and hopefully a chance to live his own life.

It wasn't that he didn't want to be Amish.

But why was everyone pushing him to choose such a narrow path so soon? The day before, he'd been in the Goshen jail. Didn't he deserve a day or two of rest? Why couldn't they just enjoy a Saturday fishing on the river?

Well, the answer was: they could.

They spent the next hour setting up their picnic area, releasing Simon the Slippery Snake and helping the girls put the fishing lines in the water. The sun was now obscured by the clouds, and a westerly wind had picked up.

"Perfect day for a picnic," he murmured, lying back on the blanket with his hat over his eyes.

"Not exactly."

"You're sweet, Susannah, but I don't think you'll melt in the rain."

"Perhaps we should start toward the house."

He tipped his hat back enough to peer at her. "Seriously? We just got here."

"The storm seems to be coming in sooner than they predicted. I wouldn't want to get caught."

"Can you stop worrying for a few minutes?"

The words came out sharper than he'd intended, and he could tell that he'd hurt her feelings by the way she pulled in a breath and sat up suddenly—her posture ramrod straight.

"Don't do that."

"Do what?"

"Get your feelings hurt because I have a big mouth."

"Oh, do you, now?"

"We both know I do." He found her hand and entwined his fingers with hers. He glanced at the girls, still

standing with their backs to them, staring at their fishing line. Could he sneak in a kiss before they turned around? Because Susannah suddenly looked quite kissable.

Susannah's voice dropped. "I do realize that I tend to be a bit too serious. You're not the first one to suggest such a thing."

"I didn't mean anything by it. Only that I wish you could relax."

"You mean you want me to be more like you?"

"Yes! Exactly. Then there would be two of us renegades in the Goshen Amish world."

When she laughed, Micah knew he was forgiven.

"Perhaps we should eat before this storm soaks everything."

Micah's stomach gurgled, and he realized he'd not eaten breakfast. He'd been too busy worrying over his *daddi*'s ultimatum. He helped her to make peanut butter and jelly sandwiches, then convinced the girls to leave their poles resting on the bank.

"What if we catch a big one?" Sharon was jerking her pole up and down in the water. "I want to be here to pull him out."

"I promise to run and catch him if some whale starts to pull your pole into the water."

Which caused Sharon to laugh. They joined Shiloh and Susannah on the blanket and the next hour was spent enjoying the food while playing a game of I Spy. It was only when he noticed Susannah attempting to hold down the corners of the blanket that he noticed the wind had picked up quite a bit.

"I truly think we should go back." Susannah began load-

ing the leftover food back into the basket, the wind tugging at her *kapp* and her skirt and the edges of the blanket.

It was in that moment that the weather abruptly changed.

"It stopped, Susannah." Sharon clapped her hands. "The wind stopped. So we can stay. Right? Please…"

But suddenly Micah wasn't thinking about fishing or picnics or even finding a private moment to kiss Susannah. He jumped to his feet and strode away from the picnic, away from the trees, where he could have a better view of the sky.

The edges of the storm had turned an ominous olive green. He checked the tops of the trees again, as if to confirm what the back of his brain was telling him. Maine only averaged two tornadoes a year, but he vividly remembered 2017, which had been one of their worst years in terms of weather. An unusually high number of tornadoes—seven in all—had touched down that year, one within sight of his parents' farm.

He knew the signs.

A green sky.

Sudden drop of wind.

Unnatural stillness.

And then he saw it, dipping down from the western sky.

"We need to go." He ran back toward the picnic, grabbed Shiloh in one arm and Sharon in the other. "Leave that, Susannah. We need to go now."

And then they were running across the field and toward the abandoned barn.

Chapter Thirteen

Susannah saw Micah running toward them, hollering at her, though she couldn't make out his words. He'd picked up the girls and was urging her to do something. She put her fingers to her ears, attempting to yawn and pop them, and that was when she heard the freight train bearing down on them.

Then he'd run back and was shouting in her ear, "We need to go."

She dropped the basket and ran with him. How was he able to carry both girls? She'd tried to pick Shiloh up just that morning, to set her on a chair and tie her shoes. They'd laughed that she'd staggered under her *schweschder*'s weight.

They were halfway across the lower field, Micah leading the way, still holding both of her *schweschdern*. Susannah stumbled, dropped to the ground, and that was when she looked back. The funnel cloud seemed to be nearly on top of them. She sat there on the ground, gawking at it, frozen.

The noise was tremendous.

The sight was terrifying.

She barely realized that Micah had once again turned back and was squatting beside her and yelling something. It was the sight of Shiloh and Sharon that brought her back to her senses. Both girls were wide-eyed, their arms wrapped around each other, tears streaming down their faces.

Susannah jumped to her feet.

"The barn," she screamed.

And then they were running, Micah again carrying Sharon and Shiloh. He didn't put them down until they'd reached the barn door. He struggled against the wind to pull it open, and Susannah thought, *This is it. We're going to die here because the door is stuck.*

Her heart cried out to God then. It wasn't so much a prayer, not words that she would later remember. It was the cry of her heart—for Shiloh and Sharon and Micah and, yes, for herself, as well. Because she realized in that moment that she wanted to live. Her fear of cancer and the uncertainties of life were whisked away and she felt an actual pain in her heart.

She wasn't ready yet.

She didn't want this to be it.

She wanted to live and embrace life and see her *schweschdern* grow into fine young women with families of their own.

The door didn't open so much as it flew out of Micah's hands, and then they were tumbling inside.

Susannah didn't know if it had been a good or bad idea to shelter in the decrepit barn, but there wasn't time to second-guess herself, and there wasn't anywhere else

to go. Her eyes met Micah's for a brief second, and she saw there the same fear and yearning and love that she was feeling.

But before she could process anything, before she could attempt to speak or reassure Shiloh and Sharon, Micah knocked them all to the ground. He threw himself on top of the three of them, and then the noise seemed to become an entity unto itself—roaring and crashing and colliding. And the structure—the barn that she had such fond memories of—simply broke apart.

She must have passed out.

She gradually became aware of Micah shaking her. She opened her eyes to find his tearstained face close to hers.

"You're alive."

"*Ya*, I think so."

She attempted to sit up. The world seemed to tilt, and she dropped her head into her hands. "I think I'm going to…"

And then she vomited up everything she'd eaten sitting on the old patchwork quilt as the girls fished in the river.

The girls…

She jerked upright, and a tremendous weight shifted from her head to her heart.

Sharon sat beside Shiloh, crying and holding her *schweschder*'s hand. Shiloh's arm was twisted at an awkward angle, but it was the blood running down her face that caused Susannah to gasp.

She didn't run so much as crawl over to Shiloh's side.

"She's still breathing." Micah squatted beside her. "I

tried… I tried to stop the bleeding." It was then she noticed he'd taken off his shirt, compressed it into a bandage and placed it against Shiloh's head. "Her arm, it's broken, but it's the cut on her head that I'm worried about."

Susannah glanced up at the roof, but it was gone. Instead of the storm they'd fled, she saw clouds broken here and there by blue sky.

"How long…"

"Fifteen minutes. I've been trying to wake you. I didn't want to leave them."

"Go. Go now."

"Are you…"

"I'm fine, Micah. Go and get help for Shiloh."

Susannah didn't watch him leave. Her attention was completely focused on Shiloh and Sharon. Shiloh had yet to move or open her eyes. Sharon was crying so hard that she'd begun to hiccup. Susannah pulled the young girl into a hug.

"She's going to be okay, Sharon. Micah has gone for help."

"I was so…so… I was so scared."

"We all were."

"Uh-uh." She wiped the back of her hand across her eyes. "You weren't scared. You stood up and ran, just like Micah. But I was so scared that Micah had to… He had to carry me. And now Shiloh is… Shiloh is dead."

She broke down into sobs. Susannah put a hand on top of her head. She'd somehow lost her *kapp*, and her hair was a tangled mess, but none of that mattered. "Micah didn't carry you because you were too scared to run."

"He didn't?"

"*Nein.* He carried you because his legs are longer, so he can move faster."

"He saved us."

"*Ya.* He did." Susannah took Sharon's hand, opened her small palm and placed it gently on Shiloh's chest. "Can you feel her breathing?"

"Uh-huh."

"She's going to be okay."

"But she's bleeding."

"Something must have hit her on the head. She's going to need stitches, and she'll probably have a big headache."

"She will?"

"*Ya.*"

"Her arm looks funny. What's wrong with her arm, Susannah?"

"It's broken."

"Broken?"

"The doctors can fix that, Sharon."

"Micah went to get help?"

"He did."

"What can we do?"

"We can pray. Do you want to do that with me?"

Sharon had been crouching on her knees. Now she plopped onto her bottom, placed her palms together and squeezed her eyes shut. Together, they began to pray.

A part of Micah's mind noted the destruction that he ran through. A line of fencing, gone. The chicken coop to the side of the garden was now sitting in the middle of the lane. He skidded to a stop at the garden, where

they had all been sitting just hours ago. It looked as if the ground had been freshly tilled. Every plant, every seedling, every tomato post had simply vanished.

Which was when he glanced up at the house and saw that the side of it facing the garden had no wall at all. He could peer inside, like an *Englisch* dollhouse he'd once seen in a store. He craned his neck back, stared up at the second floor and into Susannah's room.

What if she'd been there?

What if they'd all been there?

The question paralyzed him for a few seconds, until sirens began to echo through the air.

How many had been hurt?

Were his grandparents all right?

And how was he going to get help to Shiloh?

He sprinted to the east pasture. Percy, the buggy horse, was gone—of course he was. Susannah's parents had taken him to visit church members. He put his hands on his knees, attempting to draw in deep breaths, and when he glanced up he saw it—Susannah's bicycle leaning against the side of the barn.

Micah jumped on it and sped off down the lane.

Later he wouldn't remember bicycling the two miles or dashing into the phone booth. He didn't recall picking up the phone, dialing 911 or dropping the receiver.

The ride back to the old barn was a blur.

All he knew for certain was that he had to get back to Susannah. He had to be there with her and he needed to help with the girls.

He pumped the pedals of the bicycle, sailing back down the road, turning into the lane, jumping off when

he reached the yard and sprinting back across the field, back to the old barn.

He skidded to a stop in the doorway of the barn, though there was no longer a door. There weren't even walls so much as there were piles of debris. The roof was gone completely, the windows blown out, glass glittering on the ground.

What if the glass had blown in?

What if the entire thing had collapsed on them?

He understood in that moment that he would never forget what he saw when he stepped into the main room of the barn. Susannah was holding Shiloh in her lap. The head wound had bled through the shirt he'd pressed against her head. Shiloh raised eyes that were dazed, that seemed not to see him, but then she smiled, and the fear that had seized his heart melted away.

"Micah, I hurt my head."

"And her arm. Her arm is all wrong." Sharon darted toward him, snagged his hand and pulled him across the room—toward Shiloh and Susannah.

He knelt beside them, and that was when Susannah raised her eyes to his. When she reached out and touched his face, the tears that he'd been holding back, that had been strangling his voice and blurring his vision, began to flow freely.

Micah didn't know how long they sat there, huddled together. He was suddenly aware of the sound of a vehicle approaching and the blip of a siren. He kissed Susannah on top of the head, squeezed Shiloh's hand and said to Sharon, "Let's go tell them where we are."

By the time they stepped out of the barn, two para-

medics were jogging across the field, carrying a child's gurney and a medical box. They'd left their vehicle on the side of the road. Micah could just make out the strobe of its red lights.

It wasn't until they'd placed a splint on Shiloh's arm, put a clean compress on her head and were loading her into the back of the ambulance that Micah thought to ask, "Are there more injured?"

"We've had a lot of calls, but so far no fatalities."

Micah put a hand on the back door of the ambulance to keep the paramedic from shutting it. Sticking his head inside, he assured Susannah, "I'll stay with Sharon. We'll find your parents and tell them. We'll all be right behind you."

Susannah seemed about to say something, but instead she nodded her head and turned her attention back to Shiloh.

And then the door was slammed shut, the ambulance was pulling away and Micah was left standing on the side of the road, Sharon's hand clutching his.

Susannah knew her way around a hospital. She'd spent enough time in one when she'd gone through her cancer diagnosis and treatment. She understood the reason for the X-rays that the doctor insisted on taking. She wasn't bothered by the IV they started in Shiloh's arm or the fact that they had to shave a swath of hair to clean the wound and stitch it up.

"Now our hair will match," she assured her *schweschder*, which earned her a smile.

She was able to explain the machines that beeped,

noting Shiloh's heart rate, blood pressure, oxygen saturation, respiration and temperature.

"What does it all mean, Susannah?"

"It means you're going to be okay. Are you feeling better?"

"I didn't like that needle."

"*Ya*, needles are no fun."

"And now I'm so—" she paused for a huge yawn "—sleepy."

"Close your eyes and rest."

"But…"

"I'm not going anywhere."

"You'll wake me when *Mamm* and *Dat* get here?"

"If you want me to."

"I want you to."

Shiloh's right arm was still in a splint. She turned onto her left side, placed her hand under her cheek and closed her eyes. She was asleep before the clock on the wall had ticked off another minute.

A thousand questions crashed through Susannah's mind.

Was their house okay?

Had anyone else been hurt?

What about Percy and the chickens and the barn cats?

What about her neighbors?

For the first time in her life, she wished that she had an *Englisch* phone so that she could know what was happening. But then she realized she didn't need to know. *Gotte* knew. *Gotte* was in charge, just as He had been when He'd watched over them. She didn't need

to know every detail this minute. She only needed to trust Him.

So she did what she'd done in the barn with Sharon. She prayed—for her parents, her neighbors, for Micah and Percy and her *freinden*. She prayed for the doctors and nurses. She prayed that the break in Shiloh's arm wouldn't be too painful.

By the time the doctor came in—a young woman sporting a name tag that read Dr. Emir—Susannah felt calmer and ready for whatever news the doctor brought. She was petite with long black hair pulled back in a simple ponytail holder and large owlish glasses.

After introducing herself and confirming that Susannah was Shiloh's relative, Dr. Emir said, "Your sister was very lucky. The head wound wasn't too terribly deep, and the arm was a fairly clean break."

"So both will heal quickly?"

"It's amazing just how fast young ones heal. If it was you or me, it would take a while, but Shiloh shouldn't have any trouble at all. We'll need to cast her arm, of course."

"Her favorite color is purple."

Dr. Emir smiled. "I'll see what I can do."

Then the doctor cocked her head and asked, "Are you sure you're okay? I can have someone look at…" She raised a hand to her own face, and that was when Susannah remembered that she'd been cut from some of the debris.

"Oh, I think it's fine."

"Best to clean it up anyway. You wouldn't want infection to set in. You're going to have your hands full

taking care of your *schweschder*." And that—the doctor's use of their word—eased Susannah's heart more than she could explain. They were Amish and *Englisch*; of course they were. But they were also one community that pulled together in times of trouble.

As the doctor turned to go, Susannah asked, "Have you heard anything else? About injuries, or…" She couldn't bring herself to say the word *deaths*.

"The emergency room has been pretty busy. They're saying it was an F2 and that it left a pretty wide swath of destruction. Fortunately most of it was farmland."

Susannah nodded. She wondered how long it would be until her parents arrived and whether Micah was still with Sharon. And then her mind slipped to the realization she'd had as they ran toward the barn—that she loved Micah, that he was the person she wanted to spend the rest of her life with.

Today wasn't the time to tell him that, to explain to him how she felt, but wasn't that what she'd learned in that moment of terror when the tornado dropped out of the sky?

Life was precious, and it was best to take nothing for granted.

As a nurse stepped into the room and cleaned her wounds, Susannah promised herself that she would hold that lesson close to her heart and in the front of her mind.

She'd spent too long caught in the past. Starting this moment, she would plant her feet firmly in the present.

Chapter Fourteen

Micah wasn't sure if he should stay and wait for Susannah's parents or go check on his grandparents. Based on what he could see, the tornado had veered off in the opposite direction. He was sitting on the front porch steps with Sharon when Susannah's parents pulled up in front of the house.

Sharon flew into her mother's arms.

Micah tried to explain what had happened. He'd reached the part where the ambulance had arrived and picked up Susannah and Shiloh, when Thomas interrupted him. "Get in. You can tell us the rest on the way to the hospital."

"I should check on my grandparents."

"Of course. We'll drop you off."

"*Nein.* Go. Go to the girls, and tell them both I'll be there as soon as I can."

He realized as they pulled away that neither of Susannah's parents had commented on the destruction of their home.

Homes could be rebuilt.

Their one concern had been for their daughters.

He was thinking of that as he crossed back toward his grandparents' farm. It was the people in your life that mattered, not the things. It didn't at all matter what he wore, or whether he owned a phone, or if he drove a buggy or a car. What mattered was how you treated the people you cared about, and he realized with sudden clarity that he had not treated his grandparents well.

In fact, he'd taken them for granted—eating their food, staying in their home, allowing his *mammi* to wash his clothes and his *daddi* to provide his transportation. It was true that he'd given them money, but had he given them his respect and his gratitude? In truth, he'd thought they owed it to him, but no one really owed anyone else anything. It was their love for him that had provided for his needs.

And what had he done in return?

He'd mocked their way of life.

Shown a complete lack of respect for their years of hard work.

Argued at every possible turn.

He'd been a child, as surely as Sharon and Shiloh were children. When he'd realized that it was up to him to get Sharon and Shiloh and Susannah to safety, he'd left that side of himself behind in the path of the tornado. The storm had done more than threaten their very lives, it had pushed Micah into the world of being an adult—of being responsible for someone else and embracing that responsibility.

There would be no turning back.

He let out a breath he didn't realize he'd been holding

when he saw his grandparents' house. It was completely intact, without so much as a tree limb littering the yard.

He took the front porch steps two at a time.

His grandparents were in the living room—*Mammi* sitting next to *Daddi* on the couch, holding a glass of water and pressing it to his lips. As for his grandfather, his face was an ashen gray and his breathing seemed labored.

"What happened?"

"We heard the…the tornado. John figured you went over to Susannah's. He was going to check on you when he collapsed on the front lawn. I managed to get him inside."

"*Daddi?* Can you hear me?"

His grandfather opened his eyes, though he seemed to have trouble focusing. His breathing was ragged, and though it wasn't hot at all in the house, sweat ran in rivulets down the side of his face.

"I shouldn't…shouldn't have said…"

"Not now, *Daddi*." Micah clasped his hand. "It's forgiven and forgotten. Now, we need to get some help."

He sprinted out of the room, to the barn where he kept the replacement phone he'd purchased. He only hoped it was charged. Had he even used it since he'd arrived home from jail? He pulled it from the shelf where they kept miscellaneous tools, powered it on and ran out into the yard.

Two bars and 8 percent power.

It should be enough. It would have to be.

For the second time that day, he tapped in the number 911.

The person who answered took down the information, told him what to do and insisted on staying on the line until the paramedics arrived.

He found the bottle of aspirin in his *mammi*'s medicine cabinet. After Micah had given one to his *daddi*, the emergency dispatcher walked Micah through checking his pulse, which was weak but steady.

"It's important that you keep your grandfather calm. We have an ambulance on the way to you right now."

Five minutes passed, then ten, and then finally he heard the scream of the siren coming down their lane. He wasn't too surprised when the two paramedics who hopped out of the vehicle were the same ones he'd seen earlier.

"Busy day for you," the woman said, patting him on the shoulder before rushing past him and into the house.

They stabilized his grandfather and loaded him into the ambulance.

His *mammi* looked a bit dazed. "You can go with them, *Mammi*."

"I can?"

"I'll bring the buggy."

"*Danki*, Micah." She pulled him into a hug, clung to him fiercely for the space of three heartbeats and then she, too, was gone.

Micah wanted nothing more than to hitch up the buggy and tear out after them.

But what would his *daddi* want him to do?

After all, he would only be waiting and pacing at the hospital. They wouldn't even let him in the room for the first hour or so. Instead of rushing off, he walked

through the living room and into the kitchen. He found
a pot of red beans cooking on the stove, so he turned
the gas burner off. He covered the pot with the lid and
pushed it to the back of the stove. The clock above the
sink said that it was nearly five in the afternoon, when
his *daddi* always looked after the animals.

So Micah did those chores, too.

Finally, he walked into his grandparents' room to
see if there was anything there that they might need.
His grandmother's purse and sweater were hanging on
a hook near the door. He grabbed both and had turned
to go when he spied her worn Bible on a nightstand.
Picking it up, he ran a hand over the cover. The cor-
ners were worn and the letters on the front were barely
discernible.

Sinking down onto their bed, he opened the book
and stared at the inscription.

To Abigail, the love of my life.
John
October 15, 1978

His *daddi* had been a young man then, younger than
Micah was now if he'd done the math correctly. And
yet he'd known that Abigail was the woman he wanted
to spend his life with. He hadn't questioned his love for
her or her love for him. And look at them now. They'd
survived the terrible accident that had taken his arm,
raised a houseful of children and now they were help-
ing to raise Micah.

He realized in that moment how much he respected

his *daddi*. Micah might not always agree with his opinion on things, but he admired how he'd spent his entire life caring for and providing for his family. He recalled the look on both of their faces as *Mammi* had sat beside him holding the cup of water. There was simply no doubt how much they loved each other.

Micah wanted that.

He wanted that kind of consistency in his life.

He wanted someone who looked at him like his *mammi* looked at his *daddi*.

And he was absolutely certain he knew who that someone was.

Susannah had moved to the waiting room and was sitting with Deborah by the time Micah found her. He explained about his grandfather—the doctors had assured him that his condition was stable, but that he didn't need more visitors at the moment. "How's Shiloh?"

"*Mamm*'s in with her now, and *Dat*'s taken Sharon to get something to eat and then outside to check on the horse."

"What about you?"

"What about me?"

"Have you eaten anything?"

"Nein."

Micah reached for her hand, pulled her to her feet and then told Deborah where they were going. The room was virtually filled with *Englisch* and Amish. The latest reports were thirty-four people injured, but no fatalities. Three homes had been damaged—two Amish

and one *Englisch*, though it sounded like Susannah's had taken the most direct hit.

"I'm sure I have something to eat in this bag." Deborah hoisted her large purse off the floor and onto her lap. "*Ya.* I have gum and peanut butter crackers and…"

Micah leaned down and said, "*Danki*, but I'm going to take Susannah to the cafeteria to get her some hot food."

Deborah raised her eyes to his, glanced at Susannah and then smiled. "*Gut* idea. You should do that. I'll just stay here, and if anyone is looking for you two, I'll tell them where you are."

"*Danki*," Susannah said, enfolding her friend in her arms. She then left with Micah, tucking her hand in the crook of his elbow.

The cafeteria was staying open later than usual, owing to the aftermath of the tornado. They both grabbed sandwiches and coffee, and Micah carried their tray to a table in the corner of the room.

Susannah took a couple of bites and then sat back, studying him instead of eating.

"You should finish that. You're going to need your energy. Your *schweschdern*, they can be a handful."

She could tell he meant it in a teasing way, that he was trying to lift her mood, but she wasn't ready for that yet.

"Micah, I need to thank you."

"*Nein.* You don't." He closed his eyes and rubbed his forehead with his fingertips. Finally, he pushed his tray away, crossed his arms on the table and focused on her. "I shouldn't have talked you into going to the

river. I'm always doing that. Trying to find a way to goof off and dragging someone along with me, and today the result was that Shiloh was hurt. That's on me. That's my fault."

She could tell he was surprised when she reached across the table and covered his hands with hers. "I didn't see our house, but they told me. Half of it's gone. Is that right?"

"Ya."

"So if we'd been home, if we hadn't gone to the river, there's at least a fifty-fifty chance we'd have died in that house today."

"Please don't say that." His voice was husky with emotion, and when he raised his eyes to hers, she saw tears sparkling there.

"You saved us, Micah, and I am grateful that you did. You saved your *daddi*, too. *Gotte* has used you today, and… I'm just glad that He brought you here."

Micah swiped at his eyes, then sat up straighter and squared his shoulders. "Are you saying that you'll go fishing with me again?"

"I could be talked into it."

She'd tried to match his light tone, but it was a facade that was simply too hard to keep up. He reached for her hands, pulled them to his lips and kissed them.

"I love you, Susannah Beiler."

"You do?"

"Tell me you haven't known that for some time."

"I hoped, but *nein*, I wasn't sure."

"I let you teach me how to sew."

"You're not very good at it."

"Susannah, I'd be interested in alpacas if it meant I could spend more time with you."

"I don't have any alpacas."

"Not my point."

They sat there another ten minutes, until they became aware that others needed their table. Susannah wanted to tell him how she felt, but how was she supposed to do that in the middle of the crowded cafeteria? Then they were walking down the hall, and Micah stopped abruptly. He glanced left, then right and then pulled her into an alcove, wrapped his arms around her and held her close.

"I was so frightened," he admitted.

"Me, too."

"And when I realized…" He framed her face with his hands and kissed her softly on the lips. "When I realized that I might lose you, I understood how important you are to me. I knew when I saw that tornado dipping out of the sky that I would do anything for you, for your family, for us."

He kissed her again, then thumbed away the tears slipping down her face.

"I love you, too," she whispered.

"You do?"

"Don't act surprised."

"I thought you were dating me to keep your friends safe."

"That was the original plan."

He kissed once more, and she felt safe again. No longer worried about what might fall out of the sky. He kissed her, and she knew that somehow everything

was going to be all right. Then he pulled her back out into the hall. Together they walked toward the waiting room, knowing that whatever news they faced, they would weather it together.

Shiloh was released from the hospital the next morning.

Micah's grandfather stayed an additional three nights, and then was only allowed to go home when he promised to rest and stay off his feet. They'd put in a stent to clear up a blockage in his main artery, and the doctor had started him on a statin medication.

Micah was in the room when the cardiologist had said, "You've had a heart attack, Mr. Fisher. As we discussed, that means your heart is damaged. You're going to need to give yourself a few weeks to build your strength back up, and I expect you to be in my office in seven days for a follow-up."

Once they were home, his *daddi* insisted on sitting on the front porch while Micah unharnessed and cared for the horse. When Micah had checked everything and closed up the barn, he climbed the steps to find his *daddi* still there. The sun was dipping toward the horizon, and through the window Micah could see his *mammi* heating one of the casseroles a neighbor had left.

"I'd like to talk to you, Micah."

Instead of arguing, as he might have the week before, Micah sat in the adjacent rocker and waited.

"I meant what I said when you found me the day of the tornado. I shouldn't have spoken to you as I did that morning. I shouldn't have tried to force your path."

"You care about me."

"I do, but I see now that your path is different from mine. Doesn't mean it's wrong."

Micah fought to hide his surprise. When his *daddi* caught his eye and smiled, Micah admitted, "You're not the only one who needs to apologize. I see now that I've been bullheaded out of habit and immature because I could be."

A red bird landed in front of them in the yard, hopping back and forth as it pecked at the dirt.

"I'm going to ask Susannah to marry me."

"She'll make a fine *fraa*."

"Not yet, though. I won't ask yet. I want to give her time to recover."

His *daddi* sighed, then pushed himself up and out of the rocker. "If there's one thing I've learned, it's never assume you have more time."

Micah understood what his *daddi* was saying, but he also appreciated what Susannah had been through. He didn't want to take anything for granted, least of all her. He also wanted to be sensitive to her feelings.

Three days later, Detective Cummings stopped by to say they'd found the person who had burglarized the general store as well as quite a few others. "Not an Amish kid. He thought that by acting like one, by looking like one, he could get away with it."

"And he almost did."

"His mistake was stealing Widow Miller's buggy twice. She saw him driving out of her place, and she walked to the phone shack."

"Good thing it's across the road."

"She called the police, and we caught him as he drove into town."

Which seemed to end the matter as far as Micah was concerned.

Two weeks later, a workday was held at the Beiler place. They began before the sun came up, and by the time it was setting, a new home had been framed. They'd been staying in a *dawdi haus* over on the Hochstettler place, and Micah knew they'd be glad to move back home.

Each day of the next week, Micah went over in the afternoons to help finish the house. Each time he arrived, a different group of men were nailing up Sheetrock or painting rooms or finishing the porch. By the end of June the house was completed. They'd opted for a one-story design, since Susannah's parents didn't see themselves having any more children.

Micah tried to stay away, but he found he couldn't.

He was drawn to the Beiler place. It felt like home to him. He needed to be there.

He arrived after dinner, their first dinner in their new home. Shiloh and Sharon insisted on showing him their new room. "We have window seats," they squealed, then insisted he sit there while they brought him a pillow, blanket, three books and two dolls.

Susannah stood in the doorway laughing.

It wasn't until the girls were in bed and Susannah's parents had moved to the front porch to enjoy the cool evening, that he asked her to go for a walk. And it was there at the pasture fence, under a covering of stars, that Micah asked Susannah to marry him.

"You're sure?" She reached up and touched his face. Micah wanted to memorize the way that her fingers felt against his skin. More than that, he wanted her this close to him every day for the rest of his life.

"I've never been so sure of anything."

"Even though…"

"You can't have children? *Ya.* I'm aware."

"That's a big thing, Micah."

"It's not as big as my love for you. Now, if you said you didn't love me, that would be a big thing."

"Of course I love you."

"Then you'll marry me?" He felt as if he'd laid his heart before her. He felt as if, with Susannah by his side, he could do anything.

"*Ya*, I'll marry you."

"*Gut.*" He kissed her once, then again, and then pulled her into his arms. "We can build here or on my *daddi*'s place."

"You've thought that far ahead?"

"I need to provide for my family."

"What about Maine?"

"It'll still be there, but I can't leave now. Not with *Daddi* needing help. I don't want to leave."

"I thought you couldn't wait to get back."

"Oh, I will go back. We'll go at least once a year, and who knows—maybe someday we will move there. But not now. We'll know when the time is right."

"But…"

His kiss stopped her protests. When he finally pulled back, he craned his head back and looked up at the stars. "See those, Susannah?"

"*Ya*, I see them."

"*Gotte* did that."

"Indeed, He did."

"And if He did that, He can also provide you and me with a family. It might not be a traditional one—it could be adoption or fostering or simply kids who need a place to stay, whose families are struggling…"

"I hadn't thought of that." She snuggled in closer, pulled his arms around her and whispered, "But I'd like it. I'd like it very much."

To Micah their future seemed full of endless possibilities, like the stars that were endlessly stretched out above him. It didn't matter to him whether they ended up with a houseful of children or lived out their lives just the two of them. What mattered was that they'd found each other, that they'd been given a second chance.

It was one he didn't mean to squander.

* * * * *

AN AMISH ARRANGEMENT

Jo Ann Brown

For Leon Barkley, one of my first friends.
Together we learned softball from my dad
and basketball from your brother.
Thanks for your help with my real estate questions
and making this story possible.

A special thank-you to Tina, Melissa and Dina, who
have shared my love for the Stoltzfus family right
from the beginning and made each book better.

Then the Lord put forth His hand,
and touched my mouth. And the Lord said unto me,
"Behold, I have put My words in thy mouth."
—*Jeremiah* 1:9

Chapter One

Harmony Creek Hollow, New York

The day had started out as Jeremiah Stoltzfus had planned.

It didn't stay that way after a woman dropped into his arms.

For most men, playing the hero for a beautiful woman would have been a dream come true. But most men didn't discover that woman trespassing on a tumbledown farm in northern New York. A farm Jeremiah couldn't wait to call his own.

He'd been invited by the current owner to visit when he reached Harmony Creek. In a couple of days the farm would be his.

At dawn Jeremiah had left his family's home in Paradise Springs, Pennsylvania. He was joining others to build a new Amish settlement near the Vermont border. He'd made arrangements during the past few months, purchasing the farm based on a few photographs sent by

his Realtor. After saying goodbye to his *mamm*, brothers and sisters along with their spouses and *kinder* and knowing it was unlikely he'd see them again for a year, he'd taken a train north to Albany. There, he was met by a van, which drove him the last fifty miles to Harmony Creek Hollow.

The valley edging the creek was set outside the tiny town of Salem. Rolling hills covered with trees and meadows would support dairy farms for the Amish families moving into the area.

The owner of the sixty-acre farm he was buying, Rudy Bamberger, had invited him to stop by before the closing in two days. Jeremiah suspected the old man wanted to size him up first.

Rudy had already asked him a lot of questions through Kitty Vasic, Jeremiah's Realtor. Personal questions that Kitty told Jeremiah he didn't have to answer. However, Jeremiah had no problem with the questions, because the old man had been selling his family's farm. Jeremiah had written a long letter, explaining his background and his plans for the farm and his future. His answers must have satisfied Rudy, because the old man accepted his offer on the farm the next day.

When he'd arrived, Jeremiah had carried his two bags as he crossed the snowy yard past neglected barns. No tracks had been visible. Nothing had gone in or out of the big barn since the last snowstorm. Allowing himself a quick glance at the other outbuildings, which needed, as he'd known, a lot of repairs, he'd walked through the freshly fallen snow to the main house.

The large rambling home had a porch running along

the front and the side facing the barn. Through a stand of spruce trees, he could see another house, where a tenant family once would have lived. The few remaining shutters hung awkwardly at the windows, a sure sign the house was a fixer-upper, too.

He looked forward to beginning—and finishing—the tasks ahead of him as he made the farm viable again. His skills as a woodworker would be useful while renovating the barns and the sap house near the sugar bush farther up the hill.

Climbing onto the porch, he'd set down his bags before he knocked snow off his well-worn work boots. He'd gone directly to the side door. Rudy had told him to use that door when he arrived.

"Don't knock," the most recent letter had instructed him. "My ears don't work like they used to, and I don't want you standing in the cold while you bang and bang. Come in and give a shout."

He'd thrown the door open. "Rudy, are you here?"

A shriek had come from close to the ceiling. He'd looked up to see a ladder wobbling. A dark-haired woman stood at the very top, her arms windmilling.

He leaped into the small room as she fell. After years of being tossed shocks of corn and hay bales, he caught her easily. He jumped out of the way, holding her to him as the ladder crashed to the linoleum floor. His black wool hat tumbled off his head and rolled toward the wall.

"Oh, my!" gasped the woman.

She was, he noted because her face was close to his, very pretty. Her pleated *kapp* was flat unlike the heart-

shaped ones his sisters wore. Beneath it, her hair was so black it gleamed with bluish fire in the fading sunlight coming through the door and tall windows. Her brown eyes were large with shock in her warmly tanned face, where a few freckles emphasized her high cheekbones. She wore a pale pink dress with white and green flowers scattered across it in a subtle pattern. No Amish woman from Paradise Springs would use such fabric. It must be allowed in the new settlement along Harmony Creek. What else would be different here?

But first things first.

"Are you okay?" he asked, not surprised she wasn't the only one who sounded breathless. His heart had slammed against his chest when he saw her teetering. And from the moment he'd looked into her lustrous eyes, taking a deep breath had seemed impossible.

"I'm fine. I had just a little farther to go. Just a little…" Her voice trailed away as the shuddering ladder, which had landed on its side, clattered to the floor.

Jeremiah frowned. There was nothing on the wall to prevent her from falling. He saw the ruined wallpaper and chipped crown molding along with scraps of paper she'd already pulled off were piled on the floor. Why was she tearing off wallpaper in Rudy's house?

"Who are you?" he asked at the same time she did.

"I'm Jeremiah Stoltzfus," he answered. "You are…?"

"Mercy Bamberger." Her face shifted into a polite smile, and he guessed she'd collected her wits that had been scattered by fear. "Thanks for catching me."

"Why are you here?"

Instead of answering, she said, "You can put me down."

Jeremiah was astonished his curiosity about why she was in what would be his house had let him forget—for a second—that he was still cradling her in his arms. He set her on her feet, but caught her by the elbow when she trembled like a slim branch in a thunderstorm.

Hearing uneven thumps upstairs and hoping they heralded Rudy's arrival, he steered her to the left. There, a staircase was half-hidden behind a partially closed door. Seating her on the bottom step, he picked up his hat as he asked, "Are you all right?"

"I am."

He didn't believe her, because her skin had a gray tint and her voice quivered. He wouldn't push her, because he guessed she was embarrassed by the circumstances. But one question remained: What was Mercy Bamberger doing in his house?

"Bamberger?" he asked aloud. "Like Rudy Bamberger?"

"Yes. Do you know my grandfather?"

Well, that explained who she was and why she was in the house. Glancing up the stairs, his eyes widened when he saw a shadow slip across the top. It was far too small for a grown man and appeared to have four legs.

He watched, saying nothing as he realized the silhouette belonged to a *kind*. A little girl, who looked about seven years old, had braided hair as black as Mercy's. She leaned on metal crutches with cuffs to go around her skinny arms. Her legs were encased in plastic and

Velcro from the tops of her black sneakers to her knobby knees. Who was she?

As if he'd asked the question aloud, the little girl cried, "Mommy!" Rushing at a pace that forced his heart into his throat again, because he feared she'd fall, the *kind* flung her arms around Mercy's neck. "Are you okay?"

"I'm fine," Mercy reassured her.

The *kind* glanced at him with a scowl. "I heard the ladder fall and—"

"I'm fine, Sunni." She hugged the little girl. "Jeremiah kept me from getting hurt."

"Who?"

"Jeremiah." Mercy pushed herself to her feet and swung the little girl off the steps. She kept herself between the *kind* and him, showing she didn't trust him though he'd saved her from a broken bone or worse. "He's Jeremiah." Without looking at him, she added, "Jeremiah, this is my daughter, Sunni."

Again he fought not to ask the questions battering at his lips. The *kind* was unquestionably Asian, and her eyes, like Mercy's, glistened like dark brown mud in a sun-washed puddle. She also wore plain clothing with a small print.

Comprehension struck him. Mercy and her daughter weren't Amish. They dressed like the Mennonite women who lived near Paradise Springs. He searched his mind, but couldn't recall if his Realtor had mentioned anything about Rudy living plain. He glanced up at the electric light hanging from the ceiling. Some plain folks used electricity.

Too many questions needed answers.

Right away.

"Hi, Sunni," he said, because he didn't want to upset the little girl or her *mamm* more.

She aimed another frown at him before turning her back on him. When she didn't answer him, Mercy asked the *kind* why she'd been upstairs. He thought she was dismayed the little girl had gone on the stairs by herself until Mercy said, "Be extra careful. Don't forget the floors aren't safe."

"I stayed away from those, Mommy." Sunni raised her left crutch and tapped the floor beside her. "I do that to check before I go in." Without a pause, she asked, "Can I have a cookie?"

"One," Mercy said with a smile. "Put the bag clip on after you get your cookie."

"Okaaaay," Sunni replied in the same tone Jeremiah had used as a *kind* when his own *mamm* said something he deemed obvious.

He smiled, but again the little girl acted as if he were invisible before she drew her arms from the cuffs on the crutches. Leaning them against the wall, she hurried through a doorway to the right. He guessed it must lead to the kitchen.

His grin vanished as he glanced around the room. Rudy called it his everything room. Hooks on the wall showed where coats, hats and bonnets could be hung. The bare floor was scraped from years of barn boots on it, and the tattered wallpaper was a grubby white. It might once have been a brighter color. The room was furnished with a rickety table and a battered sofa cov-

ered with a worn blanket. A desk had a book under one leg to keep it steady on the sloping floor. The interior of the house was in worse condition than the outside. The photographs sent by the Realtor had been misleading.

Had he failed to examine them closely enough in his eagerness to buy the farm and get started on making his dream come true? No, he'd peered at each picture through a magnifying glass to discover every detail. He knew the kitchen cabinets were painted dull brown, and there was electricity in the house. He planned to remove the latter as soon as the papers were signed.

Jeremiah picked up the ladder and raised it against the wall again. Checking it was solidly in place, he looked at Mercy. He was curious why she was peeling paper off the wall in what would be his house. He could understand if she wanted to take one of the pictures of the farm hanging on a fake brick wall behind the desk, because the farm was her *grossdawdi*'s. In the silence, the *tick-tock* of a wall clock in the kitchen was loud.

Jeremiah appraised the room again. He intended to use it for the farm's office, as he guessed Rudy had. It was one plan among the many he had. His brothers teased him about having to have every detail set in place before he acted, but trying to find knots in a piece of wood before he began working on it had kept him from wasting time when building a piece of furniture. Being as cautious in his other endeavors seemed wise.

Though he knew, too well, the best of plans could fall apart. He'd thought his future was set with Emmarita Kramer, but she'd jumped the fence and married an *Englisch* guy she'd met at an auction Jeremiah had taken

her to. She never broke the courtship off with Jeremiah, just left. He should forgive her and forget his shock, but when he hadn't been able to do either, he'd decided on a clean start in the new Harmony Creek settlement.

Hearing a throat cleared and knowing Mercy was trying to get his attention, he turned. She was shorter than he'd realized. The top of her head barely reached his shoulder. As she stuck several vagrant strands of black hair beneath her pleated *kapp*, she regarded him coolly. She was, he could tell from the set of her taut lips, as curious about him as her daughter had been.

He had a lot of things he wanted to ask her, too, but he waited for her to speak first.

She took one step, then another toward him, though she was at a disadvantage because she had to tilt her head to meet his eyes. Then, seeing the determination in them, he wondered if she saw her height as a liability or a way to surprise those who underestimated her.

"You never answered my question," she said.

"Which one?" He couldn't remember what she'd asked him, and he refused to be put on the defensive in what would be his own home.

"The important one. What are you doing here?"

"I came to see Rudy Bamberger." He frowned. "You said he's your *grossdawdi*."

She nodded.

"Then I'm surprised he didn't tell you I'd be coming here today."

"Why?"

He didn't think she was being cagey on purpose.

Until now, she'd been straightforward. "He invited me to come and look around."

She shook her head. "I don't understand why."

"Didn't he tell you he's selling me his farm?"

Mercy Bamberger was shocked speechless. Had she hit her head when she'd dropped into Jeremiah Stoltzfus's strong arms after trying to grab another strip of wall-paper? She'd made a mess of this conversation from the get-go.

With the ancient Adirondacks to the west and the gentle Green Mountains to the east, the farm had been a haven for her from the first time she'd come to visit the man she called Grandpa Rudy. It offered the very thing she'd lost and didn't think she'd ever find again. Home. How desperate she'd been for a sanctuary! And how precious it seemed as the promise she'd held within her heart for the past decade was being fulfilled.

She couldn't mess it up. Already she'd made the mistake of not keeping a closer eye on Sunni. Her daughter had been born with a congenital curiosity not diminished by her physical challenges. Mercy's determination that the little girl should do anything a regular kid could allowed Sunni to indulge her quick and inquiring mind. Telling Sunni not to investigate the rooms upstairs because the floors were unsafe must have convinced her to find out how dangerous they were.

Mercy was letting herself get distracted by a handsome stranger who appeared to be a few years older than her twenty-five years. His bright blue eyes that had been shadowed by his black wool hat identified him as one

of the Amish farmers moving into the hollow. Grandpa Rudy had told her about the new settlement in one of his letters. He'd been writing to her every week since she was eleven years old, the year she'd been adopted by his son and daughter-in-law and given a chance to have a new life and the loving family she'd feared she'd never have again.

She was startled how far up she had to look to meet Jeremiah's eyes. Few Amish men she'd met had been as tall as he was. If his ruddy hair hadn't been cut in the plain style and he wasn't wearing a simple light blue shirt along with black suspenders and broadfall trousers beneath his black coat, she wouldn't have guessed this very good-looking man was Amish.

Scolding herself, she recalled how Graham Rapp was easy on the eyes, too, but he'd broken her heart by showing how much a "mama's boy" he was by choosing his mother when Mercy refused to be second. She must not let herself be beguiled by an attractive man again. Not when so much was on the line with her plans for the farm and the changes it could make in many young lives.

But the Amish were well-known for their honesty. So why was Jeremiah talking nonsense about Grandpa Rudy selling him the farm?

"I think you're mistaken," she said, hoping her voice didn't quake with the strong emotions rushing through her like lightning in a summer sky. "My grandfather didn't mention anything about selling Come Along Farm."

"Come Along Farm?"

"That's the name he gave the farm when I was little. He urged us to come along and keep up with him while he did chores, so we called it Come Along Farm."

"He didn't tell you he's selling me the farm?"

"No!"

"I'm sorry to take you by surprise," he said gently, "but I'll be closing the day after tomorrow."

"Impossible!" Her voice squeaked, and she took a steadying breath. Sounding as young as Sunni wouldn't help. And she didn't want her raised voice to bring her daughter from the kitchen to investigate. The little girl was upset enough already to have to leave their Mennonite community and Mercy's parents in central New York, and Mercy hadn't missed the glares Sunni had shot at Jeremiah. When she and Graham ended their ill-advised engagement, her daughter had been caught up in the aftermath and no longer trusted men she didn't know. Mercy's attempts to reassure Sunni that the little girl had nothing to do with the breakup hadn't helped.

"It's not impossible. I've got the paperwork in my suitcase on the porch. If you want to see it—"

"I don't have interest in seeing what can't be legitimate. It sounds as if someone has played a horrible prank on you, Jeremiah. I'm sorry." She was, because she guessed he'd traveled for hours or days to get there. "But the farm's not for sale."

He opened his mouth to protest, then closed it. Taking a deep breath, he released it. In a calm tone she doubted she could emulate, he said, "There's no sense in arguing. Why don't you get your *grossdawdi*, and we'll settle this?"

"I can't."

"Why not?"

She blinked on sudden tears. "Because he's dead."

When Jeremiah's face became ashen, Mercy wondered if she should tell him to take a seat. It must have been seconds, but it felt like a year before he asked, "Rudy is dead?"

"Yes." She swallowed hard past the lump in her throat.

"When?"

"Last week. It was a massive heart attack. He was buried the day before yesterday." As she spoke, she found it impossible to believe the vital, vigorous man was gone.

Rudy Bamberger had been more than a grandfather to her. He'd been her best friend, the one who had welcomed her into the family after her life had hit bottom. Rudy hadn't been a replacement for *Abuelita*, her beloved grandmother who had raised her when she was called Mercedes in a tiny apartment in the Bronx. *Abuelita* had died two weeks after Mercy's tenth birthday, and everything in Mercy's life had changed, including her name. Yet, Grandpa Rudy had made her feel as if she belonged among the people who were so different from those she'd known in the city. His love had been unconditional, and she'd returned it.

"I'm sorry," Jeremiah said with sincerity.

She wished he'd been trite instead of genuine, because one thing hadn't changed. He wanted to take away the farm that was her final gift from Grandpa Rudy. How often she'd sat on the old man's lap and talked

about taking care of the apple orchard or making maple syrup as he did each spring or what color she would paint the big bedroom! He'd humored her, even when her paint choices went from pink to purple to red and black over the years.

But Jeremiah was saying her grandfather had intended to sell the farm to him.

"But Grandpa Rudy told me the farm would be mine after he passed away."

"Then why would he sign a purchase agreement with me?"

Mercy shook herself from her mental paralysis. She hated admitting she couldn't guess why her grandfather would break his promise to her.

"Mommy, what's wrong?"

Shocked she hadn't noticed Sunni in the kitchen doorway, Mercy put her arm around her daughter's narrow shoulders. "Nothing that can't be fixed," she replied with a smile.

Over the child's head, she shot Jeremiah a frown, warning him not to upset Sunni. She didn't want her daughter to feel as if her world was being taken away from her—again—as it must have when Sunni traveled from Korea to what was supposed to be her forever home. It hadn't been, because her adoptive parents, who'd changed her name from Kim Sun-Hee to Sunni, couldn't handle having a daughter who wore leg braces. Sunni had been returned to social services as if she were a set of curtains that didn't match the furniture. A disrupted adoption was the name given to it. Or a failed

placement. The latter fit better, because it sure felt like a failure for the child involved.

As Mercy had learned herself fifteen years ago when she'd been the one given away by what she'd thought would be her forever family. If the Bambergers hadn't been there to take her in… No, she didn't want to think of that awful time.

Again, she warned herself to focus on the present, not the past. And her and Sunni's future. She had to stop letting her emotions take over. She needed to be logical. Building Come Along Farm into a retreat for city kids would require her to face a lot of bureaucracy on local and state levels. She must be ready to stand up for what she wanted.

"Sunni, if you go and get the book we were reading, I'll meet you in the living room once I'm finished here."

The little girl looked from her to Jeremiah, then nodded. "Okay, Mommy."

Mercy said nothing as Jeremiah watched Sunni hobble away. There was no pity in his expression, and she was grateful. Too many people felt sorry for Sunni, calling her a "poor little thing." Sunni was one of the strongest people Mercy knew and had learned to walk through perseverance and hard work. If only Mercy could help her heal from the emotional wounds she'd suffered, but those would take more time.

As soon as the little girl was out of earshot, Mercy said, "I guess I should see the purchase agreement you say my grandfather signed."

Jeremiah hooked a thumb toward the door. "Give me a minute, and I'll dig out the paperwork I've got."

She considered locking the door, but that wouldn't solve the problem. Instead, she held the door open while he brought in two scuffed duffel bags.

Closing the door, she said nothing while he opened one bag and found a manila envelope. He withdrew a sheaf of pages and sorted through them. In the middle of the stack, he pulled out several and offered them to her.

"Here's everything I got from your *grossdawdi* through my Realtor," he said without a hint of emotion.

Mercy didn't look to discover if compassion had slipped into his gaze. This time, for her. She wanted it no more than Sunni would have. When he handed her the pages, his work-roughened skin brushed against her fingers. Sensation arced between them like electricity, and she jerked her hand away. Being attracted to the man who insisted he was buying her family's farm would be stupid.

If he had the same reaction, she couldn't tell, because she carefully kept her gaze on the papers. She scanned each page, her heart sinking lower and lower. Everything looked aboveboard, and she recognized her grandfather's scrawled signature on the bottom of each page. She didn't stop to decipher every bit of legalese, but grasped enough to know Grandpa Rudy was selling the farm to Jeremiah Stoltzfus.

Just as Jeremiah claimed.

"But my grandfather died," she whispered. "Doesn't that change things?"

"I don't know. This is the first time I've ever bought property." He gave her a lopsided grin that lifted her traitorous heart once more.

Paying it no attention, she returned the papers to him and he put them in his bag. No one could answer the question gnawing at her most. Why would her grandfather promise her the property and then decide to sell it without telling her? She'd often mentioned her plans for the farm. Hadn't he read her letters? Yes, he had, because he'd responded to things in them. But never, she realized with a jolt of dismay, had he written anything about her intention to make Come Along Farm a sanctuary for city youngsters like the one she'd enjoyed when she was a Fresh Air kid years ago, escaping for two amazing weeks each summer from the steam bath of the Bronx.

"I'm not sure what we should do," he said when she remained silent.

"Me, either." For the first time she looked straight into his brilliantly blue eyes. He must realize what she was about to say she meant with all her heart. "However, you need to know I'm not going to relinquish my family's farm to you or anyone else."

"But—"

"We moved in a couple of days ago. We're not giving it up." She crossed her arms over her chest. "It's our *home*."

Chapter Two

Jeremiah had to select his words with care. He didn't know if he'd be allowed to close on the farm as scheduled. He'd never heard of a person dying before property was transferred, because in Paradise Springs most farms were handed down from one generation to the next.

As Mercy said Rudy had meant to do with this farm. He'd changed his mind, but why?

Until he spoke with Kitty Vasic, his Realtor, and got her advice, he didn't know what the outcome of this sticky situation would be. Mercy wasn't going to back down. That much was clear. If their situations were reversed, he suspected he'd be as unwilling to compromise. He *was* unwilling to compromise.

There wasn't room to. Either the farm was going to be his…or it wasn't.

"It's late," he said when he realized Mercy was waiting for him to say something. "I doubt Kitty's office is open. Do you know anyone nearby who has a phone I could use?"

As if in answer to him, a faint ringing came from

beyond the living room. He glanced at Mercy and saw she was as surprised as he was at the unexpected sound.

"Phone!" called Sunni. "I'll get it."

"No! I'll get it." Mercy spun on her heel and ran toward the sound.

Jeremiah followed, too curious to wait. He paid no attention to the large living room as he went after Mercy through what looked like a storage room and then into a bedroom. It was draped in shadows, but a single greenish light glared off to one side.

Mercy grabbed the cordless phone and jabbed at a button. Holding it to her ear, she asked, "Hello?"

The faint buzz of a voice reached him, but he couldn't discern words. His eyes widened when she held the phone out to him.

"It's for you," she said.

"For me?"

"Yes, unless you know another Jeremiah Stoltzfus."

He knew three others in Paradise Springs alone. Taking the phone, he said, "This is Jeremiah Stoltzfus."

"Hi, Jeremiah," replied a strained female voice. "This is Kitty Vasic. I know Rudy invited you to the farm, so I thought I'd catch you there. We need to talk. Rudy Bamberger is dead."

"*Ja*, I know." He glanced toward Mercy, but she'd gone to stand by a window. Talking about this was uncomfortable. For him, the farm and his future were at stake, but she'd lost her *grossdawdi*. He didn't like the idea of losing his opportunity to buy this farm, but he also disliked the idea of taking Mercy's home.

"I've got something tonight I can't get out of," Kitty said. "How about I come over tomorrow afternoon?"

"Tomorrow afternoon should be fine." What else could he say?

"Good. I'll meet you at the farm around one."

He thanked her. Tilting the phone toward the faint light coming through the window, he found the button to end the call. He set it in its holder. It chirped once, and then its glow faded.

"That was my Realtor," Jeremiah said. "She's coming over tomorrow afternoon around one to discuss what happens next."

A soft click sounded in the room before a lamp came on by the side of a bed with a headboard taller than he was. It was carved with a great tree filled with birds and other beasts gathered below it. He realized the lamp must have been connected to a timer.

"I can make myself scarce," Mercy replied.

He shook his head. "Don't. You should be here so you can ask Kitty your questions. In fact, you should contact the Realtor your *grossdawdi* used and have him here."

"I have no idea who that is."

"His name is on the paperwork I signed. Why don't I get it? It might have his phone number. You can call him and get him here, too."

She rubbed her hands together. "Thank you, Jeremiah. You're being nice about this."

"Me? You didn't throw me out on my ear when I barged in."

When she smiled, it was as if another dozen lights had turned on. "I couldn't throw you out after you saved me from my own foolishness."

The pleasant warmth buzzed through him again as his gaze connected with hers. He looked away. Until he knew what was going to happen with the farm, he needed to keep his distance.

Turning on his heel, he went to where he'd left his bags. He'd get the information she needed and then...

And then what?

Tell her he'd planned to stay here tonight? He couldn't insist Mercy and her little girl find another place tonight. He wasn't sure what, under the circumstances, would happen if he left the property before the disposition of the farm was decided. Possession being nine-tenths of the law...or something like that.

He paused as he saw an overhead photo of the farm. His gaze riveted on the tenant house. It was the answer to tonight's impasse.

Digging among the stack of legal forms, he found the purchase agreement. He paged through it to find Rudy's Realtor's name and contact information. There! He pulled a pencil out of his pocket along with the small notebook that he kept handy to take notes when someone ordered a piece of furniture. Though he planned to concentrate on farming, he knew he'd be doing woodworking on the side until he could get his first crop harvested. His hand tools and small power tools were on their way to Harmony Creek. As he wrote the name and number of Rudy's Realtor, he hoped he wouldn't have to ship those heavy crates back unopened.

He handed the information to Mercy, who nodded her thanks. Returning the papers in the envelope, he dropped it into the open bag. He drew the strings to

close it and looked at Mercy. She was as serious as a sinner confessing in front of the *Leit*. Maybe it was for the best she didn't smile again. He was too fascinated by the high arch of her cheekbones and her dark eyes.

"It's getting late," he said. "We're not going to settle this tonight. It makes sense for you and your little girl to stay here. I'll sleep in the tenant house."

Her eyes widened. "That's very kind, Jeremiah, but I'm not sure there's heat in the tenant house."

"I can figure out something." He glanced around the room. "Do you have blankets?"

"There are plenty upstairs. Help yourself." After she'd given him directions to the linen closet and he started for the stairs in the narrow space behind the door, she added, "Be careful. Like I told Sunni, the floors aren't as sturdy as they should be."

"I'll take my cue from her and test the floors before I step on them." He hurried upstairs before his grin popped out and betrayed how pleased he was to have an excuse to see more of the house he hoped would become his.

A pulse of guilt coursed through him, hot and powerful. The farm belonged to Mercy's family, and he'd be upset if someone came along and insisted his brother surrender his claim on the farm where Jeremiah had grown up. But if he walked away, he might not find another farm near Harmony Creek.

Leaving to live elsewhere might be the difference between the new settlement succeeding or failing. A settlement needed about a dozen families to prosper, and a single person not staying as agreed could doom it. He'd made a deal with the other families, and he couldn't break it without trying to stay.

Following Mercy's directions to a linen closet, Jeremiah paused whenever he heard the floor creak beneath him. Each time it wasn't anything more than the sounds made by an old building. He went to the closet beside the single bathroom on the upper floor and glanced into each room as he passed. Most were empty. Remnants of wallpaper hung in loose strips, and a damp odor filled every breath. Nibbled acorns warned squirrels had invaded. He was sure they were in the attic, too. Once it was warm enough for the squirrels to go outside, he'd check the exterior and block the holes they'd made to get into the house.

If he was here then…

He sighed. "God, You've brought me here. Help me see Your plan and the way for me to be part of this new settlement."

Selecting a couple of wool blankets and guessing there would be plenty of moth holes, he grabbed two more before he went downstairs. He could get by for a single night. If it went as he hoped, by tomorrow night he'd be able to sleep in his own house.

Mercy was waiting in the exact same spot where she'd been when he'd left. Again, guilt tormented him. Part of him wanted to walk away, but he couldn't.

"Did you find enough blankets?" she asked.

"I did."

"They may not be in good condition."

"They're *gut* enough for tonight."

She rubbed her hands together as she had before, and he realized she was as torn as he was. Turning the other cheek was the Mennonites' way, too, but he'd seen how

her eyes snapped when she spoke of him keeping her from making a home here for her and her *kind*.

"If it gets too cold," she said, "come back." A hint of a smile played along her lips. "You freezing to death would be a real complication."

When he chuckled, her smile broadened, revealing the gentle person she was.

"Don't worry, Mercy. I'll be fine." He hoped it wasn't a boast. The temperatures had been dropping fast when he came to the house. He headed for the door.

"Do you have anything to eat?" she asked.

Her question stopped him in his tracks. "No."

"Wait here." Mercy rushed into the kitchen. He heard cabinet doors opening and closing as well as drawers being slid in and out; then she returned with a plastic bag filled with odd shapes. "It's peanut butter and jelly and a few slices of the bread I brought with us. Also a couple of cans of orange juice. It's Sunni's favorite, so I always have a bunch on hand."

"It's my favorite, too."

The smile he hadn't guessed he'd see again spread across her face, adding an aura of light to her eyes and skin. "I'm glad!"

That pleasurable something uncurled within him once more as he gazed into her pretty eyes. A man could get lost in those eyes. He looked away. He hadn't come to Harmony Creek to get lost, but to find his dream.

Picking up his duffel bags, he opened one and stuffed the thin blankets inside. He felt like a hobo as he steered his bags and himself out of the house. By the time he'd reached the porch steps, he heard the dead bolt click

closed. Mercy wasn't taking any chance he'd have second thoughts and return.

He *would* be there tomorrow, he thought as he trudged through the snow. Because he wasn't ready to give up his dream…when it was within his grasp.

The next morning Mercy surveyed the wall completely stripped of ugly, peeling wallpaper. It'd taken more effort than she'd expected to get the remaining paper off. Maybe she shouldn't have done more work until she knew for certain what was going to happen with the farm. When the clock on the mantel in the living room had chimed nine o'clock, she'd used the phone in the kitchen and called Darren Paquette, Grandpa Rudy's Realtor. His office was in Glens Falls, more than twenty-five miles away, and she'd been grateful to catch him at his desk.

At least she had been until he told her not to do anything until she heard from him again. When she explained about the meeting that afternoon with Jeremiah and his Realtor, Mr. Paquette warned her to say nothing.

"A real estate transaction is adversarial at best," he'd said, "and this is far from the best situation."

"When can you come here?"

"Tell Kitty Vasic to call me, and we'll discuss it. There's no reason to involve you and Mr. Stoltzfus at this point."

"I'll tell her."

How could he say she and Jeremiah weren't involved in deciding the future of the farm? That was the silliest thing she'd ever heard.

"Are you okay, Mommy?" asked Sunni as she came downstairs.

Mercy smiled at her dear daughter, who looked adorable in her light green dress and with her black braids falling over her shoulders. The little girl was sensitive to everyone's moods, and Mercy didn't want her to get more upset.

"I'm fine, *eolin-i*." The phrase meaning "little one" was one of the few she knew in Korean.

"Is he coming back?"

"Jeremiah?"

"Yeah, him."

She got the broom she'd found in a kitchen closet and began sweeping the wallpaper scraps into a pile. "He's returning this afternoon with a friend of his."

"Is he going to make you sad again?"

Putting aside the broom, Mercy squatted until her eyes were level with her daughter's. "Jeremiah didn't intend to make me sad. But he talked about Grandpa Rudy, and that made me sad."

"Me, too." Her dark eyes glistened with tears. "I miss his water balloons."

"I don't miss that." Mercy forced humor into her voice. "You two made me your favorite target."

"It was fun to be splashed on a hot day."

"It was, wasn't it?" She hugged Sunni, being careful she didn't pull her daughter off balance.

Mercy started to add more, but the door opened. She gasped when Jeremiah walked in. Nobody ever knocked at her grandfather's door, but for the first time, having someone let himself in seemed like an invasion. From where she squatted, it appeared the top of his straw hat brushed the ceiling.

Telling herself not to be frivolous, she made sure

Sunni was steady as she came to her own feet. Paper crunched under her sneakers when she turned to him. "I thought you were coming this afternoon."

"It *is* afternoon."

"It is?"

He chuckled. "The hours pass swiftly when there's plenty of work, ain't so?"

Mercy warned herself to relax. His teasing was aimed at trying to make the situation as comfortable as possible. "There are never enough hours in a day."

"True." He turned to Sunni. "How are you doing today?"

"You aren't going to make my mommy sad again, are you?" her daughter shot back in a tone that warned Jeremiah he'd be sorry if he did that.

Though she wanted to remind Sunni of her manners, Mercy said nothing. How Jeremiah answered could tell her a lot about what he was planning to do next.

Taking off his hat, he held it by the brim. "I'm sorry if I made her sad before." He raised his eyes to meet Mercy's, and she saw his sincerity as he added, "And I don't want to make her or you sad."

"So you say," Sunni retorted, shocking Mercy again. Her daughter wasn't usually rude, but she seemed to have taken an instant dislike to Jeremiah. Should Mercy heed her daughter's instincts…which she now could see had been spot-on where her ex-fiancé had been concerned?

But being rude to someone in their home—or what she hoped would be their home—wasn't acceptable. "Sunni," she interjected in a firm tone, "it's not nice to suggest Jeremiah would do something hurtful on purpose."

As it isn't kind for me to ask why Grandpa Rudy

hid how he was selling the farm that he said would be mine. Why? Why would you change your mind without telling me?

"I'm sorry," Sunni said, but her obstinate frown countermanded her words.

"It's okay to ask questions," Jeremiah replied, "but my *mamm* says you can catch more flies with honey than with vinegar."

"Who wants to catch flies?" The little girl grimaced. "Gross."

Mercy struggled not to laugh as she explained the adage to her daughter. Looking at Jeremiah, she said, "It's past time for Sunni and I to have lunch, and I know how hungry she gets after doing her schoolwork. I'm homeschooling her." Realizing she was babbling, she added, "Have you eaten?"

"I had the last of the peanut butter for breakfast."

"You can join us if you don't mind leftover pizza."

"Leftover pizza sounds like manna from heaven."

Laughing, she said, "I didn't order the manna topping. I hope you like pepperoni."

A slow smile spread over Jeremiah's face, and her heart did a stutter step as his blue eyes shone like a cloudless summer sky. He'd been so serious during their previous discussions. Seeing him smile was like being confronted by a stranger.

He is *a stranger. A stranger who wants your farm.* Telling her heart to behave itself because it'd been so wrong about Graham, she led the way into the kitchen. She'd be a fool to listen to her heart that had believed Graham loved her. Fortunately, she'd realized in time

she always would have been a distant second in his affections after his mother.

She'd learned her lesson. Or she should have. Maybe her brain had, but her heart had a lot to learn.

Mercy used the time while she got the pizza out of the ancient refrigerator in the off-white kitchen and began warming it in the oven to regain her equilibrium. She must not be distracted by Jeremiah's beguiling smile when the future of Come Along Farm was at stake. When she got cans of soda—a special treat for Sunni—from the fridge, she listened as Jeremiah tried to engage her daughter in conversation.

Sunni was being cautious, either not replying or giving a single-word answer. It was a reminder, though Mercy didn't need one, of how her daughter had been hurt by Graham's decision to choose someone over them and walk away without a backward look. Too many people had done that to Sunni, and Mercy was determined her daughter wouldn't feel abandoned again.

They were finishing what was a very uncomfortable lunch when a knock came at the door. Mercy watched as the door opened and a woman stuck her head in.

"Anyone home?"

Mercy was on her feet as Jeremiah pushed back his chair. She saw him reach to assist Sunni and shook her head to halt him. Sunni needed to do everything as other kids did. If Jeremiah acted as if he thought Sunni couldn't do something, it would make the little girl dislike him more.

Jeremiah appeared taken aback, but drew aside his hands as Sunni pushed her chair out. When Mercy went to the door, he followed.

"Hi, Kitty," he said before introducing Mercy to his Realtor.

Kitty Vasic was the picture of an elegant, successful businesswoman. She wore a business suit of the brightest pink Mercy had ever seen, and her shoes had spiked heels that must be five inches high. Mercy was fascinated, because she expected the Realtor to topple on each step.

"Mr. Stoltzfus, how nice to meet you in person." Kitty held out her hand and when he took it, she pumped his hand vigorously. "And you, too, Ms. Bamberger."

"Please call me Mercy," she said at the same time Jeremiah was urging the Realtor to use his given name.

Jeremiah added, "Plain folks don't like to use titles."

"Oh, that's good to know." Kitty smiled. "With you Amish moving into southern Washington County, it's important to learn how to be good neighbors. Don't you agree?"

Mercy considered saying she wasn't Amish, but she didn't want to delay hearing what the Realtor had to say. "We appreciate you coming so we can get this unfortunate situation resolved right away."

Kitty's smile wavered. "Oh, dear! I'm sorry if I led you to believe this could be settled today."

"But I thought—" Jeremiah began.

"Let's talk, and I'll tell you what I do know." She grinned as Sunni appeared in the kitchen doorway. "Well, hello, young lady. You must be a Bamberger because I know Jeremiah doesn't have children."

"Sunni," Mercy said, "this would be a good time for you to finish the story we started last night."

The little girl glanced at Jeremiah's and Kitty's taut faces. Mercy guessed her own expression was as uneasy. With a nod, Sunni went into the dining room, where two overstuffed chairs were set by a fireplace that opened into the kitchen, as well. It needed to be swept because ashes had tumbled onto the floor. Something else for Mercy to add to her lengthy to-do list.

Pushing aside her longing to go with her daughter and forget about these complications, Mercy squared her shoulders. "We can sit in the living room."

Behind her, the *click-click-click* of Kitty's high heels marked her steps, but Jeremiah's boot falls were surprisingly light for such a tall, muscular man. She shook those thoughts from her head. She couldn't allow herself to become distracted.

She sat in what had been her grandfather's favorite chair by the wide window offering a view of the road through the bare branches of the maple trees. Waiting until the others chose chairs, she gazed at the green tiles on the large fireplace.

"What *can* you tell us, Kitty?" she asked.

"It's unlikely the closing will go on as planned." Kitty shot an apologetic look toward Jeremiah.

His face went as blank as the wall behind him, and his gaze refused to meet hers. The pulse of sympathy surging through her was startling. If he closed on the property, her hopes for Come Along Farm would end. Yet, he had dreams for the property, too. Oh, how she wished there was a solution that could satisfy them both.

When the Realtor spoke again, Mercy focused on her. "We'll need to consult with an attorney," Kitty said, "to

determine what New York law says. I've got to admit it's the first time I've been involved with a property transfer where one party died before closing. Mercy, I should have said this before. I'm sorry for your loss."

"Thank you."

"Your grandfather was well respected and well liked. I can't tell you how many times I enjoyed a cup of coffee with him at the Village Diner."

"Did he mention why he decided to sell?" She regretted the question. Talking about private matters when Jeremiah sat a couple of feet away was unsettling.

Kitty reached over and patted her arm. "He was selling it for you and your daughter."

"For us? But he promised…" This time she halted herself before she said too much.

"I don't know what he told you, Mercy, but Rudy mentioned that he wanted you to have a majority of the money. He hoped you'd build a nice home so you'd be close to his assisted-living apartment. He spoke often about you and your daughter and how he looked forward to spending more time with you."

"Why didn't he tell me this?"

Kitty shook her head sadly. "That's something I can't answer. I'm as perplexed as you are. I'm sure he had his reasons, but he never mentioned them to me or Darren." Her eyes narrowed. "Have you spoken with Darren?"

"I called him this morning. He said to tell you to call him."

"I see." Her lips tightened into a straight line, an expression that said as loudly as a shout she was annoyed.

"We should wait on discussing this further until Darren can be here, too, to represent Rudy's estate."

"But do *you* think the contract is valid?" Jeremiah asked.

"We should wait—"

"I think Mercy is as anxious as I am to hear your opinion. I understand we can't make decisions without Darren's input, but is the contract valid?"

"From what I've read, the answer is yes and no. In some states, the contract would be invalid upon the death of either party." She glanced from Mercy to him. "But we have leeway in New York. If the heir or heirs are willing, the contract can be completed. However, that is *my* opinion from a quick read on the internet. Until we have an opinion from an attorney, I don't think either of you should assume anything."

Jeremiah turned to Mercy. "You are your *grossdawdi*'s heir, ain't so?"

"One of them, I guess. Rudy is my father's father."

"Is your father alive?" asked Kitty.

She nodded.

"What about his brothers and sisters?"

"My father has six siblings," she replied.

Jeremiah sighed. "Kitty, when my *daed*—my dad—died, everything he had went to my mother. But if she'd died first…"

"The estate would be divided equally among his children." Kitty bit her lower lip, then said, "Unless Rudy left a written and witnessed will that specifies otherwise."

Mercy's heart sank toward her knees as she realized where the conversation was going. If Grandpa Rudy hadn't

left a valid will naming her as his heir, the property would belong to her father, her four aunts and her two uncles.

"Do you have names and contact information for your father and his siblings?" asked Kitty.

"I can find them. All but one aunt have telephones."

The Realtor smiled. "I'm glad to hear that. It'll make getting in contact with them much easier. However, paperwork will have to be mailed to them for their signatures. I'm not sure, at this point, whether the signatures will have to be notarized. The probate court will let us know."

"We have to go to court?" asked Jeremiah.

Mercy heard his consternation and understood. It usually wasn't the way of plain folks to deal with courts and lawyers. Matters were settled privately and through prayer, but estate matters were different. She wondered whom her grandfather had hired to draft his will…if he had one.

She was out of her depth. Ask her about the needs of inner-city kids and the benefits of them enjoying a summer in the country, and she could expound for an hour. Since Sunni's arrival in her life, she'd learned a lot about inter-country adoption and physical therapy and the adventures of the little girl's beloved characters in her favorite books.

But she knew nothing about what would happen with the farm.

"If you agree, Jeremiah," Kitty went on, "I'll share the contract with my agency's lawyer. I'd like him to review it and give us advice to aid us in bringing the contract to a closing." She sighed. "To be honest, this won't be quick. Obtaining an agreement from seven people will take time, and we can't be certain of the outcome."

"Is there another farm for sale in the area?" Jeremiah asked.

"None that I know of. I can make inquiries, if you'd like."

"Ja."

Her eyes cut toward Mercy. "I'll do what I can, Jeremiah, but I can't make promises. Not about this farm or any other."

"I know," he said again.

"And there's one other complication. Your money in escrow may be held by the probate court until there's an agreement among the heirs."

He blanched. "I can't put in another offer until the money is released."

"Yes, though if someone is eager to sell, we might be able to work something out." Kitty sighed. "However, like I said, I don't know of other farms for sale near Harmony Creek. There's one over by Scotts Lake, seven or eight miles from here."

"Too far for me to be part of this settlement."

"So I figured." She stood.

Mercy clasped her hands on her lap. If the closing went ahead, Jeremiah would own the farm. If the sale had to be approved by Grandpa Rudy's heirs, would Dad and his brothers and sisters decide to sell it to Jeremiah? Two of his siblings would be eager to use their share of the proceeds to invest in their businesses. What about the others? And how many had to say no before Jeremiah couldn't close on the farm? Was it a simple majority or could a single no vote give her the chance to buy the farm herself?

But how? The money she had was already earmarked to fix the house and the buildings to be approved for bringing children to visit. In addition, she needed to buy horses and other farm animals to give the youngsters a true farm experience. Perhaps she could convince her family to let her pay them bit by bit.

She heard Kitty say she'd contact them when she had further information. The *click-click-click* of Kitty's shoes headed toward the door, and Jeremiah went, too, talking with his Realtor.

Mercy didn't move. There had to be a solution to her dilemma, but what?

Unless Rudy left a written and witnessed will that specifies otherwise.

Kitty's words resonated in Mercy's head, and she gasped. What if she found a will? There were many rooms, and she hadn't dared to go into the ones with weak floors. What if she found her grandfather's will and it proved her assertion he wanted her to have the farm?

She got up and took a single step toward the formal staircase at the front of the house. Pausing, she looked over her shoulder when she heard Jeremiah's deep voice rumbling in the other room. If he knew of her intention to search the house, would he help her or try to halt her? Until she knew for sure, she couldn't let him know what she was doing. She didn't like secrets, but keeping this one might mean the difference between her dreams coming true and their destruction.

Chapter Three

Last night Jeremiah had discovered the tenant house was in worse condition than he'd guessed. It hadn't taken him long to explore it, using his flashlight. A tiny kitchen and a cozy living room filled the first floor. Upstairs were two cramped bedrooms and a bath. Every ceiling had brown water stains, and one wall of the entry hall was pulling away from the house. He'd been able to see light from the rising moon through the crack, and a puddle of slush was piled on the linoleum beside it.

This morning he woke to find the house cold and damp. He'd been grateful for a woodstove in the living room and a few logs stacked nearby. He'd used the rag rug by the stove as a mattress. He'd folded a blanket as a makeshift pillow. He'd told himself, though it wasn't likely it'd be comfortable, he'd endured worse when he'd camped in the woods when he wasn't much older than Sunni.

He'd been wrong.

Every muscle ached, and moving in the icy air seemed to make his bones creak as if he'd aged fifty years overnight. It was dark, but he guessed it was around 4:00 a.m. It was the time when he usually woke to help with chores before leaving for his woodworking shop.

His tools would be arriving today or tomorrow. He should have waited until he closed on the property before he had the crates trucked up from Paradise Springs. But how could he have imagined the debacle waiting for him in Harmony Creek?

With a groan, he pushed himself up to sit. He grimaced as the frigid air gripped him as the thick blanket fell away. Standing, he went to the stove, which was barely warm. He opened the door and saw the banked embers had burned themselves out.

Jeremiah sent up a prayer of thanks when, after he'd started a new fire in the stove, the air close to the stove warmed quickly. Something worked in the house.

After his quick inspection his first night at the house, he knew not much else did. No water had flowed into the sinks, and flushing the toilet had resulted in strange creaking sounds in the walls as if the pipes were trying to break out. The propane tanks by the back door must be empty, because the kitchen stove had refused to light.

He hoped he would have better results this morning. He opened a door to what might have been a laundry or storage room. A rusty washer lurked beneath shelves covered with dust and droppings. In a closet, he found a lantern but no kerosene.

Brushing the kitchen table off as best he could, he

grimaced when it rocked. Were the legs uneven or the floor? That answer and a whole lot more would have to wait until he could see beyond the narrow circle from his flashlight.

He made the same meal he'd eaten last night. A peanut butter and grape jelly sandwich. He thought fondly of the large meal of eggs and sausage and home fries he would have eaten at home. After he said silent grace, he ate standing up. He found a napkin Mercy had added to the bag. He sighed, wondering if it would have been much easier if she'd been rude or snarled like an angry dog. Instead, she'd made sure he had blankets to keep him warm and food to eat.

And she'd been stubborn.

Did she have ideas of her own for the farm? Most likely, as she'd started work on the house. He appreciated that, because he'd spent hours putting together his plans, something his brothers had helped him with while they teased him for trying to look at every possible angle. Taking another bite of the sandwich, he wished his brothers were nearby. He could have used their insight.

A knock startled him. Why would someone come to a house that must have been deserted for years? Setting his sandwich down, he brushed crumbs off his hands and tossed them in the sink before he went to the door.

He opened it and saw a face he recognized. The man who had recruited others to come to Harmony Creek.

"You're Caleb Hartz, ain't so?" Jeremiah asked, remembering how Caleb had spoken at a gathering in Paradise Springs, telling about the fallow farmland on

small family farms awaiting anyone who was willing to work hard to improve it.

The man nodded, then swept his too-long blond hair out of his dark green eyes. "*Ja.* I thought I'd stop by this morning to see how you're settling in." His tawny brows lowered. "I assumed you'd be at the main house, but the woman who answered the door told me I'd find you here."

"Things are a bit complicated." After he invited Caleb into the house, he gave him a quick overview of the situation.

Caleb, who would be one of his neighbors if the sale went through, listened with widening eyes. "I got to know Rudy pretty well. He was a *gut* man. He wouldn't have signed a purchase contract with you if he didn't intend for you to buy the farm."

"Maybe he should have mentioned that to his granddaughter."

Caleb's frown deepened, drawing lines into the thin angles of his face. "It's a puzzle. I've been here a little over a month. Everyone I've talked to—both Amish and *Englisch*—has praised Rudy's honesty. He sold me a battered skid loader I'll need to move hay bales. He didn't make any bones about how much work it would need, and he sold it at a fair price."

"My dealings with him were *gut*, too. I wish I knew why he didn't let Mercy know he was selling the farm."

"I hope you won't have to leave Harmony Creek. We need every family we can convince to join us in order to make this settlement a success."

Jeremiah didn't need that reminder. From the mo-

ment he'd expressed interest in joining the Hartz family and the Waglers as well as other founding members of the Harmony Creek colony, he'd been told he must be very sure about his commitment. Each family was vital to the rest.

"I'm not leaving. I'm going to farm here." Saying the words aloud was like taking an oath in the presence of the Lord, though God was well aware of what was in Jeremiah's heart.

"Aren't you a woodworker by trade?"

"*Ja*, but farming is too much in my blood." He surprised himself by chuckling. "My late *daed* would be shocked because I hated to get out of bed to do chores."

Caleb chuckled. "My *daed* used to threaten to dump cold water on me and my brothers to get us up in the morning."

"Sounds familiar."

"I can ask around and find out if anyone is thinking about selling."

"*Danki*, but I've got to wait and hear what my Realtor learns from her attorney. As my *mamm* has said more than once, there's no need to look for trouble before it finds you."

"Sounds like something my *mamm* would have said, too."

"My brothers believe *mamms* have a special language filled with platitudes for every occasion."

Caleb laughed heartily. "Why is it dark in here?"

"I couldn't find oil for the lantern."

"The house has electricity. Rudy mentioned both houses were wired." With a wave of his hand, he added,

"Let's find the fuse box and see if we can get you some light. More important is powering the well pump so you can have water."

Jeremiah followed him into the cellar. As they crossed the dirt floor to where a metal box was affixed to the wall, he wondered why he hadn't considered checking the well pump. Exhaustion could be a reason, because he felt as if he carried the house on his shoulders as he trudged after Caleb.

His neighbor whistled a single note as he popped open the door on the metal box. "A circuit breaker box. Who'd have guessed Rudy had updated his tenant house?" Reaching in, he flipped a switch.

A low rumble came from the far side of the cellar. Jeremiah aimed his flashlight in that direction and saw the well's holding tank. His fatigue fell away as he realized he could have water to brush his teeth once he'd let it run long enough to make sure any rust washed out.

"Danki," he said.

Caleb shrugged. "Glad to help. I'm sure this circuit breaker box isn't the first surprise you're going to find."

Jeremiah was tempted to say the breakers were far from the *first* surprise he'd had since his arrival, but grousing wouldn't get him anywhere. He needed to be patient until Kitty had answers for him. *That* had to be his plan. Wait and see.

A sense of calm settled over him as he realized he had a clear path…for now. He thanked God for helping him see that. He must be patient. Not an easy task when his dream was so close to realization.

Several lights were glaring against the water-stained

ceilings when he went upstairs with Caleb. He switched off everything but the fluorescent ceiling light in the kitchen, though he despised its glare.

"Let us know if you need anything before your stuff arrives," Caleb said as he reached for the doorknob. He glanced outside. "Looks like we're in for another big storm." Grimacing at the crack in the wall, he added, "We're living in the barn while we get the house repaired, and our barn is better than this. Feel free to come over if you get tired of shoveling snow out of your house."

"Danki." He knew he wouldn't abandon the house, because that might injure his fragile claim on the farm. "I appreciate it."

"We may be snowed in for a while, because we're one of the last roads plowed by the town. I don't think Rudy sold his sleigh, so if you or anyone at the main house needs something, you can use it."

"Danki." He appreciated Caleb's helpfulness, which made him more determined to be a part of the nascent community. Amish folks assisted one another. Did Mercy feel the same?

"Oh, one other thing I should let you know." Caleb turned the knob. "Wayne Flaud from the settlement north of here in Whitehall is acting as our temporary bishop. If you want me to contact him to get his thoughts on what you should do…"

"Let's see what my Realtor has to say before we bring the bishop into this. I'm sure this will work out for the best. God didn't bring me to Harmony Creek so I could turn around and leave again."

With another nod, Caleb bid him *gute mariye* and let himself out as a burst of cold and a swirl of windblown snow slipped in past him.

Jeremiah guessed Caleb believed his words. Too bad he wasn't so sure himself.

Any hopes spring might have made an early appearance overnight were dashed three days later when Mercy awoke to discover two feet of new snow. She dressed hastily, because the house was cold in the fresh light of dawn.

Peeking past Sunni's door and glad her daughter was asleep with the blankets pulled up to her chin, Mercy tiptoed down the stairs. They creaked beneath her, and she hoped Sunni wouldn't wake up until Mercy figured out what was wrong with the heat.

Despite herself, she glanced out the window that gave her a view of the trees separating them from the tenant house. She hadn't spoken to Jeremiah since he'd left after the meeting with his Realtor. She'd seen big delivery trucks in the yard the following day and watched him accept delivery of a horse, a buggy and a dozen large wooden crates, which he'd moved into an outbuilding. He'd spent time inside, coming out with pieces of wood, so she guessed he was unpacking what he'd shipped to the farm.

That was a sign Jeremiah intended to stay.

No surprise, but if he thought she'd give up because he was making himself at home, he was in for a big surprise. She'd waited years for an opportunity to host city kids on a farm.

She'd thought her grandfather comprehended her need to pay forward the gifts she'd been given. Instantly, she was contrite. She couldn't fault Grandpa Rudy for his change of heart about what should happen with the farm after he died, but she wished he'd talked to her before signing a deal with Jeremiah.

He was as much an innocent victim of this mess as she was. Of course, if he withdrew his offer, that might make a difference for her aunts and uncles. Would they be more willing to give her time to find funds to set up the farm if they didn't have an available buyer?

Mercy had discussed that with her parents last night. Her father had sympathy for how her plans for the farm might have died along with Rudy, but he'd also emphasized that he'd go along with what his siblings decided.

"I've got to admit," Dad had told her before they'd hung up, "I'd really like to have you and Sunni closer to the rest of the family."

"But there's no place near your house where I could afford to buy land." She'd tried not to sound like a petulant child who hadn't gotten her way.

"If that's what God wants you to do, He'll help you find a way."

She agreed and was sure God had led her to Harmony Creek and the farm. Otherwise, she wouldn't have uprooted Sunni, leaving behind trusted specialists and physical therapists who worked with her daughter.

Now…

Mercy winced as she entered the kitchen and felt the cold wind that had found its way into the house. Open-

ing the cellar door, she heard silence. Why wasn't the furnace running?

A quick check of the fuel tank gauge showed it was half-full. Next, she went to the furnace, which was raised up so high off the floor she had to stand on tiptoe to see the dials. Why wouldn't it start? She tried flipping the emergency switch at the top of the cellar steps.

Nothing.

If possible, it seemed colder when she returned to the kitchen. She needed help. She glanced at the snow sparkling as if stars had fallen along with the flakes. The road twisting through the hollow had vanished. If she called someone, how long would it take them to get to the house?

Her gaze settled on the tenant house. Should she ask Jeremiah to check the furnace? She'd ignored him for three days, but she wasn't sure who else would be able to help them. She didn't want Sunni getting sick from the cold.

Before she could talk herself out of it, Mercy reached for the phone, an old avocado-colored unit she'd found in a drawer. She'd hung it on the wall. The long cord allowed her to walk around the kitchen while she talked. She looked at the faded numbers on the wall beside the phone and dialed the one for the tenant house.

"Hello?" Jeremiah sounded astonished to be answering a phone.

She knew many Amish didn't keep phones in their houses, but had them in the barns or a phone shack shared by multiple families.

"Jeremiah, it is Mercy. Mercy Bamberger." Who else

named Mercy would know he was living at the tenant house?

"*Ja. Gute mariye*, Mercy." He sounded awkward and uncertain as he went on. "I hope my work hasn't disturbed you or Sunni. I—"

Not wanting to let the conversation drag along, she said, "I don't think my furnace is working. Will you look at it?"

She could almost see him nod before he told her he'd be over in a few minutes. Thanking him, she hung up.

Starting the coffeemaker, she sighed. If Jeremiah took over the farm, he'd strip the electric wires out of the house. She wondered what it'd be like to live without electricity.

A knock on the door told her Jeremiah was as good as his word. Taking a steadying breath, she opened it. She forced a smile, which she hoped looked more welcoming than it felt.

Knocking snow off his boots, Jeremiah stepped inside. He unwrapped a blue-and-green scarf from around his face and let it hang over his shoulders as he unbuttoned his black wool coat. Lifting off his hat of the same fabric, he placed it on the counter near the door.

Her heart beat a bit too fast when she stood close to him again. She'd thought of him as a problem, but with him an arm's length away, she couldn't help noticing, as if for the first time, his strong jaw and the intelligence in his compelling blue eyes. As he pulled off worn work gloves, she stared at the nicks on his knuckles and stain on his fingertips. He was a man accustomed to hard work.

Graham, her former fiancé, popped into her mind. A fastidious man, his hands always looked as if he'd just had a manicure. She'd been surprised to discover he had his nails done when he took his mother to the beauty shop. When he'd told her it made Mrs. Rapp happy, Mercy had, at first, seen it as a sign of him caring deeply about others. She hadn't guessed he'd cared more about his mother than he'd ever care for her.

"Thanks for coming over," Mercy said, holding out her hand for Jeremiah's coat.

He handed it to her, and waves of cold washed over her. It must be more frigid outside than in the house. Maybe the furnace hadn't gone out too long ago and fixing it would be easy.

"What have you done so far?" he asked, combing his fingers through his reddish hair.

"I checked the fuel oil tank." She set his coat over a kitchen chair. "There's oil in the tank, so I don't know what's wrong."

"Let me look at it."

"Thanks!" She motioned toward the cellar door. "It's down there. I'm hoping it's something simple."

"Something simple is about the extent of my skills at fixing furnaces." He gave her a grin. "Just in case, do you have the name of the person who did furnace servicing for Rudy? It's probably the same company that delivers oil."

"I probably can find it. He kept that sort of stuff in his desk." As coffee finished dripping into the clear pot, she asked, "Do you want a cup?"

"I'll have one when I'm done." Without another

word, he went to the cellar door and opened it. His work boots, which were as battered as his gloves, thumped on each step.

Mercy heard Jeremiah pull on the chain to the bare bulb near the furnace. Hurrying into the room with Grandpa Rudy's desk, she grabbed a black shawl from a peg. She threw it over her shoulders, holding it close with fingers as clumsy as a collection of icicles.

The desk was heaped with papers and envelopes her grandfather must have tossed there in the days before he died. For a moment Mercy had to blink back tears. Throughout the mess of the past days, one thing hadn't changed. She missed Grandpa Rudy, the very person she wanted to turn to now.

Mercy found a receipt from the oil company and was relieved to see it had an emergency service number at the top. Putting it in the pocket of her black apron, she hurried into the kitchen to be ready to call the oil company if Jeremiah couldn't fix the furnace.

She paused when she heard uneven steps on the stairs to the second floor. Sunni was coming down the stairs without her crutches. Mercy frowned. Her daughter had promised to use them on the stairs. Worse, the little girl had wrapped herself in a blanket that threatened to trip her.

"Sunni, you need to be careful," she chided gently.

"I was afraid of turning into an ice cube if I waited a second longer," the little girl said. "Why's it so cold, Mommy?"

"Something's wrong with the heat."

Before Mercy could say more, assertive footsteps

came from the cellar steps. She turned to see Jeremiah in the doorway.

Sunni mumbled something under her breath and scowled at Jeremiah.

His gaze followed Sunni when her daughter walked into the living room, her pose beneath the blanket one of disdain. He arched his brows at Mercy.

"Were you able to see what's wrong with the furnace?" Mercy asked.

"Nothing's wrong with it." He wiped his hands on a filthy cloth he must have found in the cellar. "Your fuel oil tank is empty."

"But I checked the tank before I called you. The gauge said it was half-full."

"The gauge is broken. The tank is completely dry."

"I never considered the gauge might be wrong."

"No reason you should."

"You did." She pushed away from the stairs and flinched when the door gave a threatening creak. One disaster at a time. Reaching under her shawl, she pulled the receipt out of her pocket. "I'll call the oil company's emergency number and see if they can deliver some oil."

He glanced out the window. "They won't be able to get in until the road is plowed."

As if on cue, the rumble of a big truck could be heard coming toward the house. She saw the huge wing of the plow as it pushed snow in large, thick chunks into the yard. She shuddered, thinking of the heavy work of clearing the driveway. Her car was stored in the rickety garage, and the old-style door opened straight out, so she was going to have to clear a large area there, too.

Mercy made the call to the oil company, who assured her they'd be there before nightfall. Apparently, she wasn't the only one needing service on the cold day.

"You can't stay here with Sunni," Jeremiah said after she hung up. "The house is going to get colder and colder. The tenant house is a bit better, but you'll get so chilled going over there, it probably won't make much difference. Isn't there a fireplace in the living room?"

"Yes."

"Did Rudy use it?"

When she nodded and Jeremiah offered to start a fire, she was relieved. She found a box of matches in the kitchen junk drawer and followed him into the living room, where he checked the fireplace, looking up at the top of the firebox where the damper opened into the chimney. He drew back, wiping soot from his trousers.

While Sunni watched from the couch, as silent as she was whenever Jeremiah was near, he quickly arranged slabs of wood in the fireplace. Mercy handed him the matches and went to sit with her daughter.

He struck one match and held it to the small bits of paper he'd stuck among the wood. Small flames rose, and Mercy resisted the yearning to hold out her half-frozen hands, knowing there wouldn't be much heat yet. She needed to wait until the fire caught on the dried wood.

Suddenly, Jeremiah jumped to his feet and staggered. Thick smoke chased him toward the middle of the room.

"Get out!" he yelled.

Chapter Four

Mercy grabbed Sunni and ran toward the living room door, but paused when she heard a window slide open with the rattle of glass behind her. Jeremiah waved the smoke from the hearth out the window. Snow fell into the house, but he ignored it as he coughed. She put Sunni down and ran into the kitchen. She filled a bucket with water.

He threw the water on the hearth, where it sizzled. He stirred the ashes, making sure the fire was completely out. Then he took the glass of water she offered him. He drained it in one gulp and coughed a couple more times.

"I told you to get out," he said. "With this dried-out wallpaper, the fire could have spread fast."

"Why would I leave you here?" she asked, annoyed he treated her as if she were Sunni's age. "Once I heard you open the window, I knew the smoke would be sucked out."

"Maybe I was planning to jump out the window. Did you consider that?"

"No."

He gave her a wry grin. "Neither did I. Once I could see through the smoke, I was able to see the fire was dying out." He raised a single finger when she started to speak. "But you and Sunni should have gotten out of the house."

"To freeze in the snow?"

He sighed as fresh air poured into the room, dispersing the smoke. "I thought you said your *grossdawdi* used the fireplace."

"He did." Mercy took the glass from him.

"Recently?"

She shrugged. "I don't know. I almost always visited during the summer vacation."

"I suspect debris in the chimney has piled up over time. After it's cleaned out, there shouldn't be a problem." He grimaced. "But right now you need heat."

"I can turn on the oven and open the door."

"Gas or electric?"

"Electric. Why?"

"I don't want you to have to deal with gas fumes." He gestured toward the kitchen. "You two go into the kitchen. Shut the doors and roll up towels and put them at the bottom. That should keep the heat in as much as possible."

"How about the fireplace between the kitchen and dining room? There are ashes on the hearth." She glanced at the smoke stains on the ceiling. "Do you think it'd be safe to try to light that one?"

"Let me check." He followed her and Sunni into the kitchen.

He knelt by the hearth as she turned on the oven and opened the door, hoping the old stove was up to heating the kitchen. Unlike the one in the living room, the kitchen fireplace was utilitarian. No fancy tiles. Just plain brick turned dark after decades of use. He reached in to check the damper. Paying no attention to the ashes, he stretched out on his back and peered into the chimney.

"It looks open." Jeremiah got up and knocked ashes off his pants. "Let me try a small fire. Got anything else to burn?"

She grabbed a handful of newspaper from the pile left by her *grossdawdi*. "How about this?"

"It'll burn long enough to see if the smoke goes up the chimney or not."

He cheered and Mercy smiled, giving Sunni's shoulders a squeeze, when the thin wisp of smoke was drawn up the chimney. Going into the living room, she realized there were only a couple of pieces of wood left. She took them into the kitchen and handed them to Jeremiah.

"You keep the fire going, and I'll get more wood," she said.

"Mercy, I can do that. It's cold outside." He started to stand.

She put her hand on his shoulder, the motion automatic. But her response to the strong sinews was anything but. Jerking her hand back, she wanted to shake it to stop her skin from tingling.

Somehow she was able to say, "No, you watch the fire. I'll be right back."

Racing to the door, she flung it open. She pulled on

her boots before she stepped into the deep snow on the porch. Quickly closing the door, she wasn't fast enough to avoid seeing Sunni's dismay that Mercy had left her with Jeremiah.

Mercy took a steadying breath as her fingers continued to quiver from the memory of Jeremiah's shoulder beneath them. Had she lost her mind? It was a big mistake to be attracted to him. Even if he didn't want her farm, she was still reeling from a broken engagement. On top of that, her daughter didn't like him.

She hurried to the split wood that had been stored on the porch to dry. She gathered pieces in her apron and turned to go inside.

She stopped as she looked across the snowy yard. It was broken by a single set of footprints. Jeremiah's.

No, she was wrong. There were other footprints. She recognized the tiny, scampering ones of a squirrel intent on finding where it had hidden its stash of acorns. A line near the pine trees separating the big house from the tenant house looked as if they belonged to deer. They would be having as difficult a time as squirrels in the deep snow. Once the house was warm, she needed to spread hay for the deer and strew a few handfuls of the birdseed she'd seen in a cupboard. Grandpa Rudy always had made sure his bird feeders were kept full, despite the concern of bears helping themselves to the seed.

All God's creatures need to eat, and we are His hands to take care of His creation.

How many times had she heard Grandpa Rudy say that? Oh, how she missed him!

A gust of wind swirled snow into her face, and

Mercy hurried inside. As she let the wood roll onto the floor beside the hearth, Jeremiah smiled at her.

"Perfect timing," he said. "I was about to go out and make sure you hadn't frozen into a chunk of ice."

"My mommy is doing the best she can!" asserted Sunni, jutting out her tiny chin. She flounced into the dining room and hid behind a book.

Mercy started to apologize to Jeremiah for Sunni's behavior.

He motioned aside her words. "She's cold, and she's scared. I should have thought before I spoke."

"You know it doesn't have anything to do with what you said." She wouldn't sugarcoat Sunni's antipathy to him. "I'm sorry she's being bratty to you." *And I know I should be honest why, but I can't when I'm too embarrassed by what happened with Graham.*

"She's a kid. I've got enough nieces and nephews to know when they get something in their head, it's not easy to get it out."

"Do you have a lot of them?"

"More all the time, thanks to my brothers and sisters." Standing, he looked at the fire crackling contentedly on the hearth. Already warmth was pushing aside the cold. "Keep feeding it wood, and it won't go out." He hesitated, then said, "I should get going."

She asked before she could halt herself, "So how many brothers do you have?"

Jeremiah wondered why Mercy was extending the conversation when it had seemed, moments ago, she couldn't wait until he left.

"Six. Three older and three younger," he said. "And two sisters. Add in their spouses and kids, and we have a full table when everyone comes together." He couldn't halt his smile. "*Mamm* is never happier than when everyone is sitting around the table together. Do you have brothers or sisters?"

"Now, but I was an only child when I lived in the Bronx."

"I can't imagine being an only." *Or living in a big city.* "I've always been surrounded by siblings, which most of the time I appreciated."

She nodded. "I know what you mean. I've learned how siblings can be your best friends, but also they know exactly how to annoy you best."

"So your family used to live in New York City? I didn't realize Mennonites lived there."

"I wasn't Mennonite then." Before he could ask what she meant, she said, "I need to make Sunni breakfast. I promised her pancakes. Would you like some, too?"

"I had some toast when I woke up, but that was several hours ago, so I'd be grateful for a second breakfast. I've got a long day ahead of me."

"Unpacking more of those big crates?" Color rose up Mercy's cheeks, and he guessed she'd blurted out the question before thinking.

"*Ja.* I had my woodworking tools sent up from Paradise Springs before I realized..." He wasn't surprised when she went to collect the makings for breakfast. Why did she act ashamed? The situation they were in wasn't her fault. She was as much a victim of misunderstandings as he was. He hurried on to fill the abrupt

silence. "I want to make sure nothing got broken between Pennsylvania and here."

"That makes sense." She took a bowl out of a glass-front hutch built into the wall opposite the fireplace. She put flour and eggs and other ingredients in the bowl and she mixed them together.

She closed the oven door and hefted a cast-iron pan out of the drawer beneath it. After heating the pan, she poured pancake batter into it.

Sunni peeked in. The frown she gave Jeremiah didn't need translation. She wished he'd go away and stay away.

Lord, help me find a way to let this kind *know I'm not her enemy. Or her* mamm's.

The little girl had to be aware of the tension between Mercy and him. Sunni was old enough to understand there was a problem, but couldn't grasp the intricacies of estate law. *He* didn't get it, either, though Kitty had explained it to him. It was too bad they couldn't help each other, but his plans for the farm and Mercy's were different.

When Mercy put pancakes on a plate and set it on the kitchen table, Sunni asked, "Can I eat in the dining room?"

Mercy hesitated; then she nodded. The little girl poured herself a glass of orange juice, picked up her plate and carried her breakfast into the other room.

"I'm sorry," Mercy said as she returned to the stove.

"It won't help to force her to spend time with me," he replied.

"True." She set a stack of lightly browned pancakes

in front of him. The edges of the pancakes were crisp, just as he liked them. As he started to say that, she interrupted him. "I need to explain why she's acting like this."

"Okay."

She faced the stove. "I was in a relationship that didn't work out, and she was upset when Graham and I went our separate ways after I realized I would always play second fiddle to his mother."

"*Danki.* I was beginning to think it was personal." He couldn't help being curious about how serious she and her Graham had been. He hoped not as serious as he'd been about Emmarita before she left her Amish life behind. He hoped Mercy didn't have as many regrets as he did.

"It's not. The move has upset her more than I'd guessed it would."

"And the possibility you won't be staying here isn't helping." He smothered the sting of Emmarita's betrayal by concentrating on the problem he and Mercy shared.

"Not a bit."

"Have you heard anything from your family?" he asked after he paused to say a silent grace. He picked up his fork so he didn't have to look at her as he waited for her answer.

"Nothing definitive. Dad said they're planning a conference call to discuss the farm." She put a cup of fragrant *kaffi* next to his plate before going to the stove to make her own breakfast. "Everyone will want to share his or her opinion."

Jeremiah waited until she brought a plate with four

pancakes to the table. She pushed two more onto his plate before she set hers down. After getting herself *kaffi* and offering him juice, which he passed on because it would taste sour after the syrup, she pulled out her chair and sat. She bowed her head, and he said nothing while she thanked the Lord for the meal.

Could she be thanking God for Jeremiah's company? Maybe she was grateful to have endured another day with him. Was she just being more polite than her daughter? Possibly, because she must want to move ahead with the farm. For the first time, he wondered if he was being shortsighted trying to stay, but what else could he do? Until his funds were released from escrow, he couldn't purchase another farm. His sole choice might be to return to Paradise Springs, and he wasn't ready to start over at square one.

Not yet.

Jeremiah looked for a safe topic to disrupt the silence. "You said you learned about siblings. It sounds as if you eventually had some."

"I had two brothers and a sister after I was adopted."

"Adopted?" He was glad she seemed focused on her food so she didn't see the astonishment on his face. No doubt she heard it in his voice.

"When I was eleven. That was after my *Abuelita*—my grandmother—died. She'd been raising me."

"What happened to your parents?"

She chased the syrup around her plate with a piece of pancake, but didn't lift it to her mouth. "A car accident when I was two years old. They were on their way to the hospital for the birth of their second child when

they were struck by another car. *Abuelita* told me the police said they died instantly. She said I needed to be grateful they never felt any pain before they went to heaven, but I couldn't be when I was a little girl who couldn't understand why God wanted to take my mama and papa and my unborn sister away."

"Mercy, I'm so sorry." He hated the sight of tears seeping into her eyes. How many had she cried through the years as she mourned those she could barely remember?

"Thank you." She dabbed a knuckle at her eye and squared her shoulders. "*Abuelita* took me in and became more like my mother than my grandmother. Everything I know of my parents is from what she told me and from the picture of them on their wedding day. I don't know what happened to that photo. To be honest, Jeremiah, it seems like someone else's past. Once I was adopted by the Bambergers, my life began anew."

"Certainly you haven't forgotten the first eleven years of your life?"

"No, but I took Grandpa Rudy's advice. He urged me to treasure the memories of those who had left me behind. I have many precious ones of *Abuelita*, and I can re-create every detail of that photo. I can even recall the name of the studio where it was taken. Lincoln Photography on Fordham Road. I remember it because I thought President Lincoln had taken their picture."

"I doubt your parents would have appreciated you thinking they were that old." He chuckled. "Kids always think their parents are ancient. Sunni probably thinks you're older than the hills."

"Thanks." A grin transformed her face, and he knew he would gladly sit and look at it for hours at a time.

Shaking his head, he warned himself not to be silly. He was the only one of his siblings not married or getting ready to marry, but now was the worst time to get involved with anyone. Most especially with the woman who held the key to his future in her slender hands.

Not Mercy, his conscience argued, *but her family.*

Jeremiah pushed his plate away enough so he could fold his arms on the table. "I was nearly grown when my *daed* died, but it wasn't easy to lose him."

"No matter what anyone says, there's no good time to lose someone we love."

She didn't seem surprised that he turned the conversation to such a sad subject. In fact, she seemed grateful he was listening and wasn't trying to relieve her pain with more jests.

Quietly, she added, "Knowing they're bound for a better place is supposed to ease the loss, but it's sad to think of not seeing them for a very long time."

"A *very* long time, I hope."

She nodded, then took a sip of her orange juice. "I should have finished that before I began the pancakes." Without a pause, she went on. "Jeremiah, I know you're as eager as I am to hear from my father and his siblings. We've got to be patient."

"I'm trying."

"Me, too." She put down her glass. "It sounds as if your family lives close together."

"Except for my oldest sister, everyone lives within a mile of where we grew up."

"Not my father's family. Shortly after they were married, my parents joined others who wanted to start a new church in western New York. That's what they told me anyhow."

"You don't believe it?"

"I'm sure they're being honest, but I think it's strange my dad's siblings moved away from Harmony Creek, and they're scattered from New York to California. I think that was one of the reasons Grandpa Rudy was glad to have me come every year. The rest of the family's visits were infrequent."

"Which explains," he said slowly, pondering the ramifications, "why nobody thought it odd Rudy was leaving the farm to you. It sounds as if none of the rest of them wanted it."

"Let's hope they still feel that way." She paused when Sunni came into the kitchen. After Mercy made more pancakes for her daughter, the little girl rushed away to the dining room as if she feared Jeremiah was infectious with a horrible disease.

He waved aside Mercy's embarrassed apology as she added another serving of pancakes to his plate. "Kids are kids. She'll accept me when she's ready."

"I pray so." As she handed him the syrup bottle, she said, "Dad hopes to get back to me in the next few days, though nothing is settled until everyone agrees. I can't imagine any of them coming here." She glanced out the window at the sparkling snow. "But then I can't imagine why they left this beautiful hollow in the first place."

"Some people need to get out from under their fam-

ily's shadow, whether it's the shadow of success or failure."

"Is that why you came here?" She put her fingers to her lips. "I'm sorry, Jeremiah. I shouldn't have asked you such a personal question."

"Why not? I've been asking you personal questions."

"I want you to know I wasn't asking why in the hope of discovering something that would give me an upper hand in claiming the farm."

He put his hand on her arm and wasn't surprised to find it trembling. What startled him was how swiftly he was suffused with warmth as if summer had arrived and flooded the house with sunshine. Knowing he should pull away, he didn't. He liked the sensation of her soft skin beneath his fingertips.

"That's not why I asked about your past, either. Mercy, we can't let this situation make us too competitive or too bitter."

"I know, but…"

He lifted his hand from her arm as she tensed beneath his fingers. "The truth of why I came here is because I wanted to start over. The woman I thought I'd marry decided to marry someone else."

"I'm sorry."

He believed her. She felt everything so deeply, and he hoped she couldn't tell he wasn't being completely honest when he said, "*Danki*, but Emmarita is in the past. I want to look to the future, so I came to Harmony Creek. Here I can be part of the building of a new settlement. It's exciting to think the steps I'm taking could lead to

a place that will provide homes for Amish families for generations to come."

She didn't reply, so he pushed back his chair. With a swift prayer of gratitude for the meal, he stood.

"If you'll excuse me," he said, "I need to see if there are usable tarps in the big barn. It looks like more snow, and the roof on the barn where my tools are has more holes than an old pair of sneakers."

"Thanks for your help, Jeremiah."

"*Danki* for breakfast."

When again she remained silent, he put his hat and coat on and turned up his collar before he opened the door. A cold blast of wind sucked him out onto the porch.

He looked across the yard toward the barns. *Lord, I could use your help in seeing the way I should go. I'm here to help make this settlement a success. How can I without this farm?*

It was possible in the coming months, after they had houses fit to live in, one of the other families might be able to offer him a place to stay. He could return to making furniture, though it would take time to establish the business, and he'd have to discover what he needed to do to open a woodworking shop in New York. Selling many of his tools in order to raise money for the farm had seemed like a *gut* choice before he found the situation was far more complicated than he'd imagined.

He did a quick inventory in his mind. He had enough tools to do simple projects. Eventually, he could buy new tools to make furniture, which would boost his profits.

But could he set aside his dream of farming? And how could he ask Mercy to put aside hers so he could have the future he wanted along Harmony Creek? He was no closer to the answer than he'd been the moment he saw her in the house.

No, he was further away because his attraction to her was sure to complicate the situation unless he was careful.

Very, very, very careful.

Chapter Five

Mercy made certain the ladder was secure against the wall before she tore off the final pieces of hideous wallpaper after lunch later that week. She was glad to toss aside the tea rose pattern and watch it flit onto the pile of scraps she'd made. If she'd had to look at the ugly wallpaper much longer, she would have had nightmares about the disgusting pink roses for a full week.

She laughed as she climbed off the ladder. Once she swept up the strips, she'd never have to see it again.

Pausing as she stepped onto the smooth wood floors, she imagined how the walls would look with a fresh coat of paint. The dark woodwork would complement it. With the variety of oak furniture in the room and forest green tiles edging the fireplace opening, the room would look inviting. She wasn't sure why her grandfather hadn't changed it years ago.

Her feeling of accomplishment faded. Was it silly to do all this work? If the farm wasn't going to be hers, she was wasting her time redoing the house to make it a home for her and Sunni.

She wasn't going to sit around and wait to hear from Dad. If they agreed to let her somehow buy the farm, she'd regret the time lost. She'd already sent a copy of the approval she'd gotten as a foster parent before Sunni was placed with her as well as other forms to county and state offices to begin the approval process for turning the farm into a summer camp for underprivileged city children.

Though it was difficult to think about warm weather when it was snowing—again!—and drifts were rising over the bottom of the porch railing. It was getting so deep Sunni didn't want to go outside. And it was cold! Even with a full tank of fuel oil, the house couldn't shake its chill. No wonder Sunni had made a tent out of blankets in the dining room to give herself a warm cocoon where she could read and color.

Chafing her cold hands, Mercy decided to do something to keep her warm, too. Not sweeping up the damp wallpaper strips. She'd turn her attention to finding the will Grandpa Rudy must have left somewhere in the house.

Two hours later she was running out of places to look on the first floor. She'd gone through the stacks of papers, mail and unread newspapers on her grandfather's desk. She'd checked every cubbyhole and drawer, including the "secret" one he'd shown her when she turned thirteen. He kept nothing in it more secret than his stash of root beer candies.

She resisted stopping to read the papers her grandfather had kept. Later...

Going to the back stairs she preferred rather than the grander front staircase, Mercy went up. The floors over the kitchen were sturdier than at the other end of the house.

Where should she begin? Where would Grandpa Rudy have put such an important document?

Mercy gnawed on her lower lip as she looked along the upper hallway. He'd told her so often that he'd made a will. Or that he was going to. If he had, wouldn't he have kept a copy somewhere in the house?

Both attorneys in nearby Salem had told her that they hadn't helped him draft a will. Why would Grandpa Rudy have been so specific about leaving her instructions on what to do after his death if he hadn't left a will somewhere? Maybe he hadn't gotten around to putting his thoughts on paper.

No, she didn't want to believe that.

Had Grandpa Rudy taken his business elsewhere? He liked to travel throughout the county as well as in the nearby hills of Vermont. His old truck had a half million miles on the odometer, proof he had friends far and wide throughout the area. Should she contact other law offices in the area?

The idea gave her a headache, because it probably would be a waste of time. Not that she didn't have time to waste. Talking to her parents last night had been as discouraging as the search for the will. Her father's siblings disagreed about what to do with the farm.

"There's no hurry," Dad had said. "Let them take the time they need to consider everything. Rushing them will annoy everyone, and making such an important decision hastily is sure to give us a reason to be sorry later."

Mercy wasn't sure if her parents were among the ones who would be irked if she pressed for an answer. She'd gently reminded them how vital it was to start the licens-

ing procedures for the farm before she could open it to children. When her mother had expressed surprise, saying she thought Mercy's foster care license would suffice, Mercy bit back her irritation. Several times before she'd left, she'd outlined for her parents what she needed to do in preparation to make Come Along Farm possible.

"I keep my important papers in my room," Mercy said aloud, smothered by the silence. "Maybe Grandpa Rudy did, too."

Pushing on the door she hadn't opened since the funeral, she started to step into her grandfather's room, then froze in the doorway. Everything about the room was a reminder of him. At the foot of the bed was the bright red-and-green afghan he'd made when he decided learning to crochet would keep his mind sharp. Two more afghans, one black-and-white and the other a gaudy yellow, were draped over an upholstered chair whose springs were gone. The seat dropped to the floor.

A low, long dresser between the room's two windows was covered with photographs. When she'd first come to the farm, the pictures had been on a table downstairs. She'd pestered Grandpa Rudy to identify each person and tell her how they were related to her until on one visit, she discovered he'd moved them upstairs. Though he'd never complained, she guessed he'd gotten tired of sharing the same stories over and over.

She stepped back. She couldn't go in and touch his things. Not yet. Not when the pain of losing him was so fresh.

Tomorrow, she promised herself. Tomorrow she would come back if she hadn't found a will in the

house. In the meantime she could look in the other rooms where the floors were solid. Perhaps up in the attic, though she shuddered at the idea of the spiderwebs in the stairwell.

"Knock, knock," came a shout from the first floor.

Even with the voice distorted by the narrow staircase, she couldn't mistake it for another or ignore how her heart began to beat a bit faster.

Jeremiah!

Since the breakfast they'd shared the day the heat went out, she'd seen him at a distance and waved when he noticed her outside. He hadn't come to the house, though she'd heard the sound of hammering, and she guessed he was doing work on the tenant house.

Hurrying down the stairs, Mercy caught sight of Sunni slipping into the kitchen. Jeremiah either hadn't noticed her or was pretending he hadn't.

Jeremiah had taken off his black felt hat, leaving his reddish-brown hair tousled. Her fingers tingled at the thought of brushing those strands into place.

He turned to her, and her breath caught. The cold wind had burnished his face, emphasizing the strong planes that realigned when he gave her a cautious smile.

Regret slashed her. In other circumstances she and Jeremiah might have become friends, but the future of the farm remained a chasm between them. She had no idea how to cross it.

And is being friends all you aspire to become with him?

She paid no attention to the soft voice from deep within her. Instantly, she wondered if doing that was a mistake,

because she hadn't heeded what it whispered when she was seeing Graham. Maybe if she'd listened then...

Jeremiah spoke, freeing her from her uneasy thoughts. "I wanted to let you know, Mercy, I've got some cattle being delivered in a couple of days."

"Cows? Here? Now?"

His face became grave. "You don't have to remind me, Mercy, how foolish I was to make these plans before the farm was officially mine. If your family decides not to sell to me, I'll have the animals removed and sold. I wanted you to know so you weren't surprised when the livestock truck backs up the drive."

"Thank you. I appreciate you letting me know." She hated how they spoke as polite strangers who intended to remain that.

"I didn't want you to think I was going behind your back."

"That never crossed my mind," she said, bowled over by his words. She'd met very few Amish people, but the ones she'd met lived a life of faith and truth.

"*Gut.*" His smile returned. "We've got to stop thinking the other one believes we have ulterior motives for everything we do or say."

"How do we do that?"

"By accepting whatever happens with the farm is God's will."

Mercy couldn't return his easy grin. God's will? Had it been God's will that her first placement had been disrupted by jealousy? Why would God allow her to fall for Graham so he could make her feel as if she was a second choice?

"Are you okay?" Jeremiah asked, his ruddy brows lowering.

"Fine. Or as fine as I can be, under the circumstances." That was the truth, and she wasn't going to spill why she couldn't accept God's will as easily as Jeremiah seemed to.

He scanned her face, puzzled and looking for answers. She wasn't going to share the details of her time in foster care when it'd seemed as if God had abandoned her. She'd told Graham about that, and he'd been shocked at first. Later, he'd acted as if her failed adoption was somehow all her fault.

Only much later had she realized he was repeating exactly what his mother had said. The woman had always been quick to point out what she saw as Mercy's shortcomings. Everything that went wrong, even rain on a day when they'd planned to go to an outdoor concert, was, in his mother's eyes, Mercy's fault. It made no sense, but Mercy would have endured it if Graham had—just once—stood up for her.

He hadn't.

Not once. He quickly agreed with Mrs. Rapp, no matter how ridiculous the older woman's opinions were.

If Graham had been willing to get out from under his mother's thumb, Mercy might not have rushed to Harmony Creek before she realized Grandpa Rudy had put the farm up for sale.

Her best friend, Erika, had warned Mercy to consider Graham's proposal very, very carefully before agreeing. "If it's a choice between what his mother wants

and what you want," Erika had told her more than once, "you're going to lose every time."

"But I love him," Mercy had argued, "and he loves me."

"I'm sure you're right, but he'll always side with his mother. Be careful."

She hadn't been. She'd given her heart totally, believing if she loved Graham enough, he'd change.

He hadn't. When the tough decision had to be made of where they'd live, he'd listened to Mrs. Rapp instead of doing what was best for his future wife and stepdaughter. His assumption Mercy was wrong for not understanding his mother's needs were most important hammered the final nail in their relationship's coffin, killing hopes she'd had of a future with him.

He hadn't come to say goodbye after she'd left a message on his phone that she and Sunni were moving to Harmony Creek. He'd never returned her call, making her feel like a fool.

One thing she knew for certain. She wasn't going to be a fool for a man ever again, no matter how handsome or nice he was.

Jeremiah couldn't help being curious what Mercy was thinking. Her face was clouded with strong emotions, which he hoped had nothing to do with the arrival of the cows he'd planned to be the beginning of the farm's dairy herd. Every instinct urged him to ask her how he could help. Even more, he yearned to pull her into his arms and offer her comfort for whatever was hurting her.

He couldn't do either.

Not letting the frustrated sigh sift past his lips, he waited for Mercy to say something.

When she did, he wasn't surprised it was a lame excuse to end their conversation. His frown returned when she mentioned going into Salem to pick up groceries.

"The roads aren't plowed yet," he said.

"Oh."

Her face was so dejected he hurried to say, "You could take the sleigh."

"Sleigh?"

He nodded. "There's one in the big barn. It's half-hidden under a blanket, but other than being covered with dust, it looks in *gut* condition. The runners may have some rust. If they do, I can sand it off, and you'll be on your way as soon as we hook up Hero to the sleigh."

"Your horse's name is Hero? Isn't that an odd name for an Amish horse?"

"It's the name he had when I bought him, and he's been my hero more than once when he got me home during a storm." He grinned. "He's very even-tempered, so you shouldn't have any problem with him."

She backed away slowly. "Thanks, but I'll make up something out of whatever is in the kitchen."

He was baffled again, but comprehension burst through him like a shooting star on a summer evening. "You don't know how to drive a horse, ain't so?"

"I never have." She glanced out the window toward where her car sat beneath deep snow. "I've been able to depend on my car to get me where I need to go."

"But you want to live on a farm with horses."

"For the children to ride."

Spying her daughter, who was peeking through the kitchen doorway, clearly eavesdropping, he acted as if he hadn't seen the *kind*. He didn't want to send her scurrying away again. "Wouldn't those *kinder* enjoy rides in a wagon, too?"

She folded her arms but laughed. "Jeremiah Stoltzfus, has anyone ever told you that once you get an idea in your head you hold on to it like a snapping turtle?"

"I'd like to think I have more sense than a turtle that won't let go even to eat." He hooked a thumb toward the door. "Might as well get started with your lessons."

"Not now."

"Why not? I've got the time, and today isn't going to be the only day you'll need the sleigh before the snow melts."

Again, she paused. Was she looking for an excuse he'd have to accept?

He realized how much he'd misconstrued her silence when she said, "I can't go outside to take driving lessons and leave Sunni alone in the house."

"Bring her along. I'll teach her, too."

"She's only seven years old."

With a laugh, he said, "I was younger than she is the first time the reins were placed in my hands." He looked straight at Sunni. "Do you want to try?" He cut his eyes to Mercy. "What do you say?"

He wasn't sure if he or Mercy was more shocked when Sunni stepped into the room and asked, "Can we, Mommy?"

Chapter Six

Mercy wanted to say no to driving lessons, but how could she when Sunni was opening up to Jeremiah for the first time? Though he might not be in their lives for long, it was good to see her daughter begin to trust another man.

But was Mercy ready to trust another man?

You're agreeing to learning to drive a sleigh, not accepting an offer to go on a date with him. That little voice was becoming more annoying, but it also was correct. *He's trying to make you less dependent on him during these storms.*

She was shocked the thought irritated her more. Poor Jeremiah! It seemed she could find an ulterior motive in whatever he did. Not his ulterior motive, but hers.

"Mommy, can we drive the sleigh?" asked Sunni, warning Mercy she'd been lost in her self-recriminating thoughts too long.

"All right." She didn't get a chance to add more before her daughter let out a cheer and began singing "Jingle Bells."

Jeremiah was grinning as broadly. "Let me get Hero hooked up to the sleigh. It may take fifteen minutes or more because I need to get the sleigh out of the barn."

"It'll give me time to make up a thermos of hot cocoa and get us bundled up," she said, excitement bursting through her. Hadn't she come to the farm to try new things? Learning to drive the sleigh would be a great place to start.

"Jingle bells, jingle bells, jingle all the way," sang Sunni at the top of her lungs as she spun about like a flat-footed ballerina.

With a wink, Jeremiah put on his hat and left. He called back that he'd pull the sleigh up to the door.

Mercy worked around her jubilant daughter and delighted in Sunni's joy. She hadn't seen her daughter so elated since before Grandpa Rudy's funeral. And Mercy was happy, too. The idea of speeding over the snow in a sleigh was exciting.

She was about to wrap a scarf around Sunni's neck when her daughter pulled away and ran to the door.

Mercy wasn't surprised to see the sleigh looked as if it'd been hit by an avalanche and buried under boulders. The paint was scraped off the dented side, but the runners were straight, and Jeremiah's horse was pulling it without too much effort.

"Ready?" she asked Sunni as she reached for her own scarf and the thermos and trio of cups.

Sunni threw open the door, then halted. "Where are the jingle bells?"

"All I could find," Jeremiah said, "was this harness."

Sunni whirled. "But, Mommy, the song is 'Jingle Bells.' We have to have jingle bells."

Before Mercy could reply, the little girl whirled and ran up the stairs at a dangerous speed for a child wearing two leg braces.

Mercy steeled herself, praying she wouldn't hear the dreadful thump that meant Sunni had fallen on the steps.

"Are you okay?" asked Jeremiah from right behind her.

She turned to discover he'd come up on the porch. "She shouldn't go so fast up the stairs."

"Words every *mamm* has said for as long as there have been stairs. We all take a few tumbles in life and are not much the worse for it, ain't so?"

"Certainly." She appreciated how he acted as if Sunni was like every other child.

"Why does she wear those braces…if you don't mind me asking?"

"I don't." She smiled. "But I don't know. We've gotten as many different opinions as we've had doctors for her. Most recently her pediatric orthopedist said we should worry less about what caused the weakness in her legs and concentrate on helping her walk better."

"And run."

Her smile broadened. "She's learned that well."

When Sunni came down the stairs at the same pace she'd gone up, both Jeremiah and Mercy jumped forward as the little girl stumbled three steps from the bottom. Between them, they caught her and set her on her feet.

"I know, I know," Sunni said before anyone could speak. "I need to go more slowly and use my crutches, but we have jingle bells." As she began singing the song again, she held up her right hand and shook it.

Jeremiah's eyes grew wide at the sound of bells jangling.

Taking the toy from Sunni, Mercy held it out to him. It was a wooden half circle into which was set a half dozen tiny metal bells.

"What is it?" he asked beneath the little girl's enthusiastic singing.

Mercy answered as softly, "A toy. Kids use them to make music in school. We got it as a therapy tool for Sunni last year. It helped strengthen her grip." Showing him how fingers wrapped around the wooden handle while the bells were shaken, she smiled. "I didn't realize she still had it."

Jeremiah raised his voice to include the little girl. "We've got our jingle bells and our cocoa, so let's go."

Mercy watched as he went outside. Sunni followed, and he swung her up onto the sleigh's bench. He sat beside her. They looked back in a silent urging for Mercy to hurry up.

She did and laughed as she hadn't in longer than she could remember when Jeremiah reached to assist her into the battered sleigh. At his touch, even through his thick gloves and hers, the day suddenly had seemed warmer.

When she sat beside him, he unlashed the reins from the dash and showed her how to hold them. He told her to loop the reins up between her pinkie and the next finger, grip them in her fist and let them go out between her thumb and first finger.

"That gives you the most control," he said, adjusting her hands slightly. "Hero is well trained, so call his name, and he'll go."

"And to stop him?"

"A simple 'whoa.' You don't have to tug on the reins. He'll stop right away." Again, he aligned her fingers. "There you go. Whenever you're ready."

She made the mistake of looking at him to ask another question. His face was so near to hers their misted breaths mingled in the cold air. As her gaze locked with his lustrous blue eyes, she knew she should look away before he got the wrong idea.

Or the right one.

Even that thought couldn't convince her eyes to turn from his handsome face. As close as they sat, she could see the faint shadow of whiskers along his jaw. Her fingers tingled, teasing her to tear off her gloves and stroke that firm line. She caught a motion from the corner of her eye. His hand was rising to cup her cheek. She leaned toward it, eager to feel him against her.

"Jingle bells! Jingle bells!" sang Sunni abruptly.

The cheerful song brought Mercy to her senses. Jeremiah, too, she guessed, because he quickly slanted away from her and urged her to give the command to go.

She did, and the horse moved at a walk toward the road. Her thoughts sped far faster as she pondered what would have happened if Sunni's innocent singing hadn't intruded. Trying to convince herself it was better she didn't know, she wondered when she'd started being dishonest with herself.

"Hold that board right there," Jeremiah urged Sunni, who kept a suspicious eye on the hammer and nail he was positioning. It was the first board for the roof of a

chicken coop. After finishing his barn chores, including milking and feeding the calves delivered earlier in the week, he'd wanted time outdoors.

He smiled at Sunni. The little girl didn't trust him completely, but she didn't scurry in the opposite direction when he approached as she had before they drove the sleigh along the twisting creek that slept beneath a sheet of ice. When, during her midmorning break from her schoolwork, she'd come to watch him building the chicken coop, a simple box with a door and shelves for the hens to lay on, he'd pretended as if nothing significant had happened. Maybe if he acted as if she'd sought him out right from the beginning, he wouldn't send her fleeing again. He kept up a steady narration of everything he did, and Sunni had inched closer and closer.

Then she began asking questions, barely giving him time to answer before she fired another one—or two—at him. She asked about the coop and the chickens that would live inside. She wanted to know what color he planned to paint it and what he intended to name the chickens. He answered questions about what the chickens would eat and where they would sleep and when the rooster would crow.

Asking her to balance the board might threaten the status quo, but Jeremiah kept reminding himself with God's help, anything was possible. Even persuading a *kind* he didn't mean her ill will. He was curious if Sunni's skittishness was for the same reason as Mercy's.

What do you know about women? he asked himself. He'd believed Emmarita when she said she was coming back. He hadn't guessed she was seeing her *Englischer*

at the same time Jeremiah was escorting her home from youth events. She'd jumped the fence, and unlike two of his brothers' wives who had done the same, she hadn't returned…though he'd waited several months to make sure. When he heard she'd married her *Englischer*, he knew he needed to put the past behind him. He listened to the hopes of having a farm of his own, the hopes God had put inside him. It was easier to heed that portion of his heart when he closed off the part filled with pain at Emmarita's betrayal.

Focusing on his work, Jeremiah made sure Sunni's fingers weren't close to where he was hammering. She'd become silent, but the fact she was standing there seemed like a precious victory.

"Mommy!" Sunni suddenly shouted and released the plank.

Jeremiah grasped the board to keep it from swinging out and striking the *kind*. His heart hitched, and he knew he couldn't blame his heart's reaction totally on fright for the little girl.

His gaze riveted on Mercy as she walked toward them. Her cheeks were burnished by the cold to the same shade as her lips, which appeared delightfully kissable. The image of his hands framing her face while he sampled her mouth was so real he lowered his eyes and swung the hammer, barely missing the nail and his thumb in his work glove. He set down the hammer, knowing, when he was that distracted, he might not miss next time.

"What are you making?" Mercy's tone hinted that she hadn't noticed how distracted he was by her.

He wasn't sure if that was *gut* or annoying.

"It's a chicken choop," Sunni answered.

"A chicken *coop*," he corrected with a smile.

"But…" Mercy looked hastily away, but not fast enough because he saw her cheeks redden more.

He wasn't going to pretend not to understand. She'd agreed on the day he taught her to drive not to look for secret intentions behind every word or deed. He wished she'd trust him.

Though he wanted to ask why she always painted him with such negative intentions, he said, "Mercy, didn't your *daed* tell you it may be several weeks before he gets an answer from his siblings?"

"He did."

"But you are working to fix up the main house. Sunni was telling me that you're painting the living room." He saw *mamm* and daughter exchange a glance, but couldn't guess what it meant. He hoped nothing. "Like you, I don't want to wait until everything is decided. If I do and they sell me the farm, I must not be so far behind on fixing up the place I can't get a decent crop in the fields or have a place to put it when it's harvested."

"I know." She raised her eyes to meet his, and he realized he'd misjudged her reaction. She wasn't angry. She was frustrated her family hadn't made their decision. "I'm sorry this is dragging on."

Stepping around the coop so it wasn't between them, he put his hands on Mercy's shoulders. "It's not your fault."

"Thanks for saying that, but every time the phone rings, I hope it's my father with news." She grimaced.

"I'm tempted to silence it and let the answering machine get the calls. That way, I'd only have to check once a day."

"Why don't you?"

Her eyes brightened. "I think I will. I'm tired of being on a ladder and having to rush down to answer it. In case it's Dad." A smile played at the corners of her mouth. "I almost tipped over the paint can yesterday. If I had, Sunni and I would be green now."

"It wouldn't be a bad color on you two," he replied in mock seriousness. "And we could use a bit more green with this snow."

The little girl giggled, and Jeremiah let his lips tilt up in a grin.

"I'll leave that to the leaves," Mercy said.

Groaning at her pun, he felt the tension dissolve around them. They might have different goals for the farm, but they were stuck in limbo together while her family debated.

"Why don't we keep doing what we've been doing?" he asked. "Any fixes we do will benefit whoever gets the farm."

"That makes sense."

"And we don't have to walk around on eggshells."

"Eggshells?" asked Sunni, looking around as if she expected to see a pile waiting to be picked up. "Where are they?"

Again, he and Mercy chuckled, and Sunni joined in.

Jeremiah rested one hand on the top of the coop. "Whether you or I or someone else ends up with the farm, me building a simple chicken coop won't make

any difference. It seems strange to live on a farm without chickens."

"You can't be thinking of putting them out here now," Mercy said, wrapping her arms around herself as a frigid gust rocked the trees beyond the barn.

He shook his head. "Ordering chicks was another thing I did before I left Paradise Springs. They'll be shipped once the weather warms up. By fall, they should be providing eggs." He gave her a wry grin. "Sorry they won't be laying in time for Easter."

"Don't worry," Mercy said. "We'll have eggs to dye for Easter."

Sunni looked relieved, but grimaced when Mercy reminded her schoolwork waited in the house.

As her daughter went inside, Mercy asked, "Do Amish kids dye eggs for Easter?"

"Some do. My *mamm* hid plastic eggs filled with jelly beans for us to find."

"I assume you have church services on Easter."

"*Ja*. Good Friday is a fast day until noon, so we can spend the morning in prayer. On Easter, we rejoice together."

"Mennonites consider it a time to be with family, and we have services on Friday and Sunday." She patted her hands together and glanced toward the house. "I should make sure Sunni is doing her schoolwork."

Gut sense told him to let her go, but he didn't want to let the moment end. "You've got a lot of questions about Amish folks."

"If I stay here, I'm going to have Amish neighbors."

He almost said if she ended up with the farm, the

settlement could be in jeopardy. He needed to stay and help it grow. There wasn't any reason to repeat what had been said already. They knew what was at stake, so why belabor it?

"Why don't you come with me to a service?" he asked. "This Sunday is a church Sunday. I think you'll get plenty of answers to your questions there."

"I didn't know your services were open to outsiders."

"They are, but few non-Amish are willing to sit on hard, backless benches for three hours to listen to sermons in High German."

"I don't understand that language."

"Visitors have someone to translate for them. I think you'd find it interesting, Mercy." *Please, God, let her say* ja. He didn't want to consider why it was suddenly so important to him that she agree, but it was.

"Thank you, Jeremiah. We'll come." Her smile banished the cold around him…and inside him.

When she walked away, he was glad she hadn't expected him to say something else. He wasn't sure what he would have said, but he was certain anything he blurted out would reveal the farm was no longer the main reason he was glad he'd come to Harmony Creek.

She was.

Chapter Seven

Jeremiah whistled one of his favorite hymns as he put the finishing touches on the chicken coop. He laughed at the sign tacked over the door.

Welkoom Hoom.

Sunni had brought it out to him right after breakfast. She'd proudly announced she'd painted it for his Amish chickens so they'd feel right at home in the coop.

It had taken every bit of restraint to keep from grinning. Not only were the words different from any he knew in *Englisch* or *Deitsch*, the everyday language of the Amish, but most of the letters had drips of green paint beneath them. He wondered if Mercy knew what her daughter had been doing.

He knew the little girl was fascinated with the idea of chickens and gathering eggs, because she'd talked of nothing else while he put the sign in place. As much as he wanted the farm to become a part of the new Amish community, he hated the idea of Sunni not having her chance to help with the new chicks.

With each passing day, the situation was becoming more of a potential disaster, no matter which one of them ended up with the farm. Did Mercy's *onkels* and *aentis* and *daed* realize that? He doubted it. Would it do any *gut* to ask Mercy to discuss it with them?

But did he want them to announce their decision if it cost him the farm?

He no longer knew.

You know, God, he prayed, *what is to come and why. Help us to walk the path You have prepared for us, even if our hearts are broken.*

He flinched. No matter what choice the Bambergers made, his heart was going to be hurt because if he took possession of the farm, Mercy's heart—and Sunni's— would be shattered. For the first time he began to wonder if he should walk away. He could have Kitty find him another place. It might take too much time and risk the success of the settlement, but how could he stand by and watch Mercy hurt?

Help me, God, to trust You have a way to resolve the unresolvable.

When Mercy heard a knock at the door that afternoon, she made sure her kerchief was in place before she answered it. She didn't want to meet one of her neighbors for the first time with her head not properly covered, because she knew Amish women always wore what they called prayer *kapps* or a kerchief like hers. Dust and spiderwebs didn't count as a proper covering, though she guessed there were plenty on the off-white kerchief.

A pulse of excitement caught her off guard as she wondered if Jeremiah stood on the other side of the door. What was she thinking? He'd been very kind to teach her to drive the sleigh so she could get to the village after a snowfall.

But he wanted her grandfather's farm, and if the family's decision went against her, he would do everything he could to buy it. Nothing had changed.

No, that wasn't true.

A few things had changed. She couldn't see Jeremiah as a rival trying to ruin her plans. Instead, her heart seemed to glow whenever he was around.

Throwing open the door, she was unprepared for the surge of disappointment when she realized it wasn't Jeremiah. She'd been silly to think he'd come to the front door and knock. He always walked in.

A woman, whose face was half-hidden by a garish purple and yellow crocheted scarf covering her mouth and nose, stood on the porch. From the top of her striped stocking cap to the tip of her boots topped by a ring of fake fur, she looked ready to go sledding on the hills beyond the barn.

The woman pulled aside her scarf to reveal the lower half of her face. "Are you Mercy Bamberger?"

"I am." Mercy motioned for the woman to come in.

Even if the woman was there to try to sell her something she didn't want, Mercy wasn't going to leave her out on the porch in the biting wind.

When the blonde woman set a briefcase on the floor and began to unzip her thick parka, Mercy asked, "What can I do for you?"

"I'm Whitney Albright with Washington County Children's Services." She opened a pocket on the side of the briefcase and pulled out a simple business card.

Mercy took it and glanced at it. The card confirmed what Whitney had said.

"I'd like to talk with you if you've got time," Whitney said.

"Certainly. Let's go into the living room."

Curiosity accompanied Mercy into the room, which was comfortably warm in the afternoon sunshine. She couldn't help being curious about whether Whitney thought of how the glass in the windows rattled whenever a strong gust struck the house. Motioning for the woman to take a seat on the couch, where the cold air seeping around the sills wouldn't reach her, Mercy took a chair facing the sofa.

"I'm sorry to come unannounced," Whitney said as she sat and set her briefcase on her knees. "I did try to call. Several times yesterday. But while I got your answering machine, I didn't want to leave a message before I had a chance to talk to you. When I tried again this morning and got the machine again, I thought maybe I'd drive over and take a chance on catching you at home."

Mercy explained how she'd turned off the phone's ringer so she wasn't interrupted while she was painting. Without giving the other woman a chance to reply, she hurried on. "If this is about my daughter not being signed up to go to public school, I made arrangements to homeschool her for the rest of this year. I plan to have her go to the Son-Rise Charter School next fall."

Whitney held up her hands and shook her head. "This isn't about your daughter, Mercy, though I'll tell you I did stop at the school in Salem to find someone who knew you. They explained to me the arrangements you'd made for Sunni. You know you can get special needs services through the public school system, though she's going to the charter school, I assume."

"Yes, because we had that arrangement with our school district where we lived."

"If anyone tells you differently, call me and I'll talk to them." She smiled, but it was cool and without humor. "Some superintendents look for ways to cut costs. Not that we've had such a problem with the Salem school district, but we like to make sure none crop up."

"I appreciate that." Curious why the woman was visiting, Mercy asked if Whitney would like something hot to drink.

"That would be nice. Coffee or tea or whatever you have."

"I have green tea."

"Perfect."

Rising, Mercy went into the kitchen and put the kettle on. She glanced into the dining room and saw Sunni curled up in a chair, sound asleep. The little girl had had nightmares last night. It was good she could catch up on her sleep today, especially until Mercy discovered why a social worker had come to the house.

Whitney took an appreciative sip of the tea, but waited until Mercy was sitting again before she opened her briefcase and pulled out a laptop. "As I said, I'm not here to speak to you about Sunni. However, I'm here

because of your daughter." The social worker looked abashed as she added, "I guess I should have told you right from the get-go I was forwarded a copy of your files and I've read them."

"I know files are shared among social workers."

"Good." Whitney relaxed a bit as she pushed the button to activate her computer. Raising her head, she wore what Mercy called a social worker's *I hope you can get me out of a jam* face.

The first time she'd seen it was when she was in the system herself. She'd forgotten about it until another social worker spoke to her about taking in Sunni on an emergency placement. Seeing it again whetted her curiosity and her trepidation.

"You are," Whitney said, "in a somewhat unique position of having exactly the experience we need."

Mercy felt her jaw drop. Another child? Here? She thought of all she'd had to do in order to be approved as a foster parent before Sunni was placed with her. There had been more paperwork and home visits and counseling when she applied to adopt her daughter. Enough to kill off a whole forest was what Dad had said with a laugh.

Glancing around the half-painted room that opened onto another where wallpaper was peeling off a wall and the floor sloping enough to send Mercy chasing after a nail when it fell and rolled away, she looked at the social worker. Was this a joke?

"I know this is unexpected," Whitney said, "and it may not be perfect timing, but I rarely find the time is

perfect when a child's placement has been disrupted and we need to find a temporary placement."

"Oh, I'm so sorry to hear about a placement falling apart."

"I know you are."

Mercy wondered exactly how much the social worker knew about her story and Sunni's. How many files had Whitney perused before she came to Harmony Creek? No doubt, there were thick files outlining how she and Sunni had come to be part of the Bamberger family.

At the thought of her family, Mercy stiffened. What was she thinking? She needed to tell Whitney, while she understood the gravity of the situation, now was the worst time for her to consider having another child placed with her family. Even a temporary one. No, most especially a temporary one, because Sunni didn't need to deal with more change.

"I know you're not ready," Whitney said in her calm voice.

Mercy bit back a laugh. "Look around you. Come Along Farm is weeks away from being ready for me to apply for approval."

"But you are a licensed foster parent?"

"I am."

"Parker, a nine-year-old boy, needs a placement." The blonde leaned forward, lowering her computer's top and putting her elbows on it. "He's a unique case because we don't get many failed international adoptions in this county. In fact, he might be the second one in sixty years. Mercy, you know how it is to be an out-

sider in a closed community, and your daughter was born in Korea as Parker was."

"Why does he need a placement?"

"His prospective adoptive parents can't deal with his many severe food allergies. You're raising a special needs child, so I can't imagine a better place for this boy while we look for another adoptive family than with you and Sunni."

Wanting to groan that Whitney was expecting too much of her and her daughter, Mercy said nothing. Instead, she prayed. *Lord, You don't have to tell me this is crazy. I know that, and I also know Your hand brought Whitney here. Come Along Farm is supposed to be a haven for children. How can I turn away the first one You present to me?*

A sensation of calm draped over her as she held out her hand. "Can I see his placement report?"

"It's on the computer." Whitney pressed several keys and then turned it so Mercy could read the report that wasn't so different from the one she'd been given with Sunni's other paperwork. It was from the Korean adoption agency and translated into sometimes confusing English. The information was sparse and included his age, gender, a couple of paragraphs outlining what his Korean caretakers had observed about him, and weight and height.

"His name in Korea was Park Jae-Eun, I see," Mercy said.

"The Kentons changed it to Parker Kenton, wanting to keep part of his Korean name as part of his new name." The social worker smiled sadly. "It'll be easier

for him in the States, I suppose, but his Korean name means talent and mercy."

"Mercy?"

Whitney nodded. "When I was looking for foster families with Korean-born children in the county, I saw your name, which was why I requested your file."

"He has several food allergies," Mercy said after finishing the two-page report from Korea, "but I don't see anything here."

"They apparently weren't discovered until he was here. He had no problem with Korean food, but Americans eat a wider variety of products."

Wondering why Parker's new family hadn't changed their own diets to accommodate the boy, Mercy looked at the list of Parker's allergies. Peanuts and shellfish were the first of nearly a dozen items, but it wouldn't be difficult to work around his allergies.

"Am I wrong," Whitney asked, "to think you make a lot of your meals from scratch? Parker seems to have extra trouble with prepared foods."

The social worker had an uncanny ability to guess what Mercy was thinking, or more likely, Whitney was very good at her job and had prepared herself for questions and concerns Mercy might have.

"I don't make as much from scratch as I normally would, because we don't have anything canned in the cellar." Second thoughts filled her. Sunni needed her during this difficult time, and bringing a second child into their family would curtail the time she had to work on the house. She couldn't reduce the time she spent teaching Sunni, and a nine-year-old would require

homeschooling, too. So much paperwork needed to be filed, and…

"You'll want to see this." Whitney held out a small photo.

Mercy looked at it and knew her protests and logical thinking were useless. The moment she saw the proud expression on the boy's face that announced he didn't need anyone's help, she recognized a kindred spirit. Especially when she noticed how his taut shoulders revealed he was trying to hide his pain of being unwanted from the camera.

Oh, how easily she remembered those feelings! And the photographs taken against an office wall while people looked on with pitying smiles. Mercy had been older than the boy the first time she'd been subjected to the humiliation of knowing she was nobody's child. When *Abuelita* had died, Mercy's sole parent had become the state government, an indifferent guardian at best. She'd been snatched from *Abuelita*'s apartment so quickly she hadn't had time to pack the photo of her parents, her most precious possession, before being bundled up and put in a car with strangers. She'd been told her personal belongings would follow. One box had…but the photo hadn't been in it. Her other box had vanished.

A chance question when she'd asked if she would be going to her Fresh Air family had saved her from what probably would have been a life in the system. A caring social worker—Mercy couldn't remember her name—had contacted the family who'd welcomed her for the previous three summers to their farm in northern New York. But the family's agreement to take her

on a trial basis hadn't been the salvation she'd expected. She hadn't been able to wait to return to the family she'd thought of constantly while she was away from it. But the fun times she'd enjoyed each summer with the two daughters had become intolerable misery when the older daughter had become wildly jealous of Mercy and the attention she'd garnered in the very conservative community.

The placement had fallen apart, and she'd found herself in a car with the social worker who'd brought her north. Returned to the city, she'd been placed with a family who used the stipend from five foster kids to help pay for their own expenses. She'd remained there, virtually ignored, for the longest four months of her life.

Then adults she hadn't known came to the house. She'd realized they were social workers, and they'd given her no warning other than she needed to pack her personal items. The other kids in the house had been told the same. Though none of them had much, they'd delayed as long as they could over the task while they'd spent time speculating about what was about to happen to them. The older children had been resigned to being put with another family in another school district, but Mercy had been terrified.

Her fear had grown when the other children were dropped off to meet other social workers so they could be introduced to their new foster families, but she'd been driven out of the city. Nobody had told her where she was going until they'd left the city behind.

She'd been taken to meet Frieda and Kevin Bamberger, a Mennonite couple whose biological children

were much older than she was. When she'd reached their comfortable home, she hadn't had high hopes. At the time it'd been another change she didn't have any say in.

But she'd been welcomed as if she'd been a part of their family her whole life. A portion of her bedtime prayers every night still included her gratitude for the two people who had stepped up to be her parents.

She had a chance to help a young child who was caught in the same trap. The Bambergers had welcomed her into their home and their hearts, giving her a new name and a new identity, though there was a remnant of Mercedes Ramirez hidden deep within her, and a family as precious to her as the one she'd shared with *Abuelita*.

"All right," Mercy whispered as she stared into the boy's face.

"All right?" repeated Whitney, astonished by Mercy's sudden about-face. "Does that mean you're willing to take Parker on a temporary basis? It could be a month or two before we find him something permanent. In the meantime, the county will provide you with an epinephrine injector in case he goes into anaphylaxis. Instructions for its use are right on the box, and you need to get familiar with them right away so you don't have to stop to read them if he has an allergy attack. Are you ready to deal with that?"

There wasn't a single doubt in her heart, though her head was blaring warnings like a fire siren. "Yes, we'll take him."

Chapter Eight

"Heard anything about what's going to happen with the farm?"

Jeremiah glanced at Caleb, who was helping him set up his woodworking equipment. For now it was a makeshift workshop, but it was in one of the sturdier outbuildings. They'd set up a portable gas generator outside to power the equipment. His neighbor had worked with him, as well, in closing up the holes in the tenant house wall so it no longer snowed indoors. In exchange, Jeremiah intended to make a few pieces for his friend's house. He'd already sketched out a large kitchen table and the benches and chairs to go with it.

"Nothing," Jeremiah said as he shifted a heavy saw a few inches to the left so there was enough space to walk past it. "I guess they're still making up their minds."

"No news is no news, ain't so?"

He grinned at his friend, who was stretched out beneath a table saw. "That's not exactly how I've heard it."

"But it's true. No news means nothing's been decided."

"You're right." Jeremiah leaned against a stack of planks as his gaze swept the workshop as if he'd entered it for the first time. He'd found the weathered boards in a small barn and brought them to his workshop. If he needed one for a project while Mercy's family discussed the farm, he'd check with her. Using Rudy's bulk tank in the barn to hold milk was one thing, but it'd be completely different to take the valuable wood without permission.

Wiping his hands on a stained cloth, Jeremiah looked out the dusty window beside him. His brows lowered at a surprising sight. He hadn't heard the late-model silver car pull into the driveway. Did Mercy have a friend visiting?

As if he'd asked the question aloud, Caleb paused in examining the underside of a piece of equipment he'd been oiling and came slowly to his feet. "What's so interesting?"

"I didn't know we had company."

Neither man spoke as a blonde *Englisch* woman came out of the house and got into the car. There was a jaunty bounce in her step.

"She sure looks happy," Caleb said. "That bolt is not turning as smoothly as it should. Want to check it?"

"Sure." Jeremiah didn't move from beside the window. "Do you know her?"

Caleb stepped closer to the window and peered out. The car was close enough so he could get a *gut* view of the woman's face before she turned to look over her shoulder while she backed the car out.

"I've never seen her before," Caleb said. "I've met

some of the *Englisch* farmers in the area, but not too many of the women. My sister said the *Englisch* women are friendly when she's gone to the store." He paused for a single heartbeat. "You seem very interested, Jeremiah. But please don't go jumping the fence after some *Englischer.* We need you to help build our settlement. We're six families since the Bowmans moved in yesterday."

Jeremiah nodded and assured Caleb that he was committed to the Harmony Creek settlement. He waited for the pain those words about jumping the fence always created. It came, but not as before. The memory of Emmarita's leaving without saying goodbye was no longer agonizing. However, Caleb's words were a reminder of what Jeremiah had tried to ignore.

Mercy was Mennonite. Getting more involved with her and her daughter would be silly. He had to ignore how his heart beat faster whenever he thought of Mercy's black hair and eyes the color of freshly overturned earth.

Had his thoughts shown on his face? Or had he revealed the truth in other ways?

Caleb gave him a sympathetic glance. "Staying separate from the world is tougher some times than others, ain't so?"

Jeremiah must have given his friend an answer, but once it'd left his lips, he couldn't recall what it was. That Caleb gave him a companionable slap on the shoulder when he left—exactly as one of Jeremiah's brothers would have—was the proof that he'd soothed his friend's concerns.

Lingering in his shop, Jeremiah knew Caleb was

worried about Jeremiah falling for a woman who should be off-limits to him. His neighbor also held the weight of the settlement's success on his broad shoulders. Adding more concern to Caleb's already overflowing plate was one of the last things Jeremiah wanted to do.

Either he or Mercy was going to be leaving the farm. Every way he looked at it, there was no future beyond friendship for them. He needed to keep that in mind.

Always.

Jeremiah's resolve lasted exactly as long as it took him to walk over to the main house.

Mercy turned from the stove as he came in. The aroma of chocolate swept through the kitchen. It wasn't as enticing as Mercy, who had a dab of flour on one cheek and a line of chocolate beneath her other eye.

Don't think of her as enticing, he warned himself, but not being honest with himself was foolish.

"I assume the other person looks worse," he said with a wink at Sunni, whose dark braid was dusted with flour.

"What?" asked Mercy.

"You look as if someone gave you a black eye."

She glanced in the mirror over the sink where Rudy must have shaved. When she gasped and reached for a washcloth to clean her face, he and Sunni laughed. Sunni giggled harder when Mercy washed the flour out of her braid.

"Call me when the cake's ready to frost," Sunni said once the last of the white was out of her hair.

"I will. You know I depend of my best spatula cleaner." Mercy bent to kiss the top of her daughter's head.

Jeremiah couldn't keep from imagining how those lips would feel against him. He composed his expression when Sunni left the room and Mercy faced him.

Her easy smile disappeared. "I'm glad you came over, Jeremiah. I need to talk to you about something important, so you're not surprised."

"You sound like I did when I told you the cows were being delivered. Are you having something delivered, too?"

His attempt at levity fell flat because she nodded.

"Did you see the car in the yard earlier?" she asked as she motioned for him to sit at the table.

"*Ja.* I assumed you had a friend visiting."

"Not a friend. Not yet anyhow. The woman who came here is Whitney Albright, and she's a social worker with the county."

"Oh." He wasn't sure what else to say. Had Whitney come for something to do with Sunni? But wasn't the little girl's adoption final? There shouldn't be a reason for a social worker to come to the house, unless...

Was Mercy already going ahead with her plans to get approval for Come Along Farm? Had her *daed* given her some hint to what his siblings had agreed to? She would have told him, wouldn't she?

"Whitney wanted to ask if I'd be willing to take in another child temporarily," Mercy said in not much more than a whisper.

"Are you going to?" He tried to ignore the cascade of relief as he realized, for now, she didn't know more about the future of the farm than he did.

No ulterior motives, he chided himself. She'd con-

curred, and he hadn't seen a sign of her reneging. He was judging her unfairly.

She wiped her hands on a towel. "As long as I've got room, I'll never turn away a child who needs a home."

When he chuckled, she frowned and asked what was so funny.

"You stating the obvious," he replied. "You want Rudy's farm so you can fill it with *kinder* every summer. It's not a big step to imagining you trying to fill this whole house with youngsters year-round."

"Not a whole houseful. Just one little nine-year-old boy who needs a home because his placement failed."

"His what failed?"

"Failed placement is a term social workers use for when a child is placed in a home with either foster parents or prospective adoptive parents and then the child needs to be removed."

"And saying it failed means the parents don't want the *kind* any longer?" He shook his head in disgust. "What were they thinking? A kid isn't something to return to the store because it's not a great fit."

Pulling out a chair, she sat facing him. "I agree, but sometimes it's for the best. If the match isn't a good one, it can be worse on the youngster than being moved somewhere else." She slid a photo toward him. "This is the boy."

Jeremiah didn't want to look. Getting more caught up in her life and her plans would complicate their already complicated situation. As he saw the determination in her eyes, he was curious why one boy she'd never met was so important to her.

He reached for the photo.

* * *

Breathe!

Such a simple order shouldn't be difficult to follow, but Mercy found it hard to draw in a breath and release it as she waited for Jeremiah's reaction to Parker's picture.

When Jeremiah smiled, she relaxed, astonished how taut her shoulders had become.

"He looks like a normal nine-year-old." Jeremiah tapped the photo. "You can tell he doesn't want to sit still for someone to snap his picture. But why did Whitney choose you? Don't take this the wrong way, but I would have thought the state would wait until a decision is made about the farm."

Standing, she got a cloth to clean off the table. "I'm a licensed foster parent, and I've taken in other children on an emergency basis until a permanent foster home could be found."

"There must be other foster families in the area."

"There are, but Whitney liked the idea of Parker being with a family who already has an Asian child."

"Parker? That's his name?"

"Yes."

"It sounds very grown-up for a kid."

"I know. It's the name his adoptive parents gave him, but it won't be legally his name until he's adopted. Until then, he's legally Park Jae-Eun."

"That's a mouthful."

"And Jeremiah isn't?"

He smiled. "I never said it wasn't."

"I wanted to let you know there's going to be another child in the house," she said.

"Why would you take on the responsibility of another *kind* when everything about the farm is up in the air?"

"Because I know how painful a failed adoption is for a youngster."

"Sunni had a failed adoption?"

"Yes. They happen more often than you'd expect." She drew in a deep breath and released it through tight lips. "The couple who were going to adopt Sunni didn't want a daughter who depends on braces."

He flinched.

"Why are you startled?" she asked.

"Amish families consider a *kind* with physical or mental challenges a gift from God who will bring a very special love to everyone."

"Do you give them physical therapy and such?"

"Of course. We may not have doctors among us, but we appreciate and admire the work they do to keep us healthy." When Jeremiah came to his feet, he said, "Be careful, Mercy. I admire your intentions, but..."

He didn't add more as he left the house.

She was not sure what he could have said. He was right. She needed to be careful with her heart. With the boy and with Jeremiah, who could break it easily.

Chapter Nine

On Sunday morning Jeremiah had Hero hitched to the buggy and ready to go a little before eight. They were going only a quarter of a mile, but a cold wind would make walking difficult. He hadn't hurried because they had the leisure of starting out later than he was accustomed to in Pennsylvania.

He shivered, pulling his coat's collar up to cover his nape. Slapping his hands together for what little warmth he could find, he was pleased when the door opened and Mercy and Sunni came out.

He wasn't surprised when Mercy picked up her daughter and half ran toward the buggy. Both were hidden beneath heavy coats, hats, mittens and scarves.

With a nodded greeting because his teeth were chattering too hard to speak, he handed Sunni and Mercy into the buggy. He jumped in on the passenger side, pushing Sunni over with a laugh toward Mercy, who had to slide into the driver's position.

"I thought you'd want to drive." He held the reins out to her.

When she didn't hesitate to take them, he motioned for her to turn the buggy with care in the shoveled area of the yard. He trusted Hero to know what to do, even if Mercy wasn't sure.

"My toes are getting warm!" Sunni stared at a metal box on the buggy's floor.

"That small heater probably won't warm much more than your toes," he said. "The bishop permits their use because of the cold, cold weather in northern New York."

"The bishop is the one who makes the rules?" Mercy looked along the twisting road, then called to Hero to go.

"The *Leit* will meet to discuss and create the *Ordnung* for our district, or we will once we have enough families to be a true district. We need about a dozen."

"What's that?" Sunni asked.

"*Leit* means our people." Jeremiah was pleased the little girl was curious about Amish ways, too. "The *Ordnung* are the unwritten rules we live by. They deal with everything from how we wear our clothes to what equipment we can use. Each item is discussed, prayed about and voted on. Our bishop helps us stick to it by defining certain aspects of life that haven't been specifically discussed. Like using small heaters in our buggies. Eventually, we'll meet to decide."

"I vote for having them," Mercy said with a laugh. "It's nice to know, even if my fingers freeze off, my toes will be safe. That is, assuming we get next door in one piece."

As they drove from sunshine to the cooler shade

where thick pine trees edged the road, Jeremiah said, "You're doing *gut* with driving."

"My mommy can do anything." Sunni's tone stated he was a *dummkopf* for not already knowing that. "When I'm having trouble with my spelling, she tells me to try. She says you can't know what you can do until you try. Right, Mommy?"

Mercy didn't shift her gaze from the ruts that could catch a buggy wheel. "That's right, *eolin-i*."

"That means 'little one' in Korean," Sunni said.

"You speak Korean?" He looked at Mercy, astonished.

"A few words. I learned them from my beautiful daughter before she forgot most of her Korean as she learned English." She winked at Sunni. "I know a lot of Korean baby talk and a couple of songs. That's about it."

Smiling, Sunni began to sing a children's hymn whose tune he recognized. When she finished the first verse, she said, "That's how Koreans sing it, Jeremiah."

"Do you know more?"

He leaned back against the seat and listened to the little girl's chirping voice singing every verse of the Korean hymn. He couldn't remember the last time he'd felt so at ease, not determined to rush off to do the next thing. It was unexpected, and he decided to enjoy the moment.

He wasn't sure when another like this one would come again.

The drive went too quickly for Mercy. She was anxious not to make a mistake and embarrass herself

and Jeremiah. What if their Amish neighbors weren't pleased he'd invited her? In the weeks she'd been living on the farm, she hadn't done more than wave to her neighbors. She knew they were as busy as she was with trying to make homes out of the mostly abandoned buildings on the farms in the hollow.

Jeremiah had told her Caleb and his sister were living in one section of their main barn while they fixed up the house, which would have fallen in a few years if they hadn't come to rescue it. So she wasn't surprised when, exchanging places with Sunni and taking the reins as Hero pulled the buggy onto a farm lane, he drove to where other buggies were parked near a barn in desperate need of paint.

Stepping out, Mercy made sure Sunni was holding her hand. A boy led Hero toward the lower portion of the barn, and Jeremiah motioned at a door on the upper level that was up a sloping concrete apron.

"Usually," he said, "we gather outside and enter in a certain order, but it's too cold for little ones and the oldsters to stay out a second longer than necessary."

"And everyone else in between," she managed to get past her teeth, which were clenched so they didn't clatter together.

Mercy didn't say anything as they entered the barn. Ropes had been hung from side to side, and bright quilts hooked to them with clothespins. It was an ingenious way to make individual rooms out of the large space. However, the center of the space was open and filled with simple benches. A dozen benches faced the other dozen, and she guessed the women sat on one side and

the men on the other. It was the same in the church she attended.

About thirty people milled around, and she was amazed they made up only six Amish families. She'd known Amish parents had many children and multiple generations lived beneath a single roof, but she was overwhelmed by the number of members attending the service. Especially when she realized most of the people were around her own age. That made sense, because it would be the young people seeking a new life by Harmony Creek.

She couldn't fail to notice the shy glances in their direction. She realized a few of the prayer coverings were quite similar to hers while the organdy on other women's heads was heart-shaped. The women must come from different church districts, maybe different states.

When a tall blonde walked toward them, Jeremiah grinned.

Mercy was shocked at the pulse of something unpleasant racing through her as the lovely woman approached. It couldn't be… No, it was impossible she was jealous of how the blonde returned Jeremiah's smile so warmly. There couldn't be any future for Mercy and Jeremiah other than as friends. She should be happy for him that a beautiful Amish woman was pleased to see him.

Lord, please keep my heart from making another mistake. I don't know if it can survive shattering again.

Jeremiah turned to her, and she schooled her face into the best imitation she could of a calm expression. His brows lowered. He was puzzled by her reaction.

So was she!

"This is Caleb's sister Miriam," he said. "She was a teacher in her old community, so I asked her to translate for you. Miriam, these are the Bambergers. Mercy and Sunni."

"We're so glad you've decided to join us for worship today." Miriam's voice was like a song, each word a pleasant note, but Mercy had noticed a flash of discomfort in her eyes when Jeremiah mentioned she'd been a teacher. Maybe she missed that job.

Mercy dampened her curiosity, knowing she couldn't pose such a personal question to someone she'd just met. Instead, she said, "Thank you. I hope I can follow along."

Miriam gave her a warm smile. "If you need help, squeeze my hand, and I'll translate or explain." She glanced at Sunni and away. "The other *kinder* are over there on the far side of the room. They're waiting for you."

Her daughter didn't need a second invitation. She crossed the space in her rolling step. Two girls close to her age met her about halfway, talking over each other in their excitement to meet her.

When it was time for the service to start, Sunni sat on one side of Mercy and Miriam on the other. Mercy tried not to stare at the massive man sitting in the first row. His gray beard reached to the center of his chest, and his deep-set eyes had an intensity that awed her.

"Is that Abraham, Mommy?" asked Sunni in a stage whisper.

Miriam had overheard Sunni's question. Her answer

was serious, though Mercy saw her eyes twinkling. "That's Wayne Flaud. He's our acting bishop."

"He looks like the picture of Abraham in Mommy's Bible."

Hushing her daughter, Mercy hoped the bishop hadn't heard her daughter's comments. If he had, he didn't react as the *Leit* stood for the first hymn.

It was sung, as Jeremiah had warned her, at a very slow pace, taking two or three times longer to sing than it would have during a Mennonite service. She bowed her head and joined in the silent prayer, grateful for this opportunity to discover more about Jeremiah's world. She hoped it would help her understand him better, because he was becoming a bigger and bigger part of her and her daughter's lives.

The afternoon sun had warmed the air considerably by the time Jeremiah drove the buggy toward Rudy's farm. Sunni was asleep, her head on Mercy's lap, exhausted from playing outside with the other *kinder* after the communal luncheon in the barn.

"What did you think of the service, Mercy?" Jeremiah asked. "Other than how uncomfortable the benches are?"

"Was I that obvious?"

He rushed to answer as he struggled to keep from laughing at her shocked and humiliated expression. "No, you weren't obvious. It's the complaint we often hear when someone who isn't Amish attends our services."

"I've got to say I missed the comfortable pews I'm

accustomed to. The way you sang the hymns was amazing. The man who started each line—"

"The *vorsinger* is what he's called."

"He kept everyone together, so nobody got too far ahead or too far behind."

He turned the buggy into Rudy's drive. Drawing back on the reins, he stared at the black car parked there. A tall, balding man was stepping out. "You've got company, Mercy."

He felt her flinch. "It's Alfred, my father's oldest brother." She hesitated, then said, "I think."

"You think?"

"I haven't seen him in ten years. He lives in California, and he only comes for funerals." She sighed. "Though he didn't come for his father's."

"Was there bad blood between them?"

"My uncle doesn't get along well with anyone in the family. He thinks nobody is ever right except him."

His brows rose in astonishment. Mercy spoke her mind and was determined to take over her *grossdawdi*'s farm, but on other subjects, she tried to look for a solution that worked for everyone involved.

Her *onkel* glanced from her to Jeremiah and Sunni, his frown deepening with each passing second, while they got out of the buggy. The little girl must have sensed the tension because she didn't say a word.

Jeremiah saw a flood of questions in the older man's expression, but her *onkel* asked, "Why is the door locked?"

Mercy took Sunni's hand before walking between the snowbanks to where her *onkel* had gone up onto

the porch. She gave the cantankerous man a kiss on the cheek.

"Why didn't you let me know you were coming, Uncle Alfred?" she asked as she pulled the key out of her purse.

Instead of answering her question, he tapped his toe impatiently. Color faded from Mercy's face.

Jeremiah struggled not to frown when he realized her *onkel* saw her as a *kind*, no older or more responsible than Sunni.

"I'm tearing down wallpaper and painting," she answered, but her voice quavered, "and I didn't want someone to walk in and trip over the mess."

"You shouldn't be doing anything to the house until its future is decided."

"Dad knows I'm working on the house, and he agreed anything I do will increase the property's value."

Onkel Alfred waved aside her words. "You shouldn't lock the door. This door was never locked while my father and mother lived here."

Doubting she'd get anywhere with her *onkel*, who wasn't interested in what she had to say, Jeremiah stepped past Mercy. He opened the door and led the way into the house. He waited for the explosion he guessed would come when her *onkel* saw the changes she'd made.

Alfred began to list everything he thought Mercy was doing wrong. She seemed to shrink within herself, and Jeremiah respected how she didn't fire protests to defend herself.

Just as an Amish woman would do, whispered his

own thoughts. Silencing them, he was shocked when a small hand slid into his.

He looked at Sunni's troubled face.

"I don't like that loud man," she whispered.

"He's your grandfather's brother."

"Still don't like him."

He gave her a quick smile. He didn't like Alfred Bamberger, either, though he'd barely spent two minutes in his company. Any man who bullied Mercy and acted as if he knew everything and she knew nothing wasn't, in Jeremiah's estimation, worth getting better acquainted with.

"Mercy, have you forgotten your manners?" demanded her *onkel*, gesturing with his head toward Jeremiah.

Her cheeks became red, but she said calmly, "Uncle Alfred, I know my parents have told you about my daughter, Sunni."

The little girl greeted him with a tentative smile.

Alfred ignored her. "And who's he?"

"This is Jeremiah Stoltzfus," Mercy said, putting her arm around Sunni's shoulders. "Jeremiah, this is—"

"Are you the one who intended to buy the farm from Rudy?" asked the older man.

Jeremiah's first reaction was to laugh at the man's hypocrisy, but he hid it, because he wasn't really amused by how Alfred Bamberger dismissed Mercy. "I am."

"You're Amish, aren't you?"

"I am." He wondered if the man was always this rude. If so, he could understand why Alfred didn't get along with his siblings.

"What did you intend to do with the farm?"

"Farm it," he said in the same clipped tone the older man used. "I've got ten dairy cows in the barn. I'd arranged for their purchase before I came here, because Rudy said it was okay."

Alfred rubbed his eyes with his thumb and finger before sighing. "That sounds like my father." He grimaced. "Father hated the idea the farm might be subdivided and sold as house lots." Again, his gaze drilled Jeremiah. "He was so eager to keep the land as a farm he would have agreed to any deal."

"The price we agreed upon was fair." He wouldn't pretend not to understand what the other man was implying.

"That's yet to be seen. On behalf of my brothers and sisters, I've come to get an appraisal done on the property. An honest appraisal, not what Rudy believed it was worth to someone who said he planned to work the land."

Jeremiah didn't wince, not outwardly, as Alfred's words slashed through his tattered hopes. That the family might demand more in exchange for selling the farm wasn't something he'd considered. He and Rudy had negotiated in *gut* faith, and the Realtors involved must have agreed it was a fair deal.

Hadn't they?

"Dad didn't mention you'd be coming," Mercy said in the same deferential tone.

"He doesn't know, but he'll be grateful when he has the facts from someone who is truly part of the family, which you aren't, Mercy."

Jeremiah looked at her in horror. How could Alfred throw in her face she hadn't been born a Bamberger? That was beyond cruel.

But Mercy motioned for him to say nothing.

Her *onkel* asked a couple more questions and walked into the living room. When they didn't follow, he bellowed Mercy's name.

Jeremiah grasped her arm as she stepped forward to follow. "He shouldn't speak to you so," he hissed, fighting to control his outrage.

"It's okay, Jeremiah." She patted his cheek gently and smiled. "I'm used to him, and it's nothing personal."

"Nothing personal? He said—"

"He's said the same thing to my sisters-in-law and my cousins' spouses. He doesn't consider anyone a true part of the family except him and his siblings, and those siblings reluctantly." Her smile broadened. "He'd prefer he was an only child."

"But—"

"Thank you, Jeremiah." She glanced at the door to the living room when her *onkel* shouted again. "But let me handle this."

She was gone before Jeremiah could agree, which was for the best, because for the next hour Alfred interrogated Mercy and him on every facet of the farm. That they could answer his questions seemed to irritate him. The man had come to the house with a chip on his shoulder. Whenever he could, Jeremiah deflected questions fired at Mercy by answering them or turning the conversation to the land rather than the house.

Alfred left with a warning not to change another

thing before the appraisal. "I'm sure the family has other plans for this property than a silly summer camp."

Jeremiah bit his lip when he saw tears blossom in Mercy's eyes. Arguing with her *onkel* could make the situation worse. When the older man shot a rancorous glance in his direction, Jeremiah knew the warning was aimed at him, as well.

When the door shut behind Alfred Bamberger, Sunni rushed to throw her arms around Mercy.

"I don't like him, Mommy," the little girl said, hiding her face in Mercy's apron. "He didn't speak to me. Not even when I said hi."

Jeremiah squatted by the *kind*. "Sunni, some people are so angry inside they can't be anything but angry on the outside. It doesn't have anything to do with you."

"That's right," Mercy said. "Uncle Alfred isn't a happy person." Helping her daughter out of her coat, she added, "I think I'll make hot chocolate for us. Do you like that idea?"

With a cheer, Sunni hugged her *mamm*, but with excitement this time. The *kind* ran into the kitchen to select the cups they'd use for the treat.

Jeremiah came to his feet as Mercy asked, "You'll stay, won't you?"

"I need to get Hero in, but then I'll come back." Putting his hands on her shoulders, he knew he might be foolish, but he couldn't let her bear the burden of her *onkel*'s threats alone. "Mercy, you can't be certain anyone else in your family will listen to what he plans."

She sighed again. "I know Uncle Alfred. That he's

talking about subdividing the land to build houses means that's what he wants to do."

"It would probably bring the greatest return to your *daed* and his siblings, but only if they sell each lot themselves. A building contractor might offer less than I did because a builder would need to make a big profit in return for his investment."

She looked out the window at rolling hills set against purplish mountains reaching up into the clouds. "I can't imagine these hills covered with houses."

"Don't worry."

"How can you say that?" she asked, looking up at him.

"Because I trust in God's plan for my life."

"I wish I could, too."

At the regret in her voice, he longed to draw her into his arms and hold her until her fears vanished. It would be a mistake because he could be jeopardizing everything he was working so hard for.

Chapter Ten

After her *onkel*'s visit and his determination to squeeze every possible penny out of the property, Jeremiah wasn't sure if either of them would end up with the farm. He didn't say that to Mercy, but he guessed, by the way she evaded his eyes, she'd had similar thoughts as she threw herself into preparations for Parker Kenton's arrival, the foster *kind* being placed with her.

She and Sunni ignored her *onkel*'s edict and painted one bedroom a fresh blue for the boy. A bed was found in another room and cleaned. After a new mattress was delivered at the beginning of the week, she topped the bed with a duvet decorated with circus animals. Rudy's black-and-white afghan was draped over the footboard.

Jeremiah was asked over and over for his opinion of the room. "Because you're a boy," Sunni said each time.

Everything in the bedroom was ready by a chilly Tuesday afternoon when a silver car rolled to a stop in the yard. When the driver got out, Jeremiah recognized her as the social worker who'd come to speak with

Mercy. She glanced at where he stood with Mercy and Sunni, but said nothing. She went to the passenger side and opened the door.

No one emerged.

The woman—her name was Whitney, ain't so?— bent and spoke quietly.

Sunni cut her eyes to Mercy, who was looking at the car with anticipation and anxiety.

Patting the little girl's shoulder, Jeremiah guessed Mercy was considering the changes another *kind* could make in their lives. Including his. The thought was a sure sign he was too involved with the Bambergers.

A boy oozed out of the car. The first word that came to Jeremiah's mind was sullen. The *kind* stared at the ground and didn't acknowledge them.

Parker was short for his age and skinny. He wore a new winter coat with blue jeans and stylish sneakers. His previous foster family must have provided for him well, though they weren't able to continue caring for him. When he pulled off his knit cap, his fine black hair danced with static electricity.

He glowered and licked his fingertips before running them over his hair. Most of the strands settled, but others stood up like insane cowlicks.

Whitney put her hand on his shoulder, but he shook it off. He walked to where Jeremiah stood with Mercy and Sunni on the front porch. He didn't say a word.

Mercy opened the door and ushered everyone through the elegant front entry and into the living room.

Whitney undid her coat and motioned for Parker to do the same. He balled up his coat and threw it on a

chair. The social worker started to reprimand him, but Mercy shook her head gently.

Arching her pale brows, Whitney said, "This is Mercy and her daughter, Sunni. Sunni was born in Korea as you were."

"Who cares about stupid Korea?" muttered the boy. His voice held the hint of an accent.

"And I'm Jeremiah Stoltzfus." He offered his hand to the boy as if Parker were a grown man.

For a second, the *kind*'s indifference cracked. He eyed Jeremiah up and down. He seemed to gather his defenses around himself and scorned Jeremiah's hand. "Why are you wearing a clown hat?"

Because of the *kind*'s accent, Jeremiah thought he said *crown hat*. He realized his mistake when Mercy replied.

"Jeremiah isn't a clown. He's Amish. Amish men wear black hats like that in the winter, Parker."

"My name isn't Parker."

Whitney's voice took on a stern edge. "We've talked about that, and you agreed, for now, you're going to stick with Parker."

The *kind* subsided, but crossed his arms over his chest and stood with his chin raised in defiance.

If the boy wanted another name, Jeremiah knew what it should be. Trouble. The boy was going to be trouble. Jeremiah hoped Mercy was prepared.

He wasn't sure he was.

Mercy was so proud of her daughter. Despite Parker's disdain for everything Sunni said and how often he called her silly or stupid, the little girl persisted.

No doubt, Sunni remembered her own rough transition into what became her permanent family. Mercy certainly recalled her own, and she knew exactly how Parker was feeling.

Unwanted. Worthless. Determined to show the world he wasn't either.

"This is for you." Sunni placed a bright blue teddy bear in Parker's hand. Her smile wavered when he didn't say anything. "It's nice to have a special friend when you're somewhere new. Blueberry has been a good friend to me, and I hope he'll be a good friend to you."

Mercy didn't catch what Parker replied under his breath. She guessed she'd be better off not knowing.

Parker tossed the bear on the bed and then picked up his suitcase. It nearly knocked him off his feet. Jeremiah slipped a surreptitious hand under one side to help guide it onto the bed. Parker shook his head when Whitney said it was time to go downstairs, but came along reluctantly upon the social worker's insistence.

Whitney stayed for several hours, then got ready to leave to allow the family to begin to adjust to each other.

When Mercy started to make supper, she asked Jeremiah if he'd like to stay.

He heard her nervous tone, and he agreed. With two *kinder*, including one who protested over anything anyone said to him, she could use another adult there.

"I'll set the table," he said as she took hamburger and potatoes out of the refrigerator. "And keep the kids away from the stove."

"They're upstairs. Sunni knows if she wants fries, she needs to stay away while I cook them."

"She's a known quantity. The other one isn't." He paused by the table. "Where do you want these papers Whitney left with you?"

"Would you mind putting them on the desk?"

"Be glad to." He began to gather them up. His eyes widened as he noticed the name on several of them. Mercedes R. Bamberger.

"Is your name really Mercedes?" he asked. "Like the fancy car?"

"Jeff and Pat have a Mercedes," said Parker, puffing out his chest and striding into the kitchen as if he owned the place. Jeremiah knew Jeff and Pat were the couple who were supposed to have adopted the boy. "Do you have one?"

"No, I've got that dented Ford out there." Mercy shot Jeremiah a glance, and he stepped between the boy and the stove.

The boy looked at Jeremiah, who said, "No car for me. But I've got a horse named Hero and a buggy."

Rolling his eyes, Parker opened cabinet doors and peered inside.

"So your name is really Mercedes?" Jeremiah asked.

She plucked the page out of his hand. "Yes, my name is Mercedes. It's Spanish for mercies, and it's the name I was given when I was born. The Bambergers asked if they could call me Mercy. I agreed, because I was getting a new life, so why not a new name?" She smiled coolly. "Especially when they didn't pronounce it as *Abuelita* did."

"I always wanted a shorter name like my brothers have. I liked my *daed*'s name. Paul. Nice and simple." He rubbed his chin. "*Mamm* always said I should em-

ulate the prophet Jeremiah and stand up and speak of the Lord."

"I didn't think the Amish evangelize."

"We don't. Or I should say, most of us don't. She meant I should proclaim God is *gut*."

"This place is ugly," Parker announced from the far corner of the kitchen.

"If you think it's ugly now," she said as she began cutting the potatoes into short lengths, "you should have seen it when I moved in here."

Mercy didn't smile when she saw the child's shock. He'd expected to annoy her with another of his insults, but she'd been a foster kid. She knew the games and the rules. Dislike everything. Push and push to see how much you could get away with.

And Parker had been yanked out of the familiar world he'd known and brought across the Pacific to a strange culture. The family that was supposed to be his forever had failed him, leaving him to be tossed into the system. Now he found himself in a plain home. That was enough to make the boy's head spin...and her heart ache.

"Can we watch TV?" the boy asked.

"We don't have one." She scraped more potatoes, figuring she'd need more than twice as many as she used when she made French fries for her and Sunni. A hardworking man and a growing boy had hearty appetites.

"How do you play video games if you don't have a TV?" His eyes widened. "Do you have a handheld?"

"No."

"Then you play on the computer."

Mercy shook her head, but Sunni, who came into the

kitchen, replied, "We don't have a computer or whatever a handheld is."

Parker stared at them as if they'd crawled out of a woodchuck hole and announced they'd been hibernating. "What do you *do*?"

"Read and color," Sunni said.

"Take care of the animals and pray," Jeremiah added.

"Teach Sunni and cook." Mercy motioned to the stove.

"Build a chicken coop." Sunni giggled and glanced at Jeremiah.

"Drive the buggy," he said with a laugh, "and teach Mercy how to drive the sleigh."

Before Mercy could think of something to add to the list, Parker threw his short arms up in the air, grumbled something and stamped away. She heard his footsteps on the stairs and overhead. She looked from the heating oil to the ceiling.

"What is it?" asked Jeremiah.

"Could you do me a favor? There's the door by Parker's room that leads into the section of the house with weak floors. I meant to lock it before he arrived."

"I'll get it."

"Be careful."

His reddish brows rose. "By that, I assume the door has to be locked from the bad side."

"Yes." She flashed him a sympathetic smile. "I've looked for the key, but I haven't found it." *Among other things, like my grandfather's will,* she wanted to say, but kept that to herself. She wasn't comfortable with Jeremiah knowing she hadn't given up the search. "Just

turn the latch on the dead bolt." As he turned to go, she repeated, "Be careful."

"I'll do my best."

"I'm sure you always do."

He paused and looked at her. The kitchen seemed to telescope, the distance between them vanishing. Everything vanished, except them. A connection, invisible and powerful, matched every breath she took to his.

She wasn't sure how long they would have stood—frozen inside a splendid moment in time—if the hot oil on the stove hadn't snapped. She turned to the stove, and Jeremiah rushed away.

Steadying her breath and her heart that seemed to be beating at fast-forward, she tried to focus on cutting the fries. She patted the potatoes dry, because she didn't want the oil to splatter.

When she heard footsteps behind her, she saw her daughter standing in the doorway but not in the kitchen.

Sunni clamped her arms over her narrow chest. "He says he's not coming down for dinner."

Mercy didn't need to ask who *he* was. "Did you ask him nice?"

"Of course." Her daughter seemed insulted at the question. "But he won't open his door."

"Did he tell you why?" Infecting Sunni with Mercy's worries that the boy might try to run away would make the situation more tense.

"No! He said bad words."

Mercy turned off the burner and sent up a quick prayer of thanks the boy was still in the house. Holding out her hand, she said, "Come with me."

She didn't want Sunni to get more upset, but she wouldn't leave her daughter in the kitchen with the hot oil on the stove. When she heard Jeremiah on the front stairs, she asked him to keep an eye on the stove. He nodded, though curiosity burned in his eyes. Again, she felt the pull of the unseen contact between them. She broke it, knowing she had to find out why Parker was refusing to come and have his supper.

He must be hungry. Whitney said she'd offered to stop to get burgers, but the boy had refused. Climbing the stairs, she went to the room between Sunni's and Grandpa Rudy's.

"Parker?"

"That's not my name!" came back a snarl.

"All right, whatever your name is." Mercy kept her voice even. "It's time for supper."

"I'm not hungry."

"Yes, you are. Have you ever had French fries before?"

"Of course!" A hint of vacillation sifted into his retort.

"Homemade ones?"

For several seconds there was no answer. The door opened slowly, enough for Parker to slip through.

As he started to close it behind him, Mercy put out her hand and kept the door from shutting. He glared at her, and she met it without comment. Finally, he lowered his eyes and stepped aside.

She pushed open the door and gasped.

The room looked as if it'd been ransacked. The drawers were pulled from the dresser. The bed had been torn

apart, and the pictures on the wall—at least the ones Parker could reach—were ripped down and tossed in a corner.

Sunni gave a soft cry of dismay and picked up the blue teddy bear she'd given Parker. Tears filled her eyes when she touched the stuffing peeking out of where the bear's ears had been.

"Why?" she asked.

"It's a stupid bear, and you're stupid for liking it. Only a cripple would like something like a stupid bear." Parker crossed his arms and raised his chin, daring them to try to make him apologize.

It was at that point Mercy knew this placement was going to be harder than she'd guessed.

A lot harder.

Jeremiah had come up the stairs after making sure nothing would burn on the stove. He didn't hesitate to step into the room as Sunni ran and threw herself in Mercy's arms. He turned to the boy, who regarded them with contempt. Parker also had, Jeremiah noticed, steeled himself as if he expected to be punished harshly for what he'd done and said.

It was *gut* the *kind* understood he shouldn't have destroyed the room and the gifts Mercy and Sunni had given him. Teaching the boy to respect those who wanted to help him would be easier if Parker knew the difference between right and wrong.

Mercy started to step forward, but Jeremiah put his hand on her arm. Warmth exploded from her skin to his. For a split second, he wanted to step out into the

hall with her and forget the angry boy and the hurt little girl. Just for a moment. A single moment while he gazed into Mercy's pretty eyes. If he bent forward, would she shy away from his lips?

Knowing he was being imprudent, especially when the *kinder* needed them, he said in a near whisper, "Let me, Mercy."

"Jeremiah, this isn't your problem." Her voice was as hushed as his while Parker's gaze moved from one of them to the other as if trying to read their lips.

"I know, but I can take him off your hands while you clean up this mess."

"He should help, so—"

"Look at him." He cut his eyes to the boy. "Everything about him says he's waiting for a fight or to be punished."

"I don't want to fight with him. I know he's scared."

"So let me give him something to take his mind off his fears."

For a moment, Jeremiah thought Mercy wouldn't trust him. She glanced between the boy and him.

"I'm not going to take him out behind the woodshed," he said quietly. "That wouldn't help anything."

"I know."

"Mercy, let me help. Can you hold dinner for about an hour?"

Indecision raced across her face, but then she nodded.

Thrilled by her trust in him, Jeremiah made sure his face remained stern as he turned to the boy. "Come with me."

"I don't want to."

"I didn't ask if you wanted to. I asked you to come with me." He kept his voice steady, wondering if *Daed* had struggled, as Jeremiah was now, when he'd needed to punish one of them.

Maybe he shouldn't have volunteered to help. He didn't know a lot about kids, other than when he spent time with his nieces and nephews. But there wasn't time for second thoughts. He'd offered, and the boy needed to learn actions had consequences, whether *gut* or bad.

Jeremiah herded the boy down the stairs. He thought Parker would argue again when told to put on his coat, hat and mittens along with his boots. The boy was reluctant but he complied and rushed out the door when Jeremiah opened it.

"Whoa, there." Jeremiah caught Parker by the hood on his coat as the *kind* started to jump into a snowbank. "If you get wet, you'll be cold by the time we finish the chores."

"Chores? What are chores?"

Surprised a nine-year-old didn't know the term, Jeremiah held the coat as Parker strained against him. "Chores are what we do to earn our keep here."

"The county is paying for me."

"And how long do you think they'll do that? A man can't depend on someone else to pay his way. Don't you want a *gut* and exciting job when you grow up?"

The boy stopped trying to pull away. Frowning, Parker said, "Sure."

"What do you want to do?"

"Be an astronaut or a fireman or maybe a policeman."

Jeremiah ignored his yearning to grin. "Those are important jobs, and they have one thing in common. They will require you to work hard to learn everything you need to know to do the job. Ever think of being a cowboy?"

"Yeah," the boy drawled, clearly suspicious.

"Here's your chance."

"Huh?"

Pretending he hadn't heard Parker's question, Jeremiah kept a hand on the boy's shoulder as they walked toward the barn. Jeremiah acted as if he didn't have a care in the world, but kept snatching glances at the *kind*'s face when they entered the barn where the cows waited to be milked.

"It smells in here," the boy said.

"It does, doesn't it?" He saw Parker's shock that Jeremiah wasn't insulted by his blunt words. "But give it a chance. Once you get used to the smell, it's kind of a nice stink."

"You're crazy!"

Jeremiah smiled. The sooner the boy learned he couldn't get a rise out of Jeremiah, the sooner Parker might start listening to him. Really listening.

"Okay," Jeremiah said, trying to sound more certain than he felt, "I'm going to milk the cows, and you're going to clean up." He pointed at the gutter behind the cows and then handed the boy a short-handled shovel. "Pick it up and put it on that pile over there." He pointed toward a stained spot on the concrete floor near the door leading into the barnyard. "It can stay there for tonight. We'll move it outside tomorrow when it's warmer."

"You want me to shovel that—?"

"Manure? *Ja*, I do."

"That's child abuse."

"Not even close." He grinned at the boy. "Once I know you can handle that, I'll let you help me milk the cows."

"I don't want to milk old, stinky cows."

"Well, that's *gut*, because these cows are neither old nor stinky."

Again the *kind* stared at him as if Parker feared Jeremiah had lost his mind.

"B-b-but…" The boy sputtered on the single word.

"You said you wanted to be a cowboy, ain't so?"

"I did, but cowboys ride horses."

"Which need to be cleaned up after, too."

"Really?"

"*Ja*, really." Smiling, Jeremiah said, "You'd better get started."

He left the boy staring at the shovel and went to get the milking equipment out of the storage room. When he returned, Parker was poking at the gutters behind the cows. Jeremiah didn't glance at him when he heard a clang as Parker started to work.

The battle wasn't over, but Parker was willing to listen to him. Maybe Jeremiah had helped Mercy tonight. He hoped so. It felt astounding, he realized, to be on the same side for once. He prayed it wouldn't be the one and only time.

Chapter Eleven

Sunni was paging through a picture book in the living room the following week, so Mercy kept Parker in the kitchen while she washed the dinner dishes. He complained about not having TV, and he couldn't seem to find anything to do. Sleet tapped at the window, and she could scarcely make out the shape of the barn on the far side of the yard.

"Can you see where Jeremiah is?" asked Parker as he set a cup of cocoa on the table.

Mercy wasn't sure what had happened in the barn the night of Parker's arrival, but whatever Jeremiah had said or done had made a huge impression on the boy. At the same time Parker looked for any chance to spend time with Jeremiah, he resisted every request she spoke, and he treated Sunni badly, making nasty comments to her over and over or stepping into her way when she was trying to navigate the stairs.

She recognized the pattern she'd seen in other foster kids. They'd shared stories about how they disrupted

a placement on purpose. Even then, she'd understood what they hadn't said. When they had no control over their lives, being pulled from one foster home to another and maybe sent home to live with one parent for a while before being dropped back into the system, they'd decided to grab what control they could. They were determined to make sure the placement didn't work, pushing their foster parents to the edge and past it with their antics. One girl she'd shared a room with for a couple of nights had put it succinctly, "I got rid of them before they got rid of me."

However, he hung on every word Jeremiah spoke. She wondered if Parker had been close to a father figure in Korea. According to the reports Whitney had left for Mercy, Parker hadn't transferred that respect to Mr. Kenton.

Yet the child admired Jeremiah and hopped to obey any request he made. She should be grateful the boy heeded one of them. Asking Jeremiah to step in made her uncomfortable because each time was a reminder that sometime, hopefully in the near future, one of them would have the farm and the other must leave.

But she knew it was more than that. She looked forward to every time Jeremiah came to the house or she ran into him in the yard. He'd had dinner and supper with them every day since Parker's arrival, and he'd lingered into the evening. His calm presence stopped arguments between the two children before they got heated.

"No, I don't see him," Mercy replied when the boy repeated the question. Louder this time. "He's smart enough not to work outside in a storm."

"Is he your boyfriend?"

"No." She ignored the regret that erupted in her at the simple answer.

"Why not?"

"He's Amish, and we're not." It was the easiest explanation to give the boy.

How could she explain to a nine-year-old about the feelings she didn't understand herself? The very thought of spending time with Jeremiah made her smile. When his hand brushed hers, even inadvertently, her heart thumped like hail on a roof. His kindness with the children touched her soul, for she couldn't help thinking of how Graham hadn't even wanted to discuss having a family. While Jeremiah spent time with Sunni and Parker, making them want to like him, Graham had barely tolerated her daughter.

But there was something else, something indefinable that drew her to him like a child to a cookie jar.

"You aren't Amish?" Parker asked, again interrupting her thoughts. "You wear a funny hat, too."

"It's my prayer covering." She put the last pot on the drainer and reached to let the water out of the sink. "The Bible asks women to cover their heads when they pray. As I pray throughout the day, I don't have to worry about my head being uncovered when I do."

"If you're not Amish, what are you?" He paused for a moment, then asked, "What's Amish?"

Mercy gave him a very brief answer, knowing, as a child who'd never encountered plain people, he wouldn't be able to handle too much information at once.

"Hey!" he shouted in the middle of her explanation.

"There's Jeremiah." He rushed to the window that gave him the best view of the barn. "What's he doing?"

Mercy walked to stand behind him. Wiping her hands on a towel, she peered through the storm that didn't seem in a hurry to abate.

Across the yard, Jeremiah was bending over a tractor parked by the barn. She'd been surprised when he drove it out of the barn until he explained he didn't plan to use it in the fields. Instead, he wanted to use the tractor's engine as a power source.

"It looks as if he's fixing the stationary engine that runs the milking machines in the barn," she said.

Parker wore an unexpected smile. "I like helping with milking. It's fun, but I wish Jeremiah had different cows."

"What kind of cows?"

"His cows give white milk. I like chocolate milk."

She drew her bottom lip between her teeth so she didn't laugh.

"Don't you?" the boy demanded.

"Certainly I like chocolate milk."

"So why doesn't he get chocolate milk cows?"

"You'll have to check with him." Putting the towel on the counter by the sink, she said, "You can ask him tonight."

"I will!"

As the boy went to the table to finish his hot cocoa, Mercy remained by the window. She watched Jeremiah's easy, economical motions as he got the tractor's engine running. When he came inside, she'd make sure

she had something warm for him to drink. She couldn't wait to tell him about chocolate milk cows.

It had been the longest conversation she'd had with Parker without him copping an attitude on her. She hoped it would be the first of many.

When Parker appeared in the barn, looking furtively over his shoulder, Jeremiah guessed the boy had snuck out of the house. He considered sending Parker back, but Mercy would know to look first in the barn if she wanted to find the boy.

She was having a rough time with her foster *kind*. Was Parker missing his adoptive *mamm* so much he was determined not to let Mercy get close? Or was he mad at the whole world? Jeremiah tried to put himself in the *kind*'s shoes. To be yanked out of what he thought was his forever home was enough to give the boy a reason to distrust everyone.

"I didn't expect you to come out in the storm," Jeremiah said as he bent to clean a cow's udder before he attached the portable milking machine.

"You're doing your chores, so I'm here to do mine." He picked up the shovel, no longer skittish around the cows. "Besides, it's boring being stuck in the house. All they want to do is read or rip off wallpaper."

With a nod, Jeremiah wished Parker would show Mercy some respect. He couldn't force the boy to do so. All he could do was be a *gut* role model for how a man treated a woman.

"Mercy said there are cows that give chocolate milk,"

Parker said a few minutes later. "How come you don't have one?"

"Because I like strawberry milk better." Without batting an eye, he pointed to a ruddy Jersey cow munching hay and ignoring them. "So that's why I have a strawberry cow."

Jeremiah fought not to laugh as Parker stared in astonishment. He'd been a lot younger than the boy when his own *daed* told him the same silly story about red cows giving strawberry milk. Most likely, he'd worn the same expression of disbelief and childish yearning to believe the story was true.

"You're kidding," Parker said.

"No. The milk these cows give can be made into chocolate milk and strawberry milk and cheese and other things."

Understanding dawned on the boy's face. "So cows are pretty important."

"Ja."

"And milking them is important?"

"Very important. They depend on us to care for them, and in return they give us milk to use." He emptied the milker into a pail to carry it to the dairy tank. "We must heed what God told Adam and Eve in the Garden of Eden."

"God?"

"Ja. God told them: *Be fruitful, and multiply, and replenish the earth, and subdue it: and have dominion over the fish of the sea, and over the fowl of the air, and over every living thing that moveth upon the earth.* That

means we need to take care of the animals and birds and fish that can't take care of themselves."

"Like cows?"

Jeremiah nodded. "Something every cowboy needs to know. You're well on your way to becoming one if you want."

Parker grinned. "Do I get a hat?"

Whipping off his black wool hat, Jeremiah set it on the boy's head. "There you go."

"This isn't a cowboy hat." He pulled it off with a disgusted frown.

"The very first cowboys wore hats very much like this one."

"Really?"

"Really."

The boy set the hat back on his head, paying no attention to how it dropped onto his nose. "Let's do the milking."

"Said just like a cowboy."

When Parker grinned, Jeremiah's heart swelled with happiness. He'd been curious how his brothers could welcome *kinder* into their lives, though they weren't the *kinder*'s biological *daeds*. They loved the youngsters as much as the *bopplin* born within their marriages. Admiring them, he'd wondered if he could open his heart so wide. He was beginning to believe he could.

Wide enough to let one naughty boy, one very opinionated little girl and one lovely woman into it.

If the situation with the farm was resolved... He might as well wish for stars to dance around the sun at noon.

*But with You, all things are possible. That's what
Jesus taught, and what I believe. All things are possible,
including finding a way out of the mess of who owns this
farm. Even falling in love with the one woman standing
in the way of me achieving that dream.*

Jeremiah began to whistle as he carried the milk can
to the dairy tank, happier than he'd been in longer than
he could recall.

He was startled when he returned to clean the next
cow and saw Mercy and Sunni walking into the barn.

Sunni rushed to him. "Can I help, too?"

He smiled. "Of course you can. The more hands to
help the faster the job goes, but you need to ask your
mamm."

"Can I help, too?" Sunni asked.

Jeremiah grinned at the little girl's excitement to
have a chance to spend time with him and Parker. After
putting up with her foster brother's pranks and scathing
comments, it was the first time since the boy's arrival
she'd asked to do something when Parker was involved.

"Certainly, *eolin-i,*" Mercy said, ruffling her daugh-
ter's hair.

Parker stared at her. "I know what that means. It's
Korean."

"I'm glad you remember your Korean." She gave him
the warm smile that lit up the recesses of Jeremiah's
heart, even when aimed at someone else. "Maybe you
can teach Sunni the language. She wasn't much more
than a baby when she came here, so she's lost most of
what she knew."

The boy's lip curled, and Jeremiah knew he was

about to say something rude. Before Parker could speak, Jeremiah said quietly, "A *gut* cowboy always helps those around him. He knows he may have to depend on others while tending the cows, so he lets others know they can depend on him."

Parker looked at him, wide-eyed, then nodded. "I'll try."

"Thank you," Mercy said. "Maybe you could help me learn, too."

"You want me to teach *you*? But you're a grown-up."

"I'm a baby when it comes to learning Korean."

The boy stared hastily at his boots, and Jeremiah would have gladly given Parker a penny—or a dollar—for his thoughts. Was Parker regretting his lack of respect toward Mercy when she treated him kindly? Or were her gentle ways tearing down the walls the boy had raised to protect himself from more hurt? Either way, Jeremiah hoped Parker realized how blessed he was to be in Mercy's care.

"Jeremiah!" Sunni's excited cry rang through the barn.

She was by the calf stall. The newest calves, four of them, had been delivered yesterday from the auction barn in Cambridge, about ten miles south. They bawled whenever he entered the barn, hoping to get his attention and something to eat.

Squatting next to Sunni, he smiled when she gazed up at him in awe.

"Look!" Her grin was almost too wide for her face. "He's sucking my fingers!"

"*She*'s hoping for milk, and she thinks your fingers

might have some because they don't look much different to her than the cow's teats."

"You can't tell a girl cow," Parker taunted, "from a boy cow. You're a stupid girl."

"Enough," Jeremiah said quietly, and the boy subsided. "You were saying, Sunni?"

Her nose wrinkled, but she hurried to ask, "When does one of the cows come over to feed them?"

"The calves don't get to drink the milk from the cows. We do."

"That's not fair! She's a baby cow. She should have first dibs."

Leaning one arm on the top of the stall, Jeremiah said, "It might not sound fair to you, but what I feed the calves provides more nutrition than cow milk. They'll grow stronger much faster with milk replacer." He motioned for Parker to join them. "Would you two like to feed them?"

Sunni cheered loudly enough so the calves jerked, staring at her with the whites of their eyes showing. Instantly, she began cooing as she tried to get them to come to her.

Parker was less enthusiastic. "You want both of us to feed them?"

"I'll help you," Jeremiah said, pretending he'd misunderstood that Parker didn't want to share the task with his foster sister.

"I don't need…" He shuffled his feet. "If you show me how to do it, I can handle baby cows."

"I'm sure you can. You, too, Sunni. That's why I asked you." Straightening, he said, "C'mon. I'll show

you how I mix up the milk replacer, and we'll fill the bottles."

Within minutes the youngsters were holding the large bottles with both hands as the calves drained them so fast the milk replacer dribbled out of the sides of their mouths. Mercy took over the task of cleaning the udders before Jeremiah hooked on the milker. They worked in easy harmony as if they'd done the tasks together a hundred times before.

Mercy paused to check the *kinder* and help refill the bottles so the other two calves could have their turns. "Are you having fun?"

Jeremiah hoped Parker would reply, but Sunni did. She nodded with a grin that revealed her loose tooth. It was her first one, and the little girl was excited about it.

Jeremiah kept hoping that while they finished the milking and other chores, Parker would say something nice to Mercy.

Nothing.

When Mercy sent the *kinder* to the house through the early evening sunshine, Parker refused to go. A single glance from Jeremiah changed the boy's mind, and he stalked out, his tightly fisted hands jammed into his coat pockets.

"Give him time," Mercy said as she wrapped a scarf around her neck.

Jeremiah reached for the light switch. "I'm trying, but how much time does he need to realize you're the best thing that could happen to him now?"

"Were you always grateful for what adults did for you? Surely you weren't that well behaved."

Closing the door behind them, he sighed as the cold scraped across his face. "I can't remember the last time I felt like a naughty kid. Not even when I was a scholar."

"That's no surprise. Were you the good boy, the one your teacher could expect to be quiet and study hard?"

"*Ja.* Sadly, I was also the one my parents seldom had to scold, though I was surrounded by siblings who enjoyed pranks and jests."

"Not sadly. It's a credit to you that you were working hard for what you wanted, even when you were a child."

"What about you? Were you the *gut* little girl?"

He was surprised when she faltered a moment before saying, "Eventually."

Wanting to kick himself for forgetting she'd endured the same uncertainty and temporary homes Parker did, he wished he could see her face better in the dim light. "I'm sorry. I shouldn't have asked that, Mercy."

"Why not? Having a wonderful childhood with siblings and two parents who were always there for you isn't anything to be ashamed of. It's something to celebrate." She looked past him to the *kinder* who were almost to the house. "It's what I'd hoped to offer Sunni here. A permanent home she knew would always be there for her." Before he could reply, she waved aside his answer. "Enough of the dreary. Let's enjoy spending time with the children."

He caught her gloved hand in his own. "And each other."

"Yes, and with each other." She smiled and squeezed his fingers as they swung their hands between them on the short walk to the barn.

Again, Jeremiah's contentment was short-lived.

Sunni suddenly ran toward them. "Mommy! Mommy! We saw kittens. Can we bring them inside?"

"If you can find them," Mercy said with a chuckle.

Ten minutes later two dejected *kinder* gave up the search. The kittens seemed to have disappeared.

"Barn cats are very, very skilled at hiding," Mercy said to console them. "I used to play hide-and-seek with the kittens in the hayloft." She laughed. "They always won."

As she continued to tell the *kinder* about when she visited her *grossdawdi*, Jeremiah kept going toward the porch. But he couldn't walk away from the truth.

Mercy's connection to the farm was real and deep. Far deeper than his own.

Lord, if You've brought me here, I know You have a reason. And I also know Your reason can't be to bring Mercy unhappiness. Look at her!

He watched as she spoke with the *kinder*. Parker was acting as if he didn't need to listen, but he was as Mercy gave them ideas on how to lure the kittens to them tomorrow with fresh milk and calm voices and no quick motions.

She's a warmhearted woman, Lord, and she's eager to do whatever she can to help anyone else, even a young boy who challenges her at every turn and other kinder *she's never met. I don't know what path You have given her to walk, but please don't let it be filled with more hurt.*

And please don't let me cause that hurt.

Chapter Twelve

Jeremiah ran his hand along the planed log. Its smooth surface would make an excellent mantel. With a few imperfections left by the growth of the tree that once had stood on the farm, the log would be the exact complement to a fieldstone fireplace. Two days ago an *Englischer* renovating a house on the road between Salem and the Vermont border had stopped by, saying he'd heard Jeremiah was a woodworker. When Jeremiah had shown him the log, the man had been skeptical…until today. After seeing the work Jeremiah had done, he'd agreed to come back tomorrow so he could get the log and have it put in place right away.

A few other commissions like that one would add to the funds Jeremiah would need to move forward with his plans to buy a farm, whether it was Rudy's or another.

The thought jolted him as he was about to pick up another piece of wood. It was the first time he'd admitted to himself that there might be alternatives if Mercy's

family decided not to accept the contract he'd signed. He hadn't spoken with his Realtor in two weeks. Maybe Kitty had learned about a nearby farm for sale.

He grimaced. If there was a farm available along Harmony Creek, he would have heard about it from Caleb or one of his other neighbors.

Could he walk away after giving his word he'd help with the settlement? Maybe one of the other families would agree to let him live with them until he found a place of his own. Mercy might be willing to rent him some of her fields to use as pasture and planting.

And he'd be able to see her and the *kinder*.

"You've gotten in too deep, Stoltzfus," he muttered to himself as he hefted the log and laid it against the wall where it would be out of the way.

The door to his workshop opened, and his heart started doing a jig in his chest at the thought of Mercy stepping out of his thoughts and into his shop.

When Parker's head appeared around the edge, Jeremiah tried to ignore the flush of disappointment. He was glad to see the boy, but...

"Can I come in?" Parker asked.

"No touching the equipment," he said.

"You tell me that every time I come in." The boy pouted.

"And you still have five fingers on each hand." He winked at Parker to soften his words. "Let's keep it that way."

Parker picked up a piece of pine and pulled out a barely sharp kitchen knife. Running it down the side of the wood, he smiled. "See? I'm careful."

"I see, but you'd do better with a whittling knife than that one." He didn't ask if Mercy had given the boy permission to take it. He knew she hadn't.

"Where can I get one?"

"We can check the hardware store in the village, but first I need to see you can be trusted with it."

"I can. I can be trusted with anything."

Jeremiah simply arched his brows, and the boy got the message. No amount of bragging was allowed in the workshop.

"Can I ask you something?" Parker lowered the knife and wood onto his lap.

"What?"

"Will you help me change my name?"

He wasn't surprised. Parker had mentioned doing that several times since his arrival. "To what?"

"I haven't decided yet. Not my Korean name. Nobody can pronounce it."

"I understand," Jeremiah said, thinking of how Mercy had said the same thing about her birth name.

"I want something other than Parker. It's a dumb name." He grimaced. "Those dumb people stuck it on me."

He frowned at the boy. "You shouldn't call the Kentons *dumm*."

"But they are. They waited and waited for a kid of their own, and then they couldn't wait to get rid of me. That's pretty dumb."

"Even so, you shouldn't call any adult *dumm*." Thinking of the names Parker had used to upset Sunni, he added quickly, "Or any *kind*, either."

"But it's okay to say Parker is a dumb name? I— Ouch!" He stared in horror at the thin red slice on his index finger. The line widened as blood ran from the cut.

Without a word as the knife clattered to the floor, Jeremiah grabbed the *kind*'s wrist. He ignored Parker's shrieks as he thrust the cut finger into a bucket of cold water he kept nearby for such emergencies. Deftly, he dabbed an antibacterial cream from his first-aid kit on the wound and bound it.

"There you go."

Tears ran down Parker's face, but he regarded his bandaged finger with as much curiosity as if it belonged to someone else. "Will I have a scar?" He raised his eyes, which sparkled with abrupt excitement. "Like the ones you have?"

Jeremiah looked at his fingers, which showcased the long hours of hard, hands-on work he'd done since he was younger than Parker. All his knuckles, including his thumbs, bore scars, and his left palm showed where a fishhook had become embedded in it when he'd been showing off for his older brothers and their friends. Each mark told a story and evoked a memory, some *gut*, some not so *gut*, especially when he'd needed stitches on his right forefinger after being bitten by a dog shortly after he'd turned ten.

"If you end up with a scar," he said as he gathered the supplies and put them in the first-aid box, "it won't be like mine, but yours will be there to remind you to be careful as mine do."

"Will girls like my scar like Mercy does yours?"

Shocked to feel heat rising up his face, Jeremiah kept his head bent so the *kind* didn't see his reaction. "I don't think Mercy cares about my scars one way or the other."

"Sure she does." Parker climbed onto the chunk of wood, but didn't reach for his knife. "I've seen her touching them. A lot. I think she likes them. A lot."

The boy was right, Jeremiah knew. About Mercy touching him when she wanted to make a point or to console him or to make a connection. He treasured each memory of her fingers against him, but he tried not to think of them too often. For all he knew, she might have another man in her life. Someone more important to her than he was. She seldom spoke of her life in central New York. Thinking of how she rushed to the mailbox as soon as the postal carrier drove past, he wondered—not for the first time—if she was eager to hear from someone special.

But he wasn't about to discuss his feelings for Mercy with a nine-year-old.

As he put the box on its shelf, he said, "You should tell God how grateful you are the injury isn't worse. Asking for healing wouldn't be a bad idea, either."

"You're always talking about God. Do you really believe in him?"

"Ja."

"Oh." The boy picked up the piece of wood he'd dropped and rolled it between his fingers. Staring off into the distance, he asked, "Aren't you going to ask me if I believe in God?"

"I figured you'd tell me if you wanted me to know."

The *kind* didn't answer quickly.

Jeremiah gave the boy time to think while he walked over to the plow he'd brought inside. He'd cleaned off the rust but needed to straighten it. The plow would be ready for him—or whoever owned the farm by the time the snow melted—to work in the fields. If he was going to be able to complete the purchase of the farm, he must buy workhorses or mules. He'd need six on a team to work on the slopes, which were far steeper than in Paradise Springs.

"I'd like to believe in God," Parker said at last. "Mercy said you Amish live as you do because you want to be close to God."

"The apostle Paul wrote in Romans 12:2: *And be not conformed to this world: but be ye transformed by the renewing of your mind, that ye may prove what is that good, and acceptable, and perfect, will of God.* That's what our ministers preach and how we try to live."

"Did the Possible Paul—"

"*Apostle* Paul." He couldn't halt his grin. "An apostle is someone who teaches us about being *gut* Christians."

"Paul, huh?" The little boy started to add more, but the sound of a car pulling into the yard intruded.

Hearing a groan from Parker, Jeremiah knew it must be Whitney's. She was scheduled to come by today for a visit to check on how Parker was fitting in.

"Let's go." Jeremiah motioned with his head toward the door.

He thought Parker might protest, but the boy walked toward the door. Every inch of the *kind* announced he wanted to go anywhere but into the house to meet with Whitney and answer her questions. Jeremiah secretly

shared the boy's dislike of someone poking and prodding into his life, but the social worker needed to be sure the placement was a *gut* one for all involved.

Jeremiah's steps faltered as he was following the boy outside. This meeting could be Mercy's chance to hand the troubled *kind* over to someone else, but he couldn't imagine she would. He'd seen the pain in her eyes whenever she mentioned Parker leaving for a permanent placement. The kid might challenge her endlessly, but she wasn't ready to give up the battle to reach him.

"Hey!" called Whitney when Parker tried to sneak past her unseen.

The boy stopped, his hands behind him and his head lowered. He didn't return the greeting.

Instead, Jeremiah did as he walked toward the silver car.

With a smile, Whitney said, "Hi, Jeremiah! Has our boy been spending time with you?"

"Ja." He crooked a finger toward Parker, who reluctantly edged forward. "You'll probably want to see this right away."

The social worker's smile faded when she saw the boy's bandaged finger. "What happened to you, young man?"

Again, Parker was silent.

Whitney's gaze shot toward Jeremiah, and he realized she was waiting for an answer.

"Parker learned a *gut* lesson about using the right tool for the job," Jeremiah replied calmly. "It's a cut."

"Does he need stitches?"

Shaking his head, he said, "No. It bled a lot, but it'll heal quickly. It's not much more than a long paper cut. He can show you in the house, and I'm sure Mercy will rebandage it for him."

"I'll do that." She flashed a quick smile at the boy. "Go and let Mercy know I'm here."

Parker took off running as best he could through the piles of snow.

Once he was out of earshot, Whitney turned to Jeremiah. He told her how Parker had hurt himself.

"He won't make the same mistake again," he finished.

"Because he won't have access to knives?"

"No, because I'm going to show him the correct way to whittle once I know he's willing to be cautious."

"I don't know," she drawled.

"This is a farm, and boys on farms learn how to whittle and use a knife as a proper tool. If he's going to be here for a while, he needs to know what the other boys do, or he'll experiment on his own. Who knows how he could hurt himself if he did that?"

Whitney nodded slowly. "I see. Does that mean you intend to remain around to teach him how to use a knife?"

He shook his head. "I honestly can't answer that. Not until Mercy's family decides what they want done with the farm."

"You know starting a children's summer camp is Mercy's dream, don't you?" Whitney asked, flashing a guilty glance at the house as if revealing an unspeakable secret.

"I know. She wants to help *kinder* enjoy getting away from the summer heat in the city."

"No, Jeremiah, it's more than that. Mercy knows her life would have been very different if she hadn't been a Fresh Air kid. She wouldn't have known the family who took her in before the Bambergers became her foster parents and then her adoptive parents. Come Along Farm is her way to repay an immeasurable debt." Whitney looked at the house again and sighed. "Will it be enough for her?"

"I don't know," he replied.

"I don't know, either, but I do know there aren't too many women her age who would have agreed to look after a very angry, very hurt, very destructive and hateful child as she has."

"Parker is a challenge, but he's not hateful." Jeremiah thought of how the *kind* was changing…slightly.

"Parker? You don't have any idea whom I'm talking about, do you?"

"No. I thought we were talking about the boy."

"No, I'm talking about Sunni."

He couldn't hide his shock. "Sunni was destructive and hateful?"

"Yes."

"But she's such a *gut* kid."

"Now." Whitney ran her fingers lightly over the handle of her briefcase. "I've probably already said too much. If you want to know more, you'll need to ask Mercy. I wanted *you* to know, other than Sunni and the rest of her family—and I'm not too sure about her family—nothing is more important to Mercy than paying

back the compassion and love she was given after her grandmother died with a bigger dose of compassion and love. Please remember that."

"I will." What else could he say as Whitney walked toward the house?

Everything and everyone kept reminding him Mercy didn't want the farm for herself. She wanted it for others.

Lord, am I being selfish to believe the farm is the only way I can help this settlement to grow and succeed? How can I stand in her way if I care for her?

And he more than cared for her, he knew. He was in danger of falling in love with her. He found it difficult to imagine a day without her being a part of it. Her smile was the last thing he thought of before falling asleep and the first thing he envisioned in the hour before dawn. The brush of her fingers set off fireworks along his skin, and the thought of kissing her left him breathless.

So how could he stand in the way of her making her dreams come true? *How, Lord?*

He turned to walk toward the barns, not sure he was ready for the answer to that question.

Mercy wasn't surprised when Jeremiah offered to help her do dishes after supper. She guessed he was curious how the meeting with Whitney had gone. She eased his concerns by telling him the social worker had been impressed with how quickly he explained what had happened to Parker's finger and why and how Jeremiah intended to prevent such things from occurring again.

"She seems very taken with you, Jeremiah," she said with a chuckle.

"I'm a very taking guy." He grimaced. "Is that even a thing?"

"Who knows? Thank you for being so up-front about Parker's injury. Once Whitney saw it was exactly as you described, she was satisfied."

"And Parker ended up with, as he described them, very cool bandages."

"Don't tell him that I bought those strips with cartoon characters for Sunni. He won't be happy then."

"I'd hoped they'd be getting along better by now."

She shrugged. "I've got to admit having him treating her badly has strengthened her." A faint smile tugged at her lips. "I suspect, in spite of my best efforts, I've babied her a bit because of her physical challenges. Parker cuts her no slack."

"That's a nice way of saying he's rude to her."

"But not to you." She smiled. "I don't know what you're doing, Jeremiah, but whatever it is, don't stop."

"I'm not planning to. By the way, I intend to start tapping the maple trees in the sugar bush tomorrow. If it's not too cold, why don't you and the *kinder* join me? I could use extra hands, and I think they'll find it fascinating. I did when I first saw sap coming out of a tree when I was a kid."

"That sounds like fun."

"It should be." He chuckled. "Do you know what Parker asked me earlier today?"

She gave a half laugh. "I don't want to try to guess. Knowing him, it could have been anything."

"He asked me if I believed in God."

Putting another stack of dirty dishes into the sink, she said, "I assume you told him you do."

"*Ja*, but I don't think he was looking for such a simple answer. He's trying to figure out why we live as we do in Harmony Creek." He picked up another plate to dry. "For a child who's so quick to anger, he can be deeply introspective when presented with a new idea. It's too bad apparently nobody has ever spoken to him about such things before he came here."

"I plan to take him to the closest Mennonite church with me on Sunday. It's about thirty miles from here." She hesitated, then asked, "Would you like to come with us?"

"You came to Sunday services with me, so I guess I should return the favor."

She faced him. "I should warn you that boys Parker's age sit with the men."

"That should make for an interesting morning, ain't so?"

Her breath grew swift as her gaze was caught by his. Strong emotions glistened in his eyes that burned a fiery blue. His fingers curved along her cheek, the warmth of his palm caressing her skin. As he stepped closer to her, he gently tilted her face toward him.

He was going to kiss her! Every nerve went on alert, and she was aware of him as she'd never been, the scent of the soap he used, the rough texture of his arms beneath her fingertips, the way his hair fell forward over his eyes as he bent to bring her lips to his.

A loud cry came from the mudroom, and Mercy

yanked herself away from him. Shoving the dishrag that had been dripping unnoticed on the floor into Jeremiah's hands, she ran to referee the latest argument between the two children. She sent Sunni to the dining room and Parker into the living room, telling them to cool off.

From behind her as she stood in the middle of the empty room, she heard Jeremiah say, "*Ja*, I think it's going to be very interesting at church." He went into the kitchen.

She was about to follow, then paused. The moment between them was gone, and she would be wise not to let it happen again. She wasn't sure she could step away without kissing him next time.

Chapter Thirteen

Mercy wasn't sure who was more excited when the next day dawned with a cloudless sky and temperatures that should rise above freezing by midday. The kids were thrilled when they heard Jeremiah's invitation to help him with tapping the maple trees. She was just as excited, praying she'd have the chance to discover if he'd truly intended to kiss her.

She had to insist the children eat a hearty breakfast. They wanted to rush out and get to work right away. She also made them show her what they were wearing. She told Parker to zip his coat and wrap a scarf around his neck. When Sunni protested wearing her snow pants, Mercy refused to let her daughter draw her into an argument. If she didn't wear them, she wasn't going.

Seeing a hastily hidden smirk on Parker's face, Mercy wanted to ask what he'd said to persuade Sunni to go out without proper clothing. She didn't. Later, when she had a chance to speak to her daughter alone, she'd find out. Why Sunni listened to him when he said

such things was a mystery to Mercy, but her own siblings were so much older than she was, so they hadn't shared growing up years with her.

Mercy found a new problem when they went outside. The snow was melting, and walking through the high piles was as difficult as slogging through knee-deep mud. Watching Sunni, she wasn't sure the little girl could trudge up the hill and into the woods.

"Who wants a ride?" asked Jeremiah as he appeared around the house with an ancient toboggan topped with buckets and spiles to use to tap the trees.

The toboggan's front was scraped as if it'd hit bushes or caromed off a tree. No cushions eased the hard seats, but he connected a new nylon rope to it.

Not waiting for an answer to his question, he bowed. "Young ladies first."

His words earned a giggle from Sunni as she climbed on, and a mouthed "Thank you" from Mercy. She was grateful for how he didn't act as if Sunni was incapable.

At first, Parker was going to ride, but he changed his mind when Jeremiah asked him to help carry the battery-operated drill he'd use to make the holes for the sap. Jeremiah grabbed two handfuls of buckets off the toboggan, leaving plenty of room for Sunni.

When Mercy urged Jeremiah and Parker to go ahead, the boy followed him toward the clump of trees halfway up the hill behind the barn. She pulled Sunni on the toboggan, following the path Jeremiah and Parker had made. It was a beautiful day, cold but the sunshine glistened on the unbroken snow. She pointed to animal tracks and had Sunni guess which animal might have

made them. Crows sang their raucous songs as they wheeled overhead, and Sunni giggled with delight at the ride through the snow.

"Just like when we went in the sleigh, Mommy!" she called out.

"Except I'm playing the horse's part."

That brought more laughter from her daughter, and Mercy's footsteps grew lighter, even as the wet snow tried to hold her back.

Jeremiah paused and let Mercy catch up. "Do you want me to take the toboggan?"

"No, I'm fine."

"That you are." He gave her a wink that made her heart dance with delight.

He went to a tree and walked around it. Looking up at the sky, he shifted partway around again. "Okay, here's the southeast side of the tree."

"Is that important?" Parker asked.

"It is. The southeast side gets sunshine first in the late winter." He held out his hand for the drill. "Stay back."

Sunni clambered off the toboggan so she could watch as the drill whirred, sending pieces of wood flying in every direction. Her eyes were wide as she leaned closer.

Mercy put her hands on her daughter's shoulders, drawing her back slightly. She didn't want the little girl hit by the debris.

Picking up a thin twig, Jeremiah showed Parker how to clean the shavings out of the hole. "This way, they won't get in the sap." He hammered a spile into the tree.

"Will the tree be okay?" Sunni asked with sudden concern. "You're not hurting it, are you?"

"It'll be fine." Jeremiah gave her a gentle smile. "We won't be greedy, so the tree will have plenty of sap to carry up its branches to grow leaves. This is a grown-up tree." He pointed to the trunk at chest height. "Once a tree is ten inches around at this height, it can share its sap with us."

He showed Mercy how to place the bucket on the hook built into the tap so it would catch the drippings. He warned her to be careful the bucket's handle wasn't in the way. When the first drop fell with a ping into the bucket, Mercy was as enthralled as the children. While Jeremiah helped Sunni set the metal "roof" over the bucket, he explained the folded piece would prevent windblown leaves and other debris from falling into the sap. Some would find their way into the bucket, but not as much as if the bucket was left open.

"It looks like it's wearing a hat," Sunni said with a grin.

Motioning for them to follow, Jeremiah began drilling another hole in the tree. He did three in the smaller trees and four in the massive ones. Each of the others had their tasks. Mercy waited while Parker cleared the hole, leaving tiny specks of wood on the snow at his feet. She and Sunni set the bucket and cover in place.

They fell into an easy rhythm as they moved from one tree to the next. After drilling holes in twenty-five trees, Jeremiah called a halt.

"If we do more," he said, "I won't have time to collect the sap, make the syrup and milk the cows." He

ruffled the top of Parker's hat, leaving it askew. "Even with my *gut* assistant here."

The boy grinned. "Can I help make syrup, too?"

"*Ja.* I'll need everyone to pitch in." He stepped aside to let Parker clear out the hole. "Wait a moment, Mercy, before you put the bucket on. Do you *kinder* want to try a sample of the sap?"

This time, Parker went first. He bent and stuck out his tongue beneath the hole exactly as Jeremiah instructed. The boy waited and waited, then frowned at Jeremiah, as if he thought the man was playing a trick on him.

"You've got to be patient," Jeremiah said with a laugh. "Sap comes out one drip at a time, and it's pretty chilly, so it's moving slowly."

"Let her try." He pointed to Sunni and stepped back, disgruntled.

"All right. Sunni, you want to have a taste?"

Mercy smiled as Sunni stepped forward to take her turn. She stood as Parker had. Silence, except for the rustle of birds in the higher branches, settled on them as she waited with her tongue poised near the hole. When she yelped in excitement, Mercy knew a drop had finally emerged.

"It's sweet!" Sunni's face glowed with happiness.

"Wait till you taste how sweet the syrup will be." Jeremiah turned to Parker as Mercy gave her daughter a hug. "You want to try again?"

"Yeah." His surly tone surprised Mercy because he hadn't used it with Jeremiah since the day of his arrival.

He stepped forward, elbowing Sunni aside. As she fell into the snow, he ordered, "Get out of my way, cripple!"

Hearing Mercy's dismayed gasp, Jeremiah grabbed the boy by his shoulders and pulled him away from the tree. Anger blared through Jeremiah, and he wasn't sure he could quiet it. Mercy's face was as pale as the snow as she lifted her daughter to her feet, and fat tears showered Sunni's cheeks. He wasn't sure if she was physically hurt or wounded by the cruel words.

"Mercy, will you and Sunni finish putting the bucket on there? We'll meet you at the house." Without another word, Jeremiah walked away, tugging Parker with him.

The boy started to speak several times as they went toward the tenant house. Each time, Jeremiah cut him off sharply.

Steering him inside, Jeremiah motioned for Parker to take a seat at the kitchen table. He half expected the boy to make a snide remark about the state of the house, but Parker stared at the floor.

"Why would you say something horrible to Sunni?" Jeremiah asked, not wanting to beat around the bush.

"I dunno," he muttered.

"I think you do. You treat Sunni and Mercy as if they're manure on the bottom of your boots."

The boy clamped his lips closed.

Knowing he needed to take another tack, Jeremiah forced his voice to be calm. The boy wasn't going to respond to anger. Parker would get defensive and close up.

Quietly, Jeremiah sighed.

The boy looked up, startled.

"Parker, I thought you wanted to be here working with me."

"I do." The boy bumped his toe against an uneven floorboard and again didn't meet Jeremiah's gaze.

"I can't work with someone who says bad things to other people."

"People say bad things to me."

He sat on a chair beside the *kind*'s. "I'm sorry to hear that, Parker. People used to say bad things about me, too."

"You?" The boy's head jerked up, revealing his shock. It made him look younger than his nine years and vulnerable. "But everyone says what a nice guy you are. When we went to the hardware store last week, I heard a man say he wouldn't be as willing as you are to wait to get what he'd signed papers for." Puzzlement threaded his brow. "What papers?"

Not wanting to be distracted from the issue at hand, Jeremiah said, "Business stuff. Nothing important now." He was astonished to realize how true his words were. As much as he wanted to own the farm, at that moment his whole attention was on the *kind*.

"What did they say about you?" Parker asked.

"I was too short. I was too chubby. I was stupid because I had a hard time alphabetizing my spelling words."

The boy's nose wrinkled. "I hate alphabetizing my spelling words, too."

"I couldn't see the point of doing it when I could be in the barn working with the cows or whittling. The cows and that stick of wood didn't care if I knew which

word should come first." He leaned toward Parker. "And they didn't care what anyone else said about me. They didn't care about anything other than I did my chores and took care of them. So that's what I did."

"Me, too."

"But as much as you and I are alike, there's one way we're different. I try never to say anything hurtful to someone else. Jesus asked us to treat everyone else the way we want to be treated."

"That's what I'm doing."

Jeremiah caught and held the boy's gaze. "Do you really want Sunni to say such nasty things to you?"

Parker's shoulders sagged. "No."

"Then why do you say them to her?"

"Sometimes I get mad."

"I know how that is."

The boy stiffened. "Do you? Sometimes I get so mad I want to hit someone."

"I know."

He frowned. "I thought Amish guys didn't fight."

"We shouldn't, but once, when I was about your age, I thought about hitting the bully who said bad things about me. I didn't."

"Why not?"

"Because I knew I was loved the way I was."

Parker shook his head. "Good for you. Nobody wants me."

"No? Mercy opened her home to you. Sunni includes you in everything she does. Don't you realize she thinks you're someone special? Haven't you noticed how she

was eager to help in the barn because you were helping there?"

He shrugged, not wanting to be swayed by Jeremiah's words. "Maybe she thought she was missing out on something."

"Maybe she did, but she didn't realize it until you showed her how much fun chores can be. She never was interested before you came here."

Tears bubbled out of the boy's eyes, and Jeremiah had to resist his immediate impulse to put his arms around Parker and comfort him. The *kind* needed to realize his mistakes and decide to change.

"I'm sorry, Jeremiah. Don't hate me, too."

"I don't hate you. Nobody on the farm hates you."

"Sunni does." He wiped his nose with his arm. "She has to. I hate me."

"If she hated you, she wouldn't want to spend time with you. And she does."

Parker dashed away more tears. "She's a silly little girl."

"Maybe, but that silly little girl doesn't hate you. I don't hate you, and Mercy doesn't." He put a hand on the boy's shoulder. "Let me tell you one more very important thing. God loves you."

"How do you know that?"

"Because His son told us so." He gave the boy a gentle smile. "He loves all his *kinder*, including when we make mistakes. I've made plenty." The image of Emmarita's face flashed through his mind, but he easily ignored it. "God chose for me to be exactly like I am, so He must love what I am. Just as he loves you. Believe

it." He tapped Parker's chest. "Right here, believe it. Next time you feel angry, give that anger over to God. He doesn't mind, and He'll ease the pain in your heart."

"He will?"

"Ja." Coming to his feet, Jeremiah said, "I think you know what you need to do."

"Apologize to Sunni?" He got up. "Will you come with me?"

"Of course."

A few minutes later Jeremiah stood beside the boy while Parker asked Sunni to forgive him. When the little girl did with a sincerity Jeremiah found endearing, he saw gratitude in Mercy's eyes. He put his arms around all of them, pulling them into a hug. Feeling Mercy's soft hand on his back, he knew he'd lost the battle to stop himself from loving her.

That made everything more difficult, and he needed to figure out what to do about it. But right now he was going to enjoy holding her—and the *kinder*—close.

Chapter Fourteen

The interior of the church could have belonged to the one Mercy had attended with her parents in central New York. Plain, whitewashed walls and simple benches. A trio of windows on either side of the pews had no stained glass like other churches in the village.

Adjusting her prayer covering, she walked with Sunni to a bench on the women's side. She glanced at where Parker sat next to Jeremiah. The boy's legs swung as he waited for the service to start. When Jeremiah bent to whisper something in his ear, Parker gave him a big grin.

How she wished she could get such a response from the boy, but he refused to trust her. She kept telling herself not to take it personally. He didn't trust any woman as far as she could see, and he had good cause. Not only had he been abandoned by his mother in Korea, left at a grocery store according to his records, but Pat Kenton had let him love her and then turned her back on him, as well.

Someday, sometime in the future when Parker was

old enough to understand, she hoped she could tell him how much she empathized with his fear of loving again. Mrs. Kenton had chosen her other life over her son's, as Graham had chosen his mother over Mercy...and her Fresh Air family had chosen their older daughter's lies over Mercy's and their younger daughter's protestations of truth.

Life wasn't fair, but it was good.

She wasn't sure who'd said that first, but she believed it with every ounce of her being. If Parker would let her closer, she might be able to convince him she knew his sense of betrayal. Maybe someday...but not today because he'd ignored Sunni and her, talking only to Jeremiah in the car. Even so, she longed to see the boy smile at something she said or did with as much joy as he did when he was with Jeremiah.

Jeremiah... Did he suspect she'd invited him to the Mennonite service hoping he'd feel comfortable enough that he'd consider putting aside his Amish life to join the Mennonites? It wouldn't be so different for him.

Except he wouldn't be part of the new community on the banks of Harmony Creek.

Praying about what to do so they could have a future together hadn't brought her any answers. Few people joined the Amish, and fewer stayed. The dedication to community and to a life separate from the rest of the world was too much for most people who hadn't been raised in it.

As well, there was the issue of Come Along Farm. Opening a summer camp for children probably wouldn't fit with the Amish ideas of staying separate. She glanced

at Sunni, who was looking everywhere but at Parker on the other side of the aisle. From Whitney, she'd learned Amish might adopt, but it was usually an internal matter. A baby born to an Amish girl who couldn't rear it would be given to another family.

But if I can't become Amish and he won't become Mennonite, there's no future for us.

That thought echoed through Mercy's head as she listened to the service but kept glancing over to where Parker sat beside Jeremiah. When the boy yawned, Jeremiah put his arm around the child and leaned Parker against him. She smiled gently before Sunni nestled against her. Pushing her worries from her mind, she gave herself over to the peace filling the sanctuary.

Mercy was smiling when, after the service, she led Sunni to where Jeremiah and Parker were waiting by her car. Urging them to get in out of the windy day, she slid behind the wheel. She turned the key to start the car and twisted the dial so the heat would fill the space. Other cars were backing up and pulling out of the parking lot, so she waited.

After turning to check both children wore their seat belts, she asked the question that weighed so heavily on her mind. "So what did you think of the service, Jeremiah?"

"The harmony when you sing the hymns is pretty. Four-part harmony, ain't so?"

"Yes, and we sing the hymns at a quicker tempo than you do. I hope that didn't trip you up."

"I was able to keep up." He gave her a smile, which did delightful things to her middle.

"You know that's not what I meant."

"Maybe I did. Maybe I didn't." He winked at the children.

Sunni began to giggle, but Parker looked baffled as if he couldn't figure out why someone would find the conversation amusing.

"I've made up my mind," he said abruptly.

"About what?" Mercy asked.

"My name."

"Is that so?" she asked, careful to make her voice sound calm. "What other name have you decided on? Or do you want to keep the one you've got?"

"Not Parker." His nose wrinkled. "I sound like someone working in a parking lot."

Jeremiah chuckled. "I had the same thought when I first heard it."

The boy remained serious. "I thought about Jerry because it's like your name, Jeremiah, but you might think Mercy is scolding you when I do something wrong."

Again, Jeremiah laughed, but Mercy could see how deeply touched he was by the child's desire to be connected to him. Her eyes were awash in tears she didn't want to let fall because the boy might think she was upset.

"So tell us your name!" Sunni leaned toward him, excited.

"I want to be Paul." He looked at Jeremiah. "I remember hearing you say the day I arrived Paul was your dad's name. That's right, ain't so? And, if I'm Paul, you won't get confused when Mercy's talking to us."

When Jeremiah nodded, Mercy realized he was so

overcome with emotion he was unable to speak. Not only was the boy picking up his way of speaking, but Parker had also chosen a name that meant so much to Jeremiah.

Clearing his throat, Jeremiah said, "You're right. Paul was my *daed*'s name, and I think he would have been happy to share it with you."

"All right. Call me Paul." Without a pause, he asked what was for lunch.

"Would you like to stop somewhere to eat?" Mercy was no longer surprised by Parker's— No, she needed to remember to call him Paul and let Whitney know about the change once she was sure the boy wouldn't pick a different name tomorrow. She was not surprised by Paul's focus on his next meal. The boy seemed endlessly hungry. "There's a nice diner between here and the farm. Grandpa Rudy used to take me there once or twice each summer when I visited him. You'll get so much to eat you'll feel like a stuffed turkey at Thanksgiving."

That brought cheers of excitement from the back seat. When she glanced at Jeremiah, he smiled.

"How could I say no when I'm outnumbered?" he asked with a chuckle.

She backed the car out, determined to enjoy the day and the company the Lord had given her.

Jeremiah wasn't surprised when Mercy walked beside him as the *kinder* raced toward the diner's door.

Slanting her head toward him, she murmured, "You do realize the importance of the name he picked, right?

It's his way of telling you he wants to be a family with you."

"It's pretty overwhelming."

"It is, isn't it?" She squeezed his arm and smiled. "You've worked wonders with him, and he knows that, though he can't—or won't—say it. Are you truly okay with him using your father's name?"

He nodded, and unabashed tears gleamed in his eyes. "My *daed* used to say that he wanted a dozen *kinder*. He and *Mamm* were blessed with the nine of us, but it feels now as if he's one more kid closer to his goal."

When she gave him a lovely smile, he wasn't sure how the day could get better. He thought about taking her hand, but they'd reached the door where Sunni and *Paul* were waiting impatiently. He opened the door and ushered them inside.

The diner was long and narrow. A single line of booths edged the windows overlooking the parking lot. Cutting the building down the middle was a curved counter. The stools were repaired with black electrical tape. However, everything was sparkling clean.

When Mercy led the way to the booth she called her favorite, he followed the *kinder*. He couldn't fail to notice the glances in their directions. They were the only plain folk in the diner.

A waitress in a simple white shirt and black pants beneath her red-checkered apron took their orders. Fortunately, the menu for *kinder* was limited, so Sunni and Paul selected quickly. Chicken nuggets for Sunni and spaghetti for Paul. After checking that none of the boy's allergies would be triggered by what he'd ordered,

Mercy asked for an open-faced hot turkey sandwich. Glad the others had ordered first, Jeremiah debated between two favorites and settled on chicken Parmesan.

The servings were as huge as Mercy recalled and as delicious. The children wasted no time cleaning their plates, their eyes continuously shifting toward the pie trolley on top of the gray counter.

When the waitress came to remove their plates, she asked if they wanted dessert. The enthusiastic response came from Jeremiah as well as the children.

The waitress smiled. "Just so you know, we get our pies from an Amish woman."

"Do you have *snitz* pie?" he asked.

"We do."

"Then two adult-size servings and two kid-size ones. Two cups of *kaffi*—coffee—and two glasses of milk."

"Chocolate?" interjected Paul.

She nodded. "Chocolate it'll be."

As she walked away, Sunni asked, "What is *snitz*?"

"Wait and see." He winked at Mercy as the kids wiggled with anticipation.

The waitress returned with their drinks before going to the counter to cut four slices of pie. She smiled as she set the plates on the table.

Paul wrinkled his nose as he looked at the dark brown filling in his serving. "What is it?"

"Is it chocolate?" asked Sunni, peering at her slice from every direction.

"It's *snitz* pie." Jeremiah grinned. "If you don't want it, I'll eat it." He held out his hand. "I never pass up a piece of *snitz* pie, especially my *mamm*'s. Ask anyone,

and they'll tell you Wanda Lapp makes the best *snitz* pie in Lancaster County. Maybe the whole world."

"Why isn't her name Wanda Stoltzfus?" asked Sunni, ever the one to try to nail down every detail.

"Because she got remarried after my *daed* died."

"My father is dead, too." The little girl's lower lip began to tremble. "And my mommy." Her gaze darted to Mercy. "Not this mommy, my before mommy."

"My whole family is dead," stated Paul, not to be outdone. As he began to tell an outrageous tale that sounded as if it'd come from a television show too violent for a child his age, he must have seen the adults weren't buying his story. "It's true!"

"But it's not *gut* conversation for the dinner table." Jeremiah caught the boy's eyes and tilted his head toward where Mercy and Sunni sat. "The ladies, you know. They don't like rough talk like cowmen use. That's very important, ain't so?"

Mercy picked up her cup of coffee and took a sip so the boy didn't see her lips twitching with a smile. When Paul agreed with Jeremiah, she guessed the child had no idea what Jeremiah meant, but he wasn't going to let anyone see that.

"But what is it?" persisted Paul.

Mercy decided Jeremiah had teased the children long enough. "Apple pie."

Paul shook his head. "It looks strange."

"Because it's made with dried apples." She looked at the boy, who was clearly torn between standing firm so he didn't look as if he was giving in to her and his obvious longing to give in to the temptation to try the pie.

"It tastes like apple butter."

"Yummy!" announced Sunni and dove into her dessert.

Not to be outdone, Paul broke off the tiniest piece with his fork and stared at it. "It's polite to eat what's put in front of me," he said, obviously repeating something he'd heard at his previous home.

Mercy exchanged a glance with Jeremiah as she wondered how many times Paul's prospective mother had uttered those words. Her sorrow at what the boy had experienced vanished when Paul's eyes lit up as he tasted the pie.

"Can we have seconds?" he asked as he jabbed his fork into the pie for another bite.

They laughed, and Mercy savored the chance to look at each of them as they all smiled at the same time. It hadn't happened often. She hoped it would more often from this point forward.

"Mommy! Stop! Now!"

When Sunni screamed, Mercy looked in the rearview mirror and saw her daughter's terror. They'd just driven out of the diner's parking lot.

Jeremiah swung around. "Mercy, pull over!"

She twisted the wheel. The car behind her honked in annoyance, but she ignored it as she jammed the shifting lever into Park. As their car rocked to an abrupt stop, she jumped out at the same time Jeremiah did.

He tore open the door on his side and leaned over Paul, who was straining to breathe. The boy's lips were

already turning blue, and his face was swollen with hives.

Grabbing her purse, she pulled out the epinephrine injector she'd been carrying since Paul joined their family. She ran around the car, pushed Jeremiah aside and flipped the top off the injector. She gripped it tightly before grabbing the fleshy part of the boy's thigh. She pressed the injector against his pants. Hearing a click, she counted off ten seconds.

"We passed an urgent care just before we pulled into the diner," Jeremiah said.

"Can you drive a car?"

He nodded. "But I haven't in a while."

"Get in and drive." She climbed between the two children, keeping her eyes on the wheezing boy. "Go!"

Jeremiah jumped behind the wheel and jammed the shift into Drive. They were thrown back against the seats as the tires squealed when he rammed the gas pedal to the floor.

"You're going to be okay," she said as she brushed Paul's bangs from his brow that was covered with cold sweat.

She heard Jeremiah praying and added her own prayers that they'd reach the urgent care quickly and— as another car blared its horn at them—without an accident.

Hours later, when Mercy sat across from Jeremiah at the kitchen table having a calming cup of tea while he drank coffee, she strained her ears to listen for foot-

steps upstairs. The children had been worn out by the day's exciting events.

"A single piece of candy with a single peanut in it." Mercy shook her head. "He didn't realize he'd grabbed one with a peanut from the bowl by the cash register. Not until it was in his mouth."

"But he's all right."

"I'd like to say my nerves are all right, too."

Jeremiah laughed quietly. "Maybe yours are. I think mine will calm down in a month or so. You were *wunderbaar*, Mercy. You didn't stop to think. You did what you had to do."

"You would have done the same."

"I'd like to think so, but I was shocked when his condition was getting more dire by the second."

Letting her shoulders sag and wincing at the ache from holding them taut for so long, she said, "Thank God it turned out all right."

"*Ja*, we must most definitely thank God. He was with us, protecting us."

"Especially when you were driving." She allowed herself a smile. "I didn't realize your previous driving experience was as a race driver."

Again, he chuckled. "Just so you know, I was praying as fast as I was driving." He sipped his coffee. His hands remained unsteady.

Just like hers. *Thank You, God, for watching over Paul today and guiding us to get help for him.*

"I hope you enjoyed the Mennonite service," Mercy said, needing to talk about something other than Paul's close brush with death.

"It was interesting. Like an Amish one, but yet n<u>o</u>t like it." He gave her a weary smile. "And I don't mean just the pace of the singing."

"If you'd like to come with us again, you're welcome." Wishing she could come out and ask him what she really wanted to know—would he ever consider becoming a Mennonite?—she couldn't. If he said no, then that ended any hopes for them to have a future together.

You're getting ahead of yourself, her conscience whispered. *He hasn't said anything about the future other than his plans for the farm. Can't you see what comes first?*

Pain twisted in her stomach. Jeremiah had been honest about the fact his dreams were his number one priority. If Graham had been so forthcoming, it would have saved them a lot of hurt.

"*Danki*," he replied, "but I may be doing some traveling."

"Really?"

"Caleb mentioned that he may need me to help him find other families for the settlement." He didn't add more, but she understood what he wasn't saying. If it wasn't God's will for him to have the farm, recruiting others to come to the Harmony Creek settlement might be the best way for him to help it thrive.

"When would you be leaving?"

"Most likely soon. Once spring comes, there won't be time for anything but fieldwork and chores." He gave her a weak smile. "Caleb suggested I go to central New York. Actually not far from where your family lives."

"You should stop in and see them if you do."

His brows lowered. "You don't think I'd try to influence them into selling me the farm?"

"I thought we weren't going to look for hidden motives." She didn't say the words harshly, because the thought had slipped through her mind, as well. "My parents would be glad to offer you a place to stay because you're my friend."

Did she see him flinch at *friend*? Or was she hoping he had? Could he feel about her as she did about him?

Her hopes he might faded when he asked, "Would there be anyone else you'd like me to take a message to? Did you leave someone special behind in central New York?"

She snorted. "How many men do you know who'd be willing to date a woman with a child, especially one with special medical needs? I could count them on the number of hairs on a bald man's head!"

"My brother Daniel married his wife, who was responsible for a *kind* with Down syndrome and her *grossmammi* Ella, who has Alzheimer's."

"Maybe so, but he's one of a kind."

He folded his arms on the table and shook his head. "Actually not. When my brothers—and sisters—have fallen in love, they haven't cared about the complications of *kinder*. Our family has grown very quickly in the past couple of years with additions, *bopplin* and older kids."

"Then your whole family is one of a kind. Most men I've met head in the other direction once they find out I have a child."

"Two."

"But for how long?" She raised her eyes toward the ceiling where the children should be asleep.

"What do you mean?"

"How long will Paul be here? There are so many reasons he could leave, some having to do with the social services. Others to…"

When her voice faded, he put his hand over her fingers on the table. "Others having to do with who ends up owning the farm? Is that what you were going to say?"

"I'm sorry, Jeremiah." She gazed at his hand on hers, confused. On one hand, she thrilled in his touch. On the other, she struggled to trust him. She knew he wasn't Graham, but her heart bore the scars of that betrayal.

"Mercy, you must realize if your family decides to sell me the farm, I'm not planning on throwing you and the kids out ten seconds later."

"I know, but you've got your plans for the farm." She slid her hand out from beneath his. Thinking clearly when his rough palm burnished her fingers was impossible.

Standing, she went to where she could look at the first stars poking through the crisp winter night. When Jeremiah moved behind her, he didn't touch her, but she was as much aware of his breathing as hers. In the silence she could hear his heartbeat matching her own. If she leaned back, even an inch, her head would be against him.

"Mercy, will you look at me?" His voice was no more than a whisper, but she could hear sorrow in it. "Tell me what you're thinking."

Facing him, she stared at the top button on his shirt. Meeting his gaze when she was so unsettled might be foolish.

"Why is it taking so long?" Not giving him a chance to answer, she added, "You've got to be asking that yourself."

"Some people need time to make an important decision. My family teases me because sometimes I'm the last one to make up my mind, but I've got to look at the decision from every angle so I know I've made the right one."

In spite of herself, she raised her eyes toward his. "Did it take you a long time to decide to buy this farm?"

"It took me a long time to realize I was happier farming than doing anything else. I immediately started looking for a *gut* place to go because I knew there weren't any farms I could afford near Paradise Springs. I wasn't sure where I'd go until Caleb talked to me about Harmony Creek. Coming here seemed the perfect answer."

"Until you got here and found us."

He arched his brows, and she saw a hint of his smile before it swiftly vanished. "I don't blame you."

"You should, you know."

"No, I shouldn't. For a reason neither of us can guess, God brought us together like this. He knows the future. We can't do anything but believe His reasons are for our *gut*, and if we continue forward toward what He has planned for us, we'll know His blessings."

"So we wait."

He shrugged, and his smile reappeared. "I don't see any alternative."

"I know." She clasped her hands behind her so she didn't reach out to throw her arms around him and beg him to hold her. "And every day we don't hear is another day Paul can stay here." She allowed herself a faint grin. "Not that any day is easy with him."

"Eventually, he'll realize what a blessing you and Sunni are for him." He went toward the door.

Had her face betrayed her longing to be in his arms? "And you. He wants your respect more than anything else now."

"Learning to respect you and Sunni would go a long way toward earning that."

"But he'd have to share you with us, and he's made it clear he doesn't want to."

He sighed and pulled his coat off the peg by the door. "He's a confused *kind*."

"I agree."

"So what can I do to help?" He reached for his scarf.

"Keep doing whatever you've been doing. I can see so many changes in him when he's with you. He listens to you."

"Sometimes."

"Which is a lot more than he listens to me. I know he craves action. That's one of the reasons he likes doing chores with you. Painting doesn't interest him."

He put his hand on the doorknob, but didn't turn it. "I'll be collecting sap and starting the evaporator to make syrup in the morning. Paul can help me."

"That should definitely keep him busy."

"Oh, I'll find lots for him to do." His eyes twinkled and then grew serious again. "He truly is blessed to have you care about him so much. Just as I am." He bent and kissed her cheek. "Sleep well, Mercy."

He was gone before she could reply. Raising her fingers to the place where his lips had grazed her face, she stared at the closed door.

He'd kissed her.

True, it'd been as chaste as a kiss he'd give the children, but he'd kissed her.

She wished she knew what it meant.

Chapter Fifteen

"Cool! Hey, Sunni! Come and see this."

Shocked by Paul's eager invitation to Sunni, whom he didn't want hanging around him, and not sure what the boy was up to, Mercy jumped up from where she was mending yet another rip in the knees of Paul's trousers. She ran to where the cellar door was open.

He stood a couple of steps below her on the stairs and looked at her with an excited grin. "Why didn't you tell me you were putting a pool in the cellar? This is the coolest house ever!"

"Pool?" She edged past him. She halted when she heard the unmistakable sound of moving water. In fact, if she hadn't known better, she would have guessed there was a waterfall in the cellar.

"How big is it? I wanna see." The boy reached for the switch to turn on the lights.

She grabbed his wrist, not wanting to risk him getting a shock.

"Go!" she cried. "Get Jeremiah. Tell him we've got

a flooded basement." Looking over her shoulder, she repeated her order.

As Paul started to go, there was a pop. Lights went out, leaving the house in a dusky twilight, and Sunni squealed from upstairs.

Mercy went up and into the kitchen. She grabbed a flashlight from the junk drawer. When she sprayed the light, she saw the water was halfway up the stairs. High enough to have flooded the electrical box and shorted it out. Boxes and other items bobbed on the rising water. She was tempted to try to snag them, but didn't want to fall into the filthy water topped by what looked like an oil slick.

It seemed forever before Paul returned with Jeremiah. When she heard Jeremiah calling, she wanted to sag with relief.

Instead, she shouted, "In the cellar!"

He hurried toward her and whistled. "I thought Paul was exaggerating. There really is a swimming pool here."

"It's rising fast."

"The snow is melting quickly, and the ground is frozen, so the water must have found its way through the foundation." He paused. "Sounds like it's pouring in over behind the fuel tank." As he started up the stairs, he said, "Let me get the generator from my workshop. We'll hook it to a pump. Rudy must have one around here."

"I'll look for it after I open the bulkhead."

"*Gut* idea. That'll give the water an exit out of the cellar."

Warning both children to stay away from the cellar steps, Mercy didn't pause to grab a coat. She stuck her feet into boots and rushed out into the evening dusk. Glancing at the workshop where Jeremiah was unplugging the generator as fast as he could, she ran through the slushy snow and deep puddles beginning to ice over again. The cold should stop the flood.

She put her foot against one side of the double doors and pulled the other. It moved with the protest of rusty hinges. She groaned when she saw another door at the base of the stairs. Water was seeping out, reaching the top of the first step even as she watched in shock.

Hurrying to where Jeremiah pushed the generator across the yard while he balanced hoses over his shoulder, she told him about the door. "If we open it, we'll get washed away."

"Look for a pump while I get the generator ready to go. You know what one looks like?"

She nodded and ran toward the garage. Her grandfather had kept a small pump on a shelf when she was a kid. Was it still there?

Finding it, her next question was if it worked. There was no way to find out without hooking it up. She handed it to Jeremiah. He deftly connected the pump to hoses and then to the generator. Yanking on the starter cord, he bent to push open one of the cellar windows. He shoved one hose inside, then started the pump.

Water whooshed out, spraying them. He switched off the pump, grabbed the hose that had showered them with dirty water and tossed it in the direction of the

road. When he restarted the pump, water erupted in a geyser again, but fell harmlessly into a snowbank.

Once assured the pump was working, Mercy followed Jeremiah into the house. He told her he had enough gasoline to keep the generator running for the next twenty-four hours.

"By then, the weather will probably have turned cold again." He sighed. "I hope so, because if it stays this warm, the sap will run too fast and won't be *gut* for syrup."

Throughout the evening, Jeremiah checked on the level of the water in the cellar. It didn't begin to lower until it was time for the children to go to bed, unhappy they'd had cold sandwiches for supper.

"Now you know how it is to live like the Amish do," Jeremiah said with a chuckle as they started up the stairs.

He got peeved looks in return, but, by the time they went upstairs, he'd brought kerosene lanterns from the tenant house and barn. Mercy helped Sunni and Paul brush their teeth, making sure they skimped on water. Until the well pump was running again, they had to conserve what was in the tank. Paul perked up, glad to skip his bath.

Mercy was relieved when Sunni and Paul went to sleep quickly. She'd piled her grandfather's crocheted afghans on top of their beds, hoping to keep them warm until morning. If it was too cold when she went upstairs, she'd carry them into her bed, where they would keep each other from freezing.

When she came into the living room, she sat on the

sofa where she'd been working what seemed like days ago. A kerosene lamp gave off more light than she'd expected. She picked up Paul's pants. She'd gotten the patch sewn on one knee and needed to finish one on the other knee.

"I don't know how he can rip out the knees of his trousers when there's a couple of feet of snow on the ground," she said wryly.

Jeremiah closed the woodworking supply catalog he'd been looking at and set it on the table beside the other end of the sofa. "The boy has a rare talent for such things."

"Another week is almost over." Her needle darted in and out of the denim, jabbing with her frustration as she added, "And nothing has changed."

"I don't want to talk about the farm and your family tonight."

"Neither do I, but the delay in getting an answer has been much on my mind, especially with the flooded cellar."

He gave her a cockeyed grin. "Me, too. That's why I don't want to talk about it. Why don't we talk about something we haven't talked about?"

"What's that?"

"Rudy." He shifted so he could look at her, leaving himself mostly in silhouette. "I never met the man, though everyone tells me about him. Everyone but you."

She frowned. "I talk about my grandfather all the time."

"Bits and pieces. Tell me about the Rudy you knew."

For a moment she was silent. Not because she wasn't

sure what to tell him. She wasn't sure what to tell him *first*. So many memories were layered on top of each other, images as clear in her mind as the photo of her parents in *Abuelita*'s apartment.

How could she explain to Jeremiah how important Grandpa Rudy had been to her? Not once had he made her feel like she was different from his other grandchildren. He didn't care she'd had other parents before the Bambergers. She was his granddaughter, and that was all that mattered.

"He loved to laugh," she said. "Apparently, he was a prankster his whole life. Any tin can could contain a fake snake. Any glass could be a dribble one, and I quickly learned to look before I sat. He really loved whoopie cushions."

"He sounds like fun."

"He was, and what he liked was for someone to play a trick on him. I spent hours before each visit trying to come up with something to surprise him and make him laugh."

"And did you?"

"I don't know if I ever surprised him, but he always laughed. He found much joy in everything. He considered everything he could see and hear and touch a gift from God, and he was thankful every day of his life." Lowering her mending to her lap, she gazed out the window toward the dark backyard. "He grew rows of rhubarb behind the house, though he was allergic to it. Touching it gave him hives, but he made sure the rhubarb grew every year and invited the neighbors to pick it."

"Why?"

"Because his wife loved rhubarb, and he'd loved her. She died quite young, so I never met her." She blinked back sudden tears. "I don't think I'd ever been so proud than when he told me, though I looked like my mother, I reminded him of his late wife." She felt her cheeks heat. "I'm sorry. I know you Amish think pride is wrong."

"I think there are exceptions to everything, even *hochmut*. It sounds as if that compliment was one." He reached across the cushion between them and took her hand. "*Danki* for sharing your love for Rudy with me, Mercy. I've known from the beginning how important the farm is to you, but I thought it was only because of your hope of helping *kinder*. I see you want the farm to be a tribute to your *grossdawdi*, who helped you find the family you thought you'd lost."

"I never thought of it that way."

When he didn't reply immediately, she realized he was giving her the chance to consider his words. And she did. Was building the farm into something special important because it symbolized what she'd found after losing everything and everyone important to her?

He shifted again, closer to her. She could see his intense expression. She dampened her lips, and his eyes followed the motion. Quickly, she looked down.

His fingers beneath her chin brought her face up. She shivered as a powerful warmth sliced through her, radiating from where his fingertips touched her. When he tilted her mouth toward his, she wondered why she was fighting what she yearned for. His face, which was

rough with a day's growth of whiskers, brushed against her when he lightly kissed her right cheek.

Her breath caught. Was another chaste kiss all he wanted? It was so sweet, but when he moved to kiss her other cheek, she caught his face between her palms. His eyes burned like the heart of a fire, sparks glinting through their shadowed depths.

"Kiss me," she whispered softly.

"I am kissing you."

"Kiss my lips."

"I want that more than you can know, *liebling*."

The gentleness of his lips mesmerized her, and she deepened the kiss. When he started to lift his mouth away, she steered it back to hers.

With a chuckle, he pulled her closer as he captured her lips again. His kiss was a delicious confirmation of the feelings she'd prayed he shared with her. She shouldn't be falling in love with him, not when he wanted to take her farm from her, but she wouldn't lie to herself or to him. Being in his arms was what she wanted right now and for the rest of...

She drew back. When he arched a brow at her, she realized he knew the course of her thoughts. Were they similar to his own?

Then she realized she didn't care. Sliding her hands up to his shoulders, she leaned forward once more. This time when he kissed her, thoughts of pulling away vanished. For one special moment, the past and the future didn't exist. Only now. The worries would return, but for now she wanted to relish his kisses.

* * *

"Danki," Jeremiah said when Mercy slid another slice of French toast onto his plate. She'd started the gas stove with a match, enabling her to make them a warm breakfast.

"You're welcome."

That was the longest sentence she'd spoken to him since Paul had insisted Jeremiah join the rest of them for breakfast. Mercy was quiet, not teasing either Sunni or Paul. Was she thinking, as he was, of the kisses they'd shared last night? She hadn't met his eyes since he came in.

He understood too well. Sleep had been elusive last night. Lying awake, he'd stared at the water-stained ceiling in the tenant house. The shadows of bare branches had rocked in the moonlight as wind groaned beneath the eaves. He'd fallen asleep a couple of times, but something jerked him awake. Finally, he realized he wanted to avoid dreaming about having Mercy in his arms.

It couldn't happen again. Well, it easily could, but he needed to make sure it didn't. Their kiss hadn't changed anything. They remained rivals for the farm, and, more important, she wasn't Amish.

If she was willing to try…

He didn't allow the thought to form. He'd seen others try, drawn by what they saw as a bucolic life. Few of them lasted more than a couple of months. Though he had no doubts Mercy could do whatever she put her mind to, her yearning to build Come Along Farm and help city kids wouldn't fit into an Amish life.

Would they?

He honestly didn't know how strict the *Ordnung* would be for the settlement because they hadn't begun discussing it yet. So far, each family was living by the rules established in their home district, and that served them well.

"Can I have more?" Paul held his syrupy plate up for another piece, too.

"You've got a hollow leg," Jeremiah said with a chuckle.

The joke fell flat when nobody else laughed.

Though he knew the French toast must be delicious, it tasted like sawdust in his mouth. He ate and then waited while the *kinder* went into the other room to do their schoolwork.

"Finished?" Mercy asked as she reached for his plate. She was stacking the dishes by the sink, planning to wash them once the electricity was on and the well pump was working again.

"Ja." He needed to build a solar setup to power the well pump so he didn't have to be dependent on the grid. He could have his younger brother come up and put a couple panels on the roof. But first he needed to check if the rafters could support the weight.

Telling Mercy why he was going up in the attic, he took the flashlight from the drawer and left the kitchen. Her urging to be careful with the weak floors sounded automatic. She said the same words each time one of the *kinder* went upstairs alone.

Floorboards creaked as Jeremiah crossed the second floor to get to the attic door. When he opened it, he

heard water dripping. He wasn't surprised there were holes in the roof. Everything about the house needed repairs.

He switched on the flashlight and aimed it at the rafters. He didn't need to test the rafters with a nail to see if there was dry rot. Several of them were bowing and one was broken. It'd dropped across the attic, crushing boxes stored there.

A scan of the boxes showed him that the contents had probably been ruined before the rafter collapsed. He calculated what the cost of replacing the broken rafter would be. Once it was in place, the other rafters should straighten. The roof could then support two solar panels.

As he started toward the stairs, the flashlight's beam flickered on a box set off by itself. It was on its side, and he guessed it had been pushed aside when the rafter broke. He froze as the light showcased the words: *Personal items of Mercedes Ramirez.*

He picked up the box, shifting it carefully so he didn't break anything in it. Or anything else, he realized when he heard the tinkle of broken glass.

Closing the attic door behind him, he took care as he crossed the creaking second floor. He rushed into the kitchen.

Mercy looked over her shoulder, and her eyes widened. "What do you have there?"

"Something you've been looking for."

She put the measuring cup she held on the counter. When he set the box on the table, he turned it so she could see the words.

She gasped and pressed her fingers to her lips. "Mer-

cedes Ramirez? This box has to be from before I was adopted."

"My guess is it's from when you first were put into the state's care."

"How do you figure that?"

He answered her question with a question. "Remember what you said last night?"

Her flush deepened, and he knew she was blushing at the thought of what had been said with words *and* kisses.

Tapping her cheek, he said, "This is charming." He didn't give her a chance to reply as he went on, "I remember how you said Rudy told you that while you resembled your *grossmammi* in temperament, you looked like your *mamm*."

"He mentioned that several times through the years."

"Don't you see what it means, Mercy? Rudy saw your *mamm*, and the only way he could have done that was by seeing the photo of your parents. The one you remember from when you were a kid." He patted the box. "It could be in here. Can I open it?"

She nodded, her teeth clamped on her lower lip.

Unfolding the flaps, he lifted out the topmost item. A stuffed rabbit made like a crazy quilt in the brightest colors he could imagine.

Mercy took it carefully. "I remember this. *Abuelita* made it for me for my fifth birthday." She touched the ears, which once had been a brilliant white and now were a sad and stained brown. "What's it doing here?"

"I don't know." He picked up a *kind*'s heavily embroidered dress. "Do you recognize this?"

"Yes," she whispered. "*Abuelita* made matching ones for me and her for a block party when I was six or seven. She said it would give her practice for when she made my *Quinceañera* gown when I turned fifteen."

"What kind of gown?"

Running her fingers along the flowers and birds stitched into the small dress, she said, "It's a Hispanic custom for a girl's fifteenth birthday. There's a big party, and she dresses like a princess in the fanciest dress you can imagine. Of course, I never had a *Quinceañera* because, by the time I was fifteen, I was living a Mennonite life."

He dug a couple of damp picture books out of the box, but they fell apart in his hands. With care, he reached for the final item in the box. It was surrounded by shards of glass. He lifted it out and discovered it was a picture encased in a cheap metal frame. The glass that once had been inserted in it was broken.

Handing it to Mercy, he said nothing.

She stared at the picture that was black with mold. Half of it had been gnawed away. Whoever or whatever was depicted in it had become an indistinct blur.

"Maybe it's not the right picture," Jeremiah said softly. "Maybe we can find the picture of your parents somewhere else upstairs."

"It's the right one." She cradled the ruined picture as if it were a *boppli*. "Look! You can make out the word 'Lincoln' on the bottom. Lincoln Photography is where the picture was taken."

"I'm sorry, Mercy. I wish we could have found it before damp and mice got to it."

Lowering the frame to her lap, she touched her chest right over her heart. "I keep my birth parents right here. Nothing's ever changed about that."

When tears flooded along her cheeks, he started to apologize.

"Thank you, Jeremiah," she said. "You've cleared up a mystery that's bothered me for years."

"I wonder why it was here."

"I don't know, but knowing the picture wasn't thrown away is a weight off my heart." She reached up and ran her fingers along his jaw.

When she guided his mouth to hers, he could think of a dozen different reasons he shouldn't kiss her. He could think of only one reason why he should. He loved her. Later he would think of the complications. Now he savored the sweet caress of her lips.

Chapter Sixteen

Jeremiah drew in a deep breath of the moist air in the sap house the next morning. The small outbuilding was barely large enough for the evaporator, the stack of wood that heated it and shelves where he'd put empty bottles and his tools. It took several hours every other day to cook the sap into syrup because he was making small batches. The sap needed to go past water's boiling point by ten degrees before it started to cook into golden maple syrup. Once it did, he filled bottles and set them on a shelf to cool.

Bending, he checked the fire under the evaporator. He shoved a couple more pieces of split wood in so the heat stayed steady. If he stayed on the farm, he would like to tap more trees. He could buy a gas-powered evaporator and make enough syrup to sell at the farmer's market in Salem. Several of the other families were already planning to set up tables once spring came, selling everything from freshly made bread to goat milk soap to eggs and dried herbs.

If Mercy's family decided to sell him the farm. If they didn't increase the price beyond what he could afford. If he was able to make a success of the property.

Why was it easier to think about the farm than Mercy's eager response to his kisses? Each time the memories tried to assert themselves, he silenced them. They were a reminder of how witless he was. He'd known right from the beginning Mercy was Mennonite. She'd invited him to her church and hadn't hid how much she hoped he'd consider being baptized as a Mennonite. The picture of her family, though it'd been ruined, was another indication she was definitely *Englisch*.

God, how have I failed to see I'm making the same mistake again? Show me a way to fix this without ruining everything.

He snorted. What made him think God was going to bail him out of this predicament? Jeremiah had gone in with his eyes open, but should have kept his heart closed. He had to find the words to tell Mercy though she was *wunderbaar* in his arms, he was committed to helping the Amish community.

For what purpose? That vexing voice was back, demanding he be honest with himself. *What purpose do you have for building a home in Harmony Creek if you're not going to share it with the woman you love?*

"Jeremiah?"

He looked up, startled to discover Sunni standing in the sap house's doorway. He'd been so lost in his thoughts he hadn't heard the door open.

The little girl was bundled up in her winter coat and snow pants and boots. Her steps were stiff as she

came in. Her motions reminded him instantly of Mercy's when she was nervous.

He wanted to put the *kind* at ease, but he couldn't when he didn't know why Sunni was there. Apparently alone, because she closed the door behind her.

"Hi, Sunni!" he said with a smile.

The little girl was adorable in her winter clothes that left only her nose and dark eyes visible between her scarf and the hood of her coat. She looked as round as she was tall. When she pulled her scarf off, she wore the most somber expression he'd ever seen on her young face.

"Are you okay?" he asked.

She nodded as she edged around the evaporator, gazing up at the steam rising into the vent and outside.

"Do you want something?" A stupid question. She wouldn't have taken the long walk from the house unless she had a reason.

He pulled a bench from beneath the shelves and motioned for her to take a seat.

She did as she loosened her coat and pulled off her mittens, shoving them into her pockets.

"Is the syrup done?" she asked.

"Another fifteen minutes should do it." He squatted in front of her. "Sunni, you look like a gal with something on your mind. Why don't you spit it out?"

Opening her mouth, she hastily closed it.

"Sometimes," he said, "the most difficult words are the first ones. Push them out, and the others will follow."

Sunni swallowed hard. "Do you like my mommy?"

"*Ja.* Your *mamm* is a nice person. I think everyone around here likes her."

The little girl shifted to perch on the very edge of the bench. "I don't mean that kind of like. I mean do you *like* her?"

"Ah…" He understood what the child was asking, but he also knew whatever he said might be repeated to Mercy once Sunni returned to the farmhouse. "I think that topic should be discussed by your *mamm* and me. Don't you think so?"

Sunni slowly nodded.

"*Gut.*" He came to his feet. "Do you want to stay until the syrup is ready?"

"Will you promise me one thing?" she asked instead of answering his question.

"Amish don't make promises. We trust our word is as *gut* as a promise."

She stared at him, baffled. Her lips moved as she repeated his words as she tried to make sense of them. The moment when she got the meaning was obvious because the lines threading her forehead vanished.

"All right. I believe you," she said.

"*Danki.*" He was amused by her stern composure. It wouldn't have been out of place for a bishop. "What did you want to ask me?"

"Please don't hurt my mommy."

He flinched at the words the *kind* spoke with a yearning from the little girl's heart. "That's the last thing I'd ever want to do, Sunni. Your *mamm* is a kind and generous woman, and I admire how hard she works."

"I know Mommy is kind, but I don't want you to hurt her."

"How do you think I'd hurt her? By buying the farm?"

Sunni shook her head. "Not that. I don't want you to hurt her like Graham did. He said he loved her and asked her to marry him. I'd hoped she'd say no, but she said yes, and then he made her cry and cry when he always did what his mother wanted. Not just once, but a lot of times because his mother didn't like Mommy. That old lady was mean to Mommy and to me."

He realized the little girl was speaking of Mercy's former boyfriend. No, Graham actually had been her fiancé. Had he missed that fact, or had she failed to mention it? Not that it mattered. From Sunni's sorrowful words, it was clear whatever had been between Mercy and Graham was over. All that remained was a little girl determined to protect her *mamm*.

He folded Sunni's small hands between his much larger ones and held her gaze. "I don't ever intend to hurt your *mamm*. I don't want to see her cry, either."

She regarded him dubiously. "Graham said that, too. More than once I heard him say that, but then Mommy cried over and over again for months. She tried to make it work because she thinks I need a daddy."

"What do you think?"

Again, the little girl took time to ponder before she answered. He wondered if she'd always been such a deep-thinking *kind*, or if her experiences in leaving Korea and coming to a new family only to have them discard her had made her question every aspect of ev-

erything around her. In so many ways, she seemed too old for such a young *kind*.

"I thought our family was perfect. Me and Mommy and Grandma and Grandpa and the rest of the family."

"Especially Grandpa Rudy?"

"Uh-huh." Sunni's eyes grew luminous with tears, and he realized he'd never given thought to how the old man's death had affected this little girl. "When Mommy told me she was going to marry Graham and he'd be my new daddy, I tried to be happy, but I didn't like him."

"For the same reason you didn't like me at first?"

"No, I didn't like him. I didn't know then how someone could be so mean and make my mommy cry. I know that now."

Jeremiah sought words to soothe the *kind*'s pain, but anything he could come up with seemed trite. He wondered if Mercy knew how badly her broken engagement had both relieved and hurt her daughter.

Sunni didn't seem to notice he hadn't answered. "But then Paul came along, and he's part of our family." Her mouth twisted. "Lots of the time, I don't like him, especially when he says bad things about me or Mommy, but I could get used to him being my brother." She sighed. "So many people come and go. I think that's what makes Mommy sad. It makes me sad, too, when people can't stay." Again, she sounded far older than her few years, but her voice cracked when she added, "Especially people like you, Jeremiah."

She jumped to her feet and left the sap house, the door slamming in her wake.

He wanted to give chase, but he couldn't leave the

evaporator. Or maybe that was an excuse, because what could he have said to the little girl?

He stared at the evaporator as an unexpected thought burst into his head. Should he leave the Amish before being baptized? Could he? Until he'd met Mercy, he'd never considered he'd ever make such a choice.

He laughed at the irony. When Emmarita had jumped the fence, he'd assumed it'd been a rash decision made to please her *Englischer*. Maybe it had been, but as he wrestled with the choice himself, he suspected she hadn't left her family and friends behind easily.

Or him.

It's long past time to forgive her. The whisper of his conscience seemed loud in the quiet. He forgave her as he comprehended what Emmarita had faced as she made her decision to leave. He knew, as he hadn't before, the choice hadn't been easy for her.

But Emmarita had made her choice. He now must, too.

Mercy picked her way through the icy patches on her way to the mailbox. She'd be so glad when spring arrived, and the last of the snow was gone. An electrician had fixed the circuit breaker box and gotten the furnace started so they had light and heat in the house. Even so, the generator sat nearby, ready to pump out water if it seeped into the cellar again. The next time she spoke with her father, she would ask him if he knew of a way to seal the rock foundation to keep water out.

She opened the metal mailbox that still had Rudy's name on the side. Pulling out the stack of mail inside,

she smiled when she saw a folded copy of the latest edition of *The Budget*. She looked at the index on the left side, and her smile broadened when she saw a listing for the Mennonite church they used to attend. Sunni enjoyed hearing news from there because sometimes her friends' names were mentioned by the correspondent. When Paul was at his worst and made fun of the names or what her friends were doing, Sunni ignored him.

That was the only time.

With a sigh, Mercy closed the box. She'd hoped by now the two children would have gotten over their obvious distaste for each other. Should she say something to Whitney? Disrupting Paul with another placement wouldn't help him, but Mercy didn't like her daughter being the target of his cruel teasing. Sunni was too young to understand why Paul was acting out, and Mercy was running out of ideas for how to bridge the gap between the two of them.

Riffling through the envelopes, she halted and stared at the return address on the bottommost one. Tucking the newspaper under her arm and the rest of the mail in her coat pocket, she ran up the slushy driveway. Mud splashed on the hem of her coat and her dress as she sped across the yard, hitting many of the puddles hidden beneath the grass that had been matted by the winter's heavy snow.

Pausing at the door of Jeremiah's shop, she peered inside. It was empty. Where was he? His buggy was in the yard, and it was too early to start the milking.

Mercy heard a thud, then a crack. He must be splitting wood on the far side of the house for use in making

the last of the maple syrup. He mentioned at breakfast the wood box was empty. As she rounded the porch, she saw him with his ax raised before he brought it down in a quick, smooth arc. The blade cut into the chunk of wood on top of a stump. Two pieces of wood tumbled to the ground.

As he bent to pick them up, he must have seen her, because he halted and called a greeting.

She didn't slow until she reached where he stood. Her face must have revealed her thoughts, because he asked what was wrong. She tried to answer, but had to take a moment to regain her breath. He waited with more patience than she would have if their situations were reversed.

Holding out the letter, she said, "It's from my family's lawyer." Her voice cracked in spite of her efforts to hide her trepidation.

"What does it say?"

"I don't know. It's addressed to you."

When he set aside the ax, leaning it against the woodpile, he took the envelope. He pulled off one work glove, then the other before he took a knife out of his pocket and slit the top of the envelope open.

She held her breath as he drew out a single sheet of paper. She couldn't guess if such a short missive was good news for her or bad.

He read it fast, then read it again.

"What does it say?" she asked as he had.

He swallowed hard. "Your family has come to a consensus about the future of the farm."

"They've decided to sell it to you, haven't they?" She

didn't know why she'd bothered to make it a question. His hesitation had told her the truth.

"I think maybe, but I'm not sure with the fancy lawyer language. Why don't you read it and tell me what you think?"

She took the letter and had to puzzle through the meaning of a couple of the long, elaborate sentences. The beginning of one seemed to contradict its ending, but she understood enough to know why the letter had been addressed to him. Her father and his siblings intended to honor the purchase contract Jeremiah had signed.

"Congratulations, Jeremiah," she said as she returned the letter. She wished she could show more enthusiasm, but how could she when she was numb? "It's okay. You can celebrate if you want."

"How can I celebrate when I know what this decision means to you and the summer camp you wanted to have for city *kinder*?" He folded the letter and put it in the envelope.

"You're going to make your dream of having your own farm come true, Jeremiah. I'm happy for you." She blinked on hot tears. "Despite what I may look like, I'm happy for you."

"You look lovely."

"I wasn't fishing for a compliment."

"I know, but I wanted to give you one I should have said long ago." When she didn't answer, he asked, "What will you do?"

"I want to build a summer camp for city kids." Her gaze swept the place that soon wouldn't be her home.

"It'll have to be somewhere else. I owe a great debt to the people who run the Fresh Air program. It's my mission. I know you may not understand because Amish don't do mission work."

"Some do."

"Not many."

He sighed. "You're right. Not many do."

"You probably want to tell Caleb you'll be staying here." She took a step back. "I need to check on the kids." Her breath caught sharply. "Paul!"

"Won't Whitney let him stay with you?"

"I don't know." Her voice broke as she added, "I don't know about anything." She raised her chin. "Congratulations, Jeremiah. I know Grandpa Rudy would be thrilled to know the plans he made with you are going to work out."

Turning on her heel, she raced around the side of the house. She heard Jeremiah call after her, but she didn't slow. She wasn't sure how much longer she could pretend she was okay with her best chance to make her dream come true being dashed.

Chapter Seventeen

Putting the last dish in the cupboard, Mercy draped the damp dish towel over the rod hanging off a cabinet. She glanced at the clock. She'd finished exactly two minutes before Whitney was supposed to arrive. Yesterday, after the letter came from the family's lawyer, Mercy had called the social worker and explained what had happened.

"Don't worry, Mercy," she'd said. "Things can be worked out in situations like this."

Mercy had prayed Whitney was right. She'd planned on talking to the social worker on her next visit about when Paul would be free to be adopted. She wanted to get her name at the top of the list of potential adoptive parents.

The crunch of tires on frozen mud in the driveway announced the social worker was punctual as always. Opening the side door, Mercy motioned for Whitney to hurry in. The day was as cold as if the thaw had never happened.

A motion in the yard caught her eyes. Jeremiah strode toward the house, and she was relieved he was going to be with her when she spoke to Whitney about Paul's future.

"Brrr," said the blonde as she unzipped her coat. "I don't think this winter is ever going to end."

"It seems that way."

"Hi, Jeremiah. Good to see you again." She pulled off her coat and looked around. "Where are the children?"

"Upstairs." Mercy took a step toward the staircase. "I can get them."

"No!" The social worker's voice was startlingly sharp. "I need to speak to you without the children first."

Mercy motioned for them to come into the kitchen. What was bothering Whitney? The blonde was usually calm, even when Paul snarled at her.

Jeremiah's brows lowered, a sure sign he was puzzled by Whitney's odd behavior, too. He sat at the head of the table, but didn't say anything.

"Want coffee, Whitney?" she asked, reaching for the pot.

"No, thank you." Putting her briefcase on the chair, Whitney stood behind it. "I think what I have to say is best said quickly."

"What's wrong?" She couldn't keep from glancing at Jeremiah, who was watching the social worker.

"The Kentons have been in contact with us for the past two weeks. Their social worker has spent time with them. She believes they're sincere in wanting their son returned to them."

Mercy stared at Whitney, sure she'd heard her wrong. Somehow, she pushed out a question. "They want him back?"

"Yes."

"Can they do that?" Mercy answered her own question before the social worker could. "I mean, I know they can ask, but why are you agreeing?"

"Parker—"

Jeremiah said with quiet dignity, "He calls himself Paul now."

"I know, but the Kentons still want to call him Parker." Whitney sighed. "I'll let them know again that he prefers the other name. Mercy, Jeremiah, I know you're attached to the boy, but he was with the Kentons for more than six months, and, though they were overwhelmed and needed a break, they've put together a support network they—and we—think will make the placement a success."

"Does he have input into the decision?" Jeremiah asked.

"He's a child." She cut her eyes to Mercy. "You know children aren't in any position to judge what's best for them in the long run."

Mercy lowered herself to a chair and clasped her hands in her lap. "I know the hurt jerking a child around can create. I had two placements before I came to the Bambergers, and I was a very angry child who didn't trust anyone." She stared at the table crisscrossed with nicks and gouges, the sign of long use. "If it hadn't been for Grandpa Rudy, I don't know if I ever would have trusted again."

When Jeremiah's hand covered hers, she knew he was offering what comfort he could.

"I understand," Whitney said as she looked from Mercy to Jeremiah.

"So do I," Mercy replied with a sigh.

Jeremiah erupted from his chair. "And that's it? You aren't going to give us time to say goodbye?"

"Of course you'll have time." Whitney sighed. "I'm not heartless, but I've got to think what's best for him."

"Staying here is best for him." Jeremiah's scowl deepened.

Mercy put her hand on Jeremiah's arm. She'd never seen him so furious and knew he was fighting to keep his temper under control. "Getting angry won't help."

"So you're going to let him go?" He snapped his fingers. "Just like that?"

"Please don't make it harder," she said.

"I don't know how it could be." Hurt blazed in his eyes as they locked with Mercy's. "Why can't he stay here with Mercy so she can adopt him?"

"We have a two-parent family who wants him," Whitney replied. "Our first choice for a child is always to have two parents."

"But they didn't want him, and Mercy does."

Knowing it was Jeremiah's grief speaking, Mercy interjected, "Whitney, will you excuse us?"

"I'll wait in the living room." She glanced at her watch. "I can give you twenty minutes. No more."

Once the social worker left the kitchen, Jeremiah came around the table so he stood beside Mercy. "I love that boy. I don't want to lose him."

"I know. I love him, too, but he has a chance for a home with two parents who love him."

"Two parents who tossed him aside like an unwanted puppy."

Wondering how she could reach through his hurt to help him understand, she knew the only way was to be honest. "Jeremiah, I don't like this any more than you do, but—"

"What if they decide they don't want him again?" He flung out his hands. "Will they throw him away again?"

"We have to pray they won't."

His shoulders dropped, and she knew she'd finally gotten him to understand. Paul's life, like theirs, was in God's hand. They had to trust God would watch over the boy.

Going to the base of the stairs, she shouted for the children. She frowned when she got no response. Paul... She'd just gotten used to calling him that, and now she had to remember to address him as Parker. He might refuse to answer her, but Sunni always came when Mercy called.

"Are you up here?" she tried again.

She heard Whitney coming from the living room and Jeremiah from the kitchen, but she ran up the stairs. Why weren't the children answering?

Jeremiah exchanged a glance with Whitney as Mercy's voice drifted to them. Before he could speak, Mercy rushed down the stairs. Her face was a sick shade.

"What's wrong?" he asked.

"Sunni and Parker have disappeared." She looked at the shocked social worker. "They aren't here."

"Let me find them," he said. "They couldn't have gone far."

"If they heard us…" Whitney choked out.

Shoving his black hat on his head, he ran out of the house. Ten minutes later he'd searched the outbuildings and the tenant house. Fruitlessly.

Mercy was waiting on the porch when he returned to the house. "Whitney wants to call the police."

"Not yet," he said. "I'll get our neighbors to help find them."

The social worker opened the door. "No, Jeremiah. The boy is my responsibility. We have to call the police before he runs away too far."

"We don't know if they've run away. They may have slipped out before you got here. I'm going to check with the neighbors. Someone must have seen them."

Whitney started to protest, but Mercy silenced her by touching her arm.

"Let Jeremiah try. Give him an hour."

"Two," he insisted. "That's enough time to check every place along the creek."

"Give him two hours," Mercy pleaded. "If the kids see policemen, they may hide instead of coming out of wherever they are."

"An hour. No longer, and it's against my better judgment." Whitney wrapped her arms around herself. "I'm risking my job on this."

"We know, and we appreciate it." Mercy kept talking to the blonde as she steered Whitney into the house.

Looking back before she closed the door, she mouthed, "Find them. Fast."

Jeremiah loped along the drive and toward Caleb's farm. As the word spread through the hollow, more and more people joined the hunt for the *kinder*. He asked everyone to check their own outbuildings and then the woods on both sides of the creek. He hoped Sunni and Paul hadn't tried to cross it because the ice was no longer thick enough to hold them.

Time sped past too fast. Ever conscious of how little time they had to search so many acres and buildings, his hope the youngsters could be found before the police were called began to fade. Leaving Caleb to direct the search as the hour elapsed, Jeremiah hurried to where Mercy and the social worker waited.

Whitney was on her cell phone as he came in. When Mercy looked at him, he shook his head, sick at heart for failing her. She'd trusted him, and he'd let her down. He thought of what Sunni had told him about Mercy's ex-fiancé not being there for her. He hadn't wanted to do the same.

She offered him a cup of cocoa, and he took it gratefully. His toes felt like a quintet of frozen blocks of ice in each of his boots. As he raised the cup to his lips, a motion outside caught his eye.

Smoke coming from the sap house? He hadn't left a fire in there after he finished the latest batch of maple syrup.

"Mercy, I think I know where they are."

"Where?" asked both women at the same time.

He pointed out the window toward the sap house.

Setting down his untasted cocoa, he grabbed Mercy's coat and thrust it into her hands. She was pulling it on as she followed him out of the house. Behind them, Whitney yelled for them to wait up. They kept going.

The ice sent Mercy skidding into him. He grabbed her hand as they climbed the hill to the small building.

When he threw open the door, heat struck his face. He stepped inside and called, "*Komm* out! I know you're in here."

Sunni peeked around the side of the evaporator. "Jeremiah!" Looking back, she motioned. "It's okay, Paul. Jeremiah will make it okay."

Mercy saw the pain on Jeremiah's face and knew he wished desperately Sunni was right. She stepped into the sap house, but halted Whitney from pushing past her.

"Let us talk to them," she said, "while you call the police and let them know the kids have been found."

For a second she thought the social worker would insist, but then Whitney nodded. "I'll meet you at the house in ten minutes."

"It may take a bit longer."

"I can't give you more time, Mercy. We're already late meeting the Kentons."

Nodding, Mercy headed for the far end of the sap house. She doubted her feet touched the floor more than twice as she bounded forward to sweep the children into her arms. Sunni clung to her, and Parker did, too. When Jeremiah put his arms around them, they stood in silence for the length of two heartbeats.

Sunni and Parker began explaining how they'd started a fire beneath the evaporator to stay warm.

"While we waited for that woman to go away." Parker shivered.

Mercy put her arm around him and gave him a comforting squeeze, knowing he wasn't cold, but scared. When Jeremiah drew the boy away and bent so his eyes were even with Parker's, she draped her arms over her daughter, clasping her hands in front of Sunni.

"If we hid, that lady couldn't take Paul away," her daughter said.

"Whitney wants the best for him," Jeremiah said.

"We're the best for him." Her daughter looked up at her. "Isn't that right, Mommy?"

"She wants to take me back to people who don't want me," the little boy insisted. "I don't want to go!"

"Would you try spending a weekend with the Kentons?" Mercy asked.

The boy and the man wore identical expressions of dismay, but understanding lit Jeremiah's eyes and he nodded.

"Just a weekend?" Parker asked, suspiciously.

"Yes, for now. Maybe it won't be as bad as you think it'll be."

"Maybe."

"You know you won't be going alone," she said softly as she reached out to take the boy's right hand. "God will be with you whether you are here or somewhere else."

"I know." He looked at Jeremiah, who took his other

hand. "I can lay my bad feelings at His feet, and He'll sweep them away with His toes."

Mercy didn't try to restrain her smile. "That's right. You're a smart boy to figure that out."

"I didn't figure it out. Jeremiah told me."

Jeremiah winked at him. "I'm glad you listened. I need to go and let the searchers know the kids have been found. I'll meet you at the house, okay? I'll be back as fast as I can."

Mercy nodded, knowing he hoped Parker would be there when he returned. She smiled. She wasn't sure how, but she'd find a way to persuade Whitney to wait.

Her concerns were needless because when she and the children entered the house, Whitney took her aside and said the Kentons had called and arranged to meet Parker the next afternoon.

"So he can stay here until then?" Mercy asked.

"If you make sure he's here when I come back."

"I'll do my best. I won't let either of them out of my sight until then."

Parker stared, openmouthed, when Whitney said he could stay overnight. He stammered out his thanks as Sunni squealed with excitement.

"Why are you sounding like a pig?" Parker asked. "Is it because you look like one?"

"Mommy!" cried Sunni. "Tell him I'm not a pig."

Knowing the kids' temporary truce was broken, Mercy herded them into the kitchen and sat them at the table once Whitney left. But she couldn't keep from smiling as they bickered. Even that annoying sound was precious while she spent these last hours with Parker.

Somehow, she managed to keep her tears hidden and her voice cheerful while they had supper and she tucked the children into bed. She kissed their freshly washed faces and wished them pleasant dreams. As she went down the stairs, she heard hushed voices and footsteps. She looked back to discover Sunni sneaking into Parker's room. She suspected when she checked later, she'd find them curled together like the litter of kittens in the barn.

Jeremiah was waiting at the bottom of the stairs. Crooking a finger, he walked into the living room. She caught up with him and put her arms around him, leaning her face against his strong back.

"Thank you," she whispered. "Thank you for finding them."

Facing her, he said, "I've been thinking, Mercy. Whitney said a two-parent family is always the best choice for a *kind*. Do you know Sunni believes you agreed to marry Graham because you wanted her to have a *daed*?"

"No." Shock raced through her. "I didn't know she knew that."

"So you were marrying him to give her a *daed*?"

"It's embarrassing to admit, but it's partly true. I did think I loved Graham."

He took her hands and led her to the sofa. Sitting beside her, he asked, "You *thought* you loved him?"

"Yes, until I realized what love really is. You taught me that."

"As you've taught me." He brushed his lips against

hers. "I need to ask you something. Would you consider staying here on the farm as my wife?"

"So we can try to adopt Parker if things don't work out with the Kentons?"

"In part, but I'm asking because I love you and I can't endure the thought of losing you." He smoothed loose strands from her face. "I thought I couldn't hurt worse than when the woman I loved jumped the fence and married an *Englischer.* But the idea of being without you is torture. Marry me, Mercy."

"Does that mean you're willing to become a Mennonite?"

"I'd hoped you would consider being baptized Amish, Mercy. You've seen how we live, and you seem comfortable with it."

She wasn't surprised at his request. And he was right. During the days when they were without electricity, she'd learned to manage the household and keep them fed. "I want to tell you yes, but I told God I'd repay the kindnesses done to me when I was little. Won't that be impossible if I became Amish?"

"I don't know, but I can present your idea for Come Along Farm to our bishop."

"But what about your plans for the farm?"

"We're two smart people. I'm sure we can figure out a way to make both our dreams come true on this farm."

"Assuming the bishop is okay with it?"

"*Ja.* I must get his opinion if it's permissible for an Amish woman to oversee a summer camp."

"Do you think he'll agree?" she asked as her heart danced within her.

"I don't know Wayne well enough to be sure, but I know he'll listen and pray for guidance."

"I have information I'd put together earlier, if you want to give it to him."

"Let's pray there will be an easy way to resolve this. If Wayne says he's okay with your plans for a summer program, we can—"

Her finger against his lips halted him. "One problem at a time, Jeremiah."

"I don't consider getting you to agree to marry me a problem." Folding her hands between his, he asked, "If we can work this out, will you marry me?"

She gave him her answer with a kiss that told him far better than words how much she loved him and wanted to be his wife.

Chapter Eighteen

The candles had been blown out, and the chocolate cake was gone except for a few crumbs on the platter. Outside the cozy kitchen, a chilly October wind whistled at the eaves.

As Mercy looked around the kitchen, she had to smile. The house didn't look different, but in the past months, it had gone through as many changes as she had. Wayne Flaud had been hesitant about Mercy being baptized. He refused to start baptism classes with her until she lived a full Amish life for six months.

She'd agreed and, with Jeremiah's assistance as well as her neighbors', complied. She attended baptism classes with the bishop, a process that took longer than usual because of the distances involved. Instead of meeting weekly with him, they met twice a month when he came to join the *Leit* for services.

And last month, at her final session with the bishop, whom she discovered wasn't as rigid and imposing as his appearance had suggested, Wayne had told her after

hours of prayer and long correspondence with other bishops, he couldn't see how it would be a problem for her to bring in Fresh Air kids for two weeks each summer. It was, he told her, no different from Amish families who took in *Englischers* in a farm-stay bed-and-breakfast for them to discover what an Amish farm was like. She'd wanted to throw her arms around him and hug him, but she'd simply said, "*Danki*, Wayne."

Mercy yawned as Jeremiah entered the kitchen. She wouldn't ever get tired of looking at the sparkle of happiness in his eyes when his gaze shifted to her.

Picking up the last of the dishes, she put them in the sink. "Next time I'm not going to plan a wedding the day after you throw a birthday party for me."

"I'd rather hoped you wouldn't ever be planning another wedding." He gave her one of the scintillating smiles she adored.

"Sunni will marry someday."

He chuckled. "Let me enjoy her being a *kind* before I think of her marrying and making me a *grossdawdi*. Now admit it. You had a *wunderbaar* time at the party."

"I enjoyed every moment of it, but the idea of another huge party tomorrow is overwhelming."

"Be grateful you're here instead of the tenant house." Jeremiah slid his arm around her waist, but kept his other hand behind his back. Was he hiding something? "I think every corner is covered with food to be served tomorrow. *Mamm* and my sisters-in-law cooked as if there were forty families here instead of seven. I don't know if they've left me a place to sleep."

"Most of my relatives will be coming in the morning.

They kindly found places to stay in the villages around here, so the house won't be filled to capacity before the ceremony begins." Her eyes widened as she recalled the service would be in High German, a language she was struggling to learn. She recognized more words every church Sunday. "Jeremiah, did you ask—?"

He tapped her nose. "All my siblings, except Isaiah who, as an ordained minister, will be helping with the service, and their spouses have offered to translate portions of the ceremony not in English as well as the songs."

"My family will know most of them, I'm sure." She smiled. "I've already warned them not to harmonize and to sing really, really, really slow."

"Look what I found!" called an excited voice from the stairs.

Sunni and the boy they again called Paul ran into the kitchen, sliding to a stop inches from Mercy. Jeremiah smiled at them. Sunni would become his daughter after tomorrow. Paul would be their son as soon as the adoption paperwork was completed in the coming weeks.

It was as if Paul had been with them his whole life. When he'd returned to the Kentons for the planned visit, Whitney returned with him only a few hours later.

"The Kentons changed their minds yet again," the social worker had said with an outraged frown. "I can assure you they won't have another chance. As you said, Mercy, jerking a child around is cruel."

Paul shoved an envelope into Mercy's hand.

"What's that?" she asked.

He shrugged. "I found it in the back of the top drawer

in my dresser when I was trying to find clean socks."
The boy's room continued to look as if a gale swept
through it twice a day. "It's got your name on it."

Mercy gasped when she recognized Grandpa Rudy's
handwriting on the envelope. Could it be the will she'd
searched in vain for? She hoped not, because that could
complicate Jeremiah's ownership of the farm he'd closed
on four months ago.

Pulling out the single sheet with quivering fingers,
she read aloud:

"My dear Mercy,
"I hope you and your darling daughter have found
the perfect home for yourselves with the proceeds
from the farm. I know you wanted the farm to
make a camp for city children, but my farm needs
too much work for you and Sunni to handle alone.
 "I have enclosed a copy of the deed for fif-
teen acres across the road from the farm. It's big
enough for you to build a house, a barn and rid-
ing area for your summer kids."

"Fifteen acres?" Jeremiah glanced at the surpris-
ingly flat fields edged by Harmony Creek. "Why didn't
we see your *grossdawdi*'s name as a neighboring land-
owner on the deed for this property when I closed on
this farm?"

"I don't know." She continued reading.

"Ask Jeremiah Stoltzfus for his help. He seems
like a good man, for my farm and for you."

She smiled at Jeremiah, who was shaking his head in amazement.

"I never guessed," he said, "why he asked me so many questions before he agreed to sell me the farm. Your *grossdawdi* was a matchmaker, Mercy."

"He knew a good thing when he saw it." She gave him a quick kiss before continuing to read Grandpa Rudy's letter.

> "The land has been held in trust for you. Make your difference, Mercy, in other lives. But remember you don't carry a debt for how your life has turned out. You may think you are beholden to us for you being a part of the family. You aren't. You weren't an obligation. You were a blessing, a gift to all of us."

It was signed "your loving grandpa."

She pressed the letter to her heart as she whispered, "I love you, too, Grandpa Rudy." Raising her eyes to Jeremiah's, she said, "We have Wayne's approval, and we can have Come Along Farm and your farm. What an amazing birthday gift!"

"Would you like another?" Sunni asked. "It's time, Jeremiah."

"Time for what?" Mercy saw the ill-concealed grins on the children's—no, she needed to use her *Deitsch*—the *kinder*'s faces.

Jeremiah took her hand and sat her at the table. "Before anything else, I want to tell you I've solved another mystery for you. When I spoke with your parents dur-

ing their visit here last month, they were as surprised as you were to learn the box of possessions from *Abuelita*'s apartment ended up in Rudy's attic. They did know about the box, because your social worker mentioned it. Apparently, your parents were in the middle of a move because your *daed* was changing jobs around the time you came to them. Your *mamm* assumes they gave your social worker this address to make sure the box was safely delivered." He drew his hand from behind his back and handed her a manila envelope. "Open it."

The envelope wasn't thick, so there couldn't be anything more than a page or two inside. Was it something to do with Paul's adoption? No, Whitney had said they'd filled out all the necessary forms, though there would be more to sign the day Paul's adoption became final.

"Open it!" Sunni urged.

"Open it!" shouted Paul, and the two *kinder* began to repeat the words over and over.

Mercy did and reached inside. She pulled out a single slick piece of paper. It was blank, so she turned it over.

"Oh, my!" she whispered as she stared at the photograph. The woman's face matched the shape of hers, and the man's eyes crinkled as hers did when she smiled. Her parents! It was the photo she'd last seen whole the day *Abuelita* died. "But how…?" She couldn't finish the question because words refused to push past the thick lump in her throat.

Jeremiah sat beside her and leaned her head against his shoulder so they looked at the picture together. "I found an address on the framed photograph. I wrote to the photography studio and asked if they were still in

business. I heard from the wife of the man who'd taken that picture. He's passed away, and their son is running the business. They searched the old files and found the negative for the picture of your parents. I had them make you a new print."

"Look!" She motioned for the children to come closer. "These are your grandparents. Gilberto and Amada Ramirez. They—" She sat up straight. "But I'm Amish since I was baptized last month, and the Amish don't like photographs."

He gave her a gentle smile. "We don't like photos taken of us. Your parents weren't Amish, so there's no problem with you having it."

"Danki," she whispered as she wept.

"Are you sad, Mommy?" asked Sunni.

"We want you to be happy," Paul quickly added.

"I'm happy. Happier than I've ever been." She hugged each of them.

Jeremiah said, "I wanted your family to be as complete as possible on our wedding day."

Holding the picture over her heart, she put her other arm around Paul and Sunni. As Jeremiah drew them closer, she said, "You've given me what I wanted my whole life. A family that's all my own."

"And my own, too," he said.

"And my own," repeated the *kinder* together.

They all laughed in the moment before Jeremiah captured her lips that would be his for the rest of their lives.

* * * * *

Grace found Nicole had pulled herself up to the front door
and was high-fiving none other than Adrian Schrock.
He'd squatted down to her level. Nicole was having a fine
old time.

Grace picked up her *doschder* and pushed open the
door, causing Adrian to jump up, then step back toward
the porch steps. It was, indeed, a fine spring day. The sun
shone brightly across the Indiana fields. Flowers colored
yellow, red, lavender and orange had begun popping
through the soil that surrounded the porch. Birds were
even chirping merrily.

Somehow, all those things did little to elevate Grace's
mood. Neither did the sight of her neighbor.

Adrian resettled his straw hat on his head and smiled.
"Gudemariye."

"Your llama has escaped again."

"Kendrick? *Ya.* I've come to fetch him. He seems to
like your place more than mine."

"I don't want that animal over here, Adrian. He spits.
And your peacock was here at daybreak, crying like a
child."

Adrian laughed. "When you moved back home, I guess you didn't expect to live next to a Plain & Simple Exotic Animal Farm."

Adrian wiggled his eyebrows at Nicole when he seemed to realize that Grace wasn't amused.

"I think of your place as Adrian's Zoo."

"Not a bad name, but it doesn't highlight our Amish heritage enough."

"The point is that I feel like we're living next door to a menagerie of animals."

"Up, Aden. Up."

Adrian scooped Nicole from Grace's hold, held her high above his head, then nuzzled her neck. Adrian was comfortable with everyone and everything.

"Do you think she'll ever learn to say my name right?"

"Possibly. Can you please catch Kendrick and take him back to your place?"

"Of course. That's why I came over. I guess I must have left the gate open again." He kissed Nicole's cheek, then popped her back into Grace's arms. "You should bring her over to see the turtles."

As he walked away, Grace wondered for the hundredth time why he wasn't married. It was true that he'd picked a strange profession. What other Amish man raised exotic animals? No, Adrian wouldn't be considered excellent marrying material by most young Amish women.

Don't miss
The Baby Next Door *by Vannetta Chapman,*
available April 2021 wherever
Love Inspired books and ebooks are sold.

LoveInspired.com

LIEXP0321

LOVE INSPIRED

INSPIRATIONAL ROMANCE

UPLIFTING STORIES OF FAITH, FORGIVENESS AND HOPE.

Join our social communities to connect with other readers who share your love!

Sign up for the Love Inspired newsletter at **LoveInspired.com** to be the first to find out about upcoming titles, special promotions and exclusive content.

CONNECT WITH US AT:

 Facebook.com/LoveInspiredBooks

Twitter.com/LoveInspiredBks

Facebook.com/groups/HarlequinConnection

LISOCIAL2020